SHATTERED LANDS BOOK 4

HEAVY
LIES THE
CROWN

TRAVIS
STARNES

Maps available at

https://tstarnes.com/book-series/shattered-lands/

Signup to get free previews of upcoming books before they're released at

http://tstarnes.com/preview-notification-newsletter/

Contents

Chapter 1

Rendalia City, Rendalia

William had spread the dispatches across the map table and weighted the corners with whatever lay near to hand: a sea-polished stone from the Chansol Ford, a bent dagger he meant to have mended, a chipped cup he had not bothered to empty. Wax seals broke and curled like red petals against Sidor's outline. Ink smudged where his thumb pressed too hard. He read the same passage twice. It did not change.

Isolde slipped in without ceremony. The lamplight caught the silk at her wrist and the dull metal of the signet he had given her after the battle at the river. She looked from the mess of paper to his face, then back again.

"You're up late," Isolde said, coming up behind him.

He didn't jump. There were guards on the keep and one on his door. He would have heard an assassin before they came in.

Still, she would have made an excellent assassin. He hadn't heard her at all, even the door opening and closing, until she'd been practically on top of him, and even then it had only been a slight whisper of her dress swishing against the floor.

Had the fire not already died down to coals and still been popping and flickering, he might not have even heard that.

He'd been focused for hours, leaning over a map that was the best representation of the forces stretched out across the River Mark and Kingsheart, based on the letters he'd received from his Aunt Alyssa, since she was the only one telling him anything worth knowing.

Which was a problem unto itself.

Sinclair, he understood. Based on everything his Uncle Aldric had told him, Sinclair was only for Sinclair, and he thought everyone else was beneath him. He'd play well with others just as long as he thought he'd get something out of it, but not a moment longer.

He'd had higher hopes for Pembroke, who'd been as much a mentor to him as Aldric had been. When he'd heard about Pembroke's departure, he'd hoped the baron would stay in contact.

He hadn't.

So he was operating on pieces of information, and those pieces weren't good.

"Late? It's barely a bell after dusk."

"You've been at it for hours. You need a break. How bad is it?"

"Bad. I have no idea how he's done it, but my father has found more men. A lot of them. We're outnumbered again and might be even if we get this entire army back to Sidor. And he's still recruiting."

"Conscripts, though," she offered.

"Volunteers, actually. If Aunt Alyssa's reports are to be believed, they've come to him in two and ten and twenty. They sign his rolls and take his coin and cheer his name. He marches through the Kingsheart towns and the men throw caps and shout for him, and when the caps fall, a hundred hands fight to keep them in the air. And it's letting him win back ground we'd taken. The rebellion's lost nearly everything it gained in the last year. They've been pushed back to the borders of Iron Keep and south of the Thunderhorn."

William pointed to one of the markers on the map that showed the current battle lines. "Without someone there to hold things together, the whole thing's going to collapse and according to my aunt, it's not just the manpower surge. Sinclair and Pembroke are spending as much time disagreeing with each other as they are fighting my father. The armies are divided and fighting their own fights, which cuts our forces in half while theirs grows."

"You're surprised that nobles are acting like nobles?" Isolde said.

William looked up at her. "What?"

"Sinclair and Pembroke have spent their entire lives building their power bases," she continued. "They've invested decades in cultivating influence, securing alliances, positioning their houses for advantage. You can't expect them to simply abandon those interests because you need them to work together."

"We're at war."

"War doesn't change a noble's nature. If anything, it amplifies it. Your uncle's death created a power vacuum and they're going to try to fill it. That's how noble houses have survived for generations, by never missing an opportunity to advance their positions."

"Even when it risks everything?"

"Especially then. The greatest rewards come from the greatest risks."

"They should be focused on achieving victory first."

"And who decides what that victory looks like? From everything you've said, Sinclair sees himself as the next duke of Iron Keep once Windermere is gone, and maybe before then. And Pembroke has always been the most powerful baron in the River Mark. For now, your aunt maintains some level of control, but she was never anointed and no one is going to follow whoever your father anoints as the next duke. If you believe he doesn't have his eyes on the duchy, then you are fooling yourself."

"Sure, Sinclair is angling for more power; it's who he is. But I expected more from Pembroke. I thought he was different from the others. More principled."

"Why?"

"Because I know him. He's always put the kingdom first, above his personal ambition. The man I know wouldn't jeopardize what we're doing here. He wouldn't abandon his responsibilities."

"He probably doesn't see it like that," she said, pulling out a chair and sitting down. "I know it's hard to think this way, but even in war, you can't just think about the war. My father may have been an evil man, but he understood how power works and would talk about it often. Even while fighting a war, you have to think about what the postwar world will look like, and arrange things so that when it ends, you are in a position to ensure your vision comes true. Sinclair and Pembroke both know this, I assure you. From how Pembroke spoke of Sinclair to me, he is almost certainly

3

worried that the man will end the war in a position of greater power. From the looks of this, he is with the Eastern barons now and has all of Iron Keep behind him. That's a larger power base than Pembroke has, giving him a leg up when it's all over. You may have the Whitton name, but other than Pembroke, do any of the barons follow you? Their knights and soldiers, yes, but none have raised a banner in your name specifically."

"If we lose, none of it will matter."

"No, but they can't think about that. The longer there is no unifying voice, the worse it's going to get. An army without clear authority will fracture. Your father knew what he was doing when he had your uncle killed."

"Which is why I need to get back. I know these men will follow me once I'm there in person. Other than my father, I have the highest claim to the throne and Aldric named me as his heir. I just hope they can hold it together until I get back."

"Until we get back."

William turned to face her fully. "What?"

"When we get back to Sidor." Isolde stood, moving closer to him. "I'm coming with you. If this rebellion succeeds, then you will have the throne. I'm your wife. I should start learning about my future people now, if I'm going to help you pull the kingdom back together."

William stared at her, realization dawning on his face. She'd been assuming all along that she would accompany him. That option hadn't even occurred to him.

"Absolutely not. It's too dangerous right now."

"I've been in danger before."

"This is different. Those times, the war came to you, you couldn't do much to stop it. But this ... we're sailing into an active war zone."

"I'm aware of the risks."

"Are you? You're not just my wife, Isolde. You're a former Lynesian princess. Edmund would see you as a prize worth any effort to capture. You'd be a weapon he could use against me and the entire rebellion."

"I'm also an asset that strengthens our position."

"Not if you're dead. Or worse, in Edmund's hands." William moved toward her, taking her hands. "Besides, our people here need you. We've just got the province established and the borders secure. Your departure would leave everything we've built vulnerable."

"We will leave it in the hands of a capable administrator."

"Administrators aren't leaders and this isn't just any province. You've shown you can balance the Lynesian and Sidorian populations; that's invaluable."

"And if the war fails, Rendalia falls anyway."

"All the more reason to keep you safe here, where you can organize defenses if needed."

Isolde's eyes flashed. "I didn't stay safe when my brother invaded."

"That was here, on familiar ground, with men who already knew your quality. This is going to be different."

"You're valuable too. If you fall, what will keep Pembroke, Sinclair, and a dozen other barons from infighting, even if the war is won? Why is the danger okay for you, but not for me?"

"That's different."

"Because you're a man? Because you're a Whitton?" She asked angrily, jerking her hands away. "I'm your partner, William. We've governed together, fought together, built this province together. Now, when you need support most, you want to leave me behind?"

"I just want to protect you."

"I don't need your protection. I need your respect. I didn't let my father treat me like some idiot fool in a dress, to be paraded out when needed and hidden away when not, and I'm not going to let you do it either."

"That's not what I'm doing."

"Good, then there's no reason for me not to come with you."

For a moment, William wasn't sure how to answer that. She was arguing him into a corner, twisting everything he said into something he didn't mean. He did trust her, but he also wasn't going to let her put herself in danger because of her stubborn pride.

"No. You're not coming to Sidor. That's my decision, and it's not open for discussion."

5

Isolde looked at him for a long moment, her expression unreadable, before finally turning toward the door.

"We'll see about that," she called over her shoulder.

She left without another word, the door closing firmly behind her. William wanted to throw something, to scream, to knock over the table. He didn't, but by the ancients, he wanted to.

Women!

Riversmeed, Barony of Yorwick, Kingsheart

The north bank of the Stonebridge River smelled of cold mud and anxious men. Garris Sinclair looked over the captains gathered in front of him, their breath plumed in the frigid air, their faces grim under the rims of their helms. They were good men. Hard men.

Men who had lost more fights lately than they had won.

It was time to change that.

"They've pushed us back far enough. I know it stings, and I feel it too. They think they can push east all the way to the Frozen Sea. They think we're weak. Defeated. It's time to show them just how wrong they are."

He gave them a final, hard look, a glance that passed from one man to the next, sealing the pact of the bloody work to come. "You have your orders. See them done."

The captains dispersed without another word, melting back into the darkness where their companies waited. Garris watched them go, the tight knot in his gut loosening just a fraction. It was a good plan. A dangerous plan, but a good one.

The preparations had taken three days. Three days of watching Crown forces tighten their grip on Riversmeed while his men worked in shifts through the freezing nights.

He made his way to the southern edge of the woods that concealed his main force, dismounting and handing his reins to a page. From a small rise, he could just make out the dark line of the enemy encampment across the frozen expanse of the Stonebridge River. Torches dotted their perimeter, small points of orange against the oppressive black of the winter night. They were comfortable. Secure. They had forgotten what it was to fear the dark.

A distant horn blast, thin and sharp in the frigid air, cut through the quiet. East. Sir Odran had begun his assault right on time. He watched the enemy line, saw a stirring of activity, torches moving in a cluster toward the eastern flank. Shouts carried faintly across the ice, indistinct but urgent. Good. They were taking the bait.

And what bait it was.

The eastern horizon erupted with fire as Odran's riders ignited prepared bundles of oil-soaked straw, hurling them at the Crown pickets.

In their redoubt on the west side of the city, it was like someone kicked over an ant-pile. Officers stumbled from their tents, bellowing orders while soldiers grabbed weapons and tried to form ranks in the chaos. The enemy had been focused on danger from inside the city but had apparently written off the idea of an attack from the outside.

The enemy sent what units they had at the ready to the east side of the city to counter the attack. Not enough, though. Fifty, maybe a hundred, rushed around to the other side of the city.

It didn't matter.

That was never the real attack. Sir Odran wouldn't even directly hit their line. He wanted them to think it was a feint, so that the next phase really sold.

Time ticked down, the sounds of distant yells meant it was working. If he was very lucky, they would push out of their siege works and try to bring Odran to grips.

He doubted they'd be that dumb and he didn't need them to be. The feint wasn't without danger. The enemy had archers on that side, firing into Odran's men, who had to be exposed for this to work.

With a nod, a runner took off, riding wide around the fortress, behind Odran, to the other side of Riversmeed. Silence was key.

No one needed to know he was here until he was ready for them to know.

He continued to wait, knowing he was losing men here or there. But the plan was to hold.

The first volley came without warning. Four hundred arrows falling from the darkness onto Crown positions. Garris couldn't see the arrows themselves from his position south of Riversmeed, only their effect: torches dropping along the distant northern line, the troops that had just started to organize falling into chaos. A second volley followed before the enemy could react, then a third.

Even from his concealed position at the Ravenswood's edge, Garris could hear officers bellowing orders. Through gaps between buildings, he glimpsed soldiers abandoning their posts.

These weren't well-trained soldiers. The king's army might have grown, but it had grown with farmers and tradesmen, not bloodied soldiers.

It took time, but the Crown officers finally managed to restore some order to a company of crossbowmen. Garris watched their torches form into rough lines, saw them loose a volley toward where they thought the arrows had originated. But they were shooting blind while Hardwick's men could see every torch-marked target. The next round of arrows came at the crossbowmen.

It ended badly for them.

If they wanted to stop the arrows, they were going to have to go out there and stop them. The Crown mounted men, while the arrows still fell, along with at least two large groups of spearmen.

At least three hundred men, maybe more.

They were ready to sweep the ice clear of the annoyance. They didn't take a lot of time to get ready. Not when they were losing men with every volley.

It wasn't a reckless charge. The men might have been green, but the Crown had given this group some good officers. You don't charge horses across frozen ground and you don't send them out away from infantry support when you don't know what you're riding into.

No, they were moving at the speed of the spearmen, keeping tight together. They could smell the ambush, since nothing followed up from the archers. Probably assumed some kind of trap for the cavalry.

They had no idea what they were riding into.

He couldn't see it, but the ice cracking and breaking under the weight of all those men and horses could be heard over everything else. He'd had his engineers out there at night for days, cutting and recutting into the ice. Sure, a lot froze over, but three days of cutting, plus the better part of this evening, had been enough to weaken it.

Pockets of air, half-frozen drill holes next to fresh ones.

It would hold one man, probably a few dozen. But not hundreds, and who knows how much horse flesh. No, the ice gave way and sent those brave men into its frozen depths.

Worse, the Stonebridge wasn't some gentle creek. It was the central river coming out of Lake Halcrest, traveling down toward the Iron Straits. The top may freeze, but below that, the river still ran its course, swift and forceful, sweeping any number of men south.

Garris couldn't see the drowning cavalry, but he could hear them. The screams carried clearly in the still air, growing more desperate before being cut short. There was something about the screams of the horses that would be hard to forget.

He just hoped Hardwick's men stayed well back, past the clear line the engineers had marked, where the ice would still be strong.

It didn't matter. A good part of the enemy's force was gone, and everyone's eyes were turned north and east. Now was the time.

Seven hundred men crouched in the tree line well short of the city and the Crown redoubt.

"Let's go," he said.

No shouts. No big speeches. They wouldn't hear his horses until he was on top of them.

And they would be surprised. Nearly every soldier had been pulled to the north side of their camp, trying to see what happened to all the men who had just marched off to their deaths.

The first Crown soldiers they encountered were support troops, cooks, quartermasters, and the infirm. These fled without fighting, throwing down their tools and running for their lives. But beyond them, a company of infantry was trying to form ranks.

Garris hit them at a sprint. A sergeant saw him coming, tried to bring his sword up, but Garris's blade found the gap below his helmet first. Hot blood sprayed across the frozen ground as the man toppled backward. The company practically crumbled as the cavalry smashed through them.

Garris's force spread through the camp, breaking to take their assigned routes. One company hit the supply wagons, cutting down guards and anyone around them. Not critical for the victory, but it was winter and it was a challenge to feed men in the field.

Another company struck at the command tents where officers were still trying to understand what was happening. Most died before they could draw their swords.

Near the north side of the camp, a young Crown lieutenant had his head about him, not running or panicking, but pulling what men he could together.

"To me! Form square! Form square!"

Crown soldiers who'd been fleeing stopped, turned, and began moving toward him, happy to have direction and leadership. Within moments, two companies of spearmen had formed a defensive square near the northern earthworks, their weapons bristling outward. More men ran to join them, seeing a point of resistance in the collapse.

Garris recognized the danger immediately. The enemy still outnumbered him, even with the men lost in the river. He was never going to kill enough of them to change that math.

What he wanted to do was rattle them and then break them with a charge. That square could ruin all of that, give the Crown forces a point to rally round, organize a real defense. Already more soldiers were running toward it, seeing safety in those ordered ranks.

Garris wheeled his horse, his guard and personal knights following him, turning a circle around the square as the infantry engaged it from the south and east. They moved through the burning camp as they circled, past abandoned tents and overturned wagons. A Crown soldier, separated from his unit, stumbled into their path. Garris's sword took him before he could cry out.

They came at the square from behind, where the spearmen were focused on the obvious threat. The lieutenant had done well, getting all the men together, but they'd made one mistake. They'd formed too close to a supply wagon, leaving a blind spot in their coverage.

They vaulted their horses over the wagon and crashed into the corner of the square. Garris's sword found the gap between breastplate and backplate on a spearman, punching through mail and flesh. The man beside him tried to turn, to bring his long spear around, but the weapon was useless at such a close range. Garris's blade opened his throat in a spray of crimson.

"The corner! They're in the corner!" The lieutenant called out, trying to shift men to meet this new threat, but that created gaps elsewhere.

Garris's main force poured through those gaps.

What had been an organized defense became a melee, spears useless in the press of bodies. The lieutenant, still trying to restore order, took a rebel's axe between his shoulder blades. He dropped to his knees, looked down in surprise at the blade protruding from his chest, then pitched forward.

Without leadership, the square disintegrated. Crown soldiers threw down their weapons and fled, tried to surrender, or simply fought until overwhelmed. Within minutes, what had been a growing defensive position was just another scene of slaughter.

To the east, new sounds of battle erupted. Sir Odran's light cavalry, seeing the complete collapse of the Crown position, had transformed their feint into a genuine assault. Not what he'd been ordered to do, but the man did have initiative.

The men inside the city walls saw their moment. The gates burst open and out poured five hundred men who'd been trapped inside for weeks, now seeing their chance for revenge.

The Crown soldiers caught between Garris's force and the garrison had nowhere to run. Some tried to form defensive lines, but they were being hit from two directions simultaneously. Others simply dropped their weapons and raised their hands, preferring captivity to death. Many weren't given the choice, in the chaos of battle, with blood running hot, quarter wasn't always given even to those who asked.

The last man standing, a grizzled sergeant with more scars than teeth, finally dropped his sword when five rebels surrounded him with spears leveled.

"I yield," he said simply.

Dawn was breaking properly now, true light replacing the gray pre-dawn. It revealed the complete scope of the victory. The Crown camps that had surrounded Riversmeed for weeks were now burning ruins. Bodies carpeted the ground, Crown soldiers who'd stood and fought, who'd run too slowly, who'd simply been in the wrong place when the rebels swept through.

The battle was over and the Crown forces defeated.

Chapter 2

Fettlesham, Barony of Hopton, Kingsheart

As his procession approached Fettlesham, Edmund surveyed the town square. Another boring town, not even a baronial seat. Once again, he wished the Key would work on a wider range and not require him to travel from town to town to gain the loyalty he needed.

Still, it was a king's duty to sacrifice for his people, and so he sacrificed.

At least Baron Danby had prepared properly for his visit, making sure that the proper displays were in place and the snow cleared.

"Your Majesty!" Danby dropped to one knee as Edmund's destrier came to a halt. "We are honored beyond measure by your presence. We are your most loyal servants, now and always."

Edmund gave a grunt as he dismounted, allowing his household guard to form a protective semicircle behind him. Twenty men in pristine mail and surcoats bearing the gold lion of his family, their weapons polished to mirror brightness.

Beyond protection, they were a sign of his station, ensuring everyone knew exactly where the power lay here.

"Baron Danby," Edmund acknowledged with a brief glance before he looked past the kneeling man to the crowd of perhaps three hundred souls packed into the town square.

"My lord, if I may present ..."

"Later," Edmund cut off whatever introduction Danby had prepared.

He had no interest in the local gentry's fawning presentations, especially Danby, the pampered son of a minor noble who'd managed to talk his grandfather into giving him a peerage for some minor accomplishment.

"Certainly, my lord. We have prepared everything as requested," Danby stammered, gesturing toward the wooden structure. "Along with wine, proper seating for the local lords ..."

"I'll stand alone on the platform," Edmund said, walking past the stunned man, sending his guards to form a barricade around the platform, both for his protection and to keep away the more annoying nobles hoping to gain his favor.

He climbed the steps slowly, dramatically, knowing all eyes were fixed on him. He could never explain to Gavric that beyond what a king did was the perception of what was done. That ruling was as much display as actual accomplishment and that, if things were presented in the right light, people would form whatever narrative you needed them to.

Reaching the center of the platform, Edmund raised his hand, bringing silence among the people. He let the moment stretch, his blue eyes moving from face to face in the front rows, making sure they knew he saw them.

Letting them connect with their king.

"Good people of Fettlesham," he started. "I come to speak about a shared purpose. For too long, the Crown has ignored you, the good people of Sidor. Has not recognized the shared triumph. The shared purpose. That ends now. The Crown needs you, the heart of our kingdom, now more than ever as we face together the greatest trial since my ancestor united the scattered kingdoms of our continent into a single whole."

He paused, letting his words sink in while he focused on the artifact hanging around his neck. He wasn't sure if he had to focus on it to make it work or not, but it was difficult not to think about it. It was like he could feel it digging into his soul every time he gave one of these speeches.

Not that he was going to stop. His armies and coffers were both filling up thanks to it. He would deal with the consequences.

"Your ancestors stood firm when the warlords spread over this land. They held on when creatures poured across the River Mark and ravaged this land before Cynewulf established his short-lived kingdom. You, each of you, are their worthy heirs. The same blood flows in your veins. The same courage beats in your hearts. And it is that heart I am here to address today. We are facing enemies more dangerous than raiders, warlords, or maw-spawned demons. Today, we face men who should be our brothers but instead want to tear our kingdom apart from within."

A murmur ran through the crowd, fear and anger mingling, more than would usually affect normal people like this. These people, or at least their ancestors, had been conquered time and again. They lived under the rule of bailiffs, barons and kings. They only cared about their children and their crops.

The rest of the world could burn for all it mattered to them.

But now they were incensed. Not just incensed. A woman near the front began to weep softly, in a level of despair that was normally reserved for much more personal things.

"So I ask, what would become of us?" Edmund continued. "If Sidor were no more? If there were no more Crown forces to guard the roads? Who would protect your daughters from bandits if ambitious lords divide the realm between them? Who would ensure that grain reaches your tables when every baron keeps his own stores? This is their vision of Sidor, a land without a rightful king. Where every baron is his own man and every inch of this country is prey every time these lords bicker and fight. There is one man above all others who bears the guilt for this suffering. My own brother. Aldric Whitton."

He paused, letting the moment hang, the words float in the air.

"It was Aldric who murdered my nephew, our young King Serwyn, a boy of sixteen years, cut down like a dog during sacred peace negotiations. My nephew's blood stained his killer's hands. The boy who should have grown to be your king now lies cold in his tomb. The ancients themselves delivered justice upon this murderer. Sir Alistair Everwood took vengeance for us all, cutting down the kinslayer where he stood."

Cheers erupted from the crowd. Edmund let the applause wash over him before continuing.

"Yet his death did not end the festering rebellion. No, it carries on, led by another usurper, Garris Sinclair of Iron Keep. An opportunist from a backwater barony who sees our division as his chance for glory. Who wants to carve himself a kingdom from our bones and call it victory?"

Now the crowd's anger had a clear target, a face to hate. He was careful to avoid William's name, not that he cared what happened to his adopted son. The problem was, his name still carried respect from the Lynese war and mentioning him might complicate his narrative. He wouldn't be able to use the Key on everyone in the kingdom, not by a long shot, so he needed those who it did affect to convince those he couldn't get to personally.

Which meant the story had to be just right.

"This is the man who brings war to your doorsteps!" His voice rose to a thunderous roar. "This is the traitor who would see Sidor broken and scattered! I name him outlaw and enemy of every true Sidorian heart!"

The square erupted. Fists shook in the air, voices raised in condemnation.

But Edmund was far from finished. He raised his hands again, and gradually the tumult subsided.

"I understand. I feel the same fire in my belly, but anger alone will not win this war," he said, his tone shifting to solemn gravity. "Anger alone will not stop this scourge. That will only be done by steel and coin."

He reached into his doublet and withdrew a heavy purse, thick with gold coins. Without ceremony, he upended it into a large wooden barrel positioned at the platform's base. The metallic clatter of the coins landing ringing across the silent square.

"I give my own gold freely to this cause, our cause. For what good is a king's treasure if his kingdom burns? But we need more than this. We need men to fight these invaders, and grain to feed them. So, I come to you, my friends, for help. Will you step up and give what you can to the cause? Your blood and your bounty?"

The common folk surged forward, pressing against the guards to reach the collection barrels that had been strategically placed around the platform. Copper coins, pieces of jewelry, warm cloaks, anything of value they had on their bodies were thrown in. Pledges were made for grain and meat for the armies. Anything they could give. The Key's influence had transformed their fear into desperate patriotism, their anxiety into the need to act, to contribute, to belong to something greater than their small, hard lives.

Along with the goods, dozens of men pressed toward the platform asking, no begging, to be allowed to volunteer. Some of the men openly wept at the idea of participating in the battle.

The fervor was palpable.

"Behold!" Edmund's voice rose above the tumult. "Behold the true spirit of Sidor! When darkness threatens, we do not cower in our homes. We stand! We fight! We defend what is ours!"

The crowd roared its approval, completely lost in the moment. The artifact's power had stripped away their individual thoughts and replaced them with collective purpose.

It took a moment for his people to set up a collection booth and a place for men to volunteer. He would leave both behind to allow people from the surrounding area to provide more donations and for the men to say goodbye to their families and march out by evening to join the armies in the east.

He'd done what he came here to do and could leave this maw-forsaken place and go back to civilization.

"Your sacrifices today will not be forgotten. With your gold, your grain, and your very lives you have purchased a better world for your children and their children after them. They will speak your names with pride, knowing their forefathers stood firm when the realm's fate hung in the balance!"

The crowd was beyond rational thought now. They chanted his name in rhythmic waves, their faces shining with tears and transcendent joy.

"Edmund! Edmund! Edmund!"

With a final wave, he turned and descended the platform, making sure enough guards were there to keep the crowd back. Not that he feared they'd try to injure him, but as worked up by the Key as they were, they were in enough of a frenzy that they might do him harm without meaning to in their rush to touch his shirt sleeve or kiss his feet.

Instead, the soldiers redirected them, pushing them to the recruiting tables, which were being mobbed by volunteers, pushing and shoving for the honor of signing their names to his cause. Mothers wept with pride as they watched their sons pledge their lives to the king. Old men pressed their life savings into the hands of his collectors, trembling with the joy of being of service.

He moved to remount his horse with the aid of a squire, so he could ride out of town, the conquering hero, before transferring to a much more comfortable carriage for the remainder of the ride, when there was a commotion among his soldiers.

Not from the crowd side, but from the direction they would be headed. A rider came tearing into town. He was wearing royal colors, but there had been enough tricks by the rebels that just because a man wore the colors did not guarantee he actually was one of their own.

He must have said the right thing because the guards let him through, once he dismounted, and the man hurried to Edmund, dropping to a knee in front of him and holding up a rolled document.

"Your Majesty! News from the east!"

Edmund took the missive and read it quickly. He'd hoped for more tales of victory after Pembroke managed to stop his people on the other side of the Thunderhorn, but his hopes were dashed.

Garris Sinclair had broken the siege of Riversmeed. The Crown forces there had been shattered in a night attack sending what remained running back to Ramsgate.

For a moment, his careful mask slipped, his nostrils flaring as he crushed the dispatch into a crumpled ball. It was all he could do not to beat the man who brought him the news.

But he was still in public, and the crowd was still worked up. The Key was magic, but even it had its limits. He had to continue the show for the rabble.

So instead, he took a deep breath, forcing his rage back. He had come too far and done too much to let a few setbacks break his control.

He had more men, and would have more each day, to replace those lost.

Time was on his side now.

North of Twyver, Dunwic's Reach, Kingsheart

Baron Pembroke raised his gauntleted hand, the signal his men had been waiting for since before dawn. Four hundred knights surged forward across the Thunderhorn Bridge, their lances lowered as one. The thunder of hooves on stone drowned out everything else as the mass of steel and horseflesh crashed into the Crown pickets guarding the eastern approach.

Pickets that had been allowed to dwindle to a small number since they were pushed out of Twyver a few weeks before.

The enemy sentries barely had time to shout a warning before the knights were upon them. One man threw down his spear and tried to run, but a lance caught him between the shoulder blades, lifting him off his feet and throwing his body twenty feet to the side. Another picket managed to thrust his pike at an oncoming horse, but the knight's lance found him first, punching through his leather jerkin as if it were parchment.

Behind the knights, nine hundred levy soldiers poured across the bridge. These weren't professional soldiers, but they were motivated, shields raised and spears ready. They swept over the scattered bodies of the pickets, securing the bridgehead while the cavalry pressed forward onto the East Road proper.

Pembroke spurred his destrier harder, leading the charge into the main body of Crown forces. The enemy, who'd been bivouacked to the side of the road, had formed a hasty line across it. It was a good effort, but he hadn't given them a lot of time and these weren't veterans.

The knights hit the enemy line like an avalanche. What defense they had set up shattered instantly. Spears were a formidable weapon against cavalry, but it took nerve for a formation of spearmen to hold. Nerve these men didn't have.

Many simply threw down their weapons and ran, trampling their own fellows in their desperation to escape. A few seasoned leaders tried to hold it together, to rally the men, but they were ridden down before they had a chance to succeed.

Pembroke wheeled his horse, but there wasn't a need to charge again. These conscripts had no stomach for real fighting. Half of them hadn't even tried to stand their ground. Bodies littered the road, most bearing wounds to their backs where they'd been cut down while fleeing.

His own men reached the melee, but there was little left for them to do. The Crown soldiers were running in every direction, casting aside shields and weapons to run faster. The problem was that most were running in the same direction, up the East Road.

Which meant they might regroup.

"Press them!" Pembroke commanded. "Don't let them reform!"

His knights needed no further encouragement. They spurred after the fleeing enemy, riding them down without mercy. The road became a killing ground, bodies sprawled in the mud and snow, blood pooling in the wagon ruts. A group of Crown soldiers tried to make a stand around their banner, but his infantry levy swarmed over them, spears thrusting again and again until none were left standing.

The entire Crown force, nearly a thousand men, turned into a panicked mob fleeing north up the road. Officers who tried to restore order were pulled from their horses and killed. Entire companies dissolved into scattered individuals running for their lives.

Pembroke felt the familiar rush of victory, the sweet taste of an enemy completely broken. His losses were minimal, perhaps a dozen men wounded, none dead that he could see. The enemy had lost hundreds already, with more falling every moment as his cavalry pursued those who tried to flee.

They would be at the Tradesway in no time, rejoined with the eastern barons, if victories like this continued.

The pursuit stretched for nearly two miles. Pembroke's knights spread out, some riding far ahead to catch the fastest runners, others sweeping the flanks to prevent any from escaping into the woods.

They rounded a wide bend in the road, the trees falling away to reveal open ground ahead. Pembroke reined in his horse so suddenly that those behind him nearly collided with his mount. There, positioned on a commanding ridge perhaps three hundred yards in the distance, stood rank upon rank of soldiers.

Formed and ready.

The last of the fleeing conscripts ran past the flanks of this new group, which opened small gaps to let them through before closing ranks again.

A well-done maneuver, and one not accomplished by rough conscripts.

"My lord," Sir Halward said, pulling up beside him. "Those aren't ..."

The trees to their left exploded with movement. Five hundred Crown knights burst from the forest where they'd been concealed, their lances already leveled. They hit Pembroke's extended column like a sword thrust into an exposed belly. The first River Mark knights didn't even have time to turn their horses before the Crown cavalry smashed into them.

Sir Morley went down immediately, a lance through his throat. His squire tried to defend his fallen lord but he was trampled under the hooves of three destriers. The knight beside him managed to parry one lance only to take another in the ribs, the force of the impact throwing him from his saddle.

"Form up! Form up!" Pembroke bellowed, wheeling his horse to face the attack.

But there was no time. His men were scattered along nearly a mile of road, some still pursuing fleeing conscripts, others looting bodies. The Crown knights carved through them, their charge perfectly timed and positioned.

Pembroke parried a lance thrust with his sword and struck back, his blade finding the gap between helmet and gorget, dropping the Crown knight from his saddle. Another enemy immediately took his place, forcing Pembroke to duck under a swinging mace.

His household guard rallied around him, twenty knights forming a desperate circle of steel. They held for a moment, their swords keeping the Crown cavalry at bay, but more enemies kept coming. The forest seemed to vomit forth an endless stream of armored horsemen.

Behind them, the levy was taking the worst of it. Caught completely in the open, they had no chance to form shield walls or pike squares.

"Their infantry's moving!" someone shouted.

Pembroke risked a glance toward the ridge. The pike blocks were advancing. They came down the slope like a steel wall. If they reached the road while his forces were still entangled with the Crown cavalry, it would be a massacre.

"Sound the retreat!" Pembroke commanded. "Back to the bridge!"

The horn call rang out. Some of his men heard it and began falling back. Others, too pressed by the enemy or too far away, fought on in isolated pockets.

Pembroke and his household guard formed the beginning of a rear guard, trying to give their retreating forces time to disengage. A Crown knight came at him with a war hammer, and Pembroke twisted in his saddle to avoid the blow, his counterstrike opening the man's thigh to the bone. Blood sprayed across his horse's flank.

"Stay together!" he shouted to his remaining knights. "Fighting withdrawal! Don't let them separate us!"

They gave ground slowly, painfully. Every yard cost them men. Now it was his men's time to abandon wounded comrades, throw away shields and spears, trying anything they could to run faster.

"My lord, we have to go!" Sir Halward shouted, parrying a sword thrust meant for Pembroke's exposed side, as his knights remained at the far back, trying to buy as much time as they could for the rest of his forces.

The baron knew he was right. The enemy infantry was less than a hundred yards away now, their pikes lowered, death for cavalry. But leaving meant abandoning hundreds of his men who were still trying to fight their way clear.

A lance caught his horse in the chest. The animal screamed and went down, throwing Pembroke hard onto the hard-packed ground. He rolled aside just as hooves crashed down where his head had been. Strong hands hauled him to his feet, Sir Halward and another knight whose name he couldn't remember in the chaos.

"Take my horse, my lord!"

Pembroke didn't argue. He swung into the saddle as more of his men fell around him. They spurred their horses toward the bridge, the thunder of pursuit right behind them.

The Thunderhorn Bridge appeared through the chaos, and Pembroke saw that some of his levy had already crossed, forming a defensive line on the western bank. Others were still streaming across, pushing and shoving in their panic. Several men fell into the icy water and were swept away by the current.

"Hold the bridge!" Pembroke commanded the men on the western side. "Spears up! Archers to the fore!"

He was among the last to cross, turning his horse on the bridge itself to strike down a Crown knight who'd gotten too close to the fleeing levy. The man's helmet split under Pembroke's sword, and he tumbled from his horse into the river below.

Once on the western bank, Pembroke quickly assessed what remained of his force. Of the four hundred knights he'd led across that morning, fewer than three hundred had made it back. The levy had fared even worse; perhaps a third of their number had fallen in the trap.

The Crown forces halted at the eastern end of the bridge and made no attempt to cross. Catching a smaller force was one thing, but on the narrow bridge, Pembroke's smaller force had the advantage.

They'd achieved their goal, caught his men and forced them back across the river, using their own conscripts as a tripwire to spring the rest of the trap.

"Where did they get so many men?" Sir Halward asked as Pembroke dismounted.

Pembroke just shook his head. The Crown had been bleeding forces for months, not even considering the losses in the peasants' revolt. The hope had been that they had bled the Crown enough that they could swat the rest away and push on to Starhaven.

And yet, somehow, the "king" had managed to find more men.

Chapter 3

Rendalia City, Rendalia

William watched the stevedores haul crates and barrels up the gangplanks of the three ships moored in the harbor. Men called orders back and forth as they loaded provisions, weapons, and armor into the holds. His armor. His weapons. His war. He had fifteen more ships, transports and not cargo ships, gathering to load up his men as soon as the maw began to close, which would be within the week.

Which meant he'd be on the waves and headed for Sidor in the week. It would be slow going, crossing the straits, but he wasn't going to risk sailing the long way around.

Hopefully, he wouldn't be too late.

"Still brooding at the water's edge?"

He turned to find Isolde approaching, her brown hair loose about her shoulders. Part of him just wanted to dive into the bay to avoid what he knew was coming.

"I'm ensuring the preparations proceed properly."

"The men know their business well enough without your supervision. Maybe you're just avoiding me."

"Maybe I'm avoiding another pointless argument."

"Pointless? I'm not sure I'd call our partnership pointless."

William turned to face her fully. "That's not what I meant, and you know it. I meant the argument about you coming to Sidor. That matter is settled."

"Nothing's settled."

A longshoreman dropped a crate nearby, the crash making them both look toward the sound before William returned his attention to his wife. "Isolde, we've been through this. Sidor is at war. I'll be marching into battle, not holding court in some peaceful castle. You'll be safer here."

"Safer, perhaps. But also useless to you and to our cause." She stepped closer. "Do you think me some delicate flower that wilts at the first sign of hardship? I've governed this province for months while you were gone. I've negotiated with the hill tribes, commanded troops, held Rendalia against invasion, and rode out of prison all the way back to you after my brother had me arrested. What more must I prove?"

"This isn't about proving anything. It's about ..."

"It's about you wanting to protect me by leaving me behind like some ornament to be kept safe in a jewelry box. I am your wife, William. Your partner. Not some prize to be hidden away while you are waging war."

William sighed, putting his hands on his hips. "You don't understand what it's like. In battle, when the swords are drawn and men are dying, I can't be thinking about whether you're safe. I can't be worrying about—"

"About me distracting you from your grand heroic destiny?"

"Ahhhh," he shouted, turning in a small circle and throwing up his hands. "Damnit, woman."

"Isn't it? You speak as though I'm some burden to be managed rather than an asset to be utilized. I dealt with Pembroke, got him to work with me. Work for me. I understand politics and diplomacy in ways that will serve you when you're trying to unite a fractured rebellion. You're a great soldier, William, but do you have those same skills?"

"It's not the same, Isolde. The nobles of Sidor are not the same as the nobles of Lynese or Rendalia. They won't accept a foreign princess telling them how to govern their kingdom."

"I'm not the first foreign bride of a king."

"And what if you're killed? What then?"

"What if you're killed?" she countered. "Should I forbid you from going because I fear for your safety?"

"That's different."

"How? Because you're a man and I'm a woman? Because you're allowed to risk your life for duty while I must cower in safety?"

William felt his own temper beginning to fray. "That's different. If you want to get on a horse and lead a charge, then have at it, but how do you think that will go? Someone has to fight! To make sure we have something worth fighting for!"

"How can you not see wars are not won by swords alone, William? You told me about your conversations with your uncle. With both of them. Didn't they teach you that wars are won by alliances, by negotiations? That is what I can do for you."

"You can do that from here, in Rendalia, where it's safe."

"Safe, yes, but useless. The nobles I need to influence are in Sidor, not here. You say you need to unite the rebellion. How do you plan to do that? I may not be from Sidor, but I pay attention. Sinclair wants the throne for himself; everyone knows it. Pembroke might be loyal to you, but he doesn't have the loyalty of everyone in the River Mark, let alone the rest of the kingdom. When your father is gone, every noble in your kingdom is gonna do what nobles always do. Look out for their own self-interest."

He looked up, toward the heavens. Toward the ancestors.

"The danger ..."

"Is mine to accept or reject. You do not get to make that choice for me. I am not asking for your permission, William. I am telling you what's going to happen."

"What do you mean?"

"I mean that I will not remain in Rendalia while you sail off to war. If you leave without me, I will commandeer the next ship I can find and follow you to Sidor. I'll cross the waters while the maw is still closing if I have to, putting myself in far greater danger than I would face traveling with you and your escort."

"You can't be serious."

"I am *completely* serious. You can take me with you, or you can force me to make the journey on my own with whatever ship I can hire. But I will not sit here like a helpless ornament while you fight for our future without me."

For a long time, he just stared at her. He could see she wasn't going to budge. He also knew she was right, in her own way.

He just wished he didn't.

"Damn woman," he said finally. "Fine. You can come."

The transformation in her expression was immediate and radiant. "Thank you for being reasonable."

"Uh-huh," he said, closing the distance between them and taking her arm. "You're right, they know their jobs. Let's get somewhere warmer."

Riversmeed, Barony of Yorwick, Kingsheart

The morning service had proceeded with the usual solemnity that marked Blessing Day. Garris Sinclair knelt with the other worshipers as the acolyte raised his hands toward the stone altar, his voice carrying the ancient words of gratitude for surviving another winter. The hall's thick walls muffled the sounds of the town outside, where his soldiers and the people of Riversmeed celebrated the end of the maw season with food and ale.

It did not muffle the sound of the bell, which rang in the middle of the acolyte's prayer, cutting off the man's words.

Garris lifted his head. The bell rang again, then again, joined by others throughout the town in a growing flood. Around him, the congregation stirred as each suddenly realized something was happening. The acolyte faltered in his recitation.

Then came the screams.

Garris surged to his feet as his personal guard moved to stand near him, pushing other worshipers out of the way in an effort to protect their liege from the unknown threat.

"Out," Garris said.

As it was the main hall, it was mostly full of nobles, people who came as much to be seen as to worship, but at least a third were officers from his army, knights and the children of lesser nobles. They all came to the realization as quickly as he had.

Riversmeed was under attack.

He hustled to the aisle, his men piling in behind him, forming a wake that washed out of the hall and into the street. Ash from the hall's incense still stung Garris's nose when he shouldered the great doors open, and cool late winter air met him like a slap. Level with the hall's steps rose the roofs of Riversmeed, a good stone town with a proud bridge, and beyond the roofs a smear of black smoke clawed at the sky from the west. More smoke lifted to the north. Shouts carried from that direction.

"Branric, you go south along Spur Lane and send any men with a badge or a blade to the north wall," Garris said. "I want Hardwick up on the west gate with bows. And get Marden ... you will probably find the man, if he still drinks, at the King's Pitcher."

"Aye," he said, grabbing several of his men and rushing north.

"Lyle, take two and ride to the barracks at Market Row. Rouse every last one of Odran's lads and have them come to the west wall."

Lyle nodded once and sprinted for the temple's side yard where three mounts stood tied under a lean-to, their reins looped over a beam for ceremony's sake. He had the good sense to drag a stable boy to help.

Garris swung up onto a bay, a plain animal with a scar on one knee from a winter fall. Two more knights mounted beside him.

"Trumpet," he said to one of the foot men behind them. "Blast for the west wall. Then run that horn to the north and sound it again."

The man wet his lips and blew until his face went dark. The clear note cut through the din.

"Move," Garris said, and set heel to horse.

They pushed into the flow of bodies. He did not have time to slow. A trap maker with stuffing in his hair clutched a cage of bristles to his chest and moved aside ... too late. The bay's shoulder clipped him and sent him spinning. Dogs ran underfoot and got kicked for their trouble.

At Spur Lane, the flow turned against them. Smoke stung his eyes. Garris's mount shoved men aside, as he shouted for them to keep to the right if they must run and give the left to soldiers. Someone overheard and bellowed it down the way, and the crush eased as the townsfolk broke to one side.

He pissed off more than a few, but he got his way.

Garris reached the western square and the staircase to the wall. Arrows hissed overhead, telling him the battle was already underway. A man toppled from the merlon and smacked into the cobbles face-first. Garris dismounted and took the steps two, then three at a time, men jammed in front of him in their own rush up or down. He heard the roars before he crested. When he gained the parapet, his breath left him.

The enemy was like wheat. Lines and lines of them in rough leather and patched wool, all with rope-tied ladders and casks and poles. Some had spears with poorly set heads. Some clutched farm hooks and stakes.

Rabble more than an army, but a huge one. And all of them were running for the wall. Behind them rode a few mounted men with short whips, trotting along and swatting shoulders to keep the flood tight.

Riversmeed's garrison still held the parapet and Hardwick was already there, his archers at the second tower, firing into the host. Men near Garris pushed the ladders away with hooks. One ladder rose, then two, then ten, slapped the stone and thudded as men below slammed them home.

"You ... you," he said, grabbing a man by his collar, militia by the look of him, still in a brown cap. "Hold that hook ready."

"They keep climbing," the man said.

"They do," Garris said.

The first head came over the edge, a youth with down on his cheek and eyes mad with something that did not look like courage. Garris buried a sword point under his chin and twisted. The boy fell without a sound and took two more with him. A hand holding a sword reached up in his place and slashed blindly. A garrison man's shield caught the blade and shoved it aside. One of his own men, a seasoned man-at-arms to his left, jammed a pike down between the rungs, then he and another heaved in time. The ladder scraped the stone and went off. Men below rushed to set it up again.

"Hooks," Garris yelled.

The brown-capped man leaned so far out Garris wanted to drag him back by the belt. He snagged a rung, then his feet slid on frost-wet stone and he had to brace. Two more pushed with him, faces purple from the strain. The ladder started to draw, then something below shoved it back up, a knot of men straining at the base. An archer to Garris's right put a shaft into one of those men, then another, but more pushed in. Garris planted his shoulder against the top stone and shoved. The ladder came up another span of hand, then slipped one back, then finally lost the fight and fell. A scream rose up and kept rising.

Three more ladders met the stone almost in front of him while the men on either side shoved theirs off. The first head over wore a cap with a feather and he had neat beard braids that made him look older. He had a knife in his teeth when he reached for the parapet with both hands, and when Branric's shield slammed him back, he spat the blade into his hand and lunged with it.

Garris stepped in and cut low from his right hip, steel biting the man's forearm to the bone. The attacker shrieked and reeled, and Garris's follow-through smashed the boss of his shield into the man's face, sending him sailing off the wall, hanging in space for a moment before smashing down into the people below.

"Hardwick," Garris called down the wall. "Shift ten to the stairs. Ladders first. Ladders only."

The bow captain did not reply. He did not need to. The flow of arrows changed while Garris watched, no shafts wasted on the rear ranks. Men on ropes and rungs jerked. A ladder fell, and men below surged to set it up again. Harwick's boys cut them down, but more ran in to replace them.

They fought like men who did not fear death. Garris had seen brave men and stupid ones; these seemed somewhere in between. Which was rare for what seemed like conscripts. Rabble.

"Baron!" a voice cried behind Garris. He ignored it until the messenger found his arm. The man bled from a cut along his hairline, and one ear hung torn. "North gate is falling. So many men ... by the ancients, so many."

"Will it hold?" Garris asked.

"I don't know, but I don't think for long. They throw bodies to fill the ditch and climb the heap."

Garris looked briefly over the wall. Things were not much better here. They were paying a price for the wall, but that cost was going to pay out. If they continued, the enemy would take the wall.

"Tell him this," Garris said. "Stand firm for as long as he can and pull off when he hears the horn. I will sound it. We withdraw together in order, shields locked, pikes to the fore."

"We withdraw? Now?"

"Go," Garris said, not explaining his thinking.

The man went. Garris spared one glance and saw the northern smoke thicken, racks of oil-fired brush going to flame along the crenels where they had stores for such days. The bells at that tower never stopped. After their last loss, he hadn't thought it possible for them to take these kinds of losses.

Garris shoved along the parapet and took the narrow steps up the nearest watchtower two at a time. The world opened when he gained the platform and leaned into the windless air. From there, he saw the whole field and wished he had not.

From the north, the ground crawled with bodies. From the west, it was the same. The ditch that ringed the wall, filled by the Stonebridge, took them by the dozens, but the dead had begun to stack deep enough in the water to create a grotesque form of land.

He turned to the south, where the fields ran to the orchard and then on to the forests. As he feared, he saw a column there, marching toward the south gate. There were probably more men ready to loop around to the east gate, sealing them in.

"How bad?" Branric asked when he returned to the wall.

"We cannot keep this," Garris said. He did not try to soften it. "They will smother us. There's a third column to the south. They will cut us off soon."

"Do we run?"

"I think we have no choice," Garris said. "Find Lyle. Find Hardwick. Odran. Have everyone pull for the east gate when the horn sounds twice. Leave three companies to hold while the rest fall back. I want the carts out on the East Road in five counts of ten."

"Three companies won't hold for long."

"They will hold long enough," Garris said. "Go. And send for Donnington."

Branric went down the steps without reply, first to the parapet, then into the tower to drop to the yard. Garris stayed, directing the fighting, shoring up the weaker parts of the wall.

Once things looked right, he moved to follow after Branric. It was time to end this.

He was halfway back to the town center when he ran into a man in blue and silver, the colors of Yorwick, who was rushing through the crowds toward him.

"Lord Sinclair," Killian Donnington said. They weren't friends, but for now, they were allies. "Will the wall hold?"

"No. Maybe an hour more, but no longer, not with the south column closing. We're going to pull out of the city, get as many soldiers as we can east to fight on as long as possible."

"We do not," Donnington said. "This is my city."

"Then you can stay here and die.

"But my people," Donnington said, sounding almost desperate.

"There is nothing we can do for them. If we delay for them, then we will lose this entire army, and they will still be in the Crown's hands. What we can do now is make sure we fight another day."

"I will not leave Riversmeed," Donnington said, angry.

"You will," Garris said. "Or you stand here and die. And your men will die. And still, your people will be under the yoke of that man on the throne. So choose."

"How dare you?" Donnington said.

"So choose or I will leave you and your men here to die because their lord wanted a piece of stone more than a living army."

Donnington's mouth worked. He had always been too gentle to rule. One of those who were born into nobility but never learned the real lessons of it.

"Damn you," he said, and the words came out low and hot. "Damn your black heart, Sinclair. Do it then ... go sound the horn. I will give the order."

"That is the first wise thing you have said today," Garris said.

He sent two runners from the tower with the words for the captains to begin pulling men back by companies at the second horn, destroying sections of the city on the way through to create barricades, slow the enemy down.

Some of the companies would get caught and cut down. Or trapped.

But that was the cost of getting the rest out.

Garris made his way to the wall, back to where the trumpeter was.

At least the one he knew about.

"Hardwick!" Garris called.

The bow captain made it to him with an arrow still held in fingers.

"You have fire?" Garris asked.

"Oil. No pitch."

"Oil will do. Soak the racks and ladders they've set. Soak the wall and the towers. Soak as much around it as you can. When the horn sounds, when we pull off, set them to burn. A hot wall is no place to climb. Give them a taste."

Hardwick grunted, understanding what the order meant. What it would cost.

Garris found the trumpeter, not far away from where the captain had been.

"Twice," Garris said. "Long. Once. Then twice again."

The boy nodded and put brass to his lips.

The sound went out along the wall. It ran in waves from tower to tower, men's heads turning. Down the wall, more trumpets sounded, passing the notes on, circling the city.

He turned and hurried, pulling men with him, heading for the east gate. Behind him, fires started to burn. Buildings started to come down.

By the time he got to the east gate, men had already started to gather, dozens, and then hundreds of men running, knowing if they were caught behind, they would be dead.

"Not many more coming," Branric said, coming from the north with almost a hundred more men.

"North falls," Branric said. "Iban pulled off in time. He left forty on the wall with pikes and hooks to hold while the rest got down. They will burn if we leave them there more than a few counts."

"Take what's here and start heading east. The river will make it hard to chase us, and the fire will make it hard for them to cross the river," Garris said.

Branric nodded, looking back at the city that would be a ruin by the time the sun went down.

Men hurried out of the city with only the armor on their backs and weapons in their hands. It would be a hungry march to Lindvale, but they had little choice. Donnington had at least been smart enough to begin pulling supplies into wagons as soon as he realized he had no choice but to give up the city, but that had been the work of minutes, not hours, and it would run out in a day, if that.

Still, better than no supplies.

"Good thinking," Sinclair said to the baron.

"My levy will not like this, Lord Sinclair," he said, still clearly not over being forced to do what he should have realized was his only choice. "They will call me craven."

"At least they will be alive to call you it," Garris said.

Now the question was, how many could he get out before the city burned around them?

Chapter 4

Starhaven, Sidor

"Your Majesty, a messenger has just arrived," one of the guards said.

Edmund squeezed his eyes, pressing the bridge of his nose. He was tired of messengers. Of messengers and favor seekers. Still, this is what being king meant.

Or so it seemed.

A moment later, the heavy doors to the throne room groaned open, admitting a man dressed in riding clothes and wearing the livery of Baron Greville, who approached the dais, falling to one knee.

"Rise," he commanded. "Speak your news."

The messenger got to his feet and said, "Your Majesty. I bring news from the east. Baron Sinclair's men have been routed from Riversmeed and Lord Greville's and Pendeen's men harry his all the way to Lindvale."

Edmund leaned forward. "Broken? Are you certain?"

"Completely, Your Majesty. The cost was high. He burnt the city down behind him and the baron apologizes for the cost, but he is confident the rebels are no longer a threat in Kingsheart."

Edmund sat back, letting the words sink in as a slow smile spread across his face. He had them. By the ancients, he had them. Pembroke was already across the Thunderhorn and now Sinclair was in flight, the heartland of his kingdom was his again. He felt a lightness, a giddy sense of triumph that he had not allowed himself to feel in months.

He turned his head to the thin, stooped man who stood in the shadows near the throne. "Did you hear that, Orlan?"

Orlan Rhys scurried forward, his watery eyes wide. "I did, Your Majesty. A great victory."

"Victory? This is not a victory. This is the end. They are shattered. Done," Edmund said, rising from his seat and descending the steps of the dais. "You have done well. Go with the guards, they will get you food and wine. You have earned it."

The man bowed, stammering his thanks, and was led away by a guard.

When he was gone, Edmund faced his aide.

"They thought they could bleed me. The great Baron Sinclair and the principled Lord Pembroke." He spat the names. "Now look at them."

"No. They could not." Edmund paced the length of the hall, his mind racing. He needed to make the most of this moment. "We need to take advantage of this, use it to quell some of the grumbling and rumors that have plagued us. Summon the court, and make sure they know any man in the city who doesn't attend will be noticed."

"At once, Your Majesty," he said, bowing low and hurrying from the hall.

Edmund stood alone in the vast space and waited. It wasn't often he called the full court, mostly because he did not want to deal with their preening and their whining.

This time, however, it was worth it.

It didn't take long for the assorted lords to assemble.

There was nothing these lords liked more than to see and be seen. The chance to preen and strut was too much for them to decline.

Within the hour, the chamber was filled with lords and ladies, resplendent in silks and velvets that were spread across hastily arranged benches for the occasion. The large space felt somehow small, so many men were in attendance. Edmund sat on his throne, trying to seem solemn, not wanting to give the game away too quickly.

When the trickle stopped and the bell rang with the attendant hour, he finally moved, no longer the statue, bringing a hush over the room. He smoothed the front of his black velvet doublet, the golden threads of the Whitton lion gleaming in the torchlight.

He stood there for a moment, looking over the gathered lords, his hands resting on the pommel of his sword.

"My lords, my ladies," he began. "I have called you here today for a reason. We have made it through another winter and we celebrate another season done. The ancients have seen fit to grant us a blessing greater than any of us could have hoped for."

He paused, letting the words hang in the air.

"I have received word from the field where our brave armies fight against the rebel hordes set on destroying our kingdom. The traitor, Rowan Pembroke, in his arrogance, thought he could bring his southerner army into our homeland. Now, his army is a ruin, his knights scattered or slain. He has been thrown back across the river, a whipped dog with his tail between his legs!"

A wave of murmurs swept through the crowd. Edmund raised a hand for silence. He waited, letting that news set in before he continued.

"And what of the great Garris Sinclair?" Edmund continued, his voice dripping with scorn. "Now we have news that the would-be kingmaker has also been beaten, crushed by Barons Pendeen and Greville. We have broken his army, taken Riversmeed, and thrown him back across the Wellspring River. More than that, we have broken his will. He continues to flee east, with our men at his heels! Kingsheart has finally been cleansed of the rebel stain!"

The hall erupted, lords clapping each other on the back, stomping in excitement. This was what they understood. Victory. Power. Being on the winning side.

"For months, I have heard that the momentum of this rebellion was theirs," Edmund shouted over the din. "Both from the rebels and, sadly, from my own people. There have been those who wanted to divide this kingdom, who thought they could take from me the right given by the ancients to rule. They were wrong."

The celebration died as men looked from one to the other. They had certainly all heard the rumors, all heard the whispers. Almost as certain, not a one of them would have hesitated to pass those rumors on. There were things they themselves had said.

"There have been questions, men who ask how we could win this war. How we could find the men and how we could pay for it, what with the coffers emptied by my brother's folly in Lynese. I know those of you saying these things would never say them to me, but I tell you ... these were wise questions to ask. A king is a shepherd to his people, but he is also a steward of his realm. When I began my recent tour of the kingdom, I confess, I had my own concerns. But what I found ... what I found was not a people weary of war. I found a people filled with a fire, and a loyalty that humbled me. In every town, in every village, they came. Not with clenched fists, but with open hands. And those people have given. They gave their coin. They pledged their grain. They sent their sons to fight for their king. For Sidor. And so I tell you this, my lords. Our coffers are not empty. Our granaries are not bare. Thanks to the unwavering devotion of the common man, the royal treasury is more full today than at any point since the war with Lynese began!"

A murmur went through the crowd. This was news even more stunning than the military victories. Wealth was security. Wealth was strength.

"The rebellion is not only broken in the field, it is bankrupt in spirit and in coin. And we ... we are stronger than ever. But, we do need victories in the field, of course," Edmund said, drawing a laugh from the crowd. "And that we now have. Such loyalty must be rewarded. The brave men who led our forces to these great victories fight still, lead men to push those fiends back to the sea and end this foolishness once and for all. While they fight, we will honor their names here, for the deeds they have done."

He reached out a hand to Orlan, who handed him a scroll he unrolled. "Let it be known that for his courage, his strategic brilliance, and his unyielding loyalty to the Crown, I hereby appoint Baron Reynard Greville of Swanstock to my council, as Master of the Hunt!"

He paused, reaching his hand out for another scroll, "And let it also be known, that for his courage, his strategic brilliance, and his unyielding loyalty to the Crown, I hereby appoint Baron Maeldaf Pendeen of Penvale as Master of the Horse!"

"A message will be sent to these brave lords at once," Edmund declared, handing the scrolls back to Orlan. "With it will go my personal thanks, and a promise. A promise that these new honors are but a taste of what is to come. I have instructed them to give the enemy no quarter, no time to lick their wounds. Once they have crossed into the lands of River Mark and Iron Keep, once they have brought the war to the doorsteps of these traitors, then their true rewards will be given. As will the rewards to any lords who serve the kingdom equally as faithfully."

He scanned the faces below him, men who had sat on the fence, men who had quietly hoped for the rebellion's success, men who feared him. He saw it all, and he felt nothing but contempt. They were sheep.

Now he would see how many could be bribed into doing their duty, when pressure wasn't working.

Eastford, Barony of Greenwood, Kingsheart

Baron Pembroke stood at the southern approach to Thunderhorn Bridge, watching the mass of humanity gathering in Twyver's blackened ruins. The Crown had spent weeks sending small groups across to probe his defenses, testing him. Or just wearing him down, but that time seemed to be past. Now they'd assembled their full strength for what could only be a major assault.

"How many?" Pembroke asked his captain.

"Three thousand at a minimum, my lord. Could be more packed in those streets we can't see. Even from the rooftops on this side, it's hard to see."

The enemy sergeants drove their men forward, although, as they had the last few weeks, the men came forward almost willingly, without the whips and curses Pembroke normally associated with conscripts. The men were most certainly armed like conscripts, at least, with cheap, hastily smithed swords and bare, unreinforced shields.

At most, he could count maybe a few hundred actual soldiers moving among them, identifiable by their mail and proper weapons.

"Signal the archers to begin," Pembroke ordered.

He was holding his archers back more and more as the weeks went by, trying to conserve ammunition. They had craftsmen continually working to make more, but with so many men now under arms, there were only so many fletchers and smiths available, and with the constant fighting, they were having trouble keeping up.

The first volley dropped two dozen men in the front ranks. Arrows punched through thin cloth and thin shields. A boy no older than fifteen took a shaft through his throat and collapsed, hands clawing at the wooden shaft. An older man beside him caught one in the eye, the point bursting out the back of his skull. The mob hesitated, watching their fellows die, then surged forward completely undeterred.

Bodies tumbled and fell, creating obstacles for those coming behind. A conscript tripped over a corpse and went down. Dozens trampled him in their rush forward, boots crushing his ribs and skull. Still they came, scrambling over the dead to reach the bridge's northern approach.

"They mean to drown us in bodies," his lieutenant said.

That was almost certainly what they wanted to happen.

The conscripts reached the bridge, inside the range of his crossbowmen and packed onto it shoulder to shoulder. Bolts flew out in response, punching through the compressed mass. A quarrel took a man through the chest, continued through him and lodged in the shoulder of the conscript behind him. Both went down screaming.

And still they pushed on.

Pembroke's knights, men-at-arms, and levy braced at the bridge's southern end. The first wave of conscripts crashed into them. Sir Aldwin's sword took a man's arm off at the elbow. The conscript stared at the spurting stump before a mailed fist crushed his face. Another knight drove his blade up under a farmer's chin, the point erupting through the top of the skull.

Crude weapons bounced off proper armor. A conscript's rusted blade shattered against Sir Morrin's breastplate. The knight's return stroke opened the man from shoulder to hip, intestines spilling onto the blood-slicked stones. His men were better armed and better trained, but numbers always told.

His losses were low, in comparison, but they were steady. And he didn't have the seemingly endless reserves the enemy seemed to possess.

An hour passed, and then another; his men worked their deadly task, but fatigue was setting in. His men swung and slashed slower, shields dropped when they shouldn't. A young knight stumbled on the blood-slick stones and a conscript's blade found the gap at his armpit, driving deep. The knight screamed and dropped his sword as two of his brothers dragged him back, allowing another to take his place.

And still they came.

Pembroke watched as another mass of conscripts pushed forward from Twyver's ruins. They had gotten tired of being picked apart by his archers and had taken to carrying doors torn off their hinges and planks from furniture, holding them above their heads as makeshift protection. His archers adjusted, aiming for legs and exposed flanks, the tactic worked and their losses to his ragged units began to lessen.

"My lord, the crossbowmen report they are running short of arrows."

Pembroke frowned but made the only choice available.

"Pull them from the line and double up the infantry."

His bowmen moved back from where they'd been shooting past the front line, making room for more soldiers. Without arrow support, the pressure on his front line increased. The wall of bodies pressed forward, making firm contact with his line for the first time during this attack.

And then things got worse.

A group of men in proper mail pushed through the mob, Crown men-at-arms finally showing themselves. Their commanders must have held them back, waiting until they had the best chance to break through and not risk them to his archers.

And it might work.

They didn't just have use of the professionals. The men-at-arms had arranged a conscript spear wall ahead of them, a disposable wedge to push into Pembroke's men. Soften up his line before the real soldiers hit.

His knights were well protected, fending off the enemy spears, but their swords couldn't get the enemy's to grips. A knight tried to bat spears aside with his shield, only to have three points find his legs simultaneously. He went down screaming. Conscripts behind the spears thrust down repeatedly, points finding every gap in his armor.

"Hold the line!"

The men tried, but the line still bent. A crisis point was approaching. He pushed through his own men and crashed into the spear points. A spear scraped across his breastplate, leaving a bright score in the metal. Another caught his pauldron but skittered off.

His blade opened the throat of the first spearman he encountered as he grabbed a spear shaft with his left hand, yanked the wielder forward, and drove his sword through the man's face. The blade punched through teeth and bone. He kicked the corpse off his sword and swung horizontally, taking another conscript's jaw off. The man dropped his spear to clutch at the ruin of his face.

His guard followed him and managed to shore up his line, his men fighting harder with their baron beside them. The enemy formation wavered, some of the men in the second and third ranks pulling back, afraid.

And then disaster struck again.

The crossbow bolt took Pembroke in the right shoulder, punching through mail and padding. The impact spun him around, his sword clattering across the cobblestone. Pain exploded through his shoulder and down his arm. His squire appeared at his side, breaking the shaft close to the armor while Pembroke fumbled for his blade with his left hand. The broken shaft ground against bone with every movement.

"Can you continue, my lord?"

"Yes."

He fought left-handed now, his stronger arm hanging useless. Each swing sent agony through his shoulder. Blood ran down his armor and dripped onto the bridge stones, mixing with the gore already there. A Crown man-at-arms recognized his weakness and came at him with an axe. Pembroke barely got his sword up in time. The axe hooked his blade and nearly tore it from his weakened grip. He stumbled backward, slipped in blood, and barely kept his feet.

The Crown men-at-arms pressed harder. A mace crashed into Sir Morrin's helmet, denting it badly. The knight dropped to his knees and a spear thrust took him through the throat before he could recover. Another knight tried to help but took a sword thrust through his knee. The joint collapsed sideways at an impossible angle. He fell screaming.

Three of Pembroke's own guard went down in quick succession as they tried to get their lord out of the melee. As quickly as the defensive line had stiffened, it began to bend backward onto the bridge itself, surrendering the southern approach they'd held for hours.

"We're losing the bridgehead!"

Pembroke knew it was ending. His men had fought beyond exhaustion, but sheer numbers would tell.

And then he heard the horns from across the bridge. The enemy smelled death and were going for an all-out push. Pembroke tried to push himself up and put himself on the line.

If his men were going to fight to the last to protect the River Mark and keep it from being overrun and taken by Edmund, he wasn't going to let them do it by themselves.

"Help me," he commanded his squire, who put his shoulder under the baron's right arm, leaving Pembroke's left to fight as best he could.

Then the unexpected happened. Instead of pressing forward, the reinforcements pushing the front line into him suddenly eased up.

Shouts erupted from the conscripts' rear ranks, screams of terror came from somewhere further back in the ranks. Everyone beyond the first few ranks seemed to freeze, looking back instead of toward their coming victory.

Men at the rear climbed over those in front, trampling their own forces in desperation to move forward, away from whatever was happening in the rear.

"Help me back to that cart," Pembroke said, gesturing to an upturned cart a dozen feet behind the front line.

His squire and one of his guards helped him struggle out of the line and back, lifting him up on the cart to get a little height over the crowd. It would have been dangerous, opening him up to being shot down by a crossbow, again, but whatever was causing them to panic had distracted their archers as well.

From his new vantage point, he could see mounted knights smashing into the enemy's rear units inside the town. For a moment, he couldn't figure out who it could be. All of the friendly banners were with him or Garris, and Garris was almost to Iron Keep, too far away with enemy armies in between them to be here. And then he saw them.

The banners.

The knights were flying a banner he'd seen popping up before he'd left Rendalia.

The banner of the Warrior Cub.

What's more, he knew the armor of the man in their vanguard. It was William. He and his men smashed into the undisciplined conscripts. More experienced men would have known how to harden their rear line, attempt to deflect the sudden appearance of a new enemy, but these weren't experienced men.

They fled. Some tried to run through the cavalry and into the infantry following behind them, others tried to cross the bridge, pressing into the men fighting Pembroke.

The majority chose that option, finding themselves crushed between two forces. It didn't help them as the cavalry punched deep into the packed bridge. Behind them came infantry in deep order.

Bodies piled up as the mob tried to escape in every direction at once. Men climbed the bridge's stone railings and jumped, choosing the fall over facing William's veterans. The Crown sergeants who'd driven them forward now tried to restore order but were cut down as soon as they presented themselves. Without leadership, thousands of conscripts became a mindless mass of flesh trying to flee.

The bridge turned impassable from corpses. William's force advanced steadily southward, climbing over bodies when necessary. Some conscripts dropped weapons and knelt. These received quarter. Anyone still holding anything that might be a weapon died where they stood.

The pressure on his line all but ceased as the enemy army crumbled, until everyone on the northern bank had either surrendered or died.

As soon as the battle ended, William's veterans began organizing prisoners into groups, binding hands and stripping weapons. They had done this before and knew what they were doing.

Not everyone died, of course. It was hard to trap three thousand men. At least a thousand ran north, probably out of Twyver entirely and along the East Road.

They'd keep running until they found more loyal forces.

But two thousand either lay dead or in chains.

"My lord, you need treatment," his squire said.

Pembroke finally let his squire lead him to where wounded knights received care while William's men continued their work.

This changed everything.

Chapter 5

Eastford, Barony of Greenway, River Mark

The makeshift aid stations sprawled across the eastern edge of the camp where wounded men lay on rough blankets and straw pallets. Isolde moved between them, a water skin in her hands with two of her personal guards trailing behind her.

This was the one thing she'd always known how to do. She might not have William's abilities on the battlefield or her father's love of the great game, as he called it, but she could take care of the people who served her.

She also relished the opportunity to spend time with the men. It was not seemly for a princess to cavort around with commoners, bolder when she wasn't married, let alone when she was, but she found soldiers to be so ... honest.

These men didn't live in the constant half-truths and double-dealing that nobles seemed to relish. For them, a man's word was his bond. Men who faced death didn't need to play petty games. They said what they meant and they meant what they said.

Maybe that's why she liked William so much. He might be from the most powerful family in Sidor, but he wasn't a dandy or a creature of the court. He was a soldier. He fought with his men, slept in the same fields they did, and bled with them.

She knelt beside a young man from her William's Rendalian army, one she vaguely recognized from previous hospital visits after the conflict with her brother. If she remembered correctly, it had been a minor wound then. This time, it looked much worse, with his left arm bound tight against his chest.

"Ivett, isn't it? My goodness, I keep seeing you in these hospitals. We need to stop meeting like this. I believe your fellows might get jealous."

"Let them," he said, wincing as he laughed. "If I knew I'd get a visit every time I got injured, I wouldn't have worked so hard to avoid that blade."

"Well, if you make it through the next battle without an injury, I will promise to visit your company at mess and make sure they know you're my favorite. How do you feel?"

"That's a deal," he said, laughing again. "And well enough. The bone's cracked but the healer says it will mend clean."

Isolde offered him water, and he drank gratefully. "You fought bravely today. All of you did."

"It was a good battle. We had them running."

"You certainly did," she said, patting him on the arm.

She moved to the next man, then the next, some she recognized and some she didn't. Some were even Lynesian, men who'd signed up for the defense of Rendalia and grown close enough to their fellow soldiers that they opted to come with their unit rather than taking William's offer to stay behind with the forces remaining in Rendalia under Sir Drummond.

Isolde approached a man with a heavily bandaged thigh who lay propped against a wooden crate. His weathered face and calloused hands marked him as a veteran, and she could see how carefully he held himself, as if any movement might send fresh agony through his leg.

"Here," she said and offered the water skin. He took it with a nod of thanks. "You were with us, on my husband's ship, for the crossing, weren't you?"

"I was, Your Highness," he said, drinking deep and then handing back the waterskin. "Nasty voyage, that. Crossed them the first time with the prince. Wish that had been it. I'd almost take the Silent Isles again over the strait."

"The storms were fierce, weren't they?" Isolde agreed.

"Storms weren't the worst of it for us. Did you see over the side? One night, water was dead calm, black as pitch beneath us. Not a breath of wind, when suddenly some of the boys started shouting. There was something moving under the ship. Something big."

Isolde had not been on deck for that, but she'd come up after the excitement. William had acted like it was nothing, but she knew at the time he was just trying to spare her being scared.

Now she had confirmation.

"I didn't see it. What was it?"

"It was one of the leviathans, like the one we saw when we chased that ship out of Werna. Massive shadow gliding under our hull. Longer than the ship, maybe twice as long. I'm glad this one wasn't hungry. If I never have to see something like that up close again, it'll be too soon."

"It was worth it, though, wasn't it? We made it in time."

"Aye, that we did, Your Highness. Still, if I'd had to choose, it's land for me from now on."

"Fair enough," she said, patting him on the arm.

She continued on, engaging the next group of men. The camp was organized chaos, with healers moving between the wounded and supplies being distributed where needed, all just outside of Eastford under tents and temporary shelters. More were in the city, in warehouses, but there were not enough of those left standing and more injured than they could hold.

This tent was for men from William's army. The bulk of the injured came from Baron Pembroke's forces, who'd taken the brunt of the damage from the battle.

She didn't know why she'd started with William's men first, maybe because they were more familiar to her and she felt safer. This wasn't like meeting Sidorians for the first time in Rendalia. There, she at least had a claim for why she was there and every other person sounded like her.

Here, she was a foreigner, and there was no escaping it.

Her guards flanked her as she left that tent and headed for another, this one flying one of the banners of Pembroke's force.

"Water?" Isolde offered, extending the water skin.

The soldier looked up at her with sharp eyes. His face was lean and scarred, marking him as another veteran.

"Obliged," he said, taking the water skin but not drinking from it immediately. Instead, he studied her face with obvious curiosity. "You sound like a Lynesian."

"I was born there."

"Thought so. That accent doesn't lie." The man's tone had changed, become cooler. "What in the depths is a Lynesian doing here?"

"I came with the army of Rendalia. I'm Princess Isolde. I married your prince and returned with him from my homeland."

A sergeant sitting nearby turned toward their conversation. His left shoulder was wrapped in bloodstained cloth, and his face carried the hard lines of a man who had seen too much death.

"Foreign whore," he said, spitting on the ground between them.

"What?" Isolde said, almost too shocked to believe what she was hearing.

"My brother died at the Doree. My cousin said he suffered for days before he finally went. Vomiting blood, burning with fever. Couldn't keep anything down, not even water."

"I'm sorry for your loss …"

"Sorry. That's what we get. Sorry."

Another wounded soldier, a much older man who had little business fighting in any army at his age, said, "A princess? My son died at Talabot. Sixteen years old and burned in your godforsaken country without getting his proper rights. Now they expect us to welcome some foreign harlot?"

The healer working on the first soldier's leg looked at her, worried, but continued to focus on his task. Disciples remained neutral, especially when it came to territorial things. They wanted to be seen as something else, something other, something above the crassness of fealty and obligation.

If things turned ugly, he would not get involved.

"I understand your anger," Isolde said carefully. "The war brought terrible losses to both sides …"

"Both sides?" The sergeant struggled to his feet despite his shoulder wound. "Your people sent a plague into our army, unleashing something so dangerous the acolytes publicly preached against your father. That's not war, that's butchery."

Galer and Lusa, the two guards with her today, took a step forward, hands moving toward their sword hilts, but Isolde held up a hand to stop them. These men were Lynesians themselves, and their intervention would only confirm every suspicion these wounded soldiers harbored.

Besides, there were hundreds of men around them. If they started a fight, it would not end well for the three of them.

"I tried to stop those tactics. I argued against them ..."

"Pretty words," the sergeant cut her off. "Pretty words don't bring back the dead. Don't help the widows feed their children or the orphans sleep at night."

More River Mark soldiers were gathering now, drawn by the raised voices. Word was spreading through the wounded; the Lynesian princess was here, the enemy's daughter walking among them as if she belonged. Isolde could see the hostility building on their faces, the way they looked at her with suspicion and barely concealed hatred.

Galer moved in closer to her. She might have held him off from physically restraining the injured men, but there was no way she was going to get him to back off completely.

A young soldier with bandages around his head pushed himself up on his elbows. "My father died at Valemonde. Cut down by Lynesian cavalry. And now his killer's daughter wants to be our queen?"

"I never killed anyone," Isolde protested. "I spent the war trying to minimize casualties ..."

"Minimize casualties?" An older man with a grizzled beard and missing fingers on his left hand struggled to sit up. "You should be in chains, not wearing a crown. Should be rotting in a dungeon for what your family did to us."

The voices were rising now, more men giving reasons why they hated her country. Hated her family. Hated her.

Isolde tried to maintain her composure as the circle of angry men grew larger. "I know you've suffered. I know there's been terrible loss. But I'm not your enemy ..."

"Not our enemy?" The sergeant's voice carried over the others. "Your blood is Lynesian. Your family was our enemy. Your brother is now and your father before that. You think a marriage ceremony changes what you are?"

A soldier with a bandaged chest wound managed to stand despite obvious pain. "What's she really doing here? Spying for her people? Do they want payback for our taking Rendalia?"

"I'm here because my husband is here," Isolde said.

Of course, she knew that wasn't the truth. At least not all of it.

William hadn't wanted her here and had warned her of this exact situation. She'd been stubborn, mostly because she'd managed to win over the Sidorians in Rendalia and she'd thought she'd be able to do the same here.

She hadn't expected this level of resistance.

The crowd was growing aggressive now, with some of the wounded soldiers attempting to move closer despite their injuries. It was impossible to miss the hatred in their faces. Behind her, she heard the soft scrape of steel as Lusa partially drew his blade.

"Stand down," she whispered urgently to her men. "Don't make this worse."

"A Lynesian has no place ruling Sidorian people," the older soldier with the missing fingers declared. "Never did, never will."

"Get out," someone called from the back of the group.

"Spy …"

"Foreign devil …"

Isolde looked around for an escape route, but the circle of angry men was tightening. Her guards had reluctantly sheathed their weapons but remained tense.

She could feel their fear.

One particularly angry soldier lurched forward, grabbing her arm.

Galer moved instantly, but Isolde pushed against him with her free hand.

"Don't," she said firmly, though whether she addressed the wounded man or her own guards was unclear.

Other soldiers were moving closer now, their voices rising to shouts. Some were calling her a traitor, others demanding she leave, still others making darker threats about what should be done with enemy royalty. The situation was spiraling beyond her control, and Isolde realized that her attempts at reconciliation had only made things worse.

She tried to back away slowly, but the man didn't let go. Didn't release her arm.

"Please," she said, but her voice was lost in the growing din of angry voices.

"What is the meaning of this?" a louder voice said from the edge of the group.

Louder and more authoritative, forcing all of the heads to turn in that direction. A group of Sidorians, veterans from the army of Rendalia, had entered the tent.

"Stand back," one of them commanded as he forced his way through the wounded soldiers standing around her.

The ten men formed a circle around her, their hands on the hilts of their weapons. The man who seemed to be their leader, an older man with River Mark heraldry on his halberd but wearing Rendalian colors on his cloak, reached for the soldier who was still holding on to Isolde's arm.

"Release her. Now."

The man glared at her, but did as he was bidden, dropping his hand and taking a reluctant step back.

"This is the Lady Whitton, wife of the Warrior Cub. Touch her again and you'll lose that hand."

"She'll never be accepted as queen. Never. Too much blood between our peoples," one of the men said.

"You know nothing of war," one of the Rendalian soldiers shot back. "You were conscripted, what, six months ago, and have spent that time guarding a bridge against other conscripts. You know nothing of real war against trained soldiers. And you know nothing of what she's done or sacrificed for Sidor. You sit here feeling sorry for yourself while she's been leading soldiers in battle."

"Leading soldiers against Sidorians, more like," the sergeant retorted.

"Against her own brother. Against Lynesian forces trying to retake Rendalia. She chose Sidor over her own blood."

The argument might have continued, but the leader of the Rendalian guards was already moving to escort Isolde away from the confrontation.

As they left the tent and started to move toward the town, the soldier who'd spoken stopped and said, "With all due respect, my lady, perhaps it would be better to limit your interactions with some of the troops."

Instead of taking her to another medical tent, however, the group of guards turned and headed back toward where row after row of tents were set up for the soldiers of the Rendalia army to stay in while they regrouped and figured out their next step.

She stopped walking. The guards around her stopped as well, making it impossible for her to turn and walk in the direction she'd intended to go.

Galer looked to Lusa, then to the Sidorians, and then back to her, clearly questioning what he should do. He was loyal to her, but he'd also come to know the men of the Rendalia army and so was suddenly concerned.

She made a calming gesture with her hand, suddenly having an inkling of what was happening. It should have occurred to her during the confrontation that these men hadn't just stumbled across her, but with everything that was happening, she'd been too distracted to consider it until now.

"Where are you taking me?" she asked.

"To your quarters, Your Highness."

"Why are we going to my quarters? You're right, I may need to pick the locations I go to slightly better, but I have work to do with the wounded, and it isn't done yet."

"I'm sorry, Your Highness, but Prince William specifically asked us to take you to your tent until he finishes his meeting with Baron Pembroke and he is able to join you. Please, Your Highness."

The man was being respectful, but she knew William's men, how fiercely loyal they were to him. She knew if he gave them clear-cut orders, they were not going to deviate from them, so she simply nodded and continued on through the encampment, to the large tent in its center that she shared with her husband.

She'd hoped, once they saw her safely in place, they would leave her there and she could continue on her way. Instead, four of the men, including their leader, positioned themselves in front of the tent while the rest left.

"Why are you not returning to your posts?"

"Prince William ordered us to remain with you until his return, Your Highness."

The senior guard held open the tent flap and gestured for her to enter.

"You're going to keep me here?"

"I apologize, Your Highness, but my orders come directly from Prince William. This is for your protection."

"And if I refuse?"

"Then we would respectfully ask you to reconsider, Your Highness."

Isolde studied the four men, all veterans who had served her faithfully since Rendalia. They avoided her eyes but maintained their positions. She looked to Galer, but he seemed fine with this, now that he realized what was happening as well. From his perspective, she was much safer in place here than getting surrounded by angry men who wanted to harm her.

With no apparent alternative, she entered the tent.

For the tent of a major noble, it was Spartan: a simple bed, a travel chest containing their personal belongings, and a campaign table covered with maps and dispatches. She knew that before she joined him, William had preferred a single cot over a bed, but had allowed for the greater comfort since she was with him.

Isolde paced the small space, frustrated. She had governed an entire province, negotiated with hostile tribes, commanded troops in battle, yet here she sat under guard like a wayward child.

Hours crawled by as Isolde alternated between reading one of the books she had brought with her and pacing the small space, rehearsing the argument she was going to have the moment William finally showed up.

It wasn't hard to tell when that moment arrived. The activity around her tent increased a hundredfold when he appeared, everyone having a duty to suddenly do what they hadn't needed to attend to for the past two hours while she'd waited.

She positioned herself in the center of the tent, arms crossed, waiting for his entrance.

He entered alone, stopping just on the threshold of the tent, still wearing his armor coated with dried blood, looking tired but determined. Part of her wanted to give him a moment's peace. They had landed in Kingsheart Bay three days prior, had ridden hard to relieve Pembroke's force, and had gone straight into combat the moment they were here. He had been pushing himself ever since the snows melted, and she knew he was exhausted.

That part, however, was overwhelmed by the part of her that had been imprisoned in this tent for two hours. Before he could speak, Isolde launched her attack.

"How dare you put me under guard like a common prisoner?"

He gave a weary smile and turned to the guards just outside the tent flap. "Thank you, Sergeant. You may return to your duties."

As the sound of the guards retreated, William entered the tent all the way, letting the tent flap fall, giving them some privacy, or as much as anyone had in a military camp like this.

"You know exactly why I did it," he said, removing his sword belt and setting it aside before addressing her anger.

"I was never in any real danger. I had my guards with me."

"That is not the way I heard it," William said as he started to remove his armor. "From what I heard, you had two dozen men crowded around you about to tear you limb from limb."

"I've dealt with hostility before. This isn't the first time I've had to win over Sidorians."

"This is a different case entirely. For one, those Sidorians were there during the peace talks, know that's why we were married and were happy to have the war over. For another, most of the men here are conscripts, not soldiers. They haven't accepted the life like the men we had with us in Lynese."

"I would have eventually won them over if given the chance," she said stubbornly.

"While I have no doubt that is true, I could not take the chance that one of them might have escalated things further before your charms had a chance to take effect."

William set down his breastplate and turned to face her fully, revealing bruises across his ribs and shoulder from the day's fighting. His armor had protected him from serious injury, but the battle had taken its toll.

"I'm sorry this was necessary and I understand why it upsets you, but I will not compromise when it comes to your safety. Which is why I'm sending you to Kenna tomorrow to stay with my Aunt Alyssa for the foreseeable future."

"No," she said, furious. "I will not be pushed aside like a child."

"This is not a punishment, Isolde," he said, surprisingly gently. "When this war ends, when my father is defeated and the kingdom is united, I'll need you beside me to rebuild Sidor just as we rebuilt Rendalia, together. But for that to work, you need to win over the Sidorian people. Not just the soldiers, but all of them. And to do that, you're going to need help."

Damn him. He was being completely reasonable and it was not the worst idea, it also infuriated her to no end. She knew she was being stubborn, but she'd been treated like this by her father, as a prop, and she was not going to let it happen a second time.

"For me to win them over, the people need to see their future queen, not have her hidden away during the kingdom's greatest crisis."

"You won't be hiding out. My uncle started this fight and my aunt is his spiritual successor. A war like this is more than just soldiers; it's all the people left behind. And the soldiers are the ones already loyal to us. I need to win over the rest of them if I'm going to be able to take over after my father is gone. I can't do that and fight the war. You said you're my partner, and you're right. But that means I need you doing the things that I can't get to, instead of duplicating the work that I'm doing. Besides, as you have so eloquently pointed out before, you are better at this kind of thing than I am. Well, I bow to your wisdom. I will win on the field, and I leave it to you to win in the homesteads."

Again, he was being damnably reasonable and using her own arguments against her.

"My Aunt Alyssa is respected throughout River Mark and Shadowhold. The people and the nobility love her. Being introduced by her will get you further with the people of the south than anything either of us could do with the army alone. It will establish you. I've already written to her about your arrival and the importance of introducing you properly to River Mark society."

"How long is this arrangement supposed to last? Am I being sent away permanently?" she asked, not ready to give in quite yet.

"Of course not. Once you and my aunt feel you have made enough headway, we will figure out the next steps, which honestly depend on how the war is going. You might rejoin me, you might go to Shadowhold to work your magic with the Duchess Blackwood, or maybe even to Iron Keep. The situation is fluid and we will have to figure out where the two of us can do the most good, and if it is together or each playing our part. Of course, once we retake Starhaven, your place will be there with me."

"Okay. I just wish you had included me in making this decision, instead of arranging everything and then presenting it as an accomplished fact. You're treating me like a subordinate rather than a partner."

"You're right," he said, closing the distance between them and putting his arms around her, crossed arms and all. "After hearing about the confrontation with the wounded, I acted without thinking. For that, I apologize. I'd promise not to do it again, but all I can do is promise to try to do my best not to."

She glared at him one more moment before dropping her arms and putting them around him, placing her cheek on his chest as he pulled her in tight.

"See that you do."

Chapter 6

Port Spofforth, Barony of Gatelake, Iron Keep

The meeting had been dragging on for over an hour, to the point where they had started to rehash the same arguments, with no one getting anywhere. It had taken a week to arrange for this council, and that had seemed like a breakneck speed considering they had to get so many people to this isolated port on the southeast corner of the duchy, deep in the Shatterstone Mountains and safe from the front lines of the conflict. Most had had to sail around Iron Keep or up from the River Mark to make it safely.

With all of that rush and urgency, William would have thought the meeting, when it finally happened, would have been more focused and productive than it was turning out to be.

"You're suggesting we abandon Iron Keep to the Icelanders?" Sinclair demanded.

"I'm suggesting we take the fight to Edmund," Pembroke said from the opposite end of the table set up in a pier-side warehouse. "Every day we delay, he grows stronger. The Tradesway runs straight to Starhaven. Now that William is here, we have the men and the momentum, but only if we move now. You have to have noticed how effective Edmund has been at conscripting men to fight. The longer we wait, the more men he'll pull in. Eventually, the numbers will flip, and we will, once again, be on the defensive to a larger force."

"Gentlemen," Duke Blackwood, who had remained passive through most of this meeting, in spite of the fact that he was the second-highest-ranking noble after William himself in the room, said. "Perhaps we should hear from Prince William. As you so rightfully pointed out, his men are why we are, once again, in a place to even consider whether to attack or to defend."

Sinclair and Pembroke, along with all of the other barons at the table, swiveled their heads to look at William, who took a moment before pushing back his chair and standing.

"You're both right," he said. "And you're both wrong."

Sinclair's eyebrows lifted. Pembroke crossed his arms.

"Baron Sinclair, you've been fighting this war for six months. What do you have to show for it?"

"I've held Iron Keep against ..."

"You've held Iron Keep. Nothing more. Baron Pembroke, you want to charge down the Tradesway. How many conscripts did my father raise since winter started?"

Pembroke shifted his weight. "The reports suggest ..."

"The reports suggest he has fifty thousand men, maybe more. You want to meet them on open ground where numbers matter most?"

"We have that many men, if we pull everyone together and fight as one," Pembroke countered.

"Barely. More importantly, my father expects us to do one of two things. Either we'll do what Baron Sinclair wants, grind away at his forces while defending our territory, or we'll do what Baron Pembroke wants, make a desperate thrust at Starhaven. Either way, he will be prepared for it. The first leaves us exhausted and spread thin. The second leaves us surrounded and cut off."

"So if neither option works, what is your plan?" Sinclair said, challenging him.

"We go where he doesn't expect us to, with a large enough force to fight if we use the terrain to our advantage. We go either north of Twin Lakes or through the gap between them and Avlan, cross the plains between that and the Stonehills, and then down the coast straight to Starhaven. We can use the forest and hills to break up their forces, and we have a larger mounted force than they do. We can move quickly. At least more quickly than untrained conscripts. We force them to fight on ground where twenty thousand conscripts are worth less than five thousand veterans. At the same time, we leave enough men to hold the crossings at the Wellspring River and the Thunderhorn. No, it will not be enough if he decides to ignore us and go for either crossing all in, but that would make our path to Starhaven even easier. And neither of you will be in your duchies, so he would get land, and nothing more. It allows us to take the fight to him and protect our rear at the same time."

"That's weeks of marching through hostile territory," Sinclair said. "More if we have to fight battles in between, which I would say is likely."

"And there are plenty of places, including the open plains east of the Twin Lake that you pointed out, where he can catch us on open ground," Pembroke added.

For once, the two barons seemed to agree on something.

"I did not say it would be easy, but my father will have his forces concentrated along the Tradesway and the southern approaches. He is not one to look at maps, and he has never had the patience for war. He will be continually demanding victories. By the time he realizes we've gone north, we'll be past his forces here and able to dictate the battle. He'll have to wheel his entire army to meet us, and conscripts don't maneuver well."

"You're gambling everything on guessing his deployments," Sinclair said.

"I'm not guessing. I know my father."

"You know your father," Sinclair repeated snidely. "That doesn't make your strategy sound. I've been fighting wars since before you could hold a sword, Prince William. Experience matters."

"You're right. You have been fighting longer." William met his gaze. "You've been fighting this rebellion for half a year with nothing to show for it but dead men. Where do you stand now that you didn't stand this past summer? If experience alone won wars, you'd be sitting in Starhaven right now."

The smile vanished from Sinclair's face.

"My lords." William looked around the table, meeting each baron's eyes in turn. "We can continue as we have been, Baron Sinclair defending Iron Keep and the River Mark holding on for dear life on the Thunderhorn. Or we can work together. One army, one purpose."

"Under whose command?" Sinclair's question cut sharply.

"Mine."

The word hung in the air. Several barons shifted uncomfortably. Baron Morley's eyes darted between Sinclair and Pembroke.

Sinclair laughed, short and bitter. "You're sixteen years old."

"I am, and I took Lynese. I marched into Valemonde and put its emperor to heel and took his daughter as my bride. I took my ancestral home from them and brought it into the kingdom. I survived the Silent Isles and sailed a ship across the Sea of Kings in winter. I crossed the Strait of Leviathan, *twice,* to bring men to aid the fight here. Do you really want to compare our accomplishments?"

Color rose in Sinclair's cheeks. "You pompous ..."

"Garris." Duke Blackwood's warning tone cut him short.

"William, no one is questioning your achievements," Pembroke said, breaking the tension. "But it is a fair question. Leading this kind of war is much different than the war in Lynese."

"You are right, of course, but my uncle also made it clear before he died that I was his successor. He said as much in word and in deed when he gifted me his sword. And as has been pointed out, more than half of the forces available to us march under my banner. Or would you prefer I take those five thousand men back to Rendalia? I can defend that province easily enough. Let you sort out my father and the Icelanders on your own."

The threat landed hard. Baron Ainsworth's face went pale. Even Duke Blackwood sat back, his gray eyes calculating.

"You wouldn't," Pembroke said.

"I came here to unite this rebellion, not to watch it tear itself apart over petty rivalries. If you won't work together under my command, then you've already lost. I won't waste my men's lives on a lost cause."

"We all want the same thing," the duke said carefully. "We all want Sidor free."

"Then act like it," William said, looking from Sinclair to Pembroke. "I'm not asking you to like me. I'm not asking you to respect my age. I'm asking you to recognize that without unity, we're *finished.* My father knows you're divided. He's counting on it."

"It could work," Pembroke said.

"You're actually considering this?" Sinclair demanded.

"Baron Sinclair," William said. "I need you. I need your counsel if this is going to work. You are an excellent tactician, and I admit that what I am proposing is risky. But I need you as an ally, not a rival."

"Pretty words," Sinclair said.

"But also true. You think I don't know I'm young? You think I don't know that half these men question whether I should be here at all?" William gestured at the assembled barons. "But I also know that my uncle trusted me with this and that I will see it done. I know that if we don't unite now, today, my father wins. I do not want to hand him victory because we could not work together."

Pembroke sighed heavily. "The boy's right."

"The prince," William corrected mildly.

"The prince is right," Pembroke said with a smile before looking to Sinclair. "I don't like it, but he's right. Garris, we've been stepping on each other's toes for months. Maybe it's time to try something different."

Sinclair's struggle was visible on his face. His brown eyes darted around the room, taking in the other barons' expressions, and he could see he'd lost them.

"If Iron Keep falls because of this plan ..." Sinclair began.

"Then the blame is mine," William said. "I'm not here for glory. I'm here to win."

"Fine," he said, which William knew was as much of an agreement as he was likely to get.

The room seemed to exhale collectively. Baron Morley actually smiled.

"Good. Then in one week, we will march for Bradford and coalesce our forces. I'll leave it to you how many men you want to bring and how many to leave behind to protect the river crossing, but the more we bring, the better chance we'll have. We will push out their forces at the crossroads, which will make my father think we are headed east, down the Tradesway. He will pull back and prepare for our attack. By the time he realizes we aren't coming, we will be north to Trentwell Hills or maybe even as far as the Blackheath Forest. Where we go from there depends on what he does in response, but it puts us in the open with options to maneuver. If he attacks either river crossing, we push hard straight for

Starhaven. Otherwise, we use the forest as best we can, cut hard for the Stonehills, and then down to Starhaven. If we get bogged down, we still have the option of the forces we left behind coming together and attacking straight down the Tradesway, which would then be left open, to take Starhaven while we have the Crown army pinned down. Either way, the capital, and my father, will be left open to us."

Several of the barons nodded along with the plan. It had flaws, William would admit. There were moves his father could make that would take the pronged options from him, and he knew better than to count on the chaos of battle not ruining his strategy, but it was a solid plan.

Garris, however, refused to be happy about it. "I hope you're right."

"Me too," William said.

Starhaven, Sidor

Edmund bent down over his desk, fingers pressed against his temples. The morning sunlight that cut through the tall windows of his office offended him. It was much too bright. His stomach rolled unpleasantly, and a small burp that threatened to be more escaped him.

And yet, for as much as the wine from the night before was affecting him, his mood could not be staunched. He replayed the events of the previous night, the feast in his honor, the toasts and praise given to him, in his mind. Finally, after months of grinding warfare, the rebellion was collapsing, and he was on the verge of having everything he ever wanted.

It was hard not to revel.

A knock came at the door, causing a wave of pain to shoot through his head as the booms reverberated through the room and his brain.

"Go away," Edmund called, not looking up. "The king is indisposed."

The knock came again, more insistent.

Edmund sighed and pushed himself up. "Unless Sinclair has come to surrender, I don't want to hear it."

He wasn't going to let anything interrupt his good mood with new problems and troubles. Not that anyone seemed to care what he wanted. The door opened anyway, and Orlan peered around the edge, his narrow face pinched with worry.

It was only Orlan, one of the few people in this ancient, forsaken city who didn't drive him to madness. A man who always knew his place.

Besides, it would give him an excellent excuse to take the one medicine known to cure a hangover.

At least temporarily.

"Orlan!" Edmund said, reaching for the corner of his desk and pulling over a bottle of Lynesian red and two goblets. "Come in, come in. Have a drink with your king. We're winning, you know. Winning at last."

Orlan Rhys slipped inside, clutching a leather portfolio against his chest. The scribe's face was pale, his eyes darting between Edmund and the floor.

"Your Majesty, I bring urgent news from the Thunderhorn."

"More victories? Has Pembroke finally surrendered? I knew he couldn't hold that bridge forever."

"No, Your Majesty. It concerns your son," Orlan said nervously.

Edmund's smile faded. "What about him?"

"He's returned from Rendalia with his army. A week ago yesterday, he attacked Baron Alton's forces at Thunderhorn Bridge."

"Attacked? Alton had three thousand men."

"Yes, Your Majesty. From the reports, the baron was on the precipice of pushing across the Eastbridge and breaking Pembroke when the prince struck them from behind. Our forces were badly mangled ... they were crushed between the two armies. Two thousand were killed or captured."

Edmund stood slowly, his hangover forgotten. "Two thousand!"

"Yes, Your Majesty. Alton was able to escape with the remaining one thousand, including most of the small number of veterans he had with him, and retreated north up the Eastroad."

"If this happened a week ago, why are we only now hearing about it?"

"The baron sent a rider instead of a wyvern. He felt it more prudent for security."

"He meant to delay reporting as long as possible, you mean."

"You are, of course, correct, Your Majesty. But ..."

Orlan paused a moment, looking around as if wanting an escape.

"What?" Edmund said, coming around the desk. "Spit it out."

"There was another message, this time by wyvern, which arrived on the heels of the first messenger, this time from Baron Greville. Baron Sinclair has pushed across the Wellspring and is fighting down the Tradesway. Greville reports that, once they learned of the fall of Alton's force, and that the baron also abandoned Ashby, it became clear that the two armies were looking to converge east of Bradford. A shot-down wyvern confirmed the two armies were coordinating. Greville was concerned that Alton would not hold Pembroke and William's forces, and that his army would be caught between the two and destroyed. He has withdrawn his forces."

"Withdrawn? On whose authority?"

"Baron Moresby feared being caught between the rebels in the north and Prince William's advancing army. He pulled back to Bradford to avoid being surrounded."

"Bradford. He retreated all the way to Bradford? Are you telling me he abandoned almost the entirety of eastern Kingsheart without a fight?"

"He believed it was the prudent ..."

Edmund's fist slammed onto the desk. Orlan jumped, papers scattering from his portfolio.

"Prudent? I had them beaten! Sinclair was running like a whipped dog, Pembroke was bleeding at the Thunderhorn. I had retaken all of Kingsheart and was on the precipice of being the one invading their lands. I should have their heads on pikes, not hearing about how we once again fall back from their armies.

We had the largest force Sidor has ever seen. How is this even possible?"

"Your Majesty, your son's veterans ..."

"My son. The ungrateful whelp returns to undo everything I've built." Edmund grabbed a wine goblet from the desk and hurled it against the wall, shattering it against the stone. "I should have strangled him when his mother died and laid him with her. Should have known the boy would grow into a viper."

Orlan bent to gather his scattered papers, hands shaking.

Edmund turned to the window, staring out at Starhaven's sprawling streets below. "What about Duke Cadogan?"

"Duke Cadogan, Your Majesty?"

"Has he sent more men south as I commanded? If he isn't going to hold Sinclair in Iron Keep, the least he could do is add his men to our forces. If he were to come down the coast of Alther Bay, we could catch them between our armies. Maybe that would give Greville the courage to stand and fight."

"No, Your Majesty. He's actually pulled his men west, gathering them along the Grimshaw."

Edmund spun around. "What?"

"He has just begun the movement and did not report it to us directly. One of our people in his camp sent notice of the movement. I hadn't brought it to your attention yet because it is unclear what his intentions with the redeployment are."

"When did this happen?"

"A week ago, Your Highness."

"I suppose I should just take it as coincidence that he began his move away from Iron Keep at the exact same time as my son's surprise appearance."

"Your Majesty, I can't see how those are connected. I'm certain Duke Cadogan remains loyal ..."

"Loyal? For two months, the man has ignored demands that he resume his assault on Iron Keep, and now he moves his troops just as my son reappears." Edmund laughed humorlessly. "Do you take me for a fool, Orlan?"

"Of course not, Your Majesty. We have no evidence ..."

"Evidence? The evidence is in their actions!" Edmund stalked back to his desk, sweeping papers aside.

"Your Majesty, perhaps Duke Cadogan simply needed to gather his strength?"

"No, this stinks of betrayal. Cadogan showing his true colors."

Orlan remained silent, clutching his portfolio.

Edmund paced the room, his voice rising. "Traitors, Orlan. I'm surrounded by traitors. Every lord who smiles at my table plots behind my back."

"Your Majesty, the lords celebrated with you just last night ..."

"Of course they did! They feast on my gold and drink my wine while sharpening their knives." Edmund kicked a chair, sending it crashing into the wall. "But I see through them. I see through all of them."

"What would you have me do, Your Majesty?"

Edmund rounded on him. "Send a wyvern to Baron Greville immediately. I want him here within the week to explain why he abandoned half the kingdom without a fight."

Orlan fumbled for a quill. "Yes, Your Majesty."

"And send word to Duke Cadogan. Tell him I require an immediate explanation for his withdrawal from Iron Keep. In person! If he refuses, we'll know where his loyalties truly lie."

"Of course, Your Majesty."

Edmund returned to the window, hands clasped behind his back. In the distance, down the Market Road, he could see merchants hawking their wares in the morning market.

"How did it all fall apart so quickly?"

"Your armies still outnumber the rebels three to one, Your Majesty," the scribe offered.

"Numbers. Yes, we have numbers. Conscripts and levies, farmers with spears, while William brings hardened veterans from Lynese." He turned to look at Orlan. "Tell me honestly, do you think they're all against me?"

Orlan wrung his hands. "Your Majesty, I ... I couldn't say."

"Can't or won't?"

"I serve only you, Your Majesty. My loyalty has never wavered."

"Your loyalty. You'd tell me the sky was green if you thought it would please me."

"Your Majesty, I speak only truth."

"Truth? Then tell me this truth, why does my own son hate me so?"

Orlan opened his mouth, then closed it.

"Even you can't spin that into something pleasant." He stood, moving to a side table where a pitcher of wine waited. His hands shook slightly as he poured. "I raised him as my own after his mother died. Gave him everything. Title, lands, the finest education. And he repays me with rebellion."

Orlan didn't say anything in reply. How could he? The boy was a traitor, and it was Edmund's fault for not seeing it firsthand. Instead of sending him to be molded and corrupted by Aldric in Lynese, he should have thrown the whelp into the straits.

"I'll prepare the messages immediately, Your Majesty," Orlan said nervously as the silence stretched between them.

Edmund set down his goblet. "Send riders to every garrison between here and Bradford. I want daily reports on William's movements. Where he camps, how many men he has, which lords ride with him."

"Yes, Your Majesty."

"Go. And find out which of these worthless nobles are plotting against me."

"At once, Your Majesty."

Orlan backed toward the door, still clutching his portfolio as Edmund turned back to the window.

The door closed softly, leaving Edmund alone with his wine and his thoughts. Outside, clouds gathered on the horizon, dark and heavy with the promise of a storm.

"Ungrateful little bastard," he muttered.

The wine tasted sour in his mouth. Last night's celebration felt like a lifetime ago. The lords who'd cheered his victories would be whispering in corners now, calculating which side would triumph. Rats, all of them, ready to flee a sinking ship.

But the ship wasn't sinking. Not yet. He still had the crown, still commanded the loyalty of most of the kingdom. And he still had the Key. He could feel its metal, cool and warm at the same time, still pressing against his chest, comforting him. Let William come. Let all the traitors reveal themselves.

Then he'd deal with them.

Chapter 7

North of the Cresswell Hills, Kingsheart

William studied the enemy formation through the morning haze, counting banners and estimating numbers. Two thousand at least, maybe more. His father seemed to have an inexhaustible supply of men.

They were still conscripts mostly, but they had a core of seasoned men-at-arms in the center who would hold them together when the killing started. He knew Edmund wasn't the man behind this, but someone on that side had a tactical mind, taking the masses his father was giving him and spreading out veterans to keep them together.

"That's a lot of men," one of his knights said.

"It is," William agreed, sounding much less worried.

He'd sent his scouts out early to initiate contact and then withdraw hastily. By now, the enemy would have marched over traces of his "main camp" which would, for all appearances, look to have been abandoned in haste, cooking fires still smoldering, tent stakes pulled up carelessly. They would see his forward positions thinly held, skirmishers spread too wide to maintain proper support.

Giving the appearance of a panicked, ramshackle army.

The Crown army's advance came with their customary confidence. The enemy commander, carrying the banner of Molesbary, one of the northern Kingsheart baronies, deployed his troops in a traditional way that worked well on level ground.

Gosforth, or one of his knights actually in charge of this group, placed his heaviest infantry in the center, a solid block of men-at-arms who could punch through most opposition. His conscript levies filled out the wings, three deep in most places, flanked by the light cavalry.

The baron himself was behind the center with a small group of knights.

The battle opened with the ritual exchange of missiles. Crown archers, advancing in loose formation ahead of their main line, let their first volley fly at two hundred paces. William's men lifted shields, hunkering down behind them. There were some losses, men screaming as arrows found limbs. His own archers replied from their thinly held positions, their arrows finding some targets among the advancing infantry, who in that position had the vulnerability of an attacker.

He didn't have enough archers to really cause damage and dissuade them from attacking.

But then, that wasn't his plan.

The real fighting began when Gosforth's spearmen reached William's forward positions. Here, the young prince had placed his most reliable veterans, men who could execute his plan and not just stand and fight. The clash of weapons rang across the valley as steel met steel in earnest.

William's leftmost company, positioned near a small stream, gave ground first. Their captain, a grizzled man named Corbin, had orders to break his formation at the first serious pressure. When a wedge of Crown men-at-arms struck his line, Corbin's men scattered up the nearest slope with just enough of them holding to keep the enemy from following in force.

Dangerous work, and some of Corbin's men gave their lives for the ruse, but that also sold it.

The sight of fleeing rebels sent ripples of excitement through the Crown ranks. Gosforth committed his reserve companies to exploit what appeared to be a breakthrough, sending fresh troops to roll up William's line as the left gave way.

The pursuit carried the men onto ground William had chosen carefully, loose scree and tangled brush that broke up the Crown formation and separated officers from their troops.

Meanwhile, William's center held just long enough to make it believable, not all falling back at once. Captain Morris, commanding the companies directly below William's position, waited until he started getting flanking pressure and then began conducting a fighting withdrawal in the same direction Corbin's men had gone. They fell back and reformed behind a low stone wall, holding until flanked again, then retreating another fifty paces to the next defensive position.

Each stage of this retreat drew the Crown forces deeper into the hills, losing sight of the open ground in the north. Gosforth's neat formations stretched and distorted as they climbed uneven slopes and tried to chase the "retreating" enemy, their intervals widening until gaps appeared between companies. Officers struggled to maintain control as their men became scattered among rocks and ravines, their voices lost in the noise of combat.

The terrain worked exactly as William had planned. He'd walked his people over the ground ahead of the fight, so they knew the footing and where to retreat to.

It was a good position. What looked like natural defensive positions to a commander on the valley floor would become traps once his troops committed to the assault. The gentle slopes that seemed easily climbable from a distance proved steep and treacherous underfoot. The scattered rocks that appeared to offer cover for advancing infantry actually created obstacles that broke up their formations.

William raised his sword when the enemy center had climbed halfway up the hillside, their formation now stretched into a vulnerable column.

"Send the signal," William commanded.

The archers struck first. From their concealed positions on the eastern heights, they loosed dense volleys into the Crown forces below. The arrows fell like deadly rain, their points finding targets among men who weren't expecting an attack from above.

The Crown forces tried to respond, raising shields and closing ranks, but their officers had lost control of the formations. Men who should have moved together became isolated in small groups, each seeking whatever cover they could find among the rocks and brush. Whatever cohesion they had disappeared as soldiers focused on their own survival.

Sir Aldwin's cavalry struck the Crown right wing, just as Gosforth was trying to rally his scattered center, pouring over a smooth, low hill into a dip where the Crown's right wing had found itself, their sudden charge shattering a company of conscripts. The psychological impact of the plummeting arrows on the left and the smashing cavalry on the right spread throughout the rest of the Crown army.

The enemy still outnumbered the smaller force William had in this fight, only half of the combined forces of the Army of Rendalia and Pembroke's men not left behind to guard the Eastbridge.

He needed to shake them, make them think they were facing something much larger than themselves.

William's crossbowmen joined the battle from their positions on the western slopes, shooting right into the veterans in the center. Their heavier bolts, fired from elevation, punched through mail and even some shields.

The battle's turning point came when Gosforth himself fell, struck down by a crossbow bolt while trying to rally his wavering center. His banner toppled with him, the sight visible across much of the battlefield.

What little remaining morale that remained went with it.

"Send a wyvern to Pembroke. He's to move his force into position."

William watched the enemy formation come apart like a tapestry with its threads cut. This was the danger of conscripts. They could fight well enough when massed and held together, but apply enough pressure and they would break where veterans would only bend.

The collapse accelerated when William's "retreating" forward companies suddenly stiffened their resistance. Captain Morris wheeled his men around and led them in a countercharge that struck the overextended Crown center, the only part of the enemy line still holding.

They broke, taking the last of the conscripts with them, throwing down weapons and running north out of the town, hoping to get back to the walls of Solestead.

The pursuit phase required as much control as the defensive battle. William's officers had strict orders to channel the fleeing enemy rather than simply slaughter them. He didn't want any of them to get the idea they had to stand and fight to the last man.

He wanted them to run.

The enemy poured out of the hills much faster than they had gone into them, and straight into the second half of William's army, now arrayed across the road back to Solestead.

The fleeing Crown forces had nowhere to go, with William's pursuit pressing from behind and Pembroke's wall blocking the road ahead.

Their rout became panic. On William's signal, Aldwin's cavalry swung wide and came in from the east, pushing the rabble west toward the Middlewood Forest far in the distance.

William spurred his horse down the slope, leaving the cleanup of the battle to his men. He found Pembroke near the center of his line, the baron's armor still pristine, not having to lift a finger to force the rout.

"Your Highness," Pembroke called as William approached. "An impressive victory. We've taken near three hundred prisoners, and the rest are scattered to the winds."

"Good." William dismounted.

Crown soldiers knelt in growing clusters under the watch of his guards, while others still fled westward across the broken ground.

"What did it cost us?" Pembroke asked.

"Light. Perhaps fifty dead, maybe twice that wounded, most to sell them on our rout."

"It was well done. You've become quite adept at this. Shouldn't we finish them off? A hard pursuit now could finish this Crown army entirely. They'll not stand again if we press them."

"No, we'll let them go. We still have a full, and even larger, Crown army building at Berkshire, and Sinclair is pushing back the men who'd held him in. It will take some time for them to integrate, and I don't want to give them enough to hound us once we cross the Tradesway. There's also a chance the men falling back from the Lindenwood might try for Solestead to reinforce it and hold us. If we move now, we can take it before word of this battle reaches the small force left behind to hold it. We can push through them and reach the Tradesway just as Sinclair does. The timing of all of this is critical."

The baron looked back toward the western hills where the last of the Crown army was disappearing. "It goes against every instinct. When your enemy breaks, you crush them."

"When your enemy breaks, you use that break to achieve your larger purpose. We're not looking to take prisoners. We're looking to win a war. My father is not among those fleeing men."

"Quite adept," Pembroke repeated, almost proudly.

South Road Cross, Barony of Merrick, Kingsheart

The columns stretched along the muddy road, the spring rains turning the South Road into a quagmire. William rode forward through the press of soldiers, his mount picking its way around supply wagons that had bogged down in the mud. The South Road Cross lay ahead, its weathered marker and the stone of the Tradesway barely visible through the mass of armed men.

Garris had beaten them here, but only by a little bit from the look of his army still marching in from the east.

"There," Pembroke said, pointing north with his good arm, his left shoulder still tight against his chest, recovering from where he'd taken an arrow at the Thunderhorn.

It was hard to miss Sinclair, sitting on his horse, towering above footmen, with the other mounted knights giving him a wide berth.

"Your Highness," Garris Sinclair said as they rode up to him. "I hear congratulations are in order for your victory."

William couldn't help but notice his saying that congratulations were in order was definitely not the same thing as giving congratulations for the victory.

Sinclair did so love his petty slights.

"The same can be said for you. Baron Greville practically ran back to Berkshire."

"Without a sword needing to be unsheathed. Not exactly a stunning victory."

"I would argue a victory without bloodshed is the best kind of victory."

"Uh-huh," Sinclair mumbled, clearly not agreeing. "We should make camp here for the night. Too much of our force is conscript and they're strung out all along the road in the march. We need to let them regroup and get started in the morning."

"No. We need to move now. We can slow to let the stragglers keep up and send some men to the rear to cajole the rest to pick up the pace. Greville will have made Berkshire by now and they will know our armies have come together. They will hold for a time, preparing for us to push on them, but it won't take long for their scouts to tell them we aren't moving down the Tradesway. My father will be pushing for results and they will have no choice but to bring the fight to us. I do not want them snapping at our heels the whole way, forcing us into a stand-up fight. When they come, I want us to take them on our own terms."

"I still say this plan is too clever by half."

"And yet it is the plan, Baron."

"Was the plan to let Gosforth's army escape untouched? You had them broken, fleeing in disorder. Any competent commander would have pursued and finished them."

William's eyes darted to Pembroke and then back to Sinclair.

"The plan was to move quickly and arrive at the same time as your forces so that we could move north the same day. Speed matters more than body counts."

"Does it?" Pembroke asked. "Those men you allowed to escape will rejoin the Crown forces in Berkshire. We'll face them again."

"Better that than being caught in the open by the eastern army while we're busy chasing stragglers through the hills."

Garris made a dismissive sound. "You had sufficient forces to do both. Send the cavalry after the routed enemy while your infantry secures the roads. Basic tactics, Prince William. Honestly, this is partially your fault, Rowan. I would have thought you would have taught him that in Lynese."

William ignored the slight. He knew bullies, and the last thing he should do is feed into his theatrics. And, as he told them, speed was of the essence.

"I learned a lot in Lynese, including that maneuvering and having the right ground was as important as having the men. Do you know why my army is full of veterans? Because I haven't bled them fighting the enemy where the enemy wanted to fight. Which is why we need to at least reach the Trentwell Hills before they figure out what's happening and catch up with us. Hell, if we're lucky, we might even make Blackheath Forest."

"You preserve your veterans like a miser hoarding gold, refusing to spend them where they might do the most good. Every enemy soldier you allow to escape is one we'll face again."

William looked between the two older men. Pembroke's expression remained neutral, but he hadn't contradicted Garris.

"Edmund's strength isn't in his armies," William said. "Don't you understand that? It's in his ability to replace losses. You must have noticed how quickly, how easily, he's been recruiting men. For every man we've killed, two more have appeared. How many armies have you routed? Trading casualties for territory is exactly what he wants us to do."

"So instead we trade territory for nothing?" Garris spread his hands in mock confusion. "Help me understand your grand strategy. We abandon defensible positions, we refuse to press advantages, we allow beaten enemies to regroup. What exactly are we accomplishing?"

"Staying alive and mobile and on the march to Starhaven."

"How do you expect to take the capital when you're afraid to properly engage the enemy?"

William's temper finally slipped. "I'm not afraid of anything."

"No? Then why do you fight this war like a merchant haggling over prices instead of a commander seeking victory?"

"Because, unlike you, I'm thinking past the next battle."

"Your arrogance will be your downfall."

"And your pride will be yours."

"You dare ..."

"I dare because I command here." William raised his voice so all could hear. "We march in the hour. Those who wish to follow, prepare your men. Those who don't, the road to Iron Keep is that way."

Garris yanked his reins hard, his horse dancing sideways. "This isn't over."

He wheeled his horse around and spurred it hard, sending mud flying as he galloped west. His officers exchanged uncertain glances before following.

Pembroke watched them go before turning to William. "That could have been handled better."

"Prepare to march," William said, ignoring the statement. "We have ground to cover before nightfall."

Pembroke said nothing, but his expression remained troubled as he turned his horse to rejoin their men.

William watched Pembroke ride away, frowning before he returned to his men as well. Pembroke and Sinclair could argue about why not do this or why not do that, but arguing would get them nowhere.

William had an army to move, and that required actual work, not just talk.

Not that he was allowed to get all the orders he needed out, to check with his quartermasters to make sure the men all had the supplies they needed for the march, or find the commander to make sure the stragglers had caught up with the main body.

As soon as he'd pulled Eskild aside to start going over what needed to be done, Baron Farrow made his way through the crowd, stopping just short of him.

"Your Highness, if I could have a word?"

William looked past the baron where men were already repacking supplies and preparing to march.

"My lord, we have a lot to do today, and not a lot of time to do it. What can I do for you?"

"It's about my lands," Farrow said. "You're taking near every fighting man from the eastern baronies and leaving very few behind. Especially from those of us in these middle baronies that will almost certainly be overrun, even if the Crown forces follow you."

"We need every sword for the march on Starhaven."

"I understand the necessity, but it leaves Merrick vulnerable. My villages, my people, they'll have no protection if Crown forces sweep through."

"I can't deny that that is a risk, but we have limited options. If we try to defend everywhere, we will end up defending nowhere."

"And if my forests burn? If my people are driven from their homes? What good does victory at Starhaven do them then?"

"They'll still have a kingdom. You, and all of the other barons, took up arms after the Crown's new restrictions, after the massive taxes they put on your people. How long could they have survived through that? Their lives were put in danger the moment you raised your banner in rebellion and they won't be safe again until we overthrow the Crown and restore sanity."

Farrow was quiet for a long moment, his amber eyes studying the camp around them.

"It's a sore peace if I'm left with a barony that has no people in it," Farrow said finally. "All of its industry burned to the ground, its villages empty."

"I understand your concerns, Baron. Truly. But there's nothing I can do. I need your men."

Farrow studied him for another moment, then nodded once.

"As you say, Your Royal Highness." He offered another precise bow. "By your leave."

The baron turned without waiting for a response, walking back toward his men with that same unhurried gait he'd maintained throughout the conversation.

"That might have been a blunder," Eskild said.

William turned sharply to the Thay sergeant. "Not you, too."

"I'm not doubting your strategy, and you're probably right, but that wasn't about tactics."

"Then what was it about?"

"Baron Sinclair, Baron Pembroke, now Baron Farrow. They're not just thinking about beating Edmund. They're thinking about what comes after."

"We have to win first before there *is* an after."

"True, but they know there will be an after. Someone will sit the throne when this ends. Someone will hand out rewards, assign new lands, settle old scores. That someone will need support to get the right to do that."

William frowned. "I'll have their support. I'm next in line for the throne and I'm Aldric's chosen successor."

"Aldric's dead," he said bluntly. "And after your cousin and then your father, how much loyalty does the Whitton name carry? Yes, by precedence and by law, you should be the next one on the throne, but precedence and law have already been thrown out. You are in open rebellion against your father who has, by precedence and by law, a right to the throne. Why do you think the thing that did not protect him from an uprising will protect you?"

"But we're allies."

"For now, but you are also a young man married to a foreign wife, and Garris has always been determined to maintain his power. When your uncle, either of your uncles, was alive, that focus was aimed at the childless duke sitting on the throne of Iron Keep, but things change, and I guarantee you Garris's goals have changed. He may not have articulated it as such, and he may not, right now, have plans to do anything about it yet, after all, he is a lot like you, thinking of the strategic over the political half the time. But it is in the back of his mind, I assure you, he is thinking about it."

William turned away, staring out at the men. "None of that matters if we lose."

"Everything matters if we win. Your uncle understood politics. It's why men followed him even when things looked darkest. He knew how to make them believe they'd be better off with him than without him."

"I'm not my uncle."

"No. You're young, and you think winning battles is enough." Eskild's tone held no judgment, just flat observation. "Sinclair knows differently. Pembroke, too, though he's subtler about it. They're already dividing up a kingdom that hasn't been won yet."

"While I'm trying to actually win it."

"And that's your weakness. You treat every problem like it's got a military solution. I need to go check with the commanders and the quartermasters."

William frowned as Eskild walked away. Maybe he should have kept Isolde with him after all.

Chapter 8

Starhaven

"Enough," Edmund yelled, slapping his palm on the desk, the crack causing the noble before him to jump, ending his protestations. "I am tired of your excuses. They grow more pathetic with every word you speak."

Baron Elstow, a portly man in his fifties, wrung his hands. "Your Majesty, my people have given all they can. Hundreds of men have joined the levy, and they have given large parts of their grain stores, which have grown very low. The winter harvest was poor, and we need men to work the fields if we are going to continue feeding the people."

"And those hundreds of men you have sent ran at the first sight of rebels. I can only wonder where they learned that kind of cowardice. The people are a reflection of their baron, and yours are not showing you in a good light. And even then, when I visited your lands two months ago, you promised me eight hundred men. So far, you delivered only four hundred, and now you claim you cannot find even four hundred more?"

"It's as I said, Your Majesty, we need men to work the fields. Planting season is well underway, and if we don't get the seeds in the ground, we will not be able to feed the men. And we've already given as many tradesmen as we are able. These men's skills take years to build, and losing them will cripple their communities."

"And how will their communities fare if the kingdom falls? Or perhaps you are looking forward to someone new sitting on the throne. Perhaps you are dragging your feet not out of incompetence, but out of disloyalty."

"No, Your Majesty. I am loyal to you, of course. I just ..."

"You just what? You didn't mean to defy your king? You didn't mean to be treasonous? I am feeling magnanimous today, so I will assume you are only incompetent and give you one more chance to do what you pledged. You will return to your barony and find me five hundred men within a fortnight. Empty your dungeons, recruit from taverns, drag them from the fields. I care not how you accomplish this task, only that you do."

Before the baron could protest again, or give more excuses, there was a knock at the door, followed by Orlan appearing in his chamber.

"Your Majesty, forgive the interruption, but the delegation from the Ice Lands has arrived."

Edmund's expression brightened considerably.

"Another incompetent come to answer for his failures," Edmund said before turning back to Elstow. "You will do as I commanded. Do not disappoint me again, Baron."

As Elstow bowed and retreated toward the doors, Edmund returned to his desk, pulling papers forward. "Send them in, Orlan. It is past time the duke explained why he has slowed, hell, stopped his attacks on Iron Keep."

Orlan looked nervous, clearing his throat. "Your Majesty, it is not Duke Cadogan who has come. His son leads the delegation."

"His son?" Edmund said, looking up.

"Yes, Your Majesty. Lord Peren Cadogan, with a small retinue of northern knights."

Edmund's face flushed red, and he stood again, angrily, "His son. Isaac sends his son. Bring the boy before me. Now."

Orlan bowed and departed, leaving Edmund alone with his fury. The duke's refusal to reopen the fight against Iron Keep had already raised questions in Edmund's mind. Yes, they had taken losses, but they still had a standing army and had barely levied their people, so his claim that his losses made it impossible to stay in the fight held little weight. And now, summoned directly to Starhaven to account for these convenient excuses, the duke sent his son like some errand boy.

The doors opened again, and Orlan returned with a young man in his mid-twenties. Lord Peren Cadogan possessed his father's imposing height and broad shoulders, though his reddish-brown hair was cropped shorter than the duke's wild mane.

"Your Majesty." Peren dropped to one knee. "I bring greetings from my father, Duke Isaac Cadogan of the Ice Lands."

Edmund remained standing, his gaze boring into the young man.

"Greetings. How ... considerate," he said, coming around the desk, walking slowly and deliberately toward him. "I am surprised to see you here since I summoned your father and not you."

Peren rose. "I know, Your Majesty. My father sends his regrets, but pressing matters in the north require his immediate attention. He felt he could not be spared from ..."

"Could not be spared?" Edmund said, his voice explosive enough that it silenced the boy, making him take a step back. "He receives a summons from his king, and he feels he cannot be spared? Tell me, boy, what pressing matters take precedence over royal commands?"

"There have been raiders from Alchmara along our coast, and the men of Iron Keep have been sinking any ship in Alther Bay and raiding some of our villages there as well. Taken together, my father feels our men have to be used to bring security back to our duchy before we can put together a new fleet of ships to carry men across the narrows and back to Iron Keep."

"He can't fight because the men from Iron Keep are fighting back? That is his excuse? What did he think they would do, just sit quietly and welcome their new overlords? Is your father that weak?"

"Of course not, Your Majesty. We, of course, foresaw the rebels fighting back, but it was ... unexpected how successful they were and the sudden aid they gained from the eastern barons of Kingsheart. With them, they control more than half of the coast of Alther Bay and the largest ports on the bay. We are not a seafaring people and do not have the men to counter that."

"So your defense is that you are not competent enough to maintain your rule? Is this what your father sent you to say? Do you take me for a fool, boy? You think I do not notice that you become so incapable precisely when my son returned from Rendalia. A curious coincidence, would you not agree?"

"I would not presume to question Your Majesty's judgment, but my father's loyalty to the Crown has never wavered. The Ice Lands were one of the first to join you in taking on this rebellion. We were among the first to put our people on the line."

"Really? Your father promised me he would take Iron Keep, and I agreed to give him dominion over it, and yet, not only does not a single man from the north still stand on that peninsula, but the pressure on the men there is so light that Baron Sinclair is in Kingsheart with nearly every single knight from that duchy along with massive levies," he said, and then paused, stepping closer to the boy, ending only a few handspans from his face. "Tell me truthfully, Lord Peren … does your father still support my rule?"

The question hung in the air between them, although the boy still had the confidence of youth and didn't shirk or look away. "My father swore an oath to the rightful King of Sidor. That oath remains unbroken."

"The rightful king. You show yourself too much, playing games with words. Not 'to you' or 'to King Edmund,' but to the 'rightful king.' One might wonder whom you consider that to be."

"Your Majesty, I …"

"Silence," Edmund snapped, taking a step back from him. "I am tired of hearing Cadogan evasions and lies. Orlan, summon Captain Drustan."

Drustan was the new captain of his guard after Colm had been elevated to a knighthood and used for more … direct actions.

"Your Majesty, I haven't done anything."

"Exactly the problem. Your family's failure to achieve any of their promises has reached the point of breaking faith. And your father well knows this, which is why he sent you to answer for his failures instead of coming himself."

"We still fight, Your Majesty. The Ice Lands stands with the Crown."

"Then let him prove it. Your father can come here himself and retrieve you if he is that willing to stand by his actions."

Captain Drustan had impeccable timing, arriving with several guards. "Your Majesty?"

Edmund pointed at Peren. "Escort Lord Cadogan to the dungeons. He will remain there until his father comes to collect him."

The guards moved forward, but Peren seemed to suddenly realize this was real and demanded, "You can't! This violates every law of ..."

"I am the law. I am the King of Sidor, and I will not tolerate treachery disguised as loyalty! Take him away."

As Drustan's men grabbed Peren and pulled him through the doors, still shouting pleas for reason. Edmund ignored him, standing there furious that Cadogan dared play these games still. He was done with the northern lord and was ready to replace him entirely.

"Orlan," he said, looking at his steward who still stood against the far wall, trying his best to stay out of the line of fire.

"Your Majesty?"

"Summon the Master of Wyverns. I have a message for Duke Cadogan."

"At once, Your Majesty."

Edmund returned to his desk, already thinking about what he'd say to bring Isaac Cadogan to heel, composing the words in his head. The duke thought himself clever; thought he could manipulate events instead of following commands directly.

He would soon learn his folly.

Trentwell Hills, Kingsheart, Sidor

The army didn't move fast enough. They'd barely made it to the Trentwell Hills before the Crown scouts started probing at the rear of their lines.

Sinclair had just had a long march, and William's forces had already had one battle in the last few days, which meant neither was going to be able to move fast enough to stay ahead of the mostly fresh Crown army.

No, he had to stand and fight.

William pulled his army up short at the southern edge of the Trentwell Hills, which folded into one another in long, stony swells, with the strip of ground between them pinched down to a throat no wider than a large farm.

The Middlewood Forest pressed hard to the southwest against the hills. The Middlewood was an old forest, thin and hard to traverse, meaning the Crown forces would have to mostly come north where the Tradesway made a bend.

Knowing this, William set his lines where the two hills made the narrows, sending the farmer who'd set up his fields between them running for Bradford, before placing his heavy foot in layered blocks across the low ground, five ranks deep at the center, then three, then reserves braced behind.

On the heights, he put all of his archers split between the two hills, with two companies in loose order on each, protected by a light rank of spearmen in front of each, although mostly the steep slope and crest would put any force advancing up it at a disadvantage.

Pembroke's knights waited behind the west hill on the reverse slope, where ground slanted away and hid the horses, while Sinclair's hid behind the same on the eastern hill on the right.

Neither had wanted to be held in reserve until William explained his plan. That was enough to mollify them, as they could see the glory in it.

If the battle went as William had laid out.

The skirmishers came first, recoiling when they came out of the trees and saw the army laid out ahead of them. Twenty minutes later, the conscripts began to push out through the lighter edge of this part of the forest, one hundred at first, then five hundred, then one thousand. The conscripts were in ragged lines, loose and not in good order.

That didn't keep them from being a threat. Conscripts might be flighty, but this many men had a bravery all of its own.

William ordered the first flag put up. On the heights, the first volley raked down, slowing the enemy advance as men hunched to avoid being hit. His archers were firing in slow volleys, enough to cause some damage but not putting on serious fire yet.

They needed to conserve their ammunition for now.

The mass pressed forward toward what they could see, the line of rebels in the field, on flat ground and straight ahead of them.

William rode behind the central ranks, not so near that a stray arrow might find him, but close enough that his men could see him when they looked back. He wanted them to hold and step when he wanted them to step, not because fear made them do either too soon.

"Look at them pack together," Eskild observed from beside William. "Too many bodies for that ground."

William agreed. The Crown commanders were pushing their conscripts forward aggressively, trying to bring their numerical advantage to bear. But the bottleneck between the hills compressed their formations. Men stumbled over each other as rear ranks pressed forward into those ahead of them.

The Crown's front surged forward, pressed on by their officers anxious to get the fight started. The pass compressed them together. The first line reached William's spears and jammed. The impact hit like a cart against a wall. Points took belly, then groin when men bent, then chest clean through when a shield slipped. The front rank died on their feet and could not fall, held up by the press from behind.

A few Crown archers let fly from the tree line, but they had a poor line and worse elevation, and were quickly countered by William's archers.

William watched the depth build. The tree line fed more bodies into the track, and the mouth jammed.

"Pull back the center," he ordered. "First position."

Drums tapped the command, short and quick, and the front row eased a cautious five paces and set up again. The second rank stepped and took the slack. The maneuver gave a little room for the Crown army, which would have felt a release of the pressure. Spearmen and pike battles were as much armies pushing each other until one or the other fled as actual fighting, and it had a rhythm of its own.

The Crown army felt the enemy give way and pushed harder, filling up the open space, their lines behind them compacting more as they felt the front move.

He let the men hold for a moment, archers firing into the massed body. He couldn't pull back too quickly, or the enemy might sense the trap they were pushing themselves into.

"Second position," he said to the drummer by the standard.

The beat rolled and the center yielded five steps again, while the flanks remained anchored on either hill, causing the line to bow inward.

Baron Greville himself led a regiment of professional infantry into the gap, their superior equipment marking them as household guards. They should have continued to hold those forces in reserve for the moment a breach opened, but they were impatient, not waiting long enough.

William wanted them in the center, in the kettle that was firming up, becoming deep enough that they were trapped between two hills and a thick line of professional soldiers.

"Third step," William commanded.

His center pulled back another five paces, maintaining formation while yielding ground. The Crown forces surged forward, believing they were breaking his forces. More enemy reserves were committed to exploit the apparent success.

William's flanks at the hill bases refused to move, creating a concave pocket that admitted the Crown forces while restricting their frontage.

The arrow storm from both hills never ceased. Rebel archers worked in shifts, one line shooting while another rested, maintaining continuous volleys. They didn't need to pick targets; the packed mass below offered nothing but opportunities. Each arrow that missed one man struck another behind him.

Crown casualties mounted faster than they could be cleared. Dead men created barriers that living soldiers stumbled over. Wounded fighters who fell were trampled by their own advancing comrades.

Finally, someone on the Crown side decided they'd had enough of the rain of arrows and decided to do something about it.

The Crown's attempt to clear the hills began as scattered efforts. Individual companies broke from the main assault and started climbing. Without coordination, they reached the slopes at different times, allowing the defenders to concentrate their efforts against each group. The first wave barely made it halfway before spear thrusts and arrows drove them back down.

Baron Pendeen, from his banner, organized a more serious effort, gathering five hundred men for a coordinated assault on the western hill. They advanced up the slope in reasonable order, shields raised against the arrow fall. The steep gradient slowed them, heavy armor becoming a burden rather than protection. By the time they reached the spearmen's line, their formation had fallen apart, their line opening up with thick gaps here and there.

The hilltop defenders had every advantage. They struck downward with limited reach, while the attackers had to thrust upward. The Crown soldiers tried to push through by weight of numbers, but the ground was uneven and had falloffs here and there, making it difficult to hold a solid line. After losing one hundred men in ten minutes, Pendeen's assault collapsed back down the slope.

Meanwhile, the main battle in the pass grew more desperate. William ordered his fourth withdrawal, pulling his center back to the final position, making a tight arc between the hill bases. The pocket was now fully formed, its mouth barely three hundred yards wide while its depth stretched nearly twice that distance.

Into this space, the Crown forces had committed thousands of men.

The compression reached critical mass. Soldiers in the middle of the Crown formation couldn't move their arms. Those at the edges were pressed against the hillsides where rebel spears thrust down at them. The rear ranks, still emerging from the forest, pushed forward unknowingly while the front ranks tried desperately to retreat.

William saw the moment their cohesion broke. The Crown army stopped being organized units and became a single mass of humanity, packed on top of each other.

If he let it hold, the rear ranks would start to panic and release the pressure, letting the army retreat out of the kettle.

That wasn't what William wanted.

The professional Crown infantry tried to restore order. They formed a wedge near the center, attempting to punch through William's line using a disciplined assault.

For a moment, they gained ground, but they advanced into a trap within a trap. The rebel center gave way slightly, drawing them deeper.

The fire from the hills had reached its maximum intensity. Rebel archers emptied their quivers into the packed mass, then resupplied from wagon loads of arrows brought up the reverse slopes.

Crown morale shattered completely. Men tried to climb over their comrades to escape. Others pressed against the edges of the pocket, clawing at the hillsides. Some Crown soldiers attacked their own officers who were trying to maintain discipline. The army devolved into a mob, then into something less than that.

"Send in the cavalry," William ordered, sending flags up, releasing the last part of his plan.

Sinclair and Pembroke had been waiting the entire battle, listening to the fight while forced to wait. It must have been torture for both barons, who would have worried their glory would pass them by.

Thankfully, both had enough self-control to hold until the moment called for them, trusting William to choose tactics over politics as usual, to not keep them out of the fight.

Now that they were released, however, both forces shot forward like a bowstring, sweeping down over the hills, the archers opening a path for them to come through down the slopes.

The twin mounted forces struck simultaneously, smashing into the sides of the army. The Crown rear guard, such as it was, dissolved before them.

It took almost no work for Pembroke and Sinclair's men to push in to each other like two pincers, snipping off the enemy force with half of it inside the pocket and the other half outside.

If they had been smart, if they'd still had cohesion, the Crown forces would have attacked the thinner line of mounted cavalry, cracking the trap open.

But they didn't have that kind of control left. Most of the veterans were inside the pocket, leaving already panicked farmers and tradesmen on the outside.

Instead of fighting to relieve their fellows, they crumbled. Men threw away weapons and shields, anything that might slow their escape, pushing back into the forest behind them, getting clogged in with their own supply wagons and support units.

The encirclement was complete.

What followed was systematic destruction. His men stopped giving up ground, and from all sides, they attacked in toward each other, slowly pressing in on the mass of men trapped in the middle. Above them, the archers in the hills continued their arrow barrage into the thick mass.

Pockets of Crown resistance formed where professional units maintained discipline. A square of Greville's household guard held for twenty minutes, their shields locked and spears bristling. But they were islands in a sea of chaos. Once isolated, rebel forces surrounded them and ground them down through attrition.

The Crown's mounted knights, at least those who'd survived the initial combat, found themselves fighting dismounted in the press. Their expensive armor became a trap when they fell, the weight preventing them from rising as the battle surged over them. Some managed to surrender, their quality equipment marking them as worth ransoming. Others died anonymously in the crush, their nobility meaning nothing in the democratic slaughter of compressed combat.

Organization on both sides began breaking down, though for different reasons. The Crown forces ceased to exist as an army, becoming thousands of individuals seeking survival. The rebel forces struggled to maintain discipline as the killing became execution rather than combat. Exhausting in its own right.

Attempts at organized surrender failed in the chaos. Groups of Crown soldiers threw down their weapons, but in the press, the gesture went unseen. Others trying to yield were cut down by rebels who couldn't distinguish surrender from tactical regrouping in the melee. The fog of battle obscured everything except immediate violence.

The pocket began to empty as Crown numbers dwindled. Where maybe three thousand had stood, now perhaps five hundred remained standing. Bodies carpeted the ground three deep in places. The wounded crawled over the dead, seeking escape that didn't exist.

Some Crown units achieved momentary breakouts. A group of a hundred managed to slip around the eastern cavalry screen, fleeing into the forest. Another of a few dozen fought their way up the western slope, preferring to face the spearmen than remain in the pocket. But these were exceptions. The vast majority found themselves trapped until death or surrender.

The battle's tempo slowed as exhaustion affected both sides. Rebels rotated fresh troops forward while tired units recovered. The Crown forces had no such luxury. Those still fighting had been in combat for over an hour without relief.

The final phase began as rebel forces systematically reduced the remaining pockets of resistance. Small groups of Crown soldiers still fought in isolated clusters, backs together in desperate last stands. The rebels surrounded each group, offering surrender or death. Most chose surrender when they recognized their situation. Those who refused were cut down without ceremony.

William swung down from his saddle only when the push on the front eased into a feed of captives.

Captain Corbin approached, his armor splattered with blood.

"You did good work, keeping the center line together." William commended him. "How are our casualties?"

"Light on our side. Maybe two hundred dead. The schiltrons absorbed most of the pressure, and our rotation kept them fresh."

William nodded, looking at the field where Crown soldiers lay in heaps. Conservative estimates suggested three thousand enemy dead in total, counting those on the hills, with another thousand wounded or captured.

Pembroke rode up, his sword bloodied and smiling ear to ear. "That was bracing."

Sinclair approached from the opposite direction, walking his exhausted horse through the carnage.

There wasn't any sign of their recent tension, both men in excellent moods. Victory had a way of doing that to a man. Especially with a victory of this magnitude.

"What about Greville and Pendeen?" William asked.

"Greville's dead," Pembroke confirmed. "Saw him go down myself when his guard tried to break out of the pocket. Haven't found Pendeen's body yet."

"He made it out. He'd been focused on the western hill when we closed the pocket. He saw the writing on the wall and pulled back, getting the remainder of the men on the outside before we could finish the pocket and chase."

William surveyed the battlefield once more. Bodies lay in a rough crescent shape where the pocket had formed, packed densest at the center where compression had been the greatest.

"One out of two isn't bad. Have the wounded separated and treated," William ordered. "Our own first, then theirs if supplies allow. Strip the enemy dead of useful equipment, especially from that group of veterans. We could use it."

The aftermath would take hours to sort through. Prisoners needed securing, wounded required treatment, and the dead demanded burial or burning, but the time pressure was less now. This was the bulk of the Crown forces in the region. Even with his father's shocking ability to recruit men, it would take time for a new army to form.

Which was good, because it would take time for him to get his own forces back together. Victories like this tended to cause chaos on all sides.

"Your uncle would be proud," Eskild said quietly.

William felt no pride, only exhaustion and a sick feeling at the scale of death. These had been Sidorian soldiers, not foreign enemies. Many were conscripts forced into service, farmers and craftsmen who'd wanted nothing more than to return home.

"Let's put some order into this chaos."

Chapter 9

Starhaven, Sidor

A month. The idea of being gone from the capital and back out among the rabble for a month ate at Edmund, but it was also clear to him that it was needed. The fervor his last tour had drummed up had faded, proving that even the Key had limitations.

In addition, demand for men and material had expanded. The losses were beginning to mount, and he needed more recruits if he was going to stop William from having any more victories.

He would have to head further north this time, to the baronies above Twin Lake. The central baronies in Kingsheart had been well gone over, and even with the Key, there weren't that many fighting-age men left who hadn't already been conscripted.

Which meant a month of travel at the very least. Not how Edmund wanted to spend his spring.

A knock interrupted his thoughts.

"Enter."

Orlan appeared in the doorway. "Your Majesty, Conservator Chatwell requests an audience."

That gave him pause. Acolytes did not ask for audiences. The members of the Covenant generally stood above the secular concerns of the world, more focused on the Ancients and cataloging the remnants from the Time of Magic. He actually couldn't think of ever hearing of an acolyte requesting an audience, even during his brother's or father's time on the throne.

And yet, he could think of something that would cause a sudden departure from tradition. That something was currently sitting in his dungeon, kept from talking to anyone lest he tell them about the Key.

Edmund had always known he was playing with fire, imprisoning an acolyte, even a lower-level one. He'd hoped he'd kept it quiet, limiting access to those most loyal, but people's faith often caused them to choose loyalty to their ancestors over more worldly loyalties.

Edmund hadn't fooled himself into thinking this day would never come, but he had hoped to put it off until after the rebellion was squashed, when he had more options.

Now, he still needed the Key, which meant Tomas had to remain in prison. To lose either was to lose the war and his throne. Not that he could say no or turn down the audience. That would only turn bad into worse.

"Send him in."

He'd only spoken to Conservator Chatwell twice that he could think of. The man stood shorter than Edmund, his frame compact beneath dark robes that bore the silver symbols of his rank, with dark, slicked-back hair and intense gray eyes.

He was one of the middle managers of the church, dealing with the day-to-day affairs of the Great Hall in Starhaven for the rapidly aging elder he served. The Acolytes operated with their own hierarchies, their own politics, which had always been uninteresting to Edmund, who preferred a more timely focus and attention.

"Your Majesty." Chatwell bowed, though not deeply. "I appreciate your willingness to receive me."

"Of course, Conservator. Please, sit." Edmund gestured to the chair across from him.

"I will not waste your time with pleasantries, Your Majesty. I come regarding Acolyte Tomas Volden."

Edmund kept his expression neutral. "I assumed as much."

"His detention has drawn attention. Questions have been raised about the circumstances."

"I understand there might be concern. Though I believe those familiar with the full context would find the situation ... understandable."

"I would welcome hearing more about that context."

This was the delicate part. He had to give enough of a reason to keep Tomas locked up and, more importantly, un-interviewed. Which was a needle he had yet to figure out how to thread.

The danger to Edmund was real. Excommunication would accomplish what William and his allies could not. It would isolate him from the spiritual authority and delegitimize his rule. Even kings required the blessing of the Ancients.

"Acolyte Volden came to my attention through certain proposals he made. Proposals that seemed inconsistent with the principles your order upholds. The sacred trust placed in those who study ancient knowledge. I have known Tomas for some time. His dedication to his work is admirable, if a bit overly focused. I did not want to see his standing in the Covenant harmed, as I know him to be a good man, and I hoped the situation might represent a temporary lapse rather than something more concerning. It seemed prudent to allow time for reflection. To prevent actions that could not be easily remedied."

The silence stretched between them. Chatwell's gray eyes remained fixed on Edmund, unreadable.

"You misunderstand me, Your Majesty."

Edmund felt a flicker of surprise. "How so?"

"I did not come to challenge your decision. Actually, quite the opposite. You have done the Hall a great service. There are those within the Covenant who have observed Volden's conduct with similar concern. Your intervention demonstrates proper regard for principles that some might otherwise overlook."

Edmund remained as still as possible. Of all the outcomes he'd gamed out, this was one he hadn't even considered.

"You were right to be cautious and circumspect, of course. There are those who might question the propriety of secular involvement in matters touching the Covenant. Others recognize that certain situations demand practical responses. The Ancients' wisdom does not always translate into simple prescriptions. As one who understands this, I knew that you, a loyal child of the Ancients, would be concerned about how your actions might be taken, and wanted to set your mind at ease, lest you feel the need to reverse your decision."

"I see."

"Of course, there is another side to this. There are considerations that must be made inside the Hall to keep those with a less flexible mindset from taking a more dogmatic view of it. There is an effort in managing questions of this nature that requires attention. Resources must be allocated, discussions conducted with appropriate discretion. Such management inevitably incurs costs."

Edmund suddenly, and very unexpectedly, found himself on ground he was much more comfortable with.

Edmund kept his voice neutral. "The Crown has always valued the Covenant's work. Supporting that work seems both appropriate and necessary."

"Your generosity has been noted." Chatwell paused. "Though circumstances change. What sufficed in quieter times may prove insufficient when matters grow more ... complex."

"Naturally. I, of course, understand that the nature of that support should reflect current circumstances."

"I am very happy to hear this. I believe we share an appreciation for what truly serves the Ancients' legacy."

Edmund gave a nod of his head, signaling his agreement. "Regarding Volden specifically, the more I consider how things have transpired so far, I imagine his situation could benefit from a more extended reflection. Time away from circumstances that might encourage further misjudgment."

"Quite so, Your Majesty. Those familiar with his conduct would likely agree that such reflection serves both his own interests and those of the Covenant. A period of seclusion often provides clarity that immediate restoration to former duties cannot."

"I am pleased we understand each other on that matter."

Chatwell inclined his head fractionally. "Your wisdom in handling this delicate situation has not gone unnoticed."

Edmund considered his next words carefully. "I wonder if there might be other instances where such understanding proves mutually beneficial. Other situations where the Crown's resources might assist in addressing other difficulties."

Something flickered in Chatwell's eyes. Interest, perhaps, or satisfaction.

"There are always challenges in maintaining proper standards," Chatwell said.

"I thought perhaps that might be true. Please know that the Covenant can count on me, should the need arise in the future."

"Your commitment honors you, Your Majesty."

"I am glad we find ourselves in agreement, Conservator."

"As am I." Chatwell paused. "I have much to do, and I understand your time is equally as limited, but perhaps we might continue such discussions through more appropriate channels."

"Indeed. I will send word when I have considered how best to demonstrate the commitment we have discussed."

Chatwell rose from his chair, pulling his robes around him as he did.

"I should return to the Hall," Chatwell said. "There are matters requiring my attention."

"Of course," Edmund said, rising from behind his desk. "Thank you for bringing this situation to my understanding, Conservator. I am grateful for the Covenant's guidance."

"Your piety honors you, Your Majesty." Chatwell bowed, deeper than when he had entered. "May the Ancients illuminate your path."

"And yours, Conservator."

Chatwell turned and departed, his steps neither hurried nor slow. The door closed behind him with a soft click.

Edmund remained standing for a moment, processing what had just occurred. This had not gone the way he'd expected at all, but he could feel the opportunity open up before him with the sudden appearance of a new ally.

Well, not an ally, exactly. Chatwell had been too careful for that, but he wouldn't have been comfortable having this conversation, as indirect as it was, unless he had support. Which meant there was something else happening in the Covenant that he hadn't realized.

The Acolytes had always been above it all. This represented a change in the very foundation of the order of the world, and such change brought opportunity.

Danger, but also opportunity.

Trentwell Hills, Kingsheart

The camp was quiet, even for as early as it was, not that he blamed them. After fighting the battle, although the enemy was retreating, William didn't want to remain where they were. So they loaded up their walking wounded and dead as quickly as possible, furloughed or enlisted those commoners who were captured and uninjured, although that was less than it was before this winter, and sent ransoms to the minor nobles they could identify before starting their march north again.

They didn't have to go far, maybe only a few miles, before they were headed in the right direction again, within the fairly safe environs of the Blackheath Forest.

For tonight, the field stretched out before the camp, which sprawled across the area, with most of the soldiers not on guard duty passing out as soon as their bedrolls were down.

The battle had been another major success. Just over one thousand enemy dead, wounded, or captured versus one hundred dead and another one hundred wounded on his side. They left their wounded and the enemy wounded with the Disciples, who'd set up a camp on the battle site and would tend to the wounded from both sides who were too hurt to walk.

He found Pembroke and Sinclair near a cluster of command tents where officers were distributing wine rations. Pembroke had already claimed a stool and held a cup. Sinclair stood, because Sinclair always stood, as if he thought chairs beneath him in more than a literal way.

Pompous to the last.

"Your Highness." Pembroke raised his cup. "A victory worth celebrating."

William accepted a cup from a serving boy and took a drink. The wine tasted sour, probably from some baron's cellar in Solestead.

"We bloodied them. That's all."

"A thousand casualties is more than bloodied." Sinclair's tone had changed since their last meeting, at least, losing much of its contempt. "I'll give you this, your strategy was sound."

"Thank you, although the terrain did most of the work."

"The terrain did what you planned for it to do." Pembroke said. "Greville was a fool. He should have seen you had the heights and refused battle until you retreated."

"Greville was never a soldier and should never have been put in charge of men," Sinclair said. "If he'd turned the command down, he'd still be alive. The rest will be more cautious now."

"Good," William said. "It will give us more time. Most of the enemy force made it back to Berkshire, and it will take them time to pull together again, which should give us enough time to make it to the forest."

"I'm still not sure what the point of that is. We hurry to make it there, and then it will take us several weeks to march through the Blackheath if we take the southern side of Twin Lake and make for Silverhall, longer if we try to swing around the north," Garris said. "That will give them plenty of time to rebuild."

"But not plenty of time to follow us. The Blackheath is thick without a large road through it. Travel will be slow for us, and even slower for the larger army they are sure to bring. And it will take time for them to come upon us. My father will almost certainly think we are making for Berkshire to follow up on our victory, which means he's going to pull back forces to block us. When we don't show, he will be slow to advance, careful. He will eventually figure out where we went, but we should be out the other side by that time with a clear path ahead of us, thanks to his caution."

"Assuming he does what you think he will," Sinclair said.

"Give the boy some credit," Pembroke, who had drained another cup, holding it up for a refill, said. "He was exactly right on what they would do today. He was right on what they would do at Cresswell and at Solestead. His successes are good."

Surprisingly, Sinclair refilled his cup now and held it up, "That is true. I might not agree, but I have to commend you for your victory."

They drank. The wine still tasted sour, but William found himself drinking deeper. Around them, the camp settled into evening routines. Fires were lit. The sounds of an army at rest, but not at peace.

"So, considering all of this you've done," Pembroke said. "You were doing well in Lynese, and made some very smart moves, but this was two battles in a row where you outmaneuvered the enemy not just strategically, but tactically. I'd like to take credit for it, but … I'm not sure I can. Where did all this strategy come from?"

"Books." William said. "I had quite a lot of time waiting for the ice to melt, and more time on the seas. I took some of my Uncle Aldric's books with me when I returned the last time, and found more in Rendalia. I spent a lot of time reading accounts of my Uncle Gavric's victories and those of his father before him, and I also found some accounts in the Halls in Rendalia of the battles of the First and Second Alliance. I studied and I applied what I've learned from you and Aldric on the battlefield."

"Books," Sinclair said, making the word sound more like a curse. "That's no way to learn warfare."

"It is not the only way I learned," William said.

Sinclair might not have been as openly hostile as before the battle, but he was still not accepting of William as a commander. That much was clear.

They drank for a while longer, but William slowed his drinking while the other two men still drank deep. He'd want his wits about him over the next few days. Just because the Crown army was defeated didn't mean it wasn't still a threat.

"We should call it an evening, gentlemen," William said finally. "We have several days of hard pushing through these hills before we reach the forest, and I'd like to be deep enough in before they start to push scouts forward."

"I still say this is a fool's errand," Sinclair said, standing wobbly. "We should just go right for them, while their army is smashed. Push through Berkshire and straight for Starhaven."

"We've been over this," William said, a little annoyed. "They will be expecting that."

"Bah!" Sinclair said, waving to his equally drunk aides and stumbling into the night.

William looked over at Pembroke, who was slumped against a chest, head lolled back, snoring. Shaking his head, William set his cup down and made his own way to his tent.

He was certain this was the right call. His father wasn't a military man. In politics, his mind might be full of twists and turns, but in the field, he thought in straight lines. In roads and sieges and cutting directly to victory.

No, he'd prepare for one thing, and William would do another.

Chapter 10

Kenna, River Mark

"Your Highness," Galer said as the carriage pulled to a stop in front of a keep that was smaller than she had expected. Sidorians preferred more functional designs without the style that Lynesians preferred.

Isolde was tired. It had been more than a week of travel to get here on roads that had been marched and fought over for several years at this point, leaving much to be desired for their upkeep.

She had put it off as long as she could, staying with the wounded, especially the men from Rendalia, until most were up and moving or sent to more permanent order hospitals.

Eventually, though, she couldn't put it off any longer and did as she was told, heading south while William rode north. *Sent away like a child who cannot be trusted with adult matters.*

"It's quaint," she said to herself as her guard helped her down.

A woman emerged from the keep's main entrance. Tall and angular, brown hair streaked with gray, she wore a simple blue dress that, while clearly made of fine material, lacked the ostentation that was prevalent in her own.

It made Isolde feel wildly overdressed.

"Isolde, it's a pleasure meeting you," the woman said, her voice warm. "Welcome to Kenna."

Isolde curtsied, though something in Alyssa's manner suggested excessive formality would be unwelcome here. "Your Grace. Thank you for receiving me."

"Come inside. You look tired, and I imagine it was a long trip." Alyssa gestured toward the keep's entrance.

They walked through corridors that felt more like a comfortable home than a fortress. Tapestries depicting hunting scenes and landscapes hung on the walls, but nothing overly elaborate.

Alyssa led her to a sitting room warmed by a fire in a stone hearth. Windows looked out over the lake where fishing boats moved slowly across the water. A servant brought wine and withdrew without being asked.

"You're angry," Alyssa said after a moment of quiet.

"I don't know what you mean."

"Yes, you do. I know William sent you away against your wishes. He mentioned it in the wyvern he sent me."

"Shouldn't I be angry about that?"

"Perhaps. What made him send you here?"

"He didn't tell you?"

"He did, but I'd like to hear your version of what happened."

Isolde found herself recounting the confrontation with the River Mark soldiers, their hostility, the threats. As she spoke, some of her anger faded. In the moment, she'd felt like she could have maintained order and kept anything bad from happening, but talking about it now, after the fact, she wasn't so sure.

"So he sent you away for your own protection?"

"Like a child."

"I'm not sure I'd go that far. He wanted to protect you. Men do that," Alyssa said with a slight smile. "Even good men. Especially when they're frightened."

"William wasn't frightened. He was angry."

"At the soldiers, perhaps. But frightened for you. You must understand, William has lost everyone he truly cared about. His mother, his uncle Gavric, and now Aldric. I'm sure part of it was fear that he would lose you as well."

"I'm not some helpless maiden who needs constant protection."

"I doubt you are, and I doubt he was making any kind of judgment on you as a person."

"It's how he sees me, though, forcing me to hide until the war ends."

Alyssa laughed, a warm sound that filled the room. "Hiding? Child, is that what you think you're doing here?"

"What else would you call it?"

"Work." Alyssa rose and moved to the window, looking out over the town. "Do you know what I've been doing while Aldric fought his battles? Managing estates, corresponding with other noble wives, making sure the people remember him as a good man, maintaining relationships with merchants and craftsmen, mediating disputes between the lesser nobles. The unglamorous business of keeping a kingdom functioning."

"That hardly seems ..."

"Important? Essential, you mean," Alyssa said, turning back to her. "Men see the glory in sword work and tactics but often miss the thousand small actions that make victory possible. William didn't send you here as punishment. He sent you here because this is where you can do the most good."

"He could have explained that instead of simply ordering me away."

"Would you have heard him?" Alyssa asked.

Isolde wanted to say, "Of course," to tell her she was being ridiculous, but ... maybe he had said something to that effect. In the moment, she'd been angry and hadn't been listening.

Hindsight again played her for the fool.

"You think I was being stubborn."

"I think you were being young," Alyssa said gently. "There's a difference, though the result is often the same."

Isolde sank back into her chair, feeling annoyed. She didn't like being talked down to, and yet Alyssa had a way about her that made it not as insulting as it would have coming from someone else.

She reminded her, in a way, of her own mother. It had been a long time since her mother died, but she remembered the way she could say things Isolde didn't want to hear, but in a way that took all the heat out of it.

"Things are very different in Lynese."

"Ah. That explains a lot. You're accustomed to being excluded from important matters, so when William makes a decision without consulting you, it feels like going back to the life you had before. But there's a difference between a father protecting his daughter and a husband making tactical decisions in wartime."

"Is there? It feels identical from where I sit."

Alyssa was quiet for a moment, considering. "When Aldric went to war years ago, when we were first married, I felt very similar to how you feel now. Not that I wanted to fight, I don't think I ever had the fire in my belly that you have, but to share in whatever he faced. Do you know what he told me?"

Isolde shook her head.

"He said that if I loved him, I would do the work only I could do rather than insisting on work we could both do. I was furious at the time. It felt like dismissal."

"What changed your mind?"

"Results." Alyssa smiled ruefully. "Within a month, I had accomplished things Aldric never could have managed from a military camp. Secured help from other barons, arranged financing."

Isolde turned this over in her mind. "You think that's what William is doing?"

"Partially, but also, I think he is looking forward to a time after the war is over, when you will have to help him rule this kingdom. You will be the first foreign queen since before Sidor was unified. You have to do the impossible, and you'll have to start the work as soon as the war is won. He is giving you the time and space to be ready for it."

Isolde hadn't thought of it like that. William had said something similar, but his way had been more ... harsh, maybe. At least not presented in the way Alyssa had.

"What should I do?"

"Start small, here in Kenna. We'll visit the people, do the work I already do, and let them see you. Once that is done, we can expand to River Mark as a whole and, if time permits, into Kingsheart and Shadowhold. We will listen to the people, help with things that the local lords can't or won't do, and prove that you are here to make the kingdom better."

"That is similar to what I did in Rendalia."

"Then you are all set for it."

The fire crackled in the hearth as they sat in silence, Alyssa giving her time to think. Outside, the afternoon light was beginning to fade, casting long shadows across the river. Isolde felt the tension that had gripped her for weeks finally beginning to release.

"Thank you," she said.

"For what?"

"For helping me understand."

Alyssa reached over and squeezed her hand. "That's what family does, child."

Family. The word carried weight Isolde hadn't expected. Her own father had always been distant, and her brother had tried to have her executed. Even before that, it had always been more of a competition between them than any kind of connection.

It had been her father's way to make them stronger. Talking to Alyssa, though, and seeing how her brother had turned out, having become a toady of Agravaine, it seemed clear it had been self-defeating.

"Now then," Alyssa said, rising from her chair. "Let me show you to your chambers. Tomorrow will be a busy day, and you'll want to be well-rested for your introduction to Kenna society."

Perhaps William had been smarter than she had given him credit for.

Near Blackheath Forest, Kingsheart, Sidor

The campfires burned low across the rebel encampment as Baron Garris Sinclair made his way between the scattered tents. The army had made good time the last few days, having moved out of the hills early that morning and was only a day's march from Blackheath Forest.

Garris found Baron Pembroke outside his pavilion, leaning back against a tree near his tent, looking up at the sky.

It was all Sinclair could do not to shake his head. While generally Pembroke was a practical man, he was taken by flights of whimsy.

His time would be better spent keeping his attention focused on what mattered.

"Baron Sinclair. I thought you'd retired for the evening," he said, hearing Sinclair approach.

"I couldn't sleep," Garris said, settling onto a camp stool without invitation. "Too much on my mind."

"Such as?"

"Our young prince."

"What about him?"

"I can't help but question his fitness to lead this endeavor."

Pembroke's expression grew guarded. "I think you would find it difficult to question his track record of success."

"Has he had success, or has he simply avoided the defeats that matter?" he said, and paused, quiet for a moment like he was waiting for the strength to say what he had really come to say. "What do you make of his refusal to pursue broken enemies? Of his willingness to let large numbers of them escape?"

"He explained that."

"I'm not sure I entirely buy his explanation. He demands we move fast to stay ahead of an enemy that he then defeats handily, and then refuses to chase those men, allowing another army to grow in our wake and follow us or face us at Starhaven. I'm not sure I ever met a commander who had so much mercy for his enemy that he would allow his own men to face them again."

Pembroke frowned. "I don't know if it's mercy. He has killed thousands of Crown soldiers. He is more concerned about preserving our veteran forces. He's explained this strategy repeatedly."

"He preserves them because he lacks the stomach for necessary sacrifice." Garris watched Pembroke's face carefully. "War demands hard choices. Sometimes you must spend men like coins to purchase victory. William refuses to make those choices."

"And you would?"

"I would do what victory requires, while William always tries to find some clever way to avoid that choice entirely."

Pembroke was quiet for a long moment. "Perhaps, but so far his cleverness has allowed us to win battles we shouldn't have."

"It's not about what he has done, it's about what he's going to have to do. The prince avoids difficult options. There's a difference. I've heard the eastern barons, some of my own, and even a few from River Mark beginning to question whether William has the resolve for kingship."

"Which barons?"

"Does it matter? The doubt exists. At some point, a king must be willing to sacrifice for the greater good. I'm not sure William will be able to do that."

Pembroke folded his hands. "It's not that simple."

"It is simple. Difficult, but simple. You send men to die when their deaths serve a purpose. You abandon positions that cannot be held. You make choices that cost lives today to save more lives tomorrow. William cannot bring himself to do any of these things."

"You would prefer he throw men's lives away in frontal assaults?"

"I would prefer he show that he can make the hard choices when necessary." Garris paused. "That's not the only problem I'm hearing from the barons. There are also questions of his ... style."

"I don't know what that means."

"When Baron Farrow raised legitimate concerns, William dismissed them. When I suggested pursuing defeated enemies, William refused to even hear arguments. Those are only a few examples."

Pembroke frowned. "I've found the prince listens to counsel."

"He listens when we agree with him. But when we offer different perspectives?" Garris shook his head. "He demands obedience rather than seeking wisdom. Tell me that doesn't remind you of his father."

"William is nothing like Edmund."

"Isn't he? Both demand unquestioning loyalty. Both dismiss concerns from experienced commanders. Both believe their judgment superior to everyone else's. I am not the only one seeing it. There are also whispers about whether we're simply replacing one tyrant with another."

"That's absurd."

"Is it? William may not be corrupt like Edmund, but he shows the same arrogance. The same refusal to admit error or accept criticism."

"William is young. He'll learn."

"Will he? Or will success convince him that he doesn't need to learn? Every victory reinforces his belief that his way is the only way. He becomes more certain, more dismissive of other views."

"You make it sound as though success is a weakness."

"For some men, it is. For men who believe their intelligence makes them infallible. William is clever, I'll grant you that. Possibly too clever for his own good."

"You've lost me again."

"Clever men often outsmart themselves. They see complex solutions where simple ones would suffice. They create elaborate plans when direct action would serve better."

"You'd prefer simple solutions and more losses?"

"I believe some problems require force rather than finesse. Some situations demand straightforward action rather than subtle maneuvering. William has never faced a problem he couldn't think his way around. What happens when he encounters one that requires different qualities?"

Pembroke folded his arms. "Such as?"

"Such as the loyalty of his own nobles. You can't outmaneuver political opposition the way you outmaneuver enemy armies. You can't read books to learn how to make nobles follow you. Kingship requires more than intelligence. The eastern barons see William's youth, his cleverness, but they are starting to wonder whether he has the strength to rule."

"And what do you see?"

"I see a brilliant young man who believes intelligence is sufficient for leadership. I see someone who mistakes complexity for wisdom and regards disagreement as disloyalty," Garris said and then paused. "I see potential but also dangerous flaws that success will only magnify."

Pembroke finally looked up. "What would you have us do?"

"Nothing, for now," Garris said, rising. "But we should keep our eyes open, listen to the other barons, and be prepared to make a hard decision. Have a good evening."

With that, Garris turned and walked back toward his own tent, leaving Pembroke alone with his thoughts. Garris knew it would take time to get the man to see reason. He was sentimental; his loyalty to Aldric making him predisposed to protect William.

He would see it eventually. Garris just hoped it wouldn't be too late.

Chapter 11

Kenna, River Mark

"Remember," Alyssa murmured as they approached the gathered lords and ladies inside the great hall. "Just be yourself."

It had taken a few days for the duchess to arrange this party and for the nobility still in the River Mark to come together for it, and Isolde had dreaded it more with each day that approached.

The assembled nobility turned as they entered. It was a smaller gathering than she would have expected, based on how similar gatherings were done in her homeland, but then they were in the middle of a war, and most of the men were off with the armies fighting in Kingsheart.

Isolde counted perhaps thirty or forty in total, dressed in their finest attire, which still felt homely and plain … again, compared to what she was used to. At Alyssa's suggestion, she was dressed in a similar drab style.

Although Alyssa would probably call it understated.

Cyril Egerton, Baron of Riverbend and Alyssa's cousin, stepped forward first.

A portly man with graying hair, he offered a respectful bow and said, "Your Grace, Princess Isolde. Thank you for the invitation."

"Thank you for coming, Cyril. It is nice to have a friendly face."

The introductions continued in formal procession. Lord Evern Halstow and his wife, Dorett from Rothpale, a minor noble of some kind, the ladies Demris Harkow, Helce Farwell, and Ismie Chamford, all older women who barely managed a curtsy in spite of Alyssa's much greater status. The names came on, one after another, and Isolde knew she wouldn't remember all of them.

She would, however, remember the coldness that most greeted her with.

"And this is Lady Thessa Dorset," Alyssa said, introducing a woman perhaps ten years older than Isolde. "Her brother is Baron of the Misty Isles, though she has remained here in Kenna since her marriage to Sir Worton."

Lady Dorset was handsome rather than beautiful, with auburn hair arranged in an elaborate style. Well, elaborate for Sidor. Her burgundy gown spoke of wealth, though its cut favored practicality over fashion.

"Your Highness," Lady Dorset said. "How unexpected to meet you here."

Isolde highly doubted that. Alyssa had been clear that the event was to welcome her new niece into Sidorian society. Isolde assumed that had also been a contributing factor to so few in attendance.

"I am glad I was able to surprise you, then," Isolde said. "I do hope we will have a chance to visit and become friends during my stay."

"Indeed." The word held no warmth. "Tell me, Your Highness, how do you find Sidorian customs? Very different from your homeland, I imagine."

"Different, yes, but I'm learning to appreciate them. Your people have a directness I find refreshing."

"Directness. How diplomatic of you to phrase it so. I suppose after what you Lynesians are used to, we must seem quite rustic."

Isolde may be new to Sidor, but she was not new to life in court, which seemed to breed the same type, regardless of where that court was located.

"I wouldn't say rustic. I would describe it more as honest. It is honestly very refreshing."

"How fortunate that you think so. Then you won't mind honest questions about matters that concern us all."

"I think maybe we should continue to circulate," Alyssa said. "There are many introductions to make."

Isolde appreciated Alyssa's attempt to rescue her, but she also knew that if she ran from this now, it would convince others they could do the same. Other guests had drawn closer, forming a loose circle around them, watching the exchange.

Better to face it head-on.

"No, that's okay," Isolde said. "I welcome honest discourse."

"Excellent. Perhaps we can discuss the Lysmir Woods then, and what happened in that forest during the war?"

There were a lot of things Isolde had expected, even a lot of things around the war, but she hadn't expected that. It was a dark day for Isolde when she failed to prevent her father's use of an ancient plague.

It was also the first contact she'd had with William, although she had yet to meet him then.

Alyssa again tried to save her. "As I understand it, Princess Isolde actually attempted to prevent what happened there, going so far as to send a letter to my nephew, who was in charge of the army there. A significant risk on her part, to try to do what's right."

"Yes, I heard of that," Demris Harkow said. "And yet she didn't stop it. Did she? It seems you were more convincing when you negotiated your marriage to the son of the man who sits on the throne, and before he was even there. Sidorian men dead, withered by a horrible disease, and you now a princess of two lands. Worked out well for you, didn't it? How convenient that opposing something in private translates to profiting from it in public."

"That's not ..." Isolde began, but Lady Harkow continued.

"And these reparations from the peace treaty, coming in after the death of Serwyn to the man who has bankrupted the realm, and being paid just at the time when he needed money to continue the war on his own people."

"Are you suggesting William, who now leads the fight against his father, was secretly arranging for money to go to his father? I admit I have much to learn about Sidorian politics, but even to me, that seems like a far stretch."

"William is young, and you are very pretty. He wouldn't be the first to be convinced to do something against his own self-interest by a pretty face," Lady Dorset added.

Isolde felt every eye upon her. She had faced hostile courts before, but this might be the worst she'd ever experienced. And that included the time her brother publicly accused her of murdering their father.

Baron Egerton cleared his throat uncomfortably. "Lady Harkow, perhaps this is not the appropriate venue ..."

"When is the appropriate venue?" Lady Harkow's voice rose. "When Prince William sits the throne with a foreign queen beside him? When Lynesian advisors whisper in his ear?"

"You think so little of my husband? You think him so easily controlled?"

"The baron's right," one of the younger ladies said. "My cousin served with him in Lynese and says that he is possibly the greatest commander he ever dealt with. He also says he takes care of his men, that he cares, more than any other high lord he's ever served with. More so than even the duke, maybe the ancients watch over him."

Lady Harkow's face flushed. "Soldiers are single-minded, but ..."

"Again, you like to talk about how little soldiers know. About how easily fooled they are. Do you think so little of the men that fight to remove the man you just said was waging war on his own people?" Isolde interrupted. "Do you think so little of your fellow countrymen?"

That elicited a few mutters in the crowd, words exchanged quietly.

"Of course not," Lady Harkow said coldly. "But you can't deny how you've benefited from ..."

"It's interesting you mention someone benefiting," Baron Egerton said. "Your brother lives on Bay Isle, doesn't he? I hear he arranged some kind of trade agreement with Rendalia to bring in Sidorian luxuries. A whole new market, and he was one of the first in the door. Quite the boon for your family. Weren't you betrothed to Master Tunridge? A tragic-looking man, but he would have brought in quite the windfall for your family since your father left so much debt. I think someone who managed to avoid that fate would not be the first to point fingers about personal gain from the treaty that married Isolde to Prince William."

Isolde had no idea what Egerton was talking about, but the rest of the crowd clearly did. The murmurs weren't as quiet as they had been, and many had turned to snickers.

"I'm certain she was not suggesting anything like that," Isolde said, not wanting to see the woman humiliated any more than she had to be. "Do you want honesty? Here it is. You're right to be suspicious. My brother tried to reject the agreement my father signed and retake Rendalia. I pulled together an army and led it against him, to keep that land as part of Sidor. I was declared a traitor to my people, and a death warrant in Lynese still sits on my head. I can never go home again. I am no longer Lynesian. And though I might be married to William, I am also not Sidorian. I am without a homeland, although I would like for Sidor to become home for me. I gave away my very identity to protect Sidorians and end the war and then to protect that which William had command over, even though he was lost at sea and presumed dead. I ask you, what have you given up for Sidor?"

The question hung in the air like a blade. Several nobles looked uncomfortable, and all eyes turned to Lady Dorset and her friends.

Baron Egerton stepped closer to Isolde. "I think that's enough, Demris."

There was a pecking order among nobles, even here, and Egerton's tone had changed from friendly to commanding. Lady Harkow and Lady Dorset looked at each other, suddenly realizing they had lost the crowd. What had begun as a bit of fun for them had turned hostile.

"I hope we get a chance to talk again," Lady Dorset said.

As benign as the statement was, the threat was unmistakable. Some of the people were looking at Isolde with much less hostility, and she had gained support by standing up to Lady Dorset and the others, but she had also made lifelong enemies.

The more things changed, the more they stayed the same.

Blackheath Forest, Kingsheart

William rode near the vanguard, watching the forest close around them as the army pushed deeper into the Blackheath. The trees here grew thick, their trunks wide enough that three men with arms outstretched couldn't circle them. Branches overhead wove together, blocking most of the daylight and turning midday into permanent dusk.

The column stretched behind him for nearly a mile, thousands of men threading through gaps between the massive trees. Progress was slow, with most of the wagons having to stick to narrow trails, bogging down several times in the tighter spots.

This was not a land made for armies to pass through quickly.

"Rider," Eskild, riding next to him, said.

Sure enough, an unarmored horse, one of the fleet ones used by messengers and scouts, came weaving through the trees.

"Your Highness." The messenger said, reining in hard. "Crown forces. Four miles back, just entering the forest and closing on us."

William's hand went to his sword hilt. "How many?"

"Hard to say through the trees, although we identified several banners that marched on us at Trentwell."

Pendeen, probably. The baron had escaped the trap at Trentwell with most of his veterans intact, leaving the center to Greville. He'd probably gathered up whatever stragglers he could before he reached Berkshire, rallied them, and hurried in pursuit.

That was why he didn't want to try to chase them to Berkshire. They would have been caught in the opposite position, in the Middlewood Forest, attacking an enemy waiting for them instead of the other way around.

Sinclair rode up, his destrier breathing hard. "Well?"

"Pendeen's got his men together and caught up to us."

"How?" Sinclair started, hopefully seeing that William had been right. Although he cleared that thought quickly. "Then we turn and fight."

Pembroke joined them, his horse picking its way carefully over a fallen log. "What's happened?"

"Crown forces behind us," Sinclair said. "We need to turn the army around and meet them."

"That would take hours. The column's stretched from here to the southern edge of the forest. By the time we reformed ranks, they'd be on top of our rearguard."

William looked around at the massive trees, the thick undergrowth, the narrow spaces between the trunks. He hadn't expected them to catch up so quickly, but it also presented an opportunity.

An idea took shape.

"We don't need to turn the whole army around. Just enough to stay mobile."

"What are you thinking?" Pembroke asked.

"They're expecting us to run or to turn and fight in open formation. We do neither." William pointed at the trees ahead. "According to the scouts, the forest gets thicker another mile north. Trees so close together cavalry can't maneuver. Undergrowth so dense infantry can't maintain formation."

"So?"

"So we pull our rearguard back fast while the front of the army and the baggage train continue on. Make it look like we're running scared. Lead them into ground where their numbers don't matter."

Pembroke nodded slowly. "An ambush."

"More than that. A killing ground." William turned to the scout. "Ride to the rear companies. Tell them to fall back quickly, but don't worry about being seen. Tell them that speed matters more than order, and to push any units ahead of them with the same order until they reach a point about a mile ahead of us. They'll know it when they get there because I'll be with the vanguard and a line will have been formed."

As the scout rode off, William began issuing orders, his mind already working through the details. He needed to position men in the densest part of the forest ahead. His veteran companies would form the core of the ambush, men who could fight independently without losing discipline.

"This is madness," Sinclair said. "You're abandoning every advantage we have. We have the weight in knights. We should use that."

"Look around you. Does this look like ground for heavy cavalry to fight?"

"Which is why we should have never come into this damned forest," Sinclair muttered.

William ignored him, riding forward with his officers, selecting the ground personally. A quarter mile ahead, the forest compressed where the trees grew particularly dense, their trunks creating a maze of natural barriers. Not impassable, of course, but it would break up formations well.

Perfect.

The positioning took almost two hours. By the time William finished, he had his entire force scattered through a space perhaps four hundred yards deep and three hundred yards wide. As the rearguard caught up, he put them on the flanks in areas with thicker undergrowth that would make them all but invisible to anyone.

Not that the enemy would look. They'd see the enemy line holding against them and focus only on that.

Men got tunnel vision in situations like this.

Then came the waiting. Time stretched on seemingly forever as they waited for the enemy to catch up to where he'd held his men.

William heard them long before he saw them. The crash of hundreds, thousands of men pushing through undergrowth.

Armies moving through places like this weren't stealthy, which is why running was never an option.

The Crown vanguard came into view first, conscripts with spears and cheap swords moving between the trees in a loose formation that was barely a formation at all. They spread out naturally as the massive tree trunks forced them apart to get around obstacles. Officers tried to keep their companies together, but the forest made it impossible.

Behind the conscripts came the Crown's better troops. Men-at-arms in proper mail moved in tighter groups, trying to maintain some semblance of order. These were the core of Pendeen's force. They navigated the forest more carefully, although even they couldn't keep it all together.

Further back, William could see the banners of Pendeen's household knights. They'd dismounted, their horses being given over to their squires to lead.

William waited. The Crown vanguard was well into the killing ground now, slowing and moving into roughly better formation, seeing his men lined up ahead of them.

The attack didn't come from his center companies. It came from his flanks, which spread out much wider than the center and were unexpected.

Pendeen's forces were not prepared for the sudden appearance of soldiers, veterans who swung down like closing doors on both sides of the Crown column.

The attacks were sudden and brutal, and the enemy was in no way prepared for them. Such a surprise that, at first, the Crown soldiers charged for his center, almost confused at where the attack came from, even though they could see his men unmoved in the center.

The Crown veterans' sudden surge, however, was slowed by the conscripts in their front, whose first response was the opposite: not to attack, but to run at the sudden contact.

The two groups smashed into each other, creating even more chaos among them, even as William's forces pressed from either side.

At the rear of the Crown column, more rebel companies blocked their retreat, cutting off the escape route. Crown forces trying to fall back found themselves facing fresh troops who'd been waiting in ambush. The rear companies weren't trying to destroy these forces, just contain them, keep them from interfering with the main battle.

William didn't have enough men here for a complete envelopment, but he made it so they couldn't scatter effectively and had to run through their own forces, spreading the chaos.

Crown officers tried to regain some control, but the panic was aided by the forest, where little in the way of coordination could work. It's why he'd kept his plan simple and didn't try for an envelopment, where he would have had to thin his line and have better coordination.

And he was using almost all veterans for his attack.

Not all the Crown forces ran, of course. A company of perhaps forty men-at-arms, Crown veterans, formed up around a particularly large tree, using its trunk as an anchor point for their defense. Shields came up, spears pointed outward. William's companies didn't charge this position directly. Instead, they moved around it, using the trees as cover to get close. Then they attacked from multiple directions simultaneously. The Crown formation held for perhaps two minutes before the pressure from all sides overwhelmed it.

Pendeen's officers were trying to organize a response. One captain managed to organize one hundred men into a larger formation, conscripts and men-at-arms mixed together. This force tried to push forward, which was the time for William to begin marching his center forward.

Not a charge that would fall apart quickly, but a steady march, applying pressure.

His men overwhelmed the group. Better armored, better trained, and more experienced, they took hardly any casualties as they smashed into the mixed unit, which broke entirely.

The Crown army, which had barely been fragmenting, fell apart as individual companies lost contact with each other. Officers couldn't coordinate between units because they couldn't see more than twenty or thirty yards in any direction.

The Crown conscripts were the first to truly break. These men had been given minimal training and now found themselves in a dark forest being attacked from every direction. They ran. Not in organized retreat, but in blind panic. They crashed through the underbrush, some running deeper into the forest in their confusion, others fleeing south back the way they'd come.

This panic spread. Other conscript companies saw their comrades running and followed. Within minutes, the entire eastern portion of the Crown force was in full rout. Hundreds of men fled through the trees, abandoning their officers and the better-trained troops.

The Crown men-at-arms tried to hold. These were the veterans; men who'd fought in multiple battles and knew how to keep their heads in chaos. They formed into small defensive clusters, backs against trees or pressed into tight circles. These positions held for a time.

William sent his veteran companies against these positions, surrounding each cluster and probing for weaknesses. When a Crown soldier became separated from his group, rebel troops would pull him down. When gaps appeared in the defensive formation, William's men would flow in. The Crown veterans fought hard, but they were outnumbered and surrounded. One by one, these defensive positions fell.

Pendeen's household knights were still fighting near what had been the center of the Crown column. The baron had perhaps fifty knights with him, along with one hundred men-at-arms. This represented the last organized resistance in the Crown army. Everyone else had either fled or been reduced to scattered groups fighting for survival.

The knights had formed a rough perimeter and held the ground stubbornly. When rebel companies tried to push, the knights would sortie out, drive them back, then retreat to their defensive positions.

William recognized he couldn't break this position with a direct assault, not without taking casualties he couldn't afford. Instead, he ordered his companies to contain it. Rebel troops surrounded the Crown position but didn't press the attack. They simply held their ground, keeping the knights penned in.

Meanwhile, the rest of William's forces dealt with the remaining Crown units.

The forest had become a maze of small, vicious fights. Crown soldiers stumbled through the trees, trying to find their units or to escape. Small squads would encounter Crown troops and either cut them down or force their surrender.

Pendeen's position held for perhaps half an hour, but the constant pressure and fighting took its toll. William had his men press and back off, press and back off, while rotating forces through so there was always a fresh group attacking.

Finally, the Crown's defense collapsed. The knights tried to fight their way out, but they were surrounded and outnumbered, and those who tried to make a break for it got brought down and killed.

Pendeen himself surrendered when his bodyguard was cut down around him. The baron threw down his sword and raised his hands. His capture signaled the end of organized Crown resistance.

The battle had lasted perhaps two hours from the first contact to the collapse of the last Crown position. It had been folly to try to pursue another force through land like this, and Pendeen had paid the price for doing it.

What remained was pursuit and cleanup. Crown soldiers who had scattered through the southern forest were hunted down by rebel companies. Some escaped, running hard and not looking back. Many didn't. William's officers knew to leave clear escape routes. Completely surrounded men would fight to the death, and William wasn't willing to sacrifice men to take down a dozen Crown soldiers here or there.

As they cleaned up the fight and began to get the prisoners and wounded together, Sinclair showed up, leading his horse carefully around a fallen log.

"You were right. An attack through a forest was a poor idea."

"Hopefully not the last time my father's armies make that mistake. Every time they give us the chance to use the terrain against them, I will take it," William said, and then flagged down a passing soldier, pointing at a group of injured Crown soldiers near a tree, guarded but otherwise unhurt. "Go get a disciple and let them know this group needs help."

Sinclair scowled at that, but William ignored him. Shortly, disciples came up and the men were carried off to the aid wagons that would take the wounded with them.

Sinclair could scowl all he wanted. William would fight the war as he saw fit, and the baron would eventually see the results of his efforts and realize that maybe William knew what he was doing after all.

Chapter 12

Starhaven, Sidor

Edmund's knuckles went white against the armrest. The messenger stood three paces from him, looking nervous.

Perhaps word had gotten out about the last several messengers to bring him unwanted news and how they joined the other traitors in the dungeons. Perhaps if enough of these cowards learned what happened when bad news was sent to him, they would start finding some good news.

"Say it again."

"Your Majesty, Baron Greville has fallen in a battle at the Trentwell Hills. Baron Pendeen, knowing you would want such an insult paid in kind, chased the usurper, but he was taken prisoner and only a portion of the force at Berkshire made it back to report on those losses. Our forces ..." The man's voice faltered.

"How many?"

"Between the two battles, fifteen hundred dead, another several hundred captured, of which many included nobles and knights, the wyverns demanding ransom already having gone out. There are perhaps a thousand men left in Berkshire, the scattered remains of Pendeen, Greville, and Gosforth's armies."

Each of those men had an army of three to four thousand men. Mostly conscripts, but still a large part of the numbers he'd been able to enlist on his last tour across the kingdom. Three armies that had been perhaps ten thousand men strong, and only a thousand remained in the field, with all of the barons who led them gone.

He was sure not that many had actually fallen. If he had to guess, probably half who were now counted as missing had taken the chance to break their oaths to him and returned home.

A job for the bailiff to deal with once things were a little more under control.

"Where is my son's army now?"

"Last reports placed them north in the Blackheath Forest, Your Majesty. We believe he's marching north, but it is hard to know. Every scout we have sent to tail him has gone missing, so we do not know the status of his army."

Damn the boy. He'd been all but set to leave on another tour of the northern Kingsheart baronies to try to recruit more men, but he could not put himself in the path of the army.

That, in fact, was probably why Pendeen and Greville had failed. They must have known he was headed north and wanted William to intercept him.

It was the only real explanation for the scale of their failures.

Perhaps they had even arranged things with William. He did not put it past the boy to have Greville killed to hide his tracks, and the 'capture' of Pendeen was a likely story.

It was a clever ruse; he had to give it to the boy. Threaten to go north to stop him from recruiting more men while planning to circle back and come up the Tradesway once Edmund panicked and sent the army at Penvale away, opening up the path for him.

Clever. But he would not fall for it.

"Leave us," he said to the messenger, who he'd honestly forgotten was still there.

The messenger departed with visible relief. Edmund remained in his chair, fingers drumming against the wood.

"Orlan," he called out, before realizing the man was hovering over his shoulder.

"Your Majesty, perhaps ..."

"It's a trick. He's trying to pull off the army at Penvale, and if that doesn't work, he's going to come out into Eddington's holdings and dash across Buckbury to take Silverhall. What a triumph that would be, taking my home seat as a prize," Edmund said, standing and starting to pace. "But he'll be clever about it. He will give himself options. If I protect Silverhall, he will take the Tradesway path; if I move men from Penvale, he will go for Silverhall. The boy thinks he has me in a noose."

Orlan had the pensive look he had when he didn't agree with something but held his peace, "What would Your Majesty have us do?"

Edmund moved to the great map that dominated the eastern wall of his chamber. His finger traced the roads and rivers, the forests and hills. The pieces were scattered, but he could still control the board. William commanded perhaps six thousand men now, maybe seven with his, Pembroke's, and Sinclair's armies. Edmund had managed to recruit thirty thousand, admittedly almost all conscripts. His problem was that he had to protect everywhere William might go, and his forces were spread across half the kingdom.

"Send word to Silverhall. The forces assembling there are to march east immediately. I want them at Omskirk within a fortnight."

"Omskirk, Your Majesty?"

"William only has three ways he can go, assuming he doesn't go east, which makes little sense because his goal has always been Starhaven. He cannot have victory while I have the throne. He could go back south to the Tradesway and then straight here; he could come out in Buckbury and make a push down the plains, north of the hills and forest but south of Twin Lake, and hit us in Penleigh; or he could go north and either take on Cadogan or travel across to the coast and then south. We must maneuver to stop all three of his options. If possible, I would like to bottle him up in those forests and starve him. How many men do we have in Penvale?"

"Almost ten thousand, Your Majesty. Baron Stourton commands them."

"They stay. William may be clever, but he's young and given to overthinking. This could be a feint, drawing forces away from the capital while his real attack comes straight down the Tradesway." Edmund couldn't afford to make that mistake. "Send riders to Berkshire. Whatever of those armies remains, I want whoever is the highest-ranking noble to pull together every able man and move northeast. They aren't to follow them into the forest, but

126

they are to act as a blocking force just where the Trentwell Hills end. I want them to keep any of the rebels from going south out of those woods. He is to conscript every peasant in those baronies if he has to, but he must have enough men to hold there."

"So you do, indeed, lock him in. Brilliant."

"It's not brilliant, just obvious, which is why I doubt how hard some of my nobles fight for the kingdom if they haven't seen this yet." Edmund turned from the map. "But it isn't complete. He still has two directions to go. If he goes east, he will eventually have to go north or south, as moving along the bay does him no good. It's the northern route I'm worried about. I sent a wyvern to Cadogan weeks ago after he tried to foist his idiot son on me, and still he hasn't replied and doesn't come as ordered. That worries me. If Cadogan is about to go to the rebels' side, it opens up the north and many options to come at the capital, and with the added forces of the Ice Lands. I want to preempt that if possible. Send a wyvern to the duke and tell him he is to put an army on the Grimshaw to counter rebel movements and then present himself here in Starhaven. If he does not, I will consider him another traitor to the Crown, execute his son, and will march my armies into his duchy next. Make it clear this is his last opportunity to prove his loyalty."

"Yes, Your Majesty."

Edmund studied the map again. The pieces were falling into place, but something nagged at him. There was more to do here than the positioning, but he did not trust his barons to fight with enough heart.

They had already lost too many battles to incompetence.

"Send for Sir Alistair Everwood."

The scribe didn't need to be told twice and scurried away. While Edmund waited, he poured himself some wine, his third cup of the afternoon. He thought he'd had everything under control once Tomas had delivered the Key to him, but it had proven not to be the answer to all his problems. He could compel loyalty with it, to some degree, and push men in the direction he needed them to go, but it could not force competence, which is obviously where the biggest weakness of his subordinates lay.

He could not trust them to win this on the field, so he had to position things to win off of it.

Alistair arrived a few minutes later. He'd considered giving this task to Colm, who had done similar work in the past, but this would require more force than Colm could put together, and it was important that it be done correctly.

Even now that he was officially knighted, the men that Colm could put together were less dependable than a more traditionally trained man like Alistair could call on, even while exiled from his barony, which was in open rebellion.

"Your Majesty." Alistair bowed, correct but not servile.

"Close the door."

The knight complied.

"Things are not going as well as we hoped in the field, and I need your assistance."

"I can ride out tonight and join the armies within the week."

"I appreciate your eagerness, but that is not what I need you for. I need you for something a lot more delicate than that."

"I am, of course, yours to command."

"I want you to take a force around the Iron Straits, head to Kenna, and collect Alyssa for me."

"Your Majesty?" he said, confused. "Considering I killed her husband, I am not sure she will welcome me into her home."

"I do not expect her to. In fact, I am certain she will not come willingly and will try to stop you, so this is not just a peaceful visit. She is to come to Starhaven as soon as you can bring her, regardless of her wishes on the matter. You are to deal with anyone who tries to stop you, although I do not want you throwing men's lives away trying to hold the city. If you should happen to see my son's foreign whore, it would be helpful if you could deal with her as well, but that is just an added bonus. Your duty is to get in, apprehend her, and get out. Take a company of reliable men, as many as you think is appropriate. It is important, above all, that she remain unharmed and make it here safely."

"I will go at once," he said, bowing deeper.

"Good. You have shown great loyalty so far, and my faith in you is high. Do not fail me now."

"I won't," he said, bowing once more and leaving.

Edmund watched him go before turning back to Orlan, who had come in shortly after the knight, and said, "I want you to begin plans for a large royal wedding."

"A wedding, Your Highness?" Orlan asked, not able to keep the shock off his face.

"Yes. I need to destabilize the River Mark. Some of those barons are on the fence already and looking for a reason to come back to the fold. I also need to find ways to put more pressure on the eastern barons and force them to accept my legitimacy as king. What better way than to have the wife of the man who previously led the rebellion join me in defeating it?"

Of course, it did not hurt that he had always carried a flame for Alyssa. Alyssa had always been beautiful, even before Aldric married her. Edmund had desired her then, had imagined what might have been if he had been the younger brother, the one free to choose his bride based on desire rather than political necessity. William's mother had been adequate, but she had never stirred his blood the way Alyssa did.

Something he had never forgiven his brother for.

"Your Majesty, of course I live to serve, but considering how she is being invited to the capital and your part in the murder of her traitor husband, I am not sure any wedding with her would be seen as legitimate. As soon as she stands to take the vows, it seems likely she will refuse and instead denounce you."

"Do not worry about that part. Once she is here, she will submit to me, that much I can promise. The hard part is getting her here, and I leave that to Alistair. What I need from you is to make sure we are able to have the wedding as quickly as possible once she is here. Also, while you are at it, we need to put additional pressure on Sinclair. Send word to our friends in Alchmara. They are to increase their raids immediately, as much as they can. Offer to increase what we will pay them. Double it, or even triple it if necessary, but I want the tempo of attacks to increase dramatically. Let them know that they will soon find the Narrows open to them so that they can get into the bay, which should allow them to better target Iron Keep and raid more cities. But, and this is key, they are only to take the fight against Iron Keep territories. Every ship, every coastal village, every target must be in Iron Keep or carrying its flag. If even one Alchmaran raider strikes at Kingsheart or Ice Lands, the gold stops permanently, and I will add the might of Sidor to chasing them down and destroying them. Make that clear. Iron Keep only."

"In addition, add this to the message you send Cadogan; I want him to release his forces from the Narrows and allow Alchmaran ships to pass through. Make sure he knows none will target his villages or ships, that they are only interested in Iron Keep."

"I understand," Orlan said, the confusion on his face making it clear he did not understand how all these different commands were related.

It did not matter; he would carry them out, and that was all Edmund truly needed.

"Good. Go."

Orlan departed quickly. Edmund stood alone again, the afternoon light fading through the windows. He hoped that would be enough. He knew he was striking out in many directions at once, but he had to do something to counter the bleeding and counter William's march, or the boy would be at the shores of Starhaven Bay, and he could not allow that.

Now he just had to hope the traitors and incompetents surrounding him were able to carry out at least some of his directives.

Kenna, River Mark, Sidor

The market square teemed with people and noise. Isolde followed Alyssa through the crowd, acutely aware of the eyes turning toward them. Conversations faltered as they passed, with people leaning together to whisper and stare.

"They're not accustomed to seeing you yet," Alyssa said quietly.

That was true, although Isolde thought the fact that she and the duchess had a considerable retinue in their wake also drew some of the stares.

"Fresh greens, Your Grace. Your Highness. First of the season."

To Isolde, this seemed like a natural exchange for Alyssa, who talked to the man about what he had for sale and instructed one of her ladies to buy some for the keep kitchens.

The merchants were clearly familiar with her and happy to see her, which meant she had come here before. Of course, most of the goods would have been purchased by her steward and her people, so Isolde assumed she did it more to see the people than for actual commerce.

Even with that as a goal, it again showed how much different governance was for Alyssa than it was at Isolde's home. Even in Rendalia, Isolde never made trips like this, and she had been much more comfortable there.

As she listened to their conversation, Isolde's attention drifted to a group of women near a seed merchant's stall. Five of them, thin and careworn, with children clutching at their skirts. They kept glancing toward Isolde, but their expressions weren't the ones of curiosity that so many had.

They were notably hostile.

One woman bent to whisper something to her companion, and both looked away quickly when Isolde met their eyes. Isolde took a few steps away from Alyssa to better hear what the women were talking to the merchant about, although trying not to seem too obvious about it.

"I understand your situation, but I've extended credit three times already. I have suppliers to pay."

"Just until the barley harvest," one of the women said, sounding tired. "We planted what we could, but without seed for the second planting ..."

"You said that last month about buying a plow horse." The merchant shook his head. "I'm sorry, Sibbe, but I can't."

The woman, Sibbe, gathered her shawl tighter and turned away. The other women followed, herding their children. One of them noticed Isolde watching and said something sharp. The others went quiet, their bodies tense.

Alyssa finished her conversation with the merchant and stopped next to Isolde, looking at her. "You look troubled."

"Those women."

"What about them?"

"They seem to be in a dire way."

"They are, and there are thousands like them throughout River Mark. The wars have stretched for several years now, and the Mark supplies more men for the armies than any of the duchies. The war has created more widows and orphans than we can count."

"How do you know they're widows?"

Alyssa's expression softened, giving her an almost patronizing look like a parent gives to a child asking questions they should know the answer to. "Come."

She led Isolde toward a baker's stall where fresh bread cooled on wooden racks. The baker, an older woman with flour dusting her apron, curtsied when she saw them.

"Your Grace."

"Good morning, Helen," Alyssa said warmly. "How is business?"

"As well as can be expected."

Before Alyssa could start her chatting again, Isolde asked, "Do you know anything about those women?"

Helen glanced over to where the group of women was walking away. "I do, my lady."

"Can you tell me?"

"Widows. They all lost men in the fighting. Sibbe's Hugh fell at Selwyn, I believe. Poor Thomas, the smith's apprentice, died in the rebellion last year, following Fletcher. The others lost husbands and sons, too. Some here, some across the sea." Helen lowered her voice. "They are a sad lot, coming to market hoping for credit or charity, but most of us struggle ourselves. I wish I could help them more, but ... such is life. Begging your pardon."

Isolde watched the women disappear into the crowd. "Thank you, Helen."

The baker nodded as Alyssa maneuvered the conversation onto less weighty matters.

"I appreciate how much you care," Alyssa said as they continued through the market. "We have charities here to help them, as do the Acolytes, but many of them are too proud to go to those and would take an offer of direct help as an insult. Even we do not have the coin to help everyone."

Isolde followed the group, which had gone to another section of the market, with her eyes. The one the merchant had called Sibbe, the woman with the baby, was arguing with a grain merchant. Her voice rose above the market noise.

"My children are eating grass porridge!"

"Then find work," the merchant said. "I'm not a charity house."

"What work? The planting's done on land I don't own. Who'll hire a woman with three little ones to mind?"

People were watching now. Some with pity, others with discomfort. A few looked toward Isolde and Alyssa, as if expecting them to intervene.

Isolde started forward, but Alyssa caught her arm.

"Wait," the duchess said. "Think first. How you handle this matters."

"They need help."

"Yes. But if you simply throw coin at them in front of everyone, what message does that send?"

Isolde considered. She couldn't just buy everyone out from under their problems. As Alyssa had said, coin was limited. Even with access to her holdings in Rendalia and William's property here in Sidor, they couldn't support every man and woman in the kingdom.

Alyssa released her arm. "I'm not saying don't help, but ... be thoughtful about how you offer it."

Isolde nodded and walked to the grain merchant's stall. The young woman with the baby had turned away, her face flushed with humiliation.

"Excuse me," Isolde said.

She turned and immediately frowned.

"Your Highness," Sibbe said.

It wasn't quite respectful. Not openly hostile either, but there was a definite hesitation.

"I overheard," Isolde said. "Forgive me for intruding, but I wanted to ... that is, I thought perhaps ..."

The words tangled in her mouth. She'd negotiated with tribal chieftains and lords, but standing here in this market square, facing these exhausted women, she felt suddenly uncertain.

"You thought you could fix our problems with a few coins?" The young woman's voice was bitter. "Like buying grain or seed makes up for everything?"

"No," Isolde said. "I know it doesn't."

"Do you?" Another woman stepped forward, her jaw set. "Do you know what it's like to tell your children there's no supper? To watch them go hungry while you stretch last autumn's stores?"

"Of course not."

People were watching them now. She'd made a mistake, said the wrong thing, and now these women looked at her with something close to contempt.

"Of course you don't know," Sibbe said, her voice rising. "You're a *lady*. What do you know about anything real?"

"I know what it means to lose," Isolde said. "My father sentenced me to death. My brother invaded ..."

"We know who you are," the freckled woman said. "My husband died at Talabot, fighting your people."

"I'm sorry, but I opposed ..."

Alyssa stepped forward then, her voice carrying authority but not anger. "Ladies, that's enough."

Their anger diverted for a moment by Alyssa's intervention, the women suddenly seemed to remember themselves and who they were talking to. They looked away, not ashamed, but concerned. Some muttered apologies.

"Begging your pardon, Your Grace," Sibbe said quickly. "I didn't mean ... we're just ..."

"I know. You have every right to be angry. But Her Highness is here to help and is my niece. She's not the enemy here."

"No, Your Grace." Thomas's widow looked at Isolde. "I'm sorry, Your Highness. That was, I shouldn't have spoken so."

The third woman nodded. "We mean no disrespect. It's just been hard."

"I understand," Alyssa said. "And I promise you we're working to make things better. The widows' fund will be replenished by month's end. I'm speaking with the guilds about apprenticeships for daughters as well as sons. It won't fix everything, but it's a start."

"Thank you, Your Grace," Sibbe said. "We know you've always looked after us as best you could."

Alyssa touched Sibbe's arm briefly. "Take your children home. There's a grain distribution at the Acolyte temple tomorrow. Tell them I sent you."

"Yes, Your Grace. Thank you."

The women curtsied, proper this time, respectful, and gathered their children. As they left, Sibbe glanced back at Isolde once. Not hostile now, just tired and wary.

Alyssa took Isolde's elbow and guided her away from the grain merchant's stall. They walked in silence for a moment, moving toward a quieter section of the market.

"I'm sorry," Isolde said quietly. "I handled that badly."

"You did," Alyssa agreed. "But your heart was in the right place. Honestly, that is an amazing place to start."

"But how do we help these people?"

"By understanding charity isn't the same as help. That good intentions aren't enough." Alyssa stopped near a stone fountain, away from the crowd. "Those women don't need a princess to buy them grain once. They need someone to ensure that systems exist to support them. The widows' fund. Guild apprenticeships. Land rights that don't disappear when a husband dies."

"But I can't change those things. I don't have that power."

"Not yet. But you will if William wins. And even now, you have influence. You can learn what needs changing. Build relationships with people who can help. Support the work already being done rather than trying to solve everything yourself. As a princess, your word carries a lot of weight."

Isolde nodded slowly. "They trusted you immediately. Listened to you."

"Because I've been here for years. I've earned that trust by doing the work, not by making grand gestures." Alyssa smiled slightly. "You'll earn it too, eventually. But it takes time, and you'll make mistakes along the way."

"I'm worried I made things worse."

"You didn't, you simply ..."

"Your Highness," a man's voice interrupted. "Forgive me for intruding."

They turned. A middle-aged man with thinning brown hair and a practical wool coat stood a respectful distance away, waiting to be acknowledged. His clothes were well-made but not ostentatious, and he had this slight smile on his face that was probably meant to be disarming but was a bit too calculating to achieve its goal.

"Yes?" Isolde said, still feeling off-balance from the confrontation.

"I'm Cornelis Roth," he said, bowing. "I have a trading concern here in Kenna. I wondered if I might have a moment of your time."

"Master Roth. You have a talent for appearing at interesting moments," Alyssa said, clearly recognizing him with a slight bit of annoyance.

"I couldn't help but observe, Your Grace," he said, before looking to Isolde. "I thought perhaps Her Highness might benefit from a different perspective. If she's willing to hear it."

"What perspective is that?" Isolde asked.

"The practical one." He gestured vaguely toward the market. "You're trying to help. That's admirable. But help comes in many forms, and not all of them involve direct charity."

"We've been through this," Alyssa said.

"We have, yes, Your Grace, but it isn't a topic I have shared with the princess or her husband, both of whom I've been keen on meeting."

"I'd like to hear him out," Isolde said.

"Thank you, Princess. I supply merchants throughout the River Mark. Wool, metalwork, some agricultural goods, bringing goods to Alchmara and Inos, and opening up those markets to our craftsmen here. Something I have spoken to Her Grace about many times is the value of reducing guild fees and the royal grants needed for both the craftsmen who make those goods, as well as the payment of the royal privilege to transport and sell them. What is, for all intents and purposes, a linear series of transactions from craftsmen to merchant, and then merchant to customer, has added layers of bureaucracy to get permission to do each of those steps, as well as duties imposed for the rights to be able to do those.

136

That added layer also adds costs to the people, such as those poor women, who then cannot afford the things they need."

"As I have said before, Master Roth, those kinds of grants of monopoly, royal grants, and prerogatives are not something we have a say in here in the duchy. I know how you feel about some of the customs duties we have imposed, but without those we would not be able to pay for the defense of the realm, unless you preferred the taxation under the Crown."

"Of course I didn't, but with the duchy in open rebellion to the Crown, prerogatives and guild fees are still being collected, and by your ministers. I can only guess those fees are not being forwarded on to the Crown like they normally would be, so there is some level of control."

"The rebellion will not last forever and come winter, when a new king sits on the throne, we would have to give those rights back and there would be a request for those monopolies and fees collected but not forwarded. The Crown will have a big job ahead of it to fix the mistakes made by the man currently sitting on the throne, so unwinding those to just put them back in place makes no sense."

"And there, exactly, is what I really wanted to talk about. Common wisdom suggests our princess's husband will be that man when the war is ended, which makes hers an ear I very much want to bend."

"To what end?" Isolde asked.

"To the end of changing things as we have always accepted them. You only have to look to Werne and Inos, who do not have the same limitations on merchants and manufacturers that we do, to see what is possible. While I know your homeland follows a similar path, those two kingdoms have no grants of monopoly or exercise guild fees for higher-end trade."

"Werne most certainly does have guild fees. Depths be, the guilds all but run their ruling council," Alyssa said. "And as for the Inos, no, they have neither, but they also lock their people to the land, allowing a peasant no freedom of movement, and locking the peasant's children to the same land. Their serfdom laws limit the upward mobility of their people and stifle any kind of innovation. You, for instance, would not have amassed your trading concern had you been born in Inos. You would live in the same hovel your father grew up in and his father before him, doing the same job, knowing your children would do the same. So perhaps let's not try to hold either up as the perfected system."

"I admit, there are drawbacks in each kingdom, but think ..."

"Think that if they did not have those limits, they would have to find other ways to fund their kingdoms, and they would have to put in new limits. There is a kingdom already run by merchants, and it has much higher customs duties than we have, and its industry is more tightly controlled by merchant factors. I think it is, perhaps, your concern is less that there is too much control and more who you think should have that control."

Isolde was getting a feeling like this argument was well-trod ground between the two, and yet she also had a sense that Alyssa liked this man and perhaps even enjoyed the sparring.

"It seems like you two have had this conversation before," Isolde said.

"You are, of course, correct," Roth said, laughing. "Her Grace and I, and the duke before her, are old sparring partners in this arena. They have yet to budge, but I shall never tire of trying to convince them of ways to make our people better."

"And yet you said you came over because you saw me, so what exactly can I do for you, aside from bear witness to this conversation, Master Roth?"

"Nothing immediate. I more wanted an introduction," he said, spreading his hands. "As I said, I do a large amount of business with some of our neighbors to the east and have built relationships over decades that could benefit the kingdom's recovery. Although it would be helpful to know the political landscape I'm navigating."

"You mean you want to know if you should bet on William winning."

Again he spread his hands, as if to say, "Of course."

"I would like to say that, of course, William will win, but then I'm sure you understand I am biased on the subject."

"As you should be, Your Highness. As I said, I mostly wanted to make an introduction and offer my counsel or services in any way that might be helpful while you are visiting our city."

"Thank you, Master Roth," Isolde said.

"Of course. I should let you continue your market tour, but I do hope we can speak again."

"We shall see," Isolde said noncommittally.

That brought a smile to the man's face. He bowed, more formally this time, and said, "Your Grace. Your Highness."

With that, he disappeared into the crowd.

"He's interesting."

"He is that," Alyssa agreed. "Cornelis is ambitious and self-serving, but he's also not stupid enough to damage relationships for short-term gain. He could be useful to you in the future."

"I will keep that in mind."

"Ready to return to the keep?" Alyssa asked.

"Yes."

Chapter 13

Blackheath Forest, Kingsheart, Sidor

They were stuck. No two ways about it. The boy had led them into this forest with plans on circling around the enemy, and instead, the enemy had bracketed them in, and they'd spent a week just sitting in these trees, eating away their supplies and waiting for the Crown forces to make a try to push them out.

"My lord," Sir Odran said, coming up behind him. "The scouts report that the northern route is still clear."

"What about that army the Ice Landers sent to the Grimshaw? Any word on that?"

"They said it moved a little further east, but it is still on the Ice Land side of the line."

"Waiting to see what we do, no doubt. If they were smart, they would come straight for us and block us off from the north, giving us only the option to run east."

"The thought is the land to the north is too open, mostly plain, giving us the advantage of the fight, unlike to the south, where the hills allow them better protection."

"Obviously," Sinclair said.

Odran opened his mouth to respond, but a man appeared out of the trees, looking around before his eyes locked on Sinclair.

"My lord," he said, bowing his head and extending a message with a seal on it.

Garris took it and waved the man away. The seal of Baron Ansell was still fixed on it, intact. Garris broke the seal and started to read through the message.

Garris had assumed the message would be bad, as it was unlike Cyneric to contact him with trivialities, but he hadn't expected anything this bad. Tales of increased Alchmaran raids, not just across the Bleakwater Straits but in Althear Bay itself. And not in just ones and twos. Not in his life, or even in his father's, had he heard of raiders making it through the narrows to attack shipping inside the bay.

And now there were descriptions of over a dozen attacks across baronies facing the bay, places like Delaney Heights, Wootan, and Everwood.

The only way it made any sense was that the Ice Landers allowed them through, opening up their side of the narrows and letting them into the bay. Not just villages, but every ship with the flag from an Iron Keep barony was apparently open season for the raiders.

More telling, as far as Ansell knew, not a single ship on the Ice Land or Kingsheart sides of the bay were touched, which meant a deal had been made.

One he couldn't ignore.

Putting that with the scouts' news that the Ice Lander army had not crossed the Grimshaw set his mind into motion. The raiders would all but freeze the shipping in the bay and be enough of a distraction to allow that army to march down the coast of Althear Bay and come in from the east.

Or more likely, get past them now that most of the fighting men were bottled up here and get into the eastern baronies and up into Iron Keep from the south.

They would lose their supply lines and starve to death in these trees. And William wouldn't see it, too invested in his own brilliance.

"Odran, go find Stanfield, Donnington, and Dunbar and have them meet me at my tent. Also, gather all of our people."

"Not Halbrok or Newberry?" Odran asked, picking up on what the names on the list had in common.

"No," he said, offering no explanation.

Odran bowed his head slightly and hurried off to carry out his duties. While he waited, Garris walked back to his tent and poured himself wine. His hands were steady despite the anger building in his chest.

They came in ones and twos over thirty minutes. The bulk of the men were from Iron Keep, but for what he was thinking, he needed more than just what he had. He needed to pull in some of the eastern barons as well.

Garris waited until they'd all found places to stand or sit, then held up Ansell's letter.

"I have dire news from home that affects not just me and mine, but any lands that touch Althear Bay. The Crown has unleashed his minions in Alchmara, opening up the narrows and sending them against us. There have been raids across the northern part of the bay, but only against baronies in open rebellion against the Crown. They're burning villages, sinking ships, killing our people. Those of you who haven't been raided yet will be."

"They opened up the narrows?" Donnington asked, shocked.

"Yes. Are you surprised? Has Edmund ever shown any care for those he thinks are below him? Which is everyone."

Donnington gave an accepting shrug.

"That's not all. We have word that Cadogan has marched his army east along the Grimshaw. I wasn't sure when I first heard, but now that I know about the raiders, I'm positive that Cadogan is going to march down the coast and come in behind us while we're trapped in this forest. How many men have you left in your baronies? How can they fight Cadogan's men and protect your coasts from raiders at the same time?"

The men all looked to each other. The answer to his questions was obvious, and they all knew how bad it would be if Cadogan's men came south.

"As I said, we have a problem."

"So what are you proposing?" Stanfield asked. "You called us here, so clearly you have something in mind."

"I'm going to William. I'm going to demand he send reinforcements east. Or better, split the army. Let him continue his march if he wants but give us enough men to defend our homes."

"He won't," Baron Dunbar said. "The prince won't divide his forces."

"Which is why I need your support. I need enough of you to back me and tell him he can either do something to keep from having our homes burned, or we march without him and leave him here while we take the fight to Cadogan directly. Before he can reach your lands. But I need to know who stands with me."

Baron Dunbar, who'd been one of the last to join the eastern barons, was the first to speak. "You have my support. He'll march through my lands first, so how could I not?"

His barons raised their voices to a man. Sinclair had suspected that. He'd spent time and effort cultivating each of them, doing favors and helping where he could, and now that support was paying off. They were loyal to him, more than to the kingdom.

"What are you going to do if he says no? This bluff only works once," Donnington said.

"Which is why I'm not bluffing. If he says no, then we march and defend our lands, just as I said."

"That's mutiny."

"That's survival," Sinclair said.

"But he's how we've held on this long. You saw how things were during the winter. We were being pushed back everywhere. Since he came back from Lynese, our fortunes have turned completely. How can we abandon him now?"

"What about the other barons? Pembroke's men almost certainly wouldn't, but some of my other barons might," Stanfield said.

"If you have pull with any of them, then talk to them and see if they would be willing to throw in with us. Cadogan has a large force, and we will need every man we can get."

"Well, Pembroke will never turn on the prince. Neither will any of the River Mark barons," Dunbar said.

"I know, and I'm not counting on them. If it's just us, then it's just us. And we will do what we have to do."

Baron Donnington looked to the other barons, and then back to Sinclair. "Everything you say is convincing, and I support your demands, but I'm sorry, I can't march with you if the prince refuses. My men are here, committed to this campaign. I can't pull them away."

"I'm sorry to hear that, but I understand," Garris said.

Donnington gave his fellows one last look, a sad look, and then left the tent.

"He has to do what he has to do, as do we. Go. Talk to those you trust and get as many as you can on our side. I want us to move soon, before the duke gets a jump on us."

The men filed out slowly, leaving Garris alone in his tent. He sat down heavily and stared at Ansell's message again. He was sure that William was making a mistake, both when he marched into the forest and holding here for so long now, but he had a lot of loyalty.

A split with him was inevitable, but he'd hoped to have more time.

Starhaven

Isaac Cadogan was in as bad a mood as he had ever been as he followed the guard up toward the throne room.

Of course, the bastard would want to have this conversation while he was sitting on his throne. He'd want to shove the trappings of his position down Cadogan's throat, to remind him of how little power he had in comparison.

And it was a terrible time for it. With all of the men he'd lost trying to take Iron Keep the previous summer, the army he'd been forced to send east represented nearly every fighting man in the duchy, all at the order of the very Crown that then commanded him to leave that army and come to the capital.

But what choice did he have? The king had his son.

"Your Majesty," he said as he marched into the throne room and stopped before the dais but did not bow.

Edmund sat upon Sidor's throne, one leg crossed over the other, and had the audacity to look the offended party. "Duke Cadogan. How gracious of you to finally accept my summons."

144

"I came for my son."

"Did you?" Edmund's mouth curved into something that might have been a smile on a different man. "Strange. The wyvern I sent requested your presence to discuss matters of loyalty and competence. I don't recall mentioning your son at all."

Isaac felt heat rise in his chest. "You want to talk about loyalty? Let's discuss that. I spent three months bleeding my forces dry in Iron Keep. Thousands of men died fighting to secure that damned peninsula because you asked me to."

"And you withdrew before the task was complete."

"I withdrew because you left me hanging there like bait on a hook." Isaac took a step forward. "Where was your promised invasion from the south? You were supposed to push through the southern entrance of the peninsula, pressing Sinclair's forces between us. Instead, you lost the eastern barons to the rebellion."

"You forget who you're addressing."

"I forget nothing. I know exactly who sits on that throne and how he got there. I supported it. Supported you. Serwyn was weak, paranoid, unfit to rule. Your removing him was the best thing that could have happened to this kingdom."

"My brother was the one who killed Serwyn."

"Yes, I understand that is the official story, and I don't care whether it is true or not. If you say Aldric killed Serwyn, then that's what happened. I have pledged my duchy to your Crown, and I remain steadfast, but I need you to do your part."

"And what part is that?"

"Stop playing defense. Stop reacting to William's movements and start forcing him to react to yours. My brother Torben will be in position along the bay in two weeks and will march as far as Ashport in a month, cutting off all of William's supply lines. He will have to retreat toward the eastern baronies, opening up River Mark for your invasion. But we have to keep him locked in the east. We have to move fast, much faster than the men you have put in charge have done so far."

"You presume to give me orders?"

"I presume to give you advice that might actually win this war. We both know you aren't your elder brother and have never taken to war. I have been leading men in fights since I could sit in a saddle. Take it or don't, but stop wasting my time and my men on half-measures and abandoned strategies."

Edmund was quiet for almost a full minute, just staring at Cadogan. The duke knew he was playing with fire, but he wasn't going to let Edmund's arrogance cost him everything.

"Your brother commands this force."

"He does."

"And he'll execute the plan as outlined?"

"He will. Torben's a better field commander than I am anyway. And he's loyal. To me, to the Ice Lands, to the Crown. In that order."

"To you?" he asked dangerously.

"To me. My brother loves me, Your Majesty. He loves his nephew Peren even more. I will speak plainly. I was concerned that if I came here, I would end up in a cell with him, and I cannot allow that to happen. I will fight your war for you, but I will not let my family rot in your dungeon. If you keep my son in a cell while Torben's fighting your battles, if you put me in a cell, he's going to hear about it eventually. And when he does, he'll have a choice to make of what force his army should support."

Edmund's eyes narrowed. "Is that a threat?"

"It's a fact. Torben won't tolerate his family being imprisoned without cause while he bleeds for your Crown. Neither will the rest of the Ice Lands." Isaac met his stare. "Right now, our interests align. We want the rebels stopped as much as you do. But turn on us, question our loyalty, and that alignment disappears."

"You overstep."

"I speak plainly. Something you need more of in this palace." Isaac gestured at Orlan. "How many people tell you what you want to hear versus what you need to know?"

"You think I don't understand the political realities of my position?"

"I think you understand them too well. You're so busy watching for knives in the dark that you're not seeing the enemy in broad daylight. I didn't come here to play word games. Release my son. Let me return to Shieldshome and lead my army. We'll do what you asked, cut off William's supplies, force a decisive battle. But

I won't do it with Peren sitting in your dungeon as some kind of surety for good behavior."

"And if I refuse?"

"Then you lose the north."

The silence stretched again.

Edmund drummed his fingers on the armrest. "Your son remains here until I'm satisfied with your brother's performance."

Isaac felt the anger surge again. "That's not acceptable."

"It's reality, Duke Cadogan. You serve at my pleasure, and Peren's comfort depends on your continued cooperation." Edmund's expression hardened. "Consider it motivation to ensure your brother's success."

"It will give me motivation, but not the motivation you want me to have."

"What?"

"You heard me."

Edmund studied him for a long moment. "Very well. You know where the dungeons are. Get your spawn and take him back to Shieldshome when you leave. But remember, Duke Cadogan, that I chose to release him when I could have kept him. Remember that I showed mercy when I could have chosen otherwise."

"I'll remember everything, Your Majesty, and when this war is over, we'll discuss what was owed and what was delivered."

"See that you do." Edmund settled back. "Go."

Isaac turned and strode toward the doors without another word. The guards opened them as he approached, and he passed through, leaving Edmund to his throne and his delusions.

Isaac descended the stone steps into the dungeons. The air grew colder with each step, helped by the fact that this was an island in the middle of a bay. For a place so far south, this almost felt like home, if not for the damp and the darkness.

The dungeons were full, more full than Isaac had ever imagined. He knew Edmund had gone power mad, but he hadn't expected it to this degree. Men sat chained to walls in clusters, their hollow eyes tracking his passage. Some wore the remnants of noble clothing, others the rough homespun of common soldiers. A few still had the look of merchants or clerks. All bore the same expression of despair.

How many had Edmund thrown down here? Isaac kept his face cold as he walked past them. The paranoid bastard saw traitors everywhere now.

He followed the directions of Orlan, who left him as he entered the underground chambers, going through several doorways as the men held in the open gave way to packed cells, gave way to many more empty cells, until he found a set of four barred doors at the end of a corridor with a set of royal guards standing outside of them.

"Open my son's cell."

The first guard hesitated. "Your Grace, we have orders."

"I am a duke of the realm and I have been given leave by the king to retrieve my son. You will open that cell and then you will leave."

"We cannot abandon our posts, Your Grace." The second guard said, his hand resting on his sword hilt. "The king himself commanded us to remain here."

Isaac took a step forward. He stood a full head taller than either of them and he let them feel the weight of that height.

"You will open that cell. You will leave this corridor or I will break you both and take the keys from your bodies."

The first guard's face went pale. "Your Grace, please. We have our orders."

"And I have given you new ones. You think the king will protect you if you stand against me? I am Duke of the Ice Lands. What are you? Sons of farmers. Open the door or die where you stand."

The second guard glanced at his companion. Something passed between them. Fear, mostly, but also calculation. They were outranked, outmatched, and they knew it.

"We will report this to His Majesty," the first guard said finally.

"Report whatever you like."

The guard fumbled with his keys, selecting one with shaking hands. The door swung wide, revealing a small cell with a single wooden bench and a bucket in the corner.

Anger boiled up in him when he saw the conditions his son had been left in.

Peren sat on the bench, his clothing dirty. He looked up as the door opened, relief flooding his features.

"Father," Peren said, standing uneasily.

Isaac rushed into the cell and grabbed his son by the shoulders, examining him. No visible injuries. No signs of torture. Edmund had kept him whole, at least.

"Are you hurt?"

"No. Hungry, mostly. And tired of staring at these walls."

"Can you walk?"

"I can, and I'll be glad to be out of here before I end up like that poor bastard in the next cell," he said, gesturing toward the solid stone wall that separated his cell from the adjacent one. "Been listening to him talk for weeks now. Half mad, I think."

"Who is he?"

"They never said. But he talks. At night, mostly. About keys and minds and corruption. He's mad."

As Isaac helped his son out of the cell, he paused to look into the next cell through the barred window in the door. It was identical to Peren's.

As Isaac turned to lead his son out, a voice came from behind the bars of that cell.

"The Key. It drives men mad. It twists them. Warps them."

Isaac looked through the window again. He could make out a figure hunched on the bench in the shadows. The man's hair hung in greasy strands, and even in the dim light, Isaac could see that his hands were shaking.

"What key?"

The man stood and moved toward the door. His face appeared at the barred window, gaunt and hollow-eyed. He laughed.

"The Key. The artifact I found in Werna. The king promised we'd study it. He lied. Don't you understand? He lied."

Peren pulled at his arm, wanting to leave this place, but he resisted. The man was indeed mad, but he mentioned Edmund, which drew Isaac's interest.

"I don't know what you're talking about."

"Of course you don't. Nobody does. That's the point, isn't it?" The man's fingers wrapped around the bars. "It's why he put me here, because people would listen to me. I thought my station as a Disciple protected me. I was a fool."

The name meant nothing to Isaac. "What artifact?"

"The Eclipse Key. It's an ancient thing, powerful and danger-ous."

"But what is it?"

"It influences minds, makes people feel things they wouldn't otherwise feel. Love. Loyalty. Devotion. All false. All manufac-tured."

Isaac glanced at Peren, who stood behind him in the corridor. His son's expression suggested he'd heard variations of this speech before, multiple times through the stone wall. To his son it meant nothing, but sudden realization dawned on him.

It explained many unanswered questions.

"You're saying the king has some magical artifact that controls people's minds."

"Not controls. Influences. Subtle. Yes. Yes. Very subtle."

Isaac studied what he could see of the man through the barred window. Mad, certainly, but there was something beneath the madness that felt true.

"You're an acolyte. What are you even doing here in the dun-geon?"

"Because I brought him the Key and he doesn't want anyone to know about it. He wants to keep it secret. He took it the moment I returned and locked me here so I couldn't tell my superiors about the Key."

"I know they prefer to hoard all of the artifacts that are found, but why would he not just petition to keep it? That has been done before."

"Because they would never let him do that once they learned about the Key. About what it does to you. It changes you, warps your sense of the world. It makes people crave the attention they get and see traitors everywhere. It creates paranoia."

Isaac frowned. "If it's so dangerous, why did you bring it to him?"

"I didn't bring it to him specifically. I brought it to Starhaven for study, for the archives. The Covenant's duty is to preserve these things, to understand them. But I would never have found it if he hadn't told me where to look. I don't know where his research came from, but he discovered where to find it and funded my expedition. He only asked that I bring it to him and let him see it before taking it to the Hall. But that was a trap. He was planning on taking it all along."

"It does explain why he's been so paranoid lately. Why the dungeons are so full. Why are you telling me this?"

"Because someone has to know, has to figure out how to get it away from him and to the elders. The longer it's used, the worse the corruption gets. He will become wild and uncontrolled and be a danger to everyone around him."

From where Isaac stood, they were already at that point.

"Father, we should go," Peren said.

Isaac stepped back from the door. The conversation was making his head ache. Half of what Tomas said sounded like the ravings of a madman. But the other half …

The other half explained much. Edmund's impossible fundraising success. The volunteers who kept appearing even as the war turned against him.

"Does the Covenant know you're here?"

"I don't think so. I think they have no idea the artifact even exists. They never believed me when I told them about it."

"You said the Key warps the user. How long until Edmund loses himself completely?"

"I don't know. Months, perhaps. Maybe less."

Isaac grabbed Peren's arm. "We need to go."

"Wait." Tomas pressed harder against the bars. "You have to free me. You have to get the Key. You have to get it before he destroys everything."

Isaac ignored the man's ravings as he pulled Peren down the corridor. He needed to get out of this city.

Chapter 14

Blackheath Forest, Kingsheart, Sidor

William sat just staring at the maps spread across the rough wooden table, candlelight throwing shadows across the terrain sketched in faded ink. There were three routes out of Blackheath Forest, unless he wanted to retreat, and his father had blocked them all.

The remnants of Baron Greville's army at Bradford had moved up and blocked the southern route out of the forest, sitting just at the edge of the Trentwell Hills where they dropped into the forest. Another force waited at Omskirk to the east, growing larger each day as fresh levies arrived from the interior baronies.

And then there was the Icelander army to the north, up on the Grimshaw. They were pushing east, but he hadn't decided yet if it was a feint to draw him out of the north end of the forest or if he was actually trying to circle around behind them.

His army numbered just over six thousand now, the same size as the Icelander army and the one at Omskirk, although the army to the east would outgrow his in the next few weeks.

The one in the south was much smaller, but he had no plan of going south again, or east. There was no going back.

The problem he had was that coming out of these trees, his columns would emerge disjointed, stretched thin and scattered while Edmund's men would be formed up, waiting. They'd choose the ground, set the terms.

He had no answer yet, and whatever he was thinking got pulled out of his head when the tent flap was jerked aside.

Baron Sinclair stepped through without announcing himself.

"I'm taking my men north," Garris said without preamble.

William prided himself on being able to roll with most changes. Adaptable. But that threw him for a second as his brain raced to catch up with what Sinclair had said.

"What?"

"The Icelander army. They're marching for Althear Bay." Garris moved to the table, jabbed a finger at the northeastern coastline. "Six thousand men and they'll burn their way through our rear if someone doesn't stop them. I'm going to be the one who stops them."

"We don't need to worry about that army."

"Don't we?" Garris's jaw tightened. "Tell that to the people in the eastern baronies. Our allies. Or my people once they round the bay and march into Iron Keep, which they've wanted all along. I will not allow my people to be slaughtered."

"They have a large army, but the ground down the side of the bay is rough and we left enough garrisons along the way, we can bleed the bastards. Slow them down."

"While my lands burn."

"While we take Starhaven." William tapped the capital on the map. "That army is out of position. If they do go for our rear, they're doing us a favor, pulling their armies out of the real battle and making our fighting with only six thousand men easier. Let them waste their strength raiding. Once we control the throne, we'll take care of them."

"Listen to yourself. Let them waste their strength. Let my people die so your strategy stays clean." He leaned across the table. "You're a weasel, boy. A clever little weasel who thinks wars are won with maps and theories."

"You're the one who said a commander has to make hard choices," William said, looking up and meeting his gaze evenly.

"And I'm making one." Garris straightened. "I'm taking my men north to stop those armies before they gut everything I've built."

"With what force?" William pushed away from the table.

"My men, Ansell's men, Dunbar's men."

"Jesus, that's two thousand men. A third of our strength, gone at the worst possible moment. We'll be outnumbered by every army

153

around us, and you're going to be a third of the size of the Icelander army. Everyone will be understrength."

"I can deal with them."

"You march north with two thousand, you'll get crushed, and you'll lose everything trying to save your holdings."

"Better than sitting here while you let them burn."

"Better? You throw away two thousand men for nothing; how does that help anyone? Your lands are gone either way, but at least if you stay, we have a chance to end this."

"I didn't come here to debate you, boy," Garris said. "You can wait for me, come with me to deal with the Icelanders, or go on without me. I'm not staying."

"Garris. This is exactly what my father wants. To divide us, make us choose between holding together and protecting our own. He's planned this."

"Maybe." Garris paused at the entrance. "Or maybe he out-planned you. Wouldn't be the first time someone underestimated what needs doing."

"This isn't a pissing contest, Garris. This is about winning a war."

"No, it's people." Garris looked back over his shoulder. "You want to play like you're your uncle, that's your choice. I'm going to save my lands."

The tent flap fell closed behind him.

William stood alone with the maps and tried not to fume.

He moved back to the table, stared at the coastline where Garris would march. Two thousand men. This was going to be a disaster.

The tent flap opened again. Pembroke stepped through, his face grave in the candlelight.

"You heard?" William asked.

"I did. Donnington came to me, said Sinclair's taking his men, Ansell's and Dunbar's," Pembroke said.

"Just them?"

"That he knows of, but he didn't discount them enlisting others."

"Can you talk to them?"

"I tried." Pembroke shook his head. "As soon as Donnington told me, I tried, but their baronies are in the path around to Iron

Keep and they're scared. They're anxious that we're just sitting here, doing nothing. I told you it was going to be a problem, and now it is."

"We need those men."

"I know. William, we can't stay here forever. This is just the beginning. The longer we just sit here, the more the eastern barons, and even some of my compatriots from the River Mark, are going to get antsy. These will just be the first we lose."

"We won't be staying here that much longer."

"Then what? There are six thousand men at Omskirk and fifteen thousand at Penvale and your army just shrank by two thousand. What can we do?"

"We can be clever," William said.

Kenna, River Mark, Sidor

Isolde slipped through the side entrance of the keep, past servants who froze in surprise seeing a noble in areas of the keep where nobles never were.

She'd brought Galer with her, because she knew he'd never forgive her if she went out on her own, and because, unlike in Rendalia, she did not feel safe on the streets here by herself.

What she didn't do was tell Alyssa what she was doing.

She knew the duchess meant the best, showing her the areas of the city that she thought Isolde should see. The problem was, Isolde wasn't sure Alyssa was showing her what she needed to see.

At one of the stops she'd made the day before, at one of the Disciple hospitals that helped soldiers with long-term wounds, she'd seen that it was a well-funded, well-run place.

And there she'd learned there were other places. Places for those who were not going to make it, wounded and lamed. People who were counting time till they died.

A disciple told her that that place was not nearly as well run. It never received visits and was perpetually underfunded.

The building stood by itself at the end of a street, far from any others, like the businesses in this city didn't want to be near it. No sign marked it as a place of healing. No signs that it housed people they owed a debt to.

Isolde pushed the door open.

The smell hit Isolde first. Unwashed bodies, old blood, the sour stench of infected wounds that had gone too long without proper care.

A man lay on a thin pallet near the entrance, his leg wrapped in bandages that had bled through days ago. No one had changed them. Three more soldiers occupied the room beyond, their faces slack with exhaustion or pain.

"Your Highness," a woman said, stopping a step inside the doorway through which she emerged from a back room, wiping her hands on an apron stained dark with old blood.

She was perhaps forty, with graying hair pulled back and lines etched deep around her eyes. The symbol of the Order of Healing hung from a chain at her throat.

"What are you ... We weren't expecting ..."

"I know, it's okay. I wanted to see for myself," Isolde said, moving past her into the main room.

Six more men lay scattered across the floor on pallets that were little more than straw wrapped in threadbare cloth. A boy, who couldn't have been more than fourteen, had his hand pressed to his side where blood seeped between his fingers. No one attended to him.

The disciple followed her. "Most of the wounded are sent to one of the larger hospitals. We take what we can here, but ..."

"But there's nothing." Isolde knelt beside the boy. His face was pale, his breathing shallow. "How long has he been like this?"

"A few weeks. The master healers said there was no repairing the wound. We sew it and treat it with herbs as best we can, but it never closes. We've done what we can."

Isolde looked at the boy's wound. She'd seen enough injuries in Rendalia to know what infection looked like. The flesh around the gash was red and swollen, the edges turning black.

"Can anything be done about his pain? There are medicines for that."

"There are, and we give some, but we don't have a large supply and must conserve it, to give at least some relief to as many as we can." The disciple's voice carried no bitterness, only exhaustion. "We do what we can with what we have."

Isolde stood. The room swam for a moment, and she realized she'd been holding her breath against the smell. Galer stood near the door, his face carefully neutral.

"Show me the rest."

The disciple led her through three more rooms. Each held the same scenes, wounded men on thin pallets, bandages that should have been changed days ago, water that looked more brown than clear in wooden buckets. In one room, a man screamed. No one went to him. There was no one to go.

"How many disciples do you have here?" Isolde asked.

"Three, Your Highness. Myself and two others. One is at the market trying to buy what supplies we can afford. Sister Maren tends to the ones who won't last the night."

Isolde's chest tightened. "That you can afford? Why are your medicines so limited? The Covenant has resources ..."

"The Covenant does what it can. But their resources aren't endless, Your Highness. They get most of their resources from tithes of the local nobles in a region. From the Crown. But the war has pressed the nobles and they can't give what they once did. And most of their funds go to the larger hospitals, the ones that treat hundreds of wounded. There isn't much left for us."

"The war takes everything."

"Yes, Your Highness."

They stood in silence for a moment. From the next room came another scream, then sobbing. Isolde forced herself not to look away from the disciple's tired face.

"I have some funds," Isolde said. "From Rendalia. I could ..."

"Your Highness is kind. But what we need isn't coin for a day or a week. We need a steady supply. Medicine. Clean bandages. Food. People to help tend the wounded. The war has taken all of that away, and until it ends," she said, and turned as the screaming from the next room intensified. "I'm sorry, Your Highness, but I have to …"

"Of course," Isolde said, waving her on. "Go."

The disciple dipped her head in a bow and hurried into the other room, leaving Isolde alone.

Isolde left the hospice with Galer and made her way back toward the keep, trying to figure out what to do. She thought of a gathering at Alyssa's, but that wasn't going to accomplish anything.

If the Duchess of River Mark hadn't addressed this problem already, it meant the duchy couldn't afford to. The war had drained every treasury, every resource. And Isolde's own funds were limited. William was a member of the royal family, but in open rebellion, he had little connection to the taxes of those properties.

They were not poor, by any means, but she needed more than pocket coin. She needed real money.

Isolde slowed and then stopped.

"Your Highness." Galer spoke quietly. "We should return to the keep."

"Not yet." Isolde turned down a different street, one that led toward the merchant quarter. "You've talked to people at the keep. Where do the nobles go for large funds? For loans on their properties? Unless things in Sidor are very different than those in Lynese, there are people who provide those services."

"There are, Your Highness," Galer said. "But, they are not the kind of people … they deal with exchequer. It is unseemly to …"

"Take me to them," she said again, giving him a serious look.

He held her gaze for a moment and then nodded once.

A moneylender named Corvin operated from a modest building in an otherwise unpresuming part of the city. From Galer's reaction, she had expected somewhere much seedier than this. If she didn't know better, she would have thought this the office of some kind of solicitor or professional.

The interior was plain but well-kept, although a pair of guards stood inside the door. They gave Galer a look over, but otherwise did nothing to stop them from going into the room at the end of the entry hall.

Inside, a desk dominated the center of the room, covered in neat stacks of papers and ledgers. The man behind it looked up as they entered, his eyebrows rising when he saw Isolde.

"Your Highness." He stood quickly, inclining his head. "I had heard you were in town but, this is ... unexpected."

"I need to borrow money," Isolde said. No point in pleasantries. "A significant amount."

Corvin was perhaps fifty, with shrewd eyes. "I suppose I should have known, you being who you are and I who I am. I am sorry, but I do not normally deal with ladies of your stature, and I am not familiar with your holdings, aside from how they connect to your husband. Pardon my crass questioning, but what security would Your Highness be offering?"

"Rendalia, the province my husband and I govern. Its revenues, its taxes, its ..."

"Your Highness," Corvin's tone was respectful but firm. "I'm afraid that won't be possible."

"Why not?" The word came out sharper than Isolde intended. "Rendalia is wealthy. Its trade revenues alone are considerable."

"I'm sure they are." Corvin gestured to one of the chairs before his desk. "Perhaps Your Highness would sit?"

Isolde wanted to refuse, but she lowered herself into the chair. Galer took up position behind her.

Corvin sat as well, folding his hands on the desk. "Your Highness must understand, lending money requires security. Certainty. A man in my position needs to know he'll be repaid."

"And I'm telling you I have the backing of Rendalia to prove I can repay whatever sum I borrow."

"Perhaps. But Rendalia is ... the situation is unclear, Your Highness."

"What situation? My husband and I control the province. We collect its taxes. We govern its people."

"For now, yes. But Rendalia only came into Sidorian hands through the peace treaty. Your Highness's own brother has recently disputed the treaty."

"That conflict is resolved. The peace holds."

"I don't doubt Your Highness's word." Corvin spread his hands. "But from a lending perspective, Rendalia remains uncertain.

It might stay in Sidorian control. It might be reclaimed by the Lynese. These are questions that affect whether debts will be honored."

"The debts would be honored. I give you my word."

"Your Highness's word is valuable. But there are other concerns. Rendalia is new to Sidorian administration. It has no established history of tax collection, no proven revenues. It's far from Kenna, difficult to reach if there were, complications with repayment."

"There would be no complications."

"And perhaps most importantly, Rendalia is not technically a barony or duchy. It exists in an unusual legal status. Until the war ends and King Edmund, or whoever emerges as the rightful king, formally recognizes its position in the kingdom's hierarchy, any debts secured against it are questionable."

"We control it. That should be sufficient."

"Control is not the same as legal ownership, Your Highness. If King Edmund were to reclaim the throne and dispute Rendalia's status, well then, a moneylender in Kenna has no way to collect debts from a province that might no longer exist under Sidorian law."

Isolde sat back in the chair. Everything he said made sense, in the cold logic of trade and coin. But men who served her husband and his people, soldiers who deserved respect, were dying in agony, and this man was telling her that uncertainty about future governance meant they would continue to suffer.

"I see." She stood. Galer moved with her. "Thank you for your time."

"Your Highness." Corvin stood as well. "I truly am sorry. If the situation were different …"

"I understand, and I appreciate your candor." Isolde turned toward the door. "Good day."

The street outside felt too bright after the dim interior of the moneylender's office.

"Your Highness. The keep?" Galer offered again.

Isolde shook her head. She thought of the disciple's tired face, the boy with the infected wound, and the man who had wrapped his own arm because no one else could. She thought of Alyssa's warnings about being a foreign queen, about winning over the people of Sidor. She thought of the nobles at the gathering, living in style and comfort.

The hospice needed resources. The Covenant had none to spare. The duchy couldn't help. Rendalia's revenues were unavailable. And borrowing was impossible because her legal status, her husband's claim, the entire future of their governance remained uncertain until this war ended.

Everything came back to the war. Always the war.

But there had to be something she could do. Some way to help that didn't require vast treasuries or legal certainty or the approval of suspicious nobles. Something immediate. Something real.

She had a thought. It wasn't a good one, but it was all she could think of at the moment.

"Your Highness, where are we going?" Galer asked as she resumed walking.

"To see about a long shot."

Chapter 15

Blackheath Forest, Kingsheart, Sidor

The barons were already in an uproar when William walked into the command tent. Twenty men, the bulk of the barons or nobles who commanded any sizable part of the army, minus Garris and the men who went with him, all stood and looked at him as he walked around to his seat at the end of the table.

"I take it from the volume of noise that you have all heard the news about Garris and a few of the other barons leaving the army?"

That was all they needed to uncork the dam again. The tent erupted as twenty men tried to talk over one another.

"Two thousand?" Baron Farrow said. "That leaves us with four thousand. Against Edmund's forces of what, six thousand men?"

"More," Baron Marlowe said. "Six thousand at Omskirk alone, with fifteen hundred more near Starhaven, not counting the recruits still streaming into Silverhall and that gaggle south of the forest."

"We're finished then. We can't fight our way through those numbers."

"We should never have come this far into the forest." Baron Donnington said. "I said as much at Bradford. Now we're trapped here with a third of our strength gone and three armies waiting to crush us, not counting the Icelanders, who outnumber Sinclair."

"Strength that Sinclair just stole," Farrow spat. "The bastard abandoned us. Left us here to die while he rides off to defend his own lands."

"Can you blame him?" Baron Donnington said. "The Icelanders are headed for the baronies along the bay, which my barony is part of. If Cadogan's army sweeps through unopposed, we will come out of this war without any barony left."

"So you'd abandon the cause, too?" Kenmore demanded. "Just walk away and let Edmund win?"

"Don't question my loyalty. I'm still here!"

"And echoing Sinclair's points for him. Your people will suffer worse under Edmund's rule," Newberry said. "We all know what he's capable of."

"Maybe so, but at least they'd be alive," Donnington replied. "What good does it do them if I die here in this forest, miles from home, while Icelanders burn their villages?"

"Then go," Farrow said. "Follow Garris north if that's what you want. But don't pretend it's about protecting anyone. It's about saving your own skin."

"Careful, Farrow."

"Or what? You'll challenge me? We're all dead anyway if we stay here."

Baron Halbrok held up his hands. "Fighting each other won't help. We need to decide what we're going to do. William, you said we'd stick to the plan, but the plan required our full numbers. With four thousand men ..."

"We could follow Garris," one of the lesser nobles said. "Keep the army together. Deal with the Icelanders first, then come back for Edmund once we've secured the east."

"By which time Edmund will have consolidated his position," another countered. "He'll have more troops, better defenses. Every day we delay makes Starhaven harder to take."

"Starhaven." Donnington laughed bitterly. "We'll never reach Starhaven. Look at the map. Edmund has us boxed in on three sides. The only way out is back the way we came, and that route's crawling with his scouts."

"So what do you suggest?" Newberry asked. "We surrender? Beg Edmund for mercy?"

"I suggest we be realistic about our situation."

"Realistic is we're trapped," Donnington said. "Trapped with dwindling supplies and an enemy that outnumbers us two to one. Maybe Blackwood's right. Maybe we should consider terms."

"Terms?" Farrow said. "Edmund murdered his own nephew and framed Aldric for it. He's executed barons for imagined disloyalty. What terms do you think he'll offer us?"

"Better than dying in this forest."

"You don't know that."

"I know I'd rather take my chances with negotiation than certain death in a hopeless battle."

Baron Newberry shook his head. "Edmund won't negotiate. Not with us. Not after everything that's happened. He'll promise safe passage and then put our heads on spikes the moment we lay down our arms. Look what happened to the peasants after their revolt."

"Then we fight our way out," Kenmore said. "Pick one of Edmund's armies and hit it with everything we have. Break through before the other two can reinforce."

"With four thousand men against three thousand?" Halbrok scoffed. "Even if we won, we'd lose most of our men doing it. And then what? The other two armies would be right behind us."

"So we split up," another baron suggested. "Small groups, moving through the forest separately."

"We can't stay in the forest forever, and it would be impossible to defend once we got out on solid ground," Halbrok replied. "We'd be picked off one by one. No, we need to stay together."

"Together doing what?" Donnington demanded. "Sitting here waiting for Edmund to starve us out?"

"Following William's plan."

"With all due respect to your plan, Your Highness, it was based on having six thousand men. We have four. The mathematics has changed."

Farrow turned toward William. "Your Highness, perhaps we should consider waiting here. Let Garris deal with the Icelanders, then rejoin us. With our full strength restored ..."

"Edmund won't wait," Halbrok interrupted. "Every day we sit here, he brings more men, more supplies. He knows we're in here. He's probably already tightening the noose."

"Then we should move now," Donnington insisted. "Either fight our way out or follow Garris north. But staying here is suicide."

William had stayed silent, letting them get as much of it out of their system as they wanted, but the argument had started to go in circles. Some wanted to just do something, some to run, others to do nothing.

None of those were good options and the arguments continued.

"Fighting our way out is suicide, too."

"So is following Garris. We'd be abandoning the campaign."

The voices rose, overlapping, each baron convinced his solution was the only viable option.

"This is pointless," someone said. "We're going in circles."

"Because there's no good option left."

"There has to be something."

"There isn't. Garris saw that. That's why he left."

"Garris is a coward."

"Garris is smart enough to know when a cause is lost."

"The cause isn't lost," Pembroke said firmly. "We've won every battle so far. Thunderhorn Bridge, Trentwell Hills, Cresswell. We've beaten Edmund's armies time and again."

"With superior numbers and good terrain," Donnington countered. "Now we have neither. Wake up, Pembroke. This campaign is finished."

"It's finished if we give up."

"It's finished either way."

Baron Farrow slammed his hand on the table. "Enough. We need to make a decision. William, you're the one who brought us here. What do you say? Do we fight, run, or surrender?"

Silence dropped over the gathering as if it were a blanket, all eyes turning to him.

"Nothing changes," William said. "We stick to the plan."

The silence lasted perhaps three heartbeats before it broke.

"Your Highness," Baron Farrow began carefully. "With respect, the plan …"

"I heard what Donnington said. I heard all of you. The numbers have changed. The situation is difficult. I know."

"Then you understand we need to reconsider," Farrow said.

"No."

"Your Highness ..." Donnington moved forward. "Perhaps we should wait for Garris to return. Once he's dealt with the Icelanders ..."

"Garris isn't coming back."

"We don't know that. If we give him time ..."

"We don't have time," William said flatly. "Every day we wait here, Edmund gets stronger. And Garris made his choice. He's not thinking about Starhaven anymore. He's thinking about his own lands."

"Can you blame him?" another baron asked quietly.

"It doesn't matter if I blame him. He's gone. We're here. And we need to finish what we started."

Baron Halbrok shook his head. "Your Grace, I understand your determination, but we need to be practical. Four thousand men against twenty thousand or more, with no clear route out of this forest ..."

"So we follow Garris north," Baron Donnington interrupted. "Keep the army together. We can always ..."

"No."

The word came out harder than William intended, but he didn't soften it. "We continue with the plan. The goal is Starhaven, not just relieving pressure from the north. Once Edmund is gone, Cadogan will have to come back into the fold. The Icelanders will withdraw. The war ends."

"If we can reach Starhaven," Blackwood said. "Which we can't."

"Your Highness," Farrow said, his tone shifting to something almost pleading. "I've followed you this far. We all have. But you're asking us to march four thousand men against impossible odds with no clear path forward. Just tell us ... what do we do?"

William looked at each of them in turn. He could see the doubt on their faces, the fear poorly hidden behind anger and frustration. These were men who'd risked everything to follow him, who'd believed in what they were fighting for. Now they stood in this tent, deep in enemy territory, afraid.

"We get some boats."

The sudden shift in topic left them momentarily confused.

"Boats?" Baron Pembroke asked.

"Yes, boats. As many as you can find, I don't care the size."

166

"But …" Baron Halbrok asked. "Your Highness, I don't understand. What do you intend to do with these boats?"

William met his eyes. "I'm going to get us out of this trap."

Kenna, River Mark, Sidor

Isolde led a nervous Galer to the eastern side of Kenna's merchant quarter, stopping in front of a nice building with a large sign out front saying, "Roth Shipping."

A significant departure from the nondescript lending house with no sign that it was even there. The two-story building of timber and stone was modest but well-maintained.

Inside, a clerk looked up from his ledger.

"I need to speak with Master Roth," Isolde said.

The clerk's eyes widened as he recognized her. He stood, nearly knocking over his stool. "Your Highness, I … Master Roth isn't expecting …"

"I know. Tell him Princess Isolde wishes to discuss a business matter."

The clerk disappeared up a narrow staircase. Isolde heard voices, then footsteps. Cornelis Roth descended a moment later looking, strangely, pleasantly surprised, as opposed to bothered by the interruption.

"Your Highness." He bowed. "This is unexpected."

"I hope I'm not interrupting your work."

"Not at all. It is always a welcome break in my day when someone such as yourself stops for a visit. Please, come upstairs." He gestured to the staircase. "We can speak in my office."

She followed him up to a room overlooking the warehouses and other buildings that made up the district. Papers covered a large desk, and ledgers lined the shelves.

Roth closed the door and offered her a chair. "May I ask what brings you here?"

"I have a business proposition."

"Really? How unexpected. I'm, of course, eager to hear what you have to propose."

"You're aware of the hospice near the eastern gate?"

"I can't say that I am."

She wasn't surprised by this.

"Well, suffice it to say there is one, and I just came from there. It is woefully underfunded. The disciples who run it lack the resources to properly care for the dying soldiers there. Worse, the duchy has no money to spare during the war, and my personal funds aren't sufficient for what's needed."

Roth nodded slowly, his face neutral.

"I went to a moneylender to see if I could borrow on Rendalia's credit to get the needed funds, but he refused me. He said Rendalia's status is too uncertain, that the war makes any loan too risky."

"I can see where someone like that would be concerned with the region's unusual status. I still am not sure what I can do to help with this."

"I'm here because I need someone willing to take that risk. Someone who can secure the loan using their own assets as collateral, with my guarantee of repayment."

Roth sat back in his chair. "You're asking me to put my trading concern at risk."

"I am."

"While I appreciate the opportunity, the moneylenders would want my ships and warehouses as security. If you couldn't repay the loan, I'd lose everything I've built. The risk of that is just too high. I'm sorry."

"I'll repay the loan. You have my word."

"Your word is worth quite a bit, Your Highness, but you're asking me to stake my family's livelihood on it. I have a wife and three children. This business represents the culmination of my life's work."

"I can appreciate the risk to you, but ..."

"Do you? Forgive me, but you're sixteen years old and married to a man fighting a civil war. Your own kingdom has exiled you. The duchy you offer is barely a year old and, as I'm sure the moneylender pointed out, it isn't clear if you actually own the duchy you are offering. Even if Lord William wins this war, there's no guarantee he'll become king. And if he doesn't, the Crown will not let his wife maintain her ownership over that province."

"Everything you've said is true, and I agree there's risk. But there's also reward. What if my husband does win and becomes king? What do my promises rate then? And at this very moment, one of his men runs the duchy, so I can deliver what I promise now. I'm not asking you to do this out of charity or loyalty. I'm willing to offer a large incentive to make the risk worth it."

"I'm listening."

"I asked around after meeting you the other day. I know you are not the largest trading concern in Sidor, but you *are* one of the largest in River Mark ... and, you're ambitious. I know you do most of your business with Inos and even Alchmara and the Thay. And I know enough about finance between the kingdoms to know that is not where the real money is. The real players in shipping are all on the western side of Sidor, because the triangular trade between Lynese, Werna, and Sidor is where the bulk of shipping in the Shattered Lands takes place, and considering you are here and not there, I am going to guess you are locked out of that trade."

"You would be correct. The Wernan concerns have been established in those ports for generations, and they do not like people taking their share of the money purse. They have connections, contracts, favorable terms with the dock masters. A new concern can't compete against that."

"And that's what I'm offering. A chance at favorable terms with at least one end of the triangle. A way to get your foot in the door."

"What do you mean?"

"I'll make your concern the primary shipping agent for Rendalia City. Any contracts for moving goods to or from the duchy will be offered to you first. You'll have the right to accept or decline before anyone else sees them. I will put in a word with the merchants in the city and make sure you get favorable terms with the dock brokers, not just in Rendalia City, but in the entire province."

Roth's expression didn't change, but the way he went stock-still said she had his attention.

"Additionally," she continued, "I'll provide you with dock space owned by the duchy itself, free of charge for five years, to help you expand. Space you can use as a warehouse for your operations."

"That's …" Roth stopped. "This would open up an entirely new market for my concern. Double my potential business, at least."

"That's my intention."

"You'd give me this for helping you secure a loan?"

"Yes."

Roth stood and walked to the window.

"How much do you need?"

"Two thousand sovereigns."

He turned back to her. "That's a substantial sum. The money-lenders would want half again that much in collateral value."

"Can you provide it?"

"I can," he said slowly, doing the math in his head. "But I need to understand that even with the extraordinary offer you are making, this is a massive risk. I do not have the liquid assets to cover that amount if you do not come through on your promise. I will lose my business."

"What is the saying merchants are so fond of? There is no reward without risk?

"And there will be a lot of reward. If this arrangement works as I expect, there will be other opportunities. Other contracts. I'm building something in Rendalia, Master Roth. Even if William wins the war and becomes king, my attention will not move away from it, for obvious reasons. I live in both worlds, and I will never lose my focus toward my homeland. I need people who can help that duchy prosper. People who have a stake in its success."

"And the loan?"

"I'll repay it within two years. You have my word, and you'll have it in writing, signed and sealed. As soon as it is, I'll send a wyvern to Sir Drummond and explain the terms and tell him to expect your representative."

After a moment, he stood and extended his hand. "You have a deal, Your Highness. I'll arrange the loan. It should take three days, perhaps four."

Isolde rose and shook his hand. "Thank you."

"I should thank you. This is an opportunity I never expected."

"One other thing. Since we are now in business together, I would like to hear what is happening in the world of commerce. Your activity will naturally bring you in contact with the Crown, while it is still separate from my husband, Lynese, Werna, along with your contacts in Inos and Thay. It would be valuable to me if you could help me understand what is happening in the world. You see things through a different lens than those who report to me directly, and I think you are a smart man."

"That is an additional risk. There are those who might not want to do business with me if they know I am reporting to you."

"And I can be discreet, but my gaining and maintaining a position to have control over Rendalia is the only way to ensure you get what you want."

"That is very clever. At no other cost to you, you get something else from me and make it sound as if it's for my own good."

"Is it not?"

"I think I may have underestimated you on our first meeting," he said, then paused in thought. After a few moments, he continued, "Fine, we have a deal. I will be in touch in the next day or two with the appropriate agreements."

She left the trading house and made her way back through Kenna's streets toward the keep. She had just made a big gamble and would have to explain it to William at some point, although she wasn't worried about him backing her.

But it was why she added the supplying of intelligence to the agreement, even if it wouldn't be in the agreement itself. It should be enough for someone like William to see the value of, even if he didn't see the value in pouring coin into charity projects.

Chapter 16

Starhaven, Sidor

Edmund waited as the nobles filed into the room, barely containing his fury at that. Forty men, none of whom would meet his eyes as they took their place in the audience chamber. Forty men who brought excuses instead of victory.

"Gentlemen," Edmund said, letting the word hang for a moment. "We are now two weeks past the point where my son's rebellion should have been crushed. Two weeks since his forces became trapped in Blackheath Forest, just waiting to be destroyed, and yet here you sit, still refusing to make progress. Still refusing to do the task set before you. I cannot help but ask myself why you have failed so spectacularly to do your duty."

"Your Majesty," the young Albert Blout, who had taken over the Barony of Langmere following the death of his father, said. "The terrain presents considerable difficulties. Baron Pendeen's attempts to pursue them into the forest resulted in ..."

"The loss of seven hundred men." Edmund finished the sentence. "Yes. I am aware. What I am unaware of, Baron Blout, is why this singular failure has prevented every other commander in my service from attempting a different approach. Surely the collective military wisdom of you all exceeds that of one unfortunate baron?"

"The forest is murder for cavalry," Lord Falkirk said. "Dense undergrowth, narrow trails. Our mounted forces provide no advantage there."

Edmund stopped his circuit of the room. "Then send infantry. Send footmen. Send peasants with pitchforks if that is all we possess. My son commands, by latest count, four thousand men. You command three times that number. The mathematics, gentlemen, seems rather straightforward."

"They have the experience, Your Majesty," Baron Crook offered. "Their veterans can fight in small units better than our conscripts, who really need to be held as a single unit to be effective."

"Excuses." Edmund's voice remained level, but something cold entered it. "You know the land, Baron Crook. Your barony sits on the eastern edge of the forest. Shouldn't the conscripts in your ranks know their own land and be able to fight in it better? No, I don't think it's about some kind of strategic advantage. Let me propose an alternative explanation for your collective inaction."

The room stilled.

"Perhaps," Edmund continued, moving behind Baron Lytle's chair, "Perhaps the issue is something far simpler. Perhaps some among you have concluded that your interests align more favorably with my son's cause than with your rightful king's."

"Your Majesty!" Baron Eddington stood. "That is an outrageous suggestion. Every man here has sworn oaths."

"Oaths." Edmund smiled without warmth. "Yes. My brother Aldric swore oaths. My nephew swore oaths. Oaths, I have learned, possess a regrettable tendency toward impermanence."

"We are losing this war," Baron Tarr said. "Not through treachery, but through the simple reality that Prince William has proven himself a capable commander. He learned his trade in Lynese well."

"My son is trapped, contained on all sides and cut off from his supply lines to River Mark and Iron Keep. He must be living off foraging at this point. His men sleep in forest camps and are outnumbered in every way. Yet somehow, they remain intact. Somehow, every attempt to engage him results in disaster for my commanders. Does this pattern not strike you as peculiar?"

"Your Majesty," Lord Tarr stepped forward. "If I may speak plainly ..."

"By all means. Plain speech seems in rather short supply of late."

"The boy is brilliant. I say that with no pleasure, but it is true. He chooses his ground, controls the pace of engagement, and withdraws before we can bring our superior numbers to bear. He is better than any of us at war."

"Brilliant." Edmund tasted the word. "Tell me, Lord Tarr, did this 'brilliant' strategy also explain why you all keep retreating like women, pulling your skirts behind you, too afraid to face him man to man? Isn't it easy to seem brilliant when your opponents refuse to fight?"

Tarr opened his mouth, then closed it.

"No answer? How unfortunate." Edmund returned to his position at the head of the table. "Let me direct your attention to a different matter. I count forty men present, yet I issued summons to fifty-three. Where, might I ask, are the absent thirteen?"

The assembled nobles exchanged glances.

"Baron Stroud sent word that illness prevents his attendance," Orlan offered from the side.

"How convenient. And the others?"

"Baron Swale has said there was an incident involving a creature coming out of the Strait of Leviathan that demanded his attention …"

"Lord Falmoth has joined the army south of the forest, adding his people to …"

"Baron Wullum felt …"

Edmund raised a hand. The explanations ceased. "Thirteen absences, each with a reasonable justification, I'm sure. Tell me, gentlemen, does it not seem odd that thirteen of our most prominent lords find themselves unable to attend a war council at the very moment when that war reaches its crisis point?"

"What are you suggesting, Your Majesty?" Baron Greystone asked.

"I am suggesting nothing, simply observing patterns, such as all the missing barons have, at various points, expressed reservations about certain of my policies. Now, either this represents an extraordinary coincidence, or it represents something else entirely."

"You think they're meeting with the rebels, Your Majesty?" Baron Crook said.

"I think the possibility merits consideration. We know that the traitor Sinclair has broken from William's army. Our scouts confirmed he marched out from the east of the forest, through the missing Baron Wullum's land. Did Wullum meet with him as he passed? Did he add his forces to Sinclair's? Have any of my other ..."

"I don't think anyone observed any contact."

"No observed contact," Edmund corrected. "Is rather different from no contact whatsoever. Tell me, Baron, how difficult would it be for messages to pass between Sinclair and my absent lords? For commitments to be made, for arrangements to be established? All while we sit here, paralyzed by our supposed tactical difficulties?"

"This is madness," Baron Harthal said.

Edmund's gaze fixed on the baron. "Is it? Then explain to me why we are losing. Explain why, with overwhelming numerical superiority, with control of the capital, with the full resources of the kingdom at our disposal, we cannot bring four thousand rebels to battle. Explain it in a manner that does not require me to conclude either staggering incompetence or deliberate sabotage."

Silence filled the chamber.

"Then give us clear orders," Baron Tarr said. "Tell us what you want done, and we shall do it."

"What I want? Very well. I want my son's army destroyed. I want Garris Sinclair's head on a pike. I want every baron who has breathed the word 'rebellion' to bend their knee or face the axe. These are my wants, Baron Tarr. Are they in any way unclear?"

"No, Your Majesty, but ..."

"But." Edmund seized on the word. "There is always a 'but' with you people. But the terrain. But the supply lines. But the tactical complexity. I begin to suspect that 'but' is the only word in your collective vocabulary. I will make myself absolutely clear, gentlemen. The time for deliberation has passed. You will march into Blackheath Forest and engage the enemy. You will bring me victory or you will bring me an explanation of why death is preferable to obedience. These are not suggestions. These are not requests open for debate. These are commands from your king."

"The losses will be substantial," Baron Tarr said.

"Then we shall replace them. I have gold. I have land. I have titles to distribute. What I lack is commanders willing to spend those resources in pursuit of victory."

"You ask us to throw men into a meat grinder," Baron Crook said.

"I ask you to do your duty."

"There is a difference between duty and suicide."

"Is there?" Edmund's smile returned. "How philosophical. Tell me, my lord, at what point does duty become suicide? When the odds are two to one? Three to one? Or perhaps duty only qualifies as duty when victory is assured, when no risk attends the task? I confess, I find your definition rather convenient. Make me understand, Lord Tarr, because at present, only two explanations present themselves. Either you are incompetent beyond measure, or you are complicit in this failure."

"Your Majesty!" Multiple voices rose in protest.

Edmund raised his hand again, but this time the room did not quiet immediately. Arguments erupted between nobles, accusations flying as the assembly fractured into competing voices. Edmund watched it unfold, something cold settling in his chest.

They were all against him. Every face, every voice, every carefully crafted argument. They plotted, schemed, worked to undermine his every command. How had he not seen it before? The signs were everywhere, in every hesitation, every qualification, every suggestion of moderation. They served him with their lips while their hearts served his enemies.

"Enough!" The room fell silent. "I see now the true nature of this assembly. You come before me speaking of tactics and strategy, of careful planning and measured response. But beneath those words lies something else. Lies cowardice. Lies treachery. You have made your choice, gentlemen. Each of you has decided that your comfort, your safety, your precious lands matter more than your oaths to your king."

"Your Majesty, please," Falkirk began.

"Be silent." Edmund's gaze found the noble. "You, Baron Falkirk, don't even control your barony anymore. You have lost the entire thing to the rebels, and yet still live."

"Your Majesty, I was with the army as it fell back, saving the men to fight again another day. I mean this with all due deference, Your Majesty, but this council cannot function if you question every man's loyalty."

"What good is a council if all it offers is protecting incompetent commanders? Stop finding reasons why my orders cannot be executed as given or admit what you truly want. Admit that you serve my enemies. That you work to ensure my defeat."

"We serve no one but you and the kingdom."

"Lies." The word snapped out. "Every word from your mouth is lies. You think me a fool? You think I cannot see how you manipulate, how you twist every discussion toward inaction and delay? You are my enemy, Baron Falkirk. You draw my gold, sit at my council table, all while working to destroy me."

"Your Majesty, I swear to you ..."

"Captain!" Edmund's voice carried to the guards outside the chamber door. "Arrest Baron Falkirk. Arrest Baron Tarr. Take them to the dungeons to await trial for treason."

Chaos erupted. Nobles shouted, some in protest, some in alarm. Barons backed away, looking stunned, as guards entered the room.

"Your Majesty, please," Tarr said. "I am innocent of these charges."

"Then you will have nothing to fear from trial. Guards, take them."

Two guards seized Tarr's arms. Others moved toward Falkirk, who stumbled backward.

"This is madness!" Baron Crook roared. "You cannot arrest your own nobles without evidence, without trial, without ..."

"Without what, my lord? Without your permission? I am king. I need no one's permission to defend my throne against traitors."

"They are not traitors!"

"That," Edmund said coldly, "remains to be determined. Let this serve as example, gentlemen. I will tolerate no further equivocation, no further delay, no further questioning of my commands. You will march into Blackheath Forest, engage my son's army, and bring me victory or you will join Tarr and Falkirk in the dungeons. Am I understood?"

No one spoke.

"I asked a question."

"Yes, Your Majesty," came the murmured response.

"Excellent. You are dismissed. Prepare your forces. I expect movement within the week." Edmund turned and strode toward the door, his mind already racing ahead to the thousand other betrayals he now saw clearly.

The absent lords meeting with Sinclair. The commanders who failed too conveniently. The nobles who counseled moderation while plotting his downfall. All of it was clear now, laid bare before him. He would root them out, every last one. He would purge the rot from his kingdom before it consumed him.

"Traitors," he muttered as he walked toward the tower and his offices.

He barely noticed the servants who pressed themselves against the walls as he passed, barely registered the nervous glances exchanged between the guards. His thoughts churned with conspiracies, connections, and patterns of betrayal.

Twin Lake, Barony of Dewsham, Kingsheart

The water lay black and still under the moonless night. William stood at the edge of Nalia's narrow beach, counting boats as they pushed off from the shore. Ninety-seven vessels had made it to the beach, in total, only one short of the ninety-eight they'd had when they'd set off from the far eastern edge of the lake where it touched the Blackheath Forest. While any casualties were lamentable, making the trip and losing only five men was an achievement.

The men were silent, and it wasn't only because of the need to remain undiscovered.

"We shouldn't have stayed here," Commander Haverhill said, appearing at William's shoulder. "The men won't say it, but they're terrified. You know what they say about this place."

William knew. Really, every child in Sidor grew up hearing tales of Keston and Nalia, the last emperor and empress from the time of magic, whose rule led to the sundering of the world, splitting it into the continents they had today.

It was said the two islands that gave Twin Lake its name were Keston's ancestral home, and the place he lived at more than at the old capital that sat where Starhaven sat today.

They also said the islands were haunted by the souls of Keston and Nalia, not allowed to join the other ancestors because of their crimes. Forever left on this world, but kept separate, each on their own island, never allowed to touch again.

William knew these tales better than most, having spent his early childhood on its shores at Silverhall, Edmund's ducal seat. His governess had told him tales of how the dead walked and the ruins sang at night, where anyone who ventured past the beach never returned.

"The ancients protected us," William said.

"Your Highness ..."

"We kept to the beach. No one went inland. The spirits have no quarrel with us."

"You worry too much, Haverhill," Eskild, unburdened by Sidorian superstition, said. "Look what we've managed. Almost a hundred boats across the lake, and no one's spotted us. It certainly does argue for your ancestors protecting you."

William smiled at Haverhill's frown. Eskild relished taking the opportunity to tweak his Sidorian comrades, poking at their 'traditionalist' views. As most Thayans, Eskild had a much less friendly view of how the ancients looked down upon their descendants. While the followers of the Acolytes saw them as protective, guiding their descendants to healthy and productive lives, the Purifiers viewed them as disappointed parents always looking for another opportunity to punish those they saw as undeserving of their lives.

"Let's chalk it up to luck," William said.

"Good planning, more like," Haverhill said. "Knowing about the morning fog and traveling only at night, tying the boats together and still making it to each island, knowing none of the fishermen would get within sight of them, and wouldn't look to the islands if they did, is how we made it."

William watched another group of vessels slide away from shore, their crews bent over oars. The ropes between the boats creating a floating chain across the water's surface, barely visible in the starlight. One boat lost meant all boats stopped. One boat discovered meant the entire fleet was exposed. But with no lights and only traveling by dark and under fog made it impossible to stay together any other way.

"My father's men watch the shores," William said. "They watch the roads. They don't watch the middle of a haunted lake at midnight."

"Because no sane commander would try it," Halbrok said as the baron joined them.

"Then it's fortunate I'm so foolish," William said with a smile before moving toward the last boats waiting on the beach. "Get the men loaded. We need to be across before dawn."

William climbed into a small fishing boat, one of the larger single ships they'd managed to acquire, holding twenty other men. The range of men carried by each boat was staggering, with the largest holding thirty, but the majority holding less than ten, and a few only simple paddlers holding two men.

Ragtag was the word that came to mind.

Yano, the man who owned this boat and one of the few who gave up their charge not only willingly, but stayed to helm it, pushed through the crowd of armored soldiers. "Last group's ready, Your Highness. Where do you want to be?"

"Middle of the line." William pointed to a cluster of vessels fifty yards out. "If the front gets spotted, I want time to react. If the rear gets caught, I want to know before they're all dead."

"Cheerful thought," Haverhill muttered.

William sat in the bow, watching the dark shapes ahead and behind. The ropes between vessels stretched and slackened as crews matched their pace. Too fast and the ropes would snap. Too slow and they'd still be on the water when the sun rose high enough to burn off the fog.

The fog arrived as William knew it would. He'd seen it a thousand mornings from Silverhall's windows, watched it roll across Twin Lake's surface like a living thing. Dense enough to hide an army, thick enough to muffle sound. But it would burn off by mid-morning, and anyone still on the water then would be exposed.

"There." Yano pointed ahead where darker shapes emerged from the gray. "The wharves."

William stood, bracing himself against the boat's rocking. Buildings materialized: warehouses, the harbor master's tower, the stone-built docks that served the city's merchant trade. Nearly no lights showed through the fog. It was still very early, and most of the city still slept.

His boat grounded against the wharf with a soft scrape. Men poured over the sides before the vessel stopped moving. Cross-bowmen first, spreading across the stone surface, then heavy infantry behind them.

Yano secured the boat to an iron ring set into the dock. William stepped onto solid ground and drew his sword. Around him, more boats beached. Men formed into their groups without orders, moving to positions they'd drilled and rehearsed for two days before they left for the attack.

A guardsman appeared between two warehouses, walking his patrol route. He stopped when he saw the boats. His mouth opened.

Crossbows snapped; bolts took him in the chest and throat. He fell backward without making a sound, but their luck had started to run short as he crashed into a stack of crates which spilled over, making enough racket to bring more guards running to see what caused the commotion.

William counted eight, maybe ten, rounding the corner. They saw the mass of armed men and started shouting the alarm. One of them turned and ran, probably to raise a warning at the keep.

He'd hoped they could get further into the city before all hell broke loose, but no plan survived the enemy intact.

The crossbowmen shot again, and most of the remaining guards dropped or stumbled, riddled with bolts. The two surviving guards turned and ran, following their fellow who'd taken off before, their hurry to raise the warning hard to distinguish from fear of watching all of their fellows slain in the span of a moment.

"Forward." William moved toward the main thoroughfare that led inland.

Behind him, fifty crossbowmen broke off and sprinted toward the bell tower and the warehouse rooftops. The rest formed a loose column, heavy infantry in front, and pushed into the city.

Bells started to ring from further in the city.

The alarm had sounded.

The street widened after a hundred yards. Shops lined both sides, their shutters closed. William heard fighting to the north, brief and sharp, then silence. The southern column would be landing now. Everything depended on speed.

A runner appeared from a side street. "Your Highness, the southern gate is down. Commander Baldwin's through with his men."

William nodded. One gate. Three more to go.

They reached an intersection where the harbor road met a wider avenue. A guard sergeant came around the corner with fifteen men. The sergeant saw William's column, and his face went white. He started shouting orders, trying to form his men across the street.

"Crossbows up," William called.

Twenty men with loaded weapons stepped forward. The range closed to thirty yards. The guards were still shuffling into position when William dropped his hand.

The volley tore into them. Bolts went through leather and padded cloth like they weren't there. Eight guards fell in the first seconds. The survivors stood frozen, staring at their dead.

"Charge," William roared, rushing forward.

The heavy infantry followed on his heels. The guards tried to fight; one managed to block a halberd swing and thrust his spear into an attacker's thigh, but they wore light armor and carried weapons meant for street patrol, not battle.

Not that any armor would stop the sword Aldric had given William. He cut down two men before his soldiers caught up to him. The melee lasted less than two minutes.

William's column had two wounded. Neither serious.

They moved again, faster now. The alarm bells were ringing across the whole city. Every guardsman would be awake, trying to respond. But respond to what? Attacks from three directions at once. The gates had already fallen. By the time they understood the situation, it would be over.

Market Square opened ahead, a broad plaza ringed by guild halls and merchant houses. Also, clearly an assembly area for the town guard which filled the space, twenty or thirty in total, plus more town militia pouring in, most still trying to get their padded gambesons pulled on, wiping sleep from their eyes.

"Take your men and circle around to the south," he told Haverhill. "Morris, take yours and swing north, cut back through that alley."

William led the rest of his men in directly, charging straight again. He had about a hundred men with him in total, and had just sent off thirty in either direction, meaning, for the moment, he had about the same number as the guards he was attacking.

With the exception that his men were heavily armored veterans and the city guard were lightly armored and more accustomed to dealing with drunks than soldiers.

Even with the same number, it would never be a fair fight.

William was again at their vanguard, not just parrying attacks but slicing clean through their weapons before slashing the holder down where he stood. The guards only held for a moment before they tried to break as his men tore into them.

Not that they had anywhere to go as Haverhill and Morris appeared with their men, smashing in from either side.

It was a slaughter.

The guard captain, William could see his better armor now, was foolish enough to stand his ground and kill an attacker with a sword thrust through the neck. Then a halberd hooked his leg, yanked him down, and a war hammer ended him.

The guards broke. Some ran, some tried to surrender. William had given orders to take no prisoners until they reached the keep. They didn't have the men to guard prisoners.

Again, the fight lasted only a few minutes, only two more of his men were wounded, and the guardsmen were slaughtered to a man.

"Hold this position," William ordered Morris. "Nothing gets through. Send runners if anything changes."

The captain saluted. William moved to the center of the square where he could see down multiple streets. This was the heart of the city. Control this, and the rest would follow.

A messenger arrived, breathing hard. "Your Highness, Commander Baldwin has the south gate with ten dead. He's holding it closed."

"Good. What about the north?"

"Still fighting, my lord. The guards are in the gatehouse towers. Baron Kenmore says he needs more men to take it."

"Tell him the second wave will reinforce him when they land."

The messenger left. William turned to Haverhill, who'd stayed at his shoulder through the fighting. "Get men into those guild halls. I want archers in every window facing the streets."

Haverhill moved off, shouting orders. Around the square, infantry took up positions in doorways and behind market stalls. Crossbowmen reloaded their weapons. The whole area stank of blood and voided bowels.

Another messenger. "Northern column reports the merchant quarter is clear. Minimal resistance. They're pushing toward the south gate now."

William looked east where the sky was beginning to lighten. The fog would hold for another hour, maybe less. The second wave should be landing at the wharves now. He needed those reinforcements to finish this.

Fighting erupted from a street to his right. William drew his sword and ran toward it. Twenty yards down, his men had encountered another guard patrol, ten or twelve, hard to see in the narrow lane. The guards fought from behind an overturned cart. Crossbow bolts flew both ways.

One of William's men went down with a bolt in his face. Another took a spear thrust through his arm. But the guards were fewer and lighter-armored. William, who'd come in from a different angle, was almost behind them.

He charged in, bellowing loud enough to startle them, getting them to turn and drop their guard. He killed two more as his men suddenly found the resistance gone and poured over the makeshift barricade.

"Keep moving," William told his men. "Don't stop for anything."

Back at the square, a knight approached. "Your Highness, the second wave is through. Six hundred men landing now."

"Send fifty to me and one hundred to the south gate; the remaining to push through to the manor. I don't know who was left in command of the city, but I want them locked in the manor."

The knight saluted and left. William paced the square's edge, watching the streets. This wasn't over, not yet. He had a rough idea of how many guardsmen were in the city, and most of the town militia wouldn't have levied yet. If he gave them too much time, they could arm themselves and organize. They couldn't actually stop the attack, not now, not with his men inside the walls. But they could exact a larger cost than William was willing to pay.

A roar came from the north. William couldn't see what caused it, but it sounded like many men fighting. Then it stopped.

A runner appeared minutes later. "The guards tried to retake the north gate, Your Highness. Came down two streets at once. Commander Baldwin caught them in the open with crossbow fire, then met them with infantry. They're dead or scattered."

William nodded. That was the push he'd been waiting for and probably the last organized guard force. Without their officers and sergeants, the remaining guards wouldn't mount another attack. They'd hide, flee, or surrender.

The sky grew brighter, now clearly visible as the fog had mostly burned away.

"A good day, My Prince," Baron Inworth said, coming out of a side street with almost a dozen men. "We have the city and the remainder are pinned inside the manor. The commander and the few household knights in the city are contained. We have the compound surrounded. They're not coming out."

"Where is the commander?"

"On the walls, watching. He hasn't tried to break out."

William considered. He estimated the man had between six and ten knights in full plate. Not enough to save the city, but if they charged together, they'd kill a number of his men before they could be stopped. But where would they charge? The city was lost. The gates were sealed. A charge would get them killed for nothing.

"Keep them contained. If they try to leave, offer terms: lives and ransom rights in exchange for surrender."

The baron nodded and headed back in the direction of the manor. Bells stopped ringing. The city fell quiet as the people hid in their homes and waited for the battle to end.

The third wave would be landing now: another five hundred men. William sent orders for them to sweep the remaining quarters systematically. Find weapons. Secure guild halls. Accept surrenders. He didn't want his men going door to door if he could avoid it. That would mean civilian casualties.

He then made his way to the manor itself. When he arrived, he saw a knight pulling a guard sergeant toward them with a crossbow bolt through his shoulder. The man was pale from blood loss but conscious.

When they saw William, the knight diverted his path from going to Inworth to bringing the man toward William.

"This one wants to talk, Your Highness."

"I'm listening."

The sergeant swallowed. "The commander's asking for terms. Wants to know what you want."

"The city. His surrender. His knights' surrender. Tell him if he surrenders there will be no reprisals against civilians. No looting. The militia can go home. But every guard still fighting needs to surrender immediately, or we'll hunt them down."

"And the commander?"

"He lives. Ransom rights. His knights, too."

The sergeant nodded. "I'll tell him."

"Can you walk?"

"I think so, my lord."

"Then go. Take the message."

The man limped away, one hand pressed to his wounded shoulder. William watched him disappear into the manor.

The fighting was all but done now, the initial blows having broken the guard to the extent that those who hadn't been directly in the fighting and the town militia had chosen to survive and not fight rather than fight to the last.

Finally, another messenger came out of the manor. "My lord is ready to surrender. He asks that you accept it in person at the manor."

William considered refusing, then reconsidered. The commander would want to surrender with dignity, in front of witnesses. Let him have that. It cost nothing and might make the occupation easier.

"Tell him to stack the weapons and have his men line up away from them. If I see a sword in a hand, we will wipe out everyone there."

The messenger left. William found Haverhill and gave him command of the square. "Hold everything we've taken. Start getting the dead cleared. Find buildings we can use for the wounded, both sides. And send a wyvern to Pembroke. Tell him we've secured the city and will march out by this afternoon. I want his men ready for their part of the plan by the day after tomorrow."

As Haverhill saluted and William turned to go take the commander's surrender, he considered that, as well as this had gone, this was the easy part of the plan.

The harder part was still to come.

Chapter 17

Kenna, River Mark, Sidor

The hospice's door closed behind Isolde, and she turned toward the keep. The disciples were floored when she came with the first part of the donation, although she wasn't just giving them money. She gave them one hundred sovereigns to get them through while she worked out the rest.

The men and women putting in their time here might be excellent healers and have good hearts, but she'd looked at what little they had in the way of books and saw immediately that, in addition to being woefully underfunded, they were making truly terrible deals, wasting money they did not have.

Today, she got a list of what they needed now and long-term, and planned to take the other one thousand nine hundred sovereigns she got from Galer and start making deals with merchants to get food and supplies at a better deal than the hospice was currently getting.

That would be a start, but it wasn't going to be enough. Two thousand sovereigns from Roth would help, but it wouldn't be enough.

She had just turned the corner when shouting erupted from within the keep's walls.

She froze, her head turning toward the sound. The shouting turned into screams and the sound of steel on steel, faint but still audible. Men's voices could be heard shouting.

She ran as fast as she could.

The gates stood open, unguarded. Wrong. That was wrong. There were always guards at the gates.

"Your Highness!"

Galer's hand clamped around her arm, jerking her to a halt before she'd taken more than a few steps through the gates. The guard's face was rigid, his other hand on his sword hilt.

"Let go!" Isolde wrenched against his grip. "Something's happening. The duchess ..."

"You can **not** go in there." Galer's voice held iron. "It's not safe for you."

Lusa appeared at Galer's shoulder, his sword was drawn as he looked to Galer to see what he should do.

Another scream echoed from inside. A woman's voice.

"They're killing people!" Isolde pleaded. "Duchess Alyssa is in there. If something happens to her, if she dies, it will be another nail in the rebellion's coffin. These people need her. William needs her. Other than his father, she is his last living relative and the only one who cares for him. She's the only thing really holding the River Mark barons together. If she dies, River Mark falls apart."

"Your Highness, it isn't safe ..."

"I'm not safe anywhere if we lose this war! My father wants me dead, William's father wants me dead. There isn't a kingdom in the Shattered Lands I can go to and not be hunted." She yanked her arm free. "I'm going. You can follow or stay, but I'm not leaving her."

The sound of fighting grew louder. Glass shattered somewhere above. Men shouted something she couldn't make out.

Galer exchanged a look with Lusa, then swore under his breath. "Behind us. Always behind us. You do not engage. Do you understand?"

"Yes."

"I mean it, Your Highness. You are the princess. You are ..."

"I understand! Just GO!"

They moved toward the entrance, Galer leading with his sword raised, Lusa at his flank, Isolde behind them both. Her hands felt empty, useless.

The entrance hall was empty, but blood marked the floor in dark splashes. A guard's helmet lay on its side near the base of the stairs. The fighting sounds came from above and to the left, toward the residential wing.

Galer started forward.

Two men rounded the corner at the far end of the hall.

They wore armor, good armor, but no River Mark insignia. No colors at all. Their swords were already drawn and bloodied.

"Back!" Galer shoved Isolde backward as the men charged.

The first attacker came at Galer with an overhead strike. Galer caught the blow on his blade, twisted, and drove his shoulder into the man's chest. They went down together, rolling across the blood-slicked floor.

The second man went for Lusa.

Lusa parried the initial strike, but his opponent was bigger, stronger. The man pressed forward, his blade battering against Lusa's guard. Lusa gave ground, his boots sliding on the stones.

Isolde pressed herself against the wall.

Galer rose to his feet, blood on his face. Not his blood, his opponent's. The other man stayed down, clutching at a wound in his side where Galer's blade had found the gap beneath his armor.

A third attacker appeared from the same corridor, this one younger, faster. He came at Lusa from the side.

"Lusa!" Isolde's warning came too late.

The new attacker's blade caught Lusa across the ribs. Not deep, his mail held, but the impact drove him sideways. He stumbled, his sword arm dropping and his weapon clattering to the floor.

The first man Lusa had been fighting saw his opening. His blade came up and around, aiming for Lusa's exposed neck.

Isolde moved without thinking.

She grabbed Lusa's fallen sword from where it lay and parried it up in time. The attacker's blade hit hers with a force that sent shock waves up her arms. Her wrists screamed in protest.

But the blow that would have opened Lusa's throat hit her blade instead.

The man's eyes widened. He'd expected an unarmed woman. He'd expected an easy kill.

Isolde drove forward.

She had no real technique, just lessons stolen here or there from soldiers and a few from William and Haverhill. But she had momentum and desperation. She thrust the blade forward with both hands.

The point caught the man below his breastplate, where the leather and mail gave way to cloth and flesh. The blade sank in. She felt the resistance as it pushed through muscle and organs. Felt the warmth of blood on her hands.

The man made a wet, choking sound. His sword falling from his fingers.

Isolde wrenched the blade free. The man collapsed.

"Get back!" Galer's roar barely penetrated her shock.

But she didn't get back. Couldn't. The younger attacker who'd wounded Lusa turned toward her now, and Galer was still engaged with his own opponent. If she ran, if she retreated, the man would reach her anyway. Or he would turn and cut Galer down from the side.

So she raised the sword again.

The young attacker grinned. He came at her with confidence, his blade moving in controlled arcs designed to test her defense.

She had no defense.

His first strike nearly tore the sword from her hands. The second made her stumble backward. The third …

Galer was there.

He hit the young attacker from the side, his blade finding the joint where arm met shoulder. The man screamed. His sword arm went limp, useless. Galer's follow-up strike caught him across the face, and he went down hard.

The second man Galer had been fighting lay motionless near the wall.

Silence descended, broken only by their ragged breathing.

"You did good," he said, putting a hand on her arm. "Are you injured?"

"No, and I did as you all taught me."

Galer nodded and turned to Lusa, "Can you stand?"

Lusa had pushed himself up to lean against the wall, one hand pressed to his ribs.

"Maybe. It's hard to breathe."

Footsteps on the stairs. Soren appeared from the direction of the guards' quarters where her men were billeted, his sword dripping.

He took in the scene, the bodies, Isolde with the sword, Lusa injured, and his expression hardened.

Isolde looked past him down the hallway and then to the stairs. She wanted to keep going, but she also felt responsible for the injured Lusa.

She saw the solution peeking out from behind a door.

"You," she shouted, pointing down the hall to where a lady-in-waiting cowered in a doorway. "It is clear behind us. Help this man out and to the healers."

The woman hesitated for a moment, clearly afraid. After looking the opposite way down the hallway to confirm it was clear, she moved quickly over to Lusa, putting his arm around her shoulders and bearing some of his weight.

That taken care of, she started toward the stairs. "We need to get to the Duchess, at least to check her chambers."

"Your Highness ..." Galer began.

"Don't." She turned on him. "Don't tell me to wait. Don't tell me it's too dangerous. They came here for her. I know it."

She didn't wait for his response. She ran for the stairs, taking them two at a time, the bloody sword still clutched in both hands. Behind her, she heard Galer swear and follow, Soren with him.

The residential wing was in chaos. Doors hung open. More servants huddled in doorways, faces white with terror. A lady's maid sobbed near one of the guest chambers.

Isolde pushed past them all.

A cry came from around the corner ahead. A woman's voice, high and frightened. Isolde rounded the corner and froze.

Lady Harkow was pressed against the wall, a man in armor pinning her there with his body. His hand was up her skirt, his other hand clamped over her mouth. Lady Harkow's eyes were wide with terror above his dirty fingers.

The man didn't hear Isolde approach, or perhaps he heard and didn't care, too focused on his prey.

Isolde didn't hesitate. Didn't think. Didn't consider.

She drove the sword into his back.

The blade punched through mail and flesh, sliding between ribs. The man arched, his body going rigid. A wet gasp escaped his throat. His hands fell away from Lady Harkow.

Isolde pulled the blade free. The man collapsed at her feet, blood spreading across the floor.

Lady Harkow stared at her, chest heaving, skirts still bunched in her hands.

"Go. To the entrance. The guards are holding there. Go now."

Lady Harkow opened her mouth. Closed it. Then gathered her skirts and ran, stumbling in her haste.

Galer and Soren caught up as Isolde started toward Alyssa's chambers.

"Your Highness." Galer's voice was strained. "Please. Let us check first."

"No time."

She pushed through the door to Alyssa's receiving room.

Two bodies lay on the floor. River Mark guards, their throats cut. A third body slumped against the wall—one of the attackers, his face frozen in death.

The door to Alyssa's bedchamber stood open.

Isolde crossed the receiving room, stepping over the bodies, and entered the bedroom.

More blood. More bodies. A River Mark guard dead near the bed. Another attacker sprawled across the threshold. But no Alyssa. The bed was unmade, sheets trailing to the floor. The wardrobe stood open, Alyssa's dresses hanging undisturbed.

The window was open.

Isolde ran to it and looked out.

Ropes. Three thick ropes, secured to the window frame, dangled down the keep's outer wall to the ground below. She looked out, across the garden behind the keep toward the nearby Von River.

She saw six men hurrying toward the river. One in the center wore a knight's surcoat over his plate that she recognized. Sir Alistair Everwood. She'd seen him at William's side in Lynese, had dined with him, had heard him called Aldric's most trusted knight.

He carried Duchess Alyssa in his arms. She wasn't moving.

"No!" The word tore from Isolde's throat. "Stop! Guards! To the river!"

The men below didn't slow. They ran for the docks where a small boat waited, already pulling away from its moorings. River

Mark guards engaged them, but there were only three against five unburdened men.

Isolde turned from the window and ran for the door.

Galer caught her arm. "You can't ..."

"Let go!" She tried to wrench free, but his grip held firm.

"Look!" He dragged her back to the window, forced her to see what she'd missed in her panic.

The boat was already in the water. The men had reached it, were climbing aboard even as the River Mark guards tried to stop them. One guard fell to a sword thrust. Another went down under a mailed fist. The remaining guard pulled back, outmatched.

Alistair handed Alyssa's limp form up to someone already in the boat. Then he climbed in himself. The boat pulled away from the dock, oars dipping into the Von River's current.

"We have to go after them!" Isolde turned to Galer. "We need boats. We need ..."

"Your Highness." Galer's voice was gentle but firm. "Look at their lead. Look at the river."

She looked.

The boat was already thirty yards from the dock and moving fast. The oarsmen knew their work, pulling in a synchronized rhythm. The Von's current was with them, carrying them downstream toward where the river widened and deepened.

"By the time we organize a pursuit, they'll be well on their way to Albion Bay, where I guarantee they have a larger ship waiting."

"I don't care!" Isolde's voice was wild with panic. "We have to try! She's ... without her, William can't ..."

She stopped, breathing hard, staring at the boat as it grew smaller with distance.

She drew herself up, getting herself back under control, calming herself enough to think instead of react.

"We need to find the captain of the guard. Now!"

Heartland Plains

William saw the Royal forces spread across the plain like a dark stain. He knew what he'd been walking into as he marched out of Silverhall the day after he'd taken it, abandoning the city after killing all its wyverns to keep the Crown forces from learning what was happening too soon.

He'd immediately swung east onto the Heartland Plains, the fertile open farmland that lay between Twin Lakes and the forests far to the south. He knew the army from Omskirk was out here, trying to keep him from coming out of the Blackheath forest, not realizing that he had already done so.

Or at least some of his men, anyway.

Not that they could miss almost fifteen hundred infantry marching toward them out of the west. They may be poorly led, but even this commander was smart enough to have scouts out.

So they were ready for him, deployed in a wide, thin line that stretched north to south, trying to use numbers to overwhelm through sheer frontage.

It was a good plan for someone who didn't take the effort to count the number of men facing him.

"He's taken the bait," Commander Haverhill said from beside him.

William nodded. His thirteen hundred and fifty heavy infantry stood in a formation eight men deep, shields locked together. The crossbowmen crouched in the gaps between companies, already loading their bolts. They looked like a fist compared to the enemy's open hand.

"Keep the reserves close," William said. "When men fall back exhausted, fresh troops push into the gaps."

"Aye, Your Highness."

The Royal archers came first, three hundred of them jogging forward in a loose screen. They stopped at two hundred yards and loosed. Arrows arced overhead. Most clattered off shields. A man three ranks behind William took a shaft through his thigh and went down screaming. Another dropped without a sound, an arrow through his eye.

William's crossbowmen replied. The quarrels flew flat and fast, punching through the archers' leather jerkins, aimed well, dropping dozens of archers. The survivors scattered back toward their own lines.

"Here they come," someone muttered.

The conscripts advanced in ragged blocks, four thousand farm boys and shopkeepers pressed into service. They had swords, spears, and axes, but most wore only padded cloth for armor or nothing at all. Behind them came the Royal heavy infantry, six hundred men in mail with proper shields and swords. William could see the enemy knights in the rear, a small knot of mounted men near the command banners.

"Steady," William called. "Let them come to us."

The ground shook. The conscripts broke into a run the last fifty yards, screaming to drive out their fear. They hit the shield wall like a wave against stone. Spears and swords jabbed forward. The first conscript to reach William's position took a spear through his stomach and folded over it. The man behind him tried to jump the body and caught two spears in his chest. A third conscript swung a sword at the shield wall. The blade clanged off iron and the man's arm went numb. A sword took him in the throat before he could recover.

William held the Whitton Sword in his right hand, holding his place in the wall. His commanders had argued hard for him to be back with the rest of the command group, but everything depended on his men holding this line and not folding to what would feel like overwhelming odds. If they broke, this entire battle would fail, and his army, both halves, would be destroyed.

A conscript with an axe broke through the shields to his left, swinging wildly. William stepped forward and cut with his sword. The blade passed through the axe handle, through the man's collarbone, through his ribs. Blood sprayed hot across William's face. The conscript dropped.

Another came at him from the right, thrusting a spear. William caught it on his shield and pushed it wide, then brought Marrow's Bane around in a horizontal cut that took the man's head off his shoulders. The body stood for a moment, blood fountaining from the neck, before collapsing.

The conscripts kept coming. They had to; the ones behind pushed the ones in front, and the ones in front had nowhere to go but into the Sidorian steel.

The fighting became chaos as bodies piled up at the base of the shield wall, making the ground slick. A conscript tried to climb over the dead to reach William. He made it halfway before a spear caught him in the armpit and he tumbled back down. Another conscript slipped in blood and went to his knees. Three spears found him before he could rise.

A Royal man-at-arms in mail pushed through the conscripts, sword raised. He knew what he was doing; he kept his shield up, moved with purpose. William caught his first strike on his own shield, felt the impact jar his arm to the shoulder. The man-at-arms pulled back and thrust low, trying for William's legs. William dropped his shield to block it, and the man reversed his grip and swung high. William ducked. The blade passed over his head close enough to feel the wind of it. He came up inside the man's guard and drove Marrow's Bane through the mail shirt, through the gambeson underneath, through flesh and organs. The man-at-arms coughed blood and collapsed.

More Royal heavy infantry carved through the conscripts to reach William's line. That's when the real killing started. These men had armor and training. They formed a wedge, shields overlapping, swords and axes striking in coordinated rhythm. The shield wall contracted as men fell, but others pushed forward from behind to fill the gaps. A Sidorian soldier to William's right took an axe to the shoulder that split his collarbone. He dropped. Another man shoved past William to take his place.

The enemy heavy infantry formed a tighter wedge, trying to drive into the center where William fought, which meant that someone on the other side had realized he was fighting on the front lines and had gotten smart. That explained why the heavy infantry was trying to push through now, going so far as to trample conscripts and weaken the center of their line to get to him. They decided if they could kill the commander, his army would break. William set his feet and waited. Conscripts still swarmed around the edges, dying in dozens, but the real threat was the wedge. Fifty Royal men-at-arms, maybe sixty, all focused on one point.

They hit like a hammer.

The first man reached William with a longsword, blade raised for an overhead strike. William stepped into the blow instead of away from it. Got inside the man's reach. Marrow's Bane came up and across, cutting through the man's wrists. Both hands, still gripping the sword, fell to the ground. The man stared at the stumps. William kicked him backward into the next man.

The wedge pushed forward, hitting his line hard. A man William didn't know took a sword through his gut and was replaced by another man pushing into the spot, but they were being pushed back hard by the better-armed and experienced heavy infantry.

The fighting had already lasted for almost thirty minutes straight, which was an eternity to be engaged in heavy combat. William's arms ached and his lungs burned. All he could do was focus on the man in front of him. Block. Strike. Step.

Someone to his left went down. William couldn't see who. Couldn't spare the attention. A conscript came at him swinging a woodcutter's axe. William stepped inside the swing and took off the man's head. Then a Royal man-at-arms thrust at his face, but William deflected it with his shield and hooked Marrow's Bane through the man's knee. As his leg gave out and he fell, William stabbed him through the back of the neck.

Time became meaningless. William's world was three feet in every direction. They fought hard, but the enemy kept coming. An endless wave of men to be killed.

A roar erupted from the east.

William couldn't see what was happening, but he heard it. Screaming, not the battle screams of men fighting, but the terror screams of men dying without warning. The enemy formation shuddered. Men in the rear ranks started turning, trying to look behind them, but the press was too tight. They were packed shoulder to shoulder, a thousand pounds of flesh and steel with nowhere to go.

William knew what it meant, however. Pembroke had arrived.

"Push them!" William shouted. "Forward!"

The noise from the east grew louder. Pembroke's heavy infantry was driving through the Royal rear like a spear. William heard officers shouting commands, heard the screams of men being slaughtered without warning, heard the crash of formations breaking. The enemy had been watching west, focused on William's force. They'd never seen Pembroke coming, and Pembroke came with almost every mounted knight of their army.

Through gaps in the press, William caught glimpses of Pembroke's knights sweeping around the northern edge, slashing through the enemy formation and coming back out, just to do it again, taking chunks of soldiers out of the line each time.

They were defending on two sides, and no army could do that.

The enemy commander's banners went down. William saw it happen through the thinning press, saw the pole topple, saw the surge of Pembroke's troops where the command post had been. Without the banners, without orders, the last shred of enemy cohesion evaporated.

Bodies covered the ground. Conscripts mostly, piled three deep in places, scattered among them was the gray and blue of Sidorian dead. It was deepest along the line William had been holding. A wall of bodies marking where the fighting had been. The air stank of blood, shit, and fear.

The fighting slowed, then stopped. The Royal heavy infantry were dead or dying, surrounded and cut down. The conscripts weren't fighting anymore. Thousands of them just stood there, hands empty or raised, waiting. Some wept. Some prayed. The ones who tried to run got cut down or trampled.

"Hold!" William shouted. "Hold positions!"

His voice was raw. His throat burned. His soldiers heard him anyway, or enough of them did. Here and there, fights still raged where isolated Royal men-at-arms refused to surrender, but those ended quickly. One man couldn't stand against twenty.

William lowered his sword. He was tired. His arms shook. His legs barely held him up. Blood dripped from his shield onto his boots. Not his blood, or not much of it. The scrape along his ribs burned now, but it felt shallow. He'd been lucky.

Pembroke appeared through the crowd on foot, his armor splattered red, his sword still in his hand.

"Your Highness."

"My lord," William said. His voice came out hoarse. "Well struck."

"They never knew we were there until we struck." Pembroke looked around at the carnage. "A lot of prisoners, maybe a thousand or fifteen hundred, mostly conscripts. We'll need to count the dead."

William nodded. His vision swam. He locked his knees to keep from falling. "How many did we lose?"

"Sixty on my side. Yours?"

"I have no idea." It would take time to count the dead. Time they didn't have.

From a first glance, however, his part of the army seemed mostly intact. If Pembroke only lost sixty, then the victory had been massive.

"What now?" Pembroke asked.

William looked west. The sun was past its peak, sliding toward evening. They'd been fighting for hours. It felt like minutes and years at the same time.

"We need to move fast. I want to be to the Stonehills before the capital hears about this loss. They have fifteen thousand at Penvale, and if they catch us in the open, we will be crushed."

Pembroke nodded. "I'll spread the word."

William walked through the aftermath. Wounded men cried for water, for their mothers, for gods who didn't answer. The dead stared at the sky. Sidorian soldiers stripped corpses of weapons and armor, cut purses from belts, pulled rings from fingers. William didn't stop them. They'd earned it.

Haverhill found him near what used to be the enemy center. "Captains are asking what to do with the prisoners."

"Collect all of their weapons and send the conscripts and lowborn soldiers home. Bind any nobles and bring them with us for ransom."

"They might rejoin Edmund's forces. The soldiers at least."

"There aren't many of those left. They lost most in that wedge trying to break my line. Go, get it started. I want us at the march in the next hour. Get our wounded up on wagons. Send those too injured to the Disciple camp back in the forest under minimal men. All the walking wounded come with us."

Corbin left. William kept walking. He was tired. Too much fighting, too many kills. He should have fallen back at some point, let fresh men hold the line. But officers were supposed to lead from the front. That's what Aldric had taught him.

William found a wagon and lowered himself under it, pulling his tabard up from the back and over the top of his head to block the sun, and closed his eyes.

Some time later, someone kicked his foot.

"Hey. Get up. We're marching. Stop lollygagging."

It took a second for William to get his wits about him, enough time for the man to kick his foot and repeat what he'd said. William sighed and pushed himself up, letting the tabard fall back.

"Your Highness," the now completely mortified guard said, taking an instinctive step back. "I'm so sorry. I had no ..."

"Don't apologize, Sergeant. You were doing your job and doing it well. How are we looking?"

"The men are mostly formed up and ready to march, Your Highness."

William looked up at the sky again, doing a rough estimate. He'd slept maybe an hour.

"Good. Very good. Let's get going, shall we?"

Chapter 18

Kenna, River Mark, Sidor

The small council chambers of Kenna Keep still smelled of smoke and blood. Isolde stood at the head of the long oak table, her dress still marked with dark stains from the morning's violence. It had taken hours to get things under control after the attackers had fled.

Hours they didn't have.

As soon as they'd gone to alert the guards, they had realized that the attackers had not just killed everyone they found in the keep, from guards to servants, but they had set a series of fires, probably to further distract from their escape.

And it had worked. The first boat didn't get on the water to chase them for almost forty minutes, and it was a small river boat that wouldn't make it to the sea, which was the most likely destination, since it seemed impossible for Alistair and his men to make it overland unnoticed.

They'd also sent riders to try and intercept them, but the land favored the water route, forcing the riders to take a circuitous enough path that they were unlikely to reach the kidnappers either.

Which meant if they were going to catch Alistair and rescue the duchess, it was going to happen at sea.

That was more than the local guard force could handle, so she'd called in all the highest-ranking nobles she could find, who had now gathered here, in the council chambers, to discuss what was going to happen. Around the table were four barons and seven knights who'd remained in the duchy and were near enough to the capital to get to her summons in time.

These were all the men she could get who controlled enough armed forces to do something about this.

Baron Egerton spoke first. "Your Highness, I heard from Lady Harkow how you killed the guard and saved her. That was very brave."

"Not just one," corrected Sir Malvin from down the table. "I talked to some of the injured guards, who said you slew at least one other. These men served under a knight of the kingdom and were well-trained. An impressive feat."

"I did what anyone would have done," she said, cutting off any more praise. They didn't have time for this. "What matters now is that Duchess Alyssa has been taken and is, at this moment, heading downriver toward Albion Bay where they clearly have a ship waiting to take them out to sea and back to Starhaven, most likely. We need to pursue them immediately."

The nobles exchanged glances. Baron Calthorpe cleared his throat. "Your Highness, we're grateful for your actions today. You fought when others might have fled. But pursuing the duchess ..."

"Is our duty," Isolde finished. She planted both hands on the table. "Alyssa is your duchess, your liege lady. She was kidnapped from her own keep and people who served this community slain. We cannot let them get away with that."

"The princess is right," Baron Egerton said. "The Duchess must be recovered."

Baron Norcross crossed his arms and said, "And how do you propose we do that, Your Highness? Most of our fighting men are with Prince William in Kingsheart. I have perhaps fifty fighting men in my barony and only ten or so with me right now."

"We don't need many men. They only have the five that escaped plus whoever's waiting on their ship, but I don't think it will be a lot. This was a fast raid, not a landing. We just need to get to them with one or two dozen trained men, and we can take them," Isolde said. "But we cannot delay. Alistair has hours on us, but we could ride for the port on the bay and maybe beat him, as the mouth of the Von is not a completely straight line. If we move quickly, we can catch them before they get through the Iron Straits and into open water."

Sir Tormal shook his head. "Your Highness, with respect, we don't have the men here in the city. Most of our men are back in our holdfasts."

"We don't need many." Isolde's voice rose. "Whatever ship we commandeer will have a crew, and there are at least ten lords in this city with guards. If we pool enough together, we will have the men we need to take their ship and rescue her."

"Your Highness, what if this is exactly what Edmund wants?" Baron Calthorpe asked. "What if this attack was designed to draw us out and pull enough of our men out to sea while he tries to come in and retake the land? If they came down Kingsheart Bay in the northwest, they could be in the heart of the duchy before the men we have at the Eastbridge can respond. And if they do, that would open us up to invasion from that direction. Your husband has pulled north, allowing the Crown forces back into Ambleton and Dunwic's Reach. We need every man we have ready to counter an assault."

"I'm only asking for a dozen men and a ship," Isolde countered. "I'm not asking for you to pull men from your holdings. Depths, we don't even have time for that. We have to go with those we have here in town or those between us and the port on Albion Bay."

"Your Highness," Baron Calthorpe said. "I just don't see how we can do that and still protect our people."

"But she's your duchess!" Isolde said in complete disgust that she would even have to have this conversation.

"Is she?" Baron Norcross asked.

"What?"

"Is the Duchess still our liege lady?" Norcross asked again. "Duke Aldric is dead, and Prince William is the heir to the throne of the kingdom, but he is not in direct line for succession of the duchy. His father is. Even if we accepted him as the heir to Aldric's seat, which has little precedence, he has bigger things on his mind and still, his aunt would not be our duchess. Some of us aren't certain who we owe fealty to anymore."

"I can't believe what I'm hearing."

"We question nothing about Duke Aldric's memory," Baron Calthorpe said. "But the Duke is dead. These are questions that must be asked, Your Highness."

"Now? You have to know this now, when she was kidnapped this morning?" Isolde's voice cracked. "You didn't question this yesterday, or the day before. Why now? Surely whatever legal questions you have about succession can wait until after we rescue her from Edmund's clutches."

"Can they?" Sir Norcross stood. "Your Highness, I'm sorry, but we can't get past this point. If we commit to this pursuit and leave our lands defenseless, and Edmund attacks, we lose everything. Every baron at this table is responsible for thousands of souls. We cannot abandon them on a rescue mission that may be a trap."

"So you abandon Alyssa instead?"

"We make impossible choices." Baron Calthorpe said. "That's what it is to rule. You of all people should know that."

"Your Highness, if circumstances were different ..." Sir Malvin said, holding up his hands.

"But they're not." Isolde cut him off. She was done listening to excuses. "The circumstances are that your duchess was kidnapped this morning, that the 'king' violated every law and custom to do so, and that a good woman needs help. Those are the circumstances. Everything else is just fear dressed as wisdom. When William returns, when he asks what happened to his aunt, I'll tell him the truth. That the nobles of River Mark chose safety over honor, clutching their skirts instead of what their position and honor demanded of them."

"That's not fair," Baron Calthorpe protested.

"Isn't it?" Isolde looked back. "You speak of responsibilities and risks, but Alyssa had the same responsibilities. Every time Aldric rebelled, every time she supported William, she risked everything. She pulled enough of you together to stop the king's army from marching into this land just last fall. There are risks worth taking. If you don't understand that, then you've learned nothing from this war."

She opened the door and left them all behind her, sitting in their shame. Worthless, the lot of them. They sat in safety and spoke of risks and legal precedents while Alyssa was being carried away by that assassin.

"Your Royal Highness!"

She paused and looked behind her. Baron Egerton hurried after her, although it was hard for a man of his age and size to hurry. He caught up as she reached the top of the stairs, one hand pressed against the stone wall, breathing hard.

"Please, I must apologize for my fellows."

"Apologize?" Isolde turned on him. "For cowards? They were never going to listen, were they?"

"No." Egerton shook his head. "They're too scared of losing their positions, now more than ever. They support William and Pembroke, but these are not men who put their lives on the line. Even the knights ... they earned their honor through favors, not fighting."

"And you? Were you too afraid? Is that why you're still here?"

"That's a fair question, Your Highness. In my heart, I wanted to, and I would have if I were a younger man, but I'm too old to be charging off into battle. I would have only slowed them down; gotten better men killed trying to protect me. But I sent nearly every man I have with your husband. Three hundred soldiers from my lands, led by my son, left to fight for your husband. In all of River Mark, I have only ten men left, and four of those are back at my estate guarding my daughter-in-law, who is managing things while I am here."

That was no small commitment. Isolde's anger faltered.

"The other six are here with me," Egerton continued. "It's not enough, I know. But they're yours if you'll have them."

Six men wouldn't make a difference. With Galer and Soren, that made eight. Not enough by far.

"First, I have to find a ship."

"I assume that's where you're going now?"

"Yes." She started down the stairs. "Though it's a long shot."

"I have faith in you, Your Highness." Egerton's voice followed her. "I'll go to the nobles' quarter now and call my men in. I'll have them armed and ready."

She stopped and turned back. "Thank you, Baron. And I'm sorry for what I said."

"You have nothing to apologize for. I understand your anger. Now hurry."

Isolde descended the rest of the stairs and crossed through the keep's lower halls. Guards stood at their posts, most still looking shaken by the sudden violence. Servants moved around them, cleaning blood from the stone floors.

Isolde went away from the keep and back to the merchants' quarter, still not having changed out of her blood-covered clothes, now dried and stiff. People stared and whispers followed her. She ignored them all.

She returned to Roth Shipping where she had made a deal just a week ago, when all she had to worry about was her home and injured men.

The clerk behind the desk looked up, and his face went pale.

"I need to see Master Roth."

"He's ... Your Highness, are you ..."

"Now."

The clerk scrambled from his seat and disappeared through the back door. Isolde stood in the small front room, her hands clenched at her sides. Blood crusted under her fingernails. She'd washed her hands after the attack, but some had remained in the creases of her skin.

The door opened. Cornelis Roth emerged, took one look at her, and stopped.

"Your Highness." His voice carried genuine shock. "Are you okay? Are you injured? I heard there was an attack at the keep."

"Yes."

"But your dress ..."

"The Duchess was taken."

Roth's expression shifted. "Oh no. Your Highness, I'm so sorry."

"I need your help."

He gestured toward his office. "Of course. Please, come in."

She followed him into the small room. He closed the door, moved to his desk but didn't sit.

"I'm so sorry to hear about Her Grace, but I'm not sure what I can help with ..."

"The nobles still in the duchy have decided it's too risky to go after her abductors." Isolde couldn't keep the anger from her voice.

207

"They'll wait to see what happens. They'll do nothing while she is taken, probably to Starhaven to be used as a bargaining chip."

Roth stared at her. "They won't go after her?"

"No. That's why I'm here."

"I don't know what I can do, Your Highness."

"I need a ship." She moved closer to his desk. "And any guards you can muster. I don't need many. I only have eight men at my disposal, so I will need a few more. But mostly, I need a ship."

Roth's face went through several expressions. Surprise. Calculation. Something that might have been concern.

"Of course I can supply you with a ship," he said. "That's simple enough. But guards ... Your Highness, I don't have much in the way of fighting men. A handful at most. My business doesn't require ..." He trailed off. "You said you had eight men?"

"Yes, two of my own guards and six from Baron Egerton."

"That isn't very many. Pursuing men who were able to assault the keep and escape with the Duchess with eight men is ..."

"Suicide? Maybe. But I won't sit in Kenna while Alyssa is taken, ancestors know where. I won't do nothing."

"No, I can see you won't. Of course I will help. I have four men who work security for my warehouses. Former soldiers, mostly. They're a bit long in the tooth, but they are experienced and still very capable, and they're yours."

"Twelve men." It wasn't enough. It would never be enough. But it was what she had. "I'll take the ship and go with what I have."

Behind her, the office door opened.

"Your Highness?"

Isolde turned. Lady Harkow stood in the doorway, her face still bruised from the attack. Unlike Isolde, at least, she had changed her clothing into a simple, but untorn, dress.

"I have some men." Lady Harkow stepped into the office. "I heard what you said to Baron Egerton and followed you here. I assume that is what you are doing, getting more men? I don't have many, but I told my husband we must help and forced him to agree. I have ten guards you can have. I apologize for the small number."

"You ... you want to help?" Isolde asked, surprised.

Lady Harkow had made it very clear when she had first come to Kenna that Isolde was not welcome here. Now she was offering up what was probably every guard in her family's service.

"You saved my life, Your Highness. I will be forever indebted to you. If you can save the Duchess, then I want to help. I owe you that much."

Twenty-two men. Not enough to storm a fortress or fight a large force, but enough, perhaps, to intercept and board a ship.

Isolde turned back to Roth. "That should be enough."

Roth nodded. "I'll prepare the ship immediately. The *Wayfarer*. She's fast, one of my best. Where did they take her?"

"Down the Von River. Sir Everwood, the fiend that took her, had a boat waiting. They were heading east when I last saw them."

"The Von feeds into the Albion," Roth said, already moving toward his maps. "From there, they could go east, down the Iron Straits and out to the sea. I know the Crown has ties to raiders in Alchmara, but there are many Iron Keep boats patrolling there lately, thanks to all the attacks, so he will probably head south, try to avoid them and take the long way round, back to Starhaven."

"If we leave now and push hard, we might catch them before they make it out of the straits. From there, if we guess wrong, we will have lost her. But Your Highness, even if we catch them, Sir Everwood is a skilled knight. He'll have guards with him."

"Which is why I needed men." She met his eyes. "Are you coming?"

"Me?" Roth seemed genuinely surprised. "Your Highness, I'm a merchant, not a soldier. I wouldn't be much help in a fight."

"You know ships, you know these waters, and you know your men."

"I have men who can ..."

"I need someone I can trust." Isolde didn't move. "Someone who has as much to lose as I do if this fails. You've tied your fortune to mine, Master Roth. If Edmund wins and William falls, our deal will mean little for you and the money you loaned me will be in jeopardy."

She let the words hang.

Roth's jaw worked. He looked at his office, at the ledgers stacked on his desk, then back at her.

"You're very persuasive, Your Highness."

"Is that a yes?"

"It's a statement of fact. Yes. I'll go. I'll need to speak with my first mate, get a crew together. Good men who can handle trouble."

"How long?"

"An hour. Maybe less."

"Make it less."

"Your Highness," He stopped. "If we do catch them, what's your plan?"

"We get Alyssa back and kill every man that took part in the raid."

Roth blanched slightly at the expression on her face, but only nodded. "I'll gather the crew. The *Wayfarer* is at the third dock from the bridge."

"We'll meet you there."

Lady Harkow spoke up. "I'll go and get my men now. They'll be at the dock within the hour.""Thank you, both of you." Isolde looked between them. "Now, we need to hurry."

Chapter 19

Heartland Plains, West of the Twin Lakes, Kingsheart

The wounded had slowed them.

William knew it before the first hour passed. Men with slashed arms and cracked ribs couldn't march at the pace he needed. The surgeons worked stitching gashes and binding broken bones in the wagons while the army pressed west across the plains.

"Can't keep this up," Pembroke said. "The men fought hard. They need rest."

"They'll rest in the Stonehills. My father's army on the Tradesway is already on the move northwest, trying to intercept us."

"How many?"

"Enough to crush us if they catch us here."

The plains stretched out around them, flat and open. No trees. No rivers deep enough to matter. Nothing but grass and the occasional village. The Stonehills were still three days west if they marched hard, two if they abandoned the wounded. William wasn't going to abandon anyone.

"The flanking scouts have reported riders following us. Sure as death, it's Crown scouts shadowing us, keeping track of where we're going so they can get the angle on us."

"How far?"

"Close enough to watch us, but they're maintaining enough distance to keep from getting swept up."

Pembroke nodded, understanding what that meant. There was only so far ahead scouts could ride before they were of no use to the army they were the eyes for, which meant the actual army was not far behind. Maybe a day, if they were lucky, and if they could cut the angle, they could shorten that.

For them to get this close, they had to have started out almost as soon as the Battle of the Plains concluded, maybe even before.

Probably before.

There was no kind of organized resistance, and it was a day's ride to Omskirk from where the fight had happened, so the knowledge hadn't come from the retreating men.

More likely, they'd either missed a wyvern in Silverhall or one of the river traders had landed at the city and sent their own wyverns back to Starhaven.

He had to give credit to whoever was in charge of that army. They certainly hadn't dithered or delayed.

They hadn't seen the enemy army yet, but it would be at least five thousand men, and probably closer to ten. While it was still possible for him to double back and come down the Tradesway, which is where his father seemed certain the attack would come, he'd held those fifteen thousand men in place, but with Garris off in the far northeast and William and Pembroke now cutting to the north side of the capital, he'd have reevaluated.

If William had to guess, Edmund would have required a third to hold just in case there was a trick he couldn't see, but this move was enough for him to send the other two-thirds after William.

And ten thousand versus four was not a battle William could win. Not on open ground like this.

"I've doubled the scouts, and they have orders to take out any of the enemy scouts they can, but I don't think we'll have that chance. They know that's what we're going to do."

"We could turn and fight," Pembroke offered.

"We'd lose."

"Not if we chose the ground."

"What ground?" William gestured at the plains. "It's all the same. Flat grass for miles. They'd flank us, surround us, and grind us down. We need the hills. Something to maneuver around."

The baron fell silent. William knew what he was thinking. The hills were three days away, and the Crown army moved faster than wounded men could march. Every hour that passed brought Edmund's soldiers closer.

He was saved from further thought as a messenger came riding toward him, leather wyvern tube in his hands.

"Message from Baron Sinclair, Highness," the man said, handing it over.

Sure enough, the tube had the Sinclair seal, which William broke, pulling the small script from inside.

Victory at Brennan's Fork. Crown force routed. Marching for Grimshold. — Sinclair

Short and blunt, just like the man who wrote it. William folded the message and tucked it into his belt. Well, at least that was something. He would have preferred to have Sinclair's men with him to help even the odds, but at least he was winning.

"What news?" Pembroke asked.

"Sinclair took Brennan's Fork."

"That's good."

"It's a waste. Cadogan was already committed to going south along the bay, so he wasn't going to be able to intervene here against us one way or another. Yes, it would hurt those barons whose holdings got ravaged by his forces, and people would die, but we'd have two thousand more people to make this work. Considering how outnumbered we already are, every man would count. And would give us more options when we finally do have to face them."

Pembroke just nodded. He knew all of that before William said anything, but he also knew that sometimes the need to do something overrode what was the smart thing to do.

So they did the only thing they could do. They marched.

Through the afternoon and into the evening, he pushed his men hard, causing the line to spread out over almost two miles, which was not ideal. Even then, many of the walking wounded collapsed and had to be helped along by their comrades.

But they covered twelve miles by the time the sun set. It still wasn't enough. William called a halt when the light faded, and the men collapsed where they stood. No tents. No fires. Just exhausted soldiers lying in the grass. The small support group pulling up the rear did the best they could to provide food for the men, but most had to make do with the dry, hard bread and a little dried meat they carried on them.

Once they were in the hills, he could slow down and feed them properly.

William hunted down Pembroke near the center of the formation. The baron sat on the ground, his armor removed, his hands wrapped around a waterskin.

"We need to move faster," William said.

"We're moving as fast as we can."

"It's not fast enough."

Pembroke drank and then passed the skin to William. "You want to push them harder, we're going to have to leave the wounded behind."

"I want to avoid that, if I can."

"I'm not sure you can. It's actually the walking wounded that are slowing us down the most. The more serious are in wagons, and so keep going at the pace of the army. But it's doing them no good. If we left them behind, let the acolytes set up a temporary aid station in a village, we could load the walking wounded who might recover before this is over into the wagons and keep going. The rest of the men won't be slowed then."

William just nodded, but he wasn't agreeing. He was thinking. Pembroke was right, of course, but he didn't trust the men his father put in charge not to come across their aid station and slaughter all of the men in the camp.

In days past, and even in the war with Lynese, he could be sure that being under the protection of the Acolytes would be enough to protect them, but these were not normal times.

His father had killed Serwyn and Aldric. A man who could murder his family like that could do anything.

And yet.

"Is there any other choice?"

"Leave the walking wounded; they're the ones who are slowing the army down, but that's not what I'd pick."

"Yeah," William said. "Fine. Send some scouts ahead and see what they can find, a village or something, and get with the

Disciples of Healing and see if they'd be good with us leaving them behind with some supplies. I'd hope Baron Stroud, when he realizes they are here, would at least let the disciples get supplies from their order hospital in Silverhall."

"He might," Pembroke said, sounding like he thought that was as unlikely as William did.

"Yeah. See if the disciples can go ahead tonight and set up. I'd be willing to give up an hour this morning to transfer off the seriously injured and load up the walking wounded on the wagons, but that's all. After that, we need to get the men moving again."

"I'll see what I can do," Pembroke said. "I'm sorry it came to this."

"Me too," William said.

Not that he had a choice. He didn't want to send men to their deaths, but if he delayed and tried to protect everyone, his men would be caught in the open, and he'd be sending a lot more with them.

The burdens of command, as his Uncle Aldric had said.

Iron Straights

The *Wayfarer* cut through the gray water, its bow rising and falling with each swell as they neared where the Iron Straits poured into the Eastern Sea. Isolde stood near the starboard rail, one hand wrapped around a stay line for balance, her eyes fixed on the eastern horizon where sea met sky in an indistinct blur. Two days. Two days since they'd left Kenna, and still no sign of the ship carrying Alyssa.

The wind pulled at her cloak and tugged strands of hair loose from the practical braid she'd adopted, and she had to keep wiping salt mist from her face.

She'd ignored it the same way she ignored the hollow ache in her stomach from the constant moving of the ship.

"Princess," Roth said, coming up beside her, close enough that she could hear him over the wind but not so close as to crowd her. "We need to talk about what happens when we reach the Eastern Sea."

"We keep chasing them, if we haven't caught them by then," she said, although her tone made it clear she was losing faith that such a thing was possible.

"We've closed the distance."

"Have we?"

Roth's face showed the strain of two days at sea, lines deeper around his eyes and mouth, his jaw shadowed with stubble he hadn't bothered to shave. But his expression remained calm, certain in a way that made her want to believe him.

"We've seen nothing," she continued. "Not since yesterday morning when one of your men thought he spotted a sail."

"He spotted them. A single-masted vessel, square-rigged, matching the description we had from the harbormaster at Kenna."

"A description that could fit a dozen ships."

"In these waters? At this time of year?" Roth shook his head. "The Straits aren't crowded this early in spring. Most merchant captains wait until after the spring storms pass before venturing into the Eastern Sea."

"Then why can't we see them? Why haven't we caught them?"

"Because it's clear whoever is captaining that ship knows these waters. He's running with full sail, taking risks with the current that I won't match because I don't want to crack our mast or lose a man overboard. But he can't maintain that pace forever. The wind's shifting. By afternoon, it'll be coming more from the north, and that favors us. By afternoon, we could be out of the Straits entirely. This morning, an hour before dawn, my lookout spotted them again. They were perhaps five miles ahead, maybe six. Close enough to see their sail against the sky."

Isolde's breath caught. "Why didn't you tell me?"

"Because you were below, and because there was nothing for you to do about it. You needed the sleep. We're gaining. When we first left Kenna, they were almost four hours ahead. Now it's less than two. Maybe less than one, depending on how hard they push. We're faster, Princess. That's a fact. And unless Everwood's captain works some miracle, we'll have them in another day or two."

The words should have brought relief, but they didn't.

"And then what? When we reach the end of the Straits? We don't have them in sight, so what if they turn north and we turn south?"

"Then we would lose them, which is why I just sent a wyvern to Salt Tower. I know some of the men there; I've done some trading with them. They'll keep an eye out and tell me which direction their ship turns."

A sailor called out something from the rigging above them. Roth glanced up, nodded, then returned his attention to Isolde.

"Can't they sail faster once they're out of the Straits?"

"They can go under fuller sail, yes. Most of the wind blows south/southeast, which is one of the reasons people prefer to take the path around Thay and across the Great Expanse rather than going up past Alchmara and around the Frozen Sea. But that's not why I think he'll go south."

"Because of raiders?"

She was well aware of the Alchmara raiders. Her father had always had good relations with the family that ruled the island nation, which had always been isolated by Sidor's sphere of influence, something they wanted badly to get out from under.

Which her father had used to great effect many times, and ultimately had led to the Sidorian invasion of Lynese.

"Raiders are a problem in both directions. Thay has as many raiders as Alchmara, and both ours and Everwood's ships are exactly what the raiders look for, but no, that's not why I think he'll turn south."

That wasn't exactly encouraging, but Isolde asked, "Then why?"

"Because he has to sail past Iron Keep if he goes north, and they have a lot of ships in the water. No one in Inos or Thay cares about a single Sidorian ship, aside from the raiders, but if he turns north, it would be easy for you to send a wyvern to the coastal barons along Iron Keep and have them put out ships to interdict Everwood. He knows that and won't risk it."

The logic made sense. "So he'll turn south."

The wind gusted harder, making the ship heel slightly to port. A sailor shouted something, and others moved to adjust the rigging. Isolde watched them work while she thought through what Roth had said.

"When will we know?" She asked. "When will the message from Salt Tower arrive?"

"Soon, I hope. By this evening, probably. It depends on how close he wants to take the cut south and if he goes around Widow's Island or between it and the Gloom Peaks. If he wants speed, he'll go between them, but that's bad sailing. A lot of reefs and sandbars. We will have to go around; I don't trust sailing through there."

"But if he goes between them and doesn't hit anything, he'll be able to pick up time on us. I can't allow that."

"I understand your frustration, but we can't chance it. He'd have to be very lucky to go that way and get through without problems, even with a pilot on board, and there are scant few of those for hire. If we followed and reefed, we would never be able to catch them."

Isolde nodded absently. He was probably right, but it didn't make the decision sit better knowing that. "I hate waiting."

"I know."

"We will catch them, Princess. The Salt Tower can see if he cuts sharp enough for the faster route, so we'll know, and I have a few tricks still up my sleeves once we're out in the open sea. I won't let you down."

Chapter 20

Stonehills, Kingsheart, Sidor

William stood on the ridge crest and watched three thousand Crown soldiers pour into the valley below. He had finally stopped running the night before and set his men up. They were just inside the Stonehills, but the Crown forces had been getting closer and closer with each day, and he was worried another day of travel deeper into the hills would have him overrun by the Crown forces' lead elements.

And he had been proven right, as they had come into sight within an hour of his men halting, before they were even all the way in position. A more veteran army would have either held back and been cautious, sensing the still-deploying nature as some sort of trap, or charged in headlong, realizing it was not a trap but just a sign of how close they were to their enemy.

This army had done neither. It had come in at a slow pace, starting and stopping as the army accordioned behind it, not having found a rhythm to their march even after days.

Which explained how nine thousand men chasing him was only three thousand in front of him. The other six thousand were scattered across almost two miles of plains.

This was not just poor soldiery, but poor leadership all the way down the line.

They had been chasing him long enough that they were excited to cram themselves into the terrain, once again giving away all of their advantage in numbers in a headless attack straight ahead.

The valley floor rolled and dipped, cut by shallow ravines and studded with boulders. No room for their cavalry to form proper charges. No space for their infantry to deploy in the wide formations that might overwhelm his smaller force through sheer mass.

"Archers ready on both slopes, and the infantry is holding the crest line," Commander Baldwin said, joining him on the ridge.

The Crown vanguard had reached the valley floor and began forming rough lines, separated by the landscape, while the remainder still pushed in through the entrance behind them, clumping up.

"Wait until their center reaches the base of our slope. This is less than half their army, and I want them to fully commit before we start."

His own force held the high ground in a curved line along the ridge. Thirteen hundred heavy infantry formed the center and right, shields locked and pikes angled forward. Another five hundred infantry anchored the left wing where the ground rose more steeply. Scattered among them, positioned on the upper slopes, two hundred archers waited with them. Not enough bowmen to decide the battle through firepower alone, but enough to bleed them.

And somewhere beyond the eastern ridge, hidden in a lateral ravine, Pembroke waited with a thousand men.

At some point, they should stop just looking at the army in front of them, count, and realize that there was a separate force out there, waiting to flank them. It was the first thing William did in battle, if his scouting reports had any kind of count of the army facing them, because it would tell the truth when the formations he could see lied.

True, he was using the hills to make it hard to count clearly, but he had not needed it in the flat plains before this and doubted he actually needed it this time.

Not that poor generalship on their side excused sloppy work on his.

The Crown vanguard organized itself into three broad columns and started forward. Conscript infantry mostly, although behind them came the better troops.

"Their scouts never found Pembroke," Eskild murmured.

"They were not looking for him. They think we are running. They probably have not heard details of the battle yet, and might even assume there is another army marching to join them. They keep marching without intel," William said, as much to himself as to Eskild, before turning to one of the runners. "Let the archers know they can begin phase one."

A handful of minutes later, the first arrows fell among the Crown ranks. Not volleys, just harassing fire from his scattered archers. Men stumbled and dropped, but the shots were not dense enough to make the enemy hesitate or waver.

The Crown forces reached the steeper section of slope, and their advance slowed. The ground here rose at a sharp angle, forcing men to lean forward as they climbed. Their broken columns came apart even more as soldiers were forced to pick individual paths up the incline. Some veered toward easier grades. Others clustered behind rocks that offered momentary protection from arrows, turning the entire mass into a mob.

"Signal for phase two," William said.

Horns blew along his line. The scattered archer fire became focused volleys, with the other half of his archers, all crossbowmen, who had not been involved yet, joining their bows to the fight. Instead of dropping arrows down on the enemy in indirect fire, these men, interspersed at the moment with the line along the top of the hill line, put direct, aimed fire into the enemy, shooting down into them so if they missed one, they would hit someone behind him.

The effect was not devastating, but it was enough that the conscripts were starting to waver.

Another mistake for their commander. William understood the impetus, not wanting to waste veterans on the initial push, but untrained men could not take the punishment that often happened before the initial engagement, collapsing when they hit opposition.

"Keep firing," William said. "Make them pay for every step."

The Crown officers drove their men forward despite the arrows. Conscripts died, but more took their places, driven by threats and physical force from behind. The mass of bodies simply absorbed the losses and kept climbing. William watched them come and calculated ranges. Forty yards. Thirty. Twenty.

"Infantry, ready! Send the runner to Pembroke; it is time for him to start his assault."

His heavy infantry shifted, shields coming up, pikes and axes preparing for contact. These were veterans from the Lynesian campaigns, and the last several months of fighting here in Sidor. They had seen dozens of battles and knew their business. No shouting, no bravado, just silent readiness.

The first Crown soldiers reached the crest. A wave of conscripts breathing hard from the climb, stumbling into William's waiting line.

The slaughter began.

His veterans drove forward in a compact mass. Shields slammed into the exhausted men who had spent their strength on the climb. Pikes punched through cheap leather armor. Men who were not killed outright were pushed down into the men behind them, like flailing boulders.

The Crown soldiers who reached the crest died or broke, and those behind them had to climb over corpses and push the men falling into them to continue the assault. William watched the pattern repeat. A cluster of Crown troops would fight their way to the top, struggle against his line for desperate seconds, then fall or flee. Each wave weakened itself in the climb and broke against fresh defenders who held the advantage of height and position.

But the Crown could absorb the deaths. Even as the men fought here, more were still coming into the valley, a constant stream of meat for the grinder. For every man who died or ran, two more climbed to replace him. The casualties meant nothing if they could sustain this pressure long enough to exhaust William's smaller force.

"They are forming on the left," Eskild said sharply.

William turned his attention to the valley floor where Crown officers had managed to organize a proper formation. Five hundred men-at-arms in decent armor in the vanguard. Behind them, a reserve of conscripts waited to exploit any breakthrough. The column started up the slope in good order, shields overlapping, moving at a steady pace that preserved their formation.

This was the real threat. These troops would not break easily against his line.

"Concentrate arrows on that column," William ordered. "Break their formation before they reach the crest."

Every archer on the left slope turned their fire toward the advancing shield wall. Arrows hammered down, finding the gaps between shields, striking helmets and shoulders. Men fell, but the formation held. The soldiers behind simply closed ranks and kept climbing. The column absorbed the punishment and maintained its cohesion, approaching William's left wing where his line thinned.

William felt the first flicker of doubt. This column had a chance to actually punch through, and once they broke his line, the whole position could collapse.

"Baldwin, shift two hundred men from the center to reinforce the left."

"Your Highness, that will thin our middle."

"Do it."

Baldwin ran to relay the orders. William watched his center contract as men hustled toward the threatened flank. The movement created small gaps in his line, but the conscripts still scrambling up the slope did not recognize the opportunity.

The Crown shield wall hit his left wing.

The impact drove William's troops back as the lines smashed together, pikes thrust between gaps in the others' line of shields. Men shouted and cursed and died on both sides. The Crown soldiers, still relatively fresh despite their climb, pressed hard. William's veterans gave ground grudgingly, their own formation starting to bow inward under the pressure.

The reinforcements arrived and crashed into the flank of the Crown column. Two hundred men hit the enemy formation from the side, breaking its neat shield wall into a confused melee. The Crown advantage evaporated. Both forces hacked at each other in brutal close combat where armor and experience mattered more than numbers.

It was costly, but his line held. Barely.

The Crown kept feeding more troops up the slope. The valley floor below him churned with soldiers organizing for the next assault. They had enough men to try this a dozen times. He had enough men to stop them once, maybe twice more.

Where was Pembroke?

The battle ground on. His infantry killed, bled, and died but refused to break. The slope in front of them disappeared under bodies. Crown soldiers slipped on blood and corpses as they climbed. The arrows never stopped falling. Neither did the Crown attacks.

"Movement on the right," someone said.

William turned. A new threat emerged on the valley floor. Two hundred Crown cavalry had found space to form up between the rock outcrops. Not enough room for a proper charge, but they could still ride up one of the gentler slopes and hit his line. And cavalry against infantry, even uphill, William's right wing would fold.

"We need those horses stopped."

"We don't have cavalry in reserve," Eskild reminded him.

"I know." William scanned the battlefield, his mind racing through options. "Pull back the right wing. Refuse the flank. Make them ride uphill into a bent line where we can hit them from two sides."

"That gives them ground."

"It gives them a trap. Send a runner. When they strike, I want the wing to swing back like a door on a hinge."

The horns signaled the maneuver. His right wing pulled back in stages, maintaining formation but creating an angled position. The Crown cavalry saw the movement as weakness and spurred forward. They came up the slope at a trot, lances lowered, heading straight for what looked like a collapsing flank.

William's infantry on the right contracted into a tight wedge. The cavalry hit the point of the wedge and its pikes and stopped dead. Horses reared. Lances broke against shields. And then William's left center pivoted inward and struck the cavalry from the side.

The cavalry charge dissolved into chaos as panicked animals tried to turn in a space too narrow to maneuver. Some riders broke through and fled back down the slope. Others died.

But the victory cost time and blood. William's right wing had taken casualties holding that position. And the center had thinned further to execute the flanking attack. Every tactical success carved away a piece of his shrinking force.

The Crown commanders saw it too and formed a new assault. This time, they massed every available man into a single column aimed straight at his thinnest point.

"They're going to break us," Baldwin said.

William ignored him, watching two thousand Crown soldiers start up the slope in a packed formation four men deep. Too many. His center couldn't hold against that weight, not with his line stretched so thin.

He needed Pembroke. Now.

The Crown column climbed steadily, learning from previous failures. They moved at a sustainable pace. They kept formation despite arrow fire. Officers rode behind them, preventing flight. And they were coming as a mass, large enough to wrap over the sides of the hill and surround him.

"Prepare to retreat," William said.

Baldwin stared at him. "What?"

"If the center starts to waver, start a fighting retreat down the back slope in stages. Don't let them encircle us."

"Your Highness, we can't abandon this position. They'll be attacking downhill and have position on us."

"And if we stay where we are, we will be crushed under their weight. Dead is dead. This, at least, gives us a chance."

William gripped the pommel of his sword and watched the Crown column approach. Fifty yards. Forty. His archers fired as fast as they could, but the column kept coming. Thirty yards. His infantry braced for impact.

A horn blew. Not his horn.

The sound came from the east, from beyond the ridge where Pembroke should be. Every head on the battlefield turned toward that sound. For one frozen moment, the entire battle paused.

Then Pembroke's cavalry appeared.

They came down the ravine trail at a gallop, five hundred men on horseback spilling onto the valley floor directly behind the

Crown army's right flank, with five hundred heavy infantry following behind.

The effect was immediate.

The Crown rear formations collapsed. Pembroke's cavalry cut through reserve troops and archers, overrunning them completely. They drove straight for the command group where banners marked the enemy's leadership.

The assault on William's center faltered as men looked back over their shoulders and saw disaster unfolding below them. The tight column wavered. Gaps opened in the formation. William saw his moment.

"Forward! Drive them down!"

His entire line surged downhill. Exhausted infantry found new strength and threw themselves at an enemy who'd lost cohesion. The Crown soldiers who'd been seconds from breaking William's center now broke themselves. They turned and ran back down the slope, colliding with men still trying to climb up.

The Crown army imploded.

Pembroke's cavalry rolled up their right flank while William's infantry hammered their front. The Crown center, still organized and dangerous, found itself trapped between two forces with no room to maneuver in the confining valley. Officers tried to rally squares and defensive positions, but terrain that had hampered their attack now prevented their defense.

William descended the slope, following his advancing troops. He passed through the killing ground where bodies lay three deep. Blood made the rocks slick. The grass had been trampled into mud that stank of iron, shit, and death.

The Crown army wasn't fleeing yet. Couldn't flee. Too many men crammed into too small a space. They fought because running meant pushing through their own ranks to reach the valley exit behind them.

William's veterans exploited the confusion. They moved in tight groups, hitting isolated enemy formations and destroying them before moving on to the next target. No grand charges or heroic duels. Just methodical butchery of an army that could no longer coordinate its defense.

Pembroke's cavalry had reached the Crown command group. William saw the banners fall. The enemy officers died or fled, and with them went any hope of organized resistance. The Crown soldiers, leaderless and trapped, began surrendering by the dozen. By the hundred.

"Your Highness!" Captain Baldwin appeared, blood on his surcoat and a grin on his face. "We have them!"

"Where are their escape routes?"

Baldwin pointed toward the valley entrance. "That narrow defile. They're trying to pull back through it, but it's jammed with bodies and panicked men."

William scanned the battlefield. The Crown army had collapsed, but it wasn't destroyed. Thousands of men still fought or tried to flee. If they escaped and regrouped, they'd return with reinforced numbers.

He couldn't let that happen.

"Get me Sir Alwin and whatever cavalry we have left."

Baldwin ran to obey. William continued down the slope, watching the battle fragment into a hundred smaller fights. His troops had the advantage everywhere, but the Crown still had more men on the field. If they stabilized, if they found space to reform …

Alwin arrived with a hundred cavalry, all that remained uncommitted from William's force.

"Your Highness."

"Take every mounted man we have. Circle around the northern edge of the valley and cut off the escape route through that defile. Seal it shut. I want them trapped in here."

Alwin nodded and spurred his horse. The cavalry thundered away, following the valley rim where the ground rose high enough for the horses to move freely. William watched them go and then turned his attention back to the valley floor.

Pembroke had linked up with William's infantry on the Crown army's right. The enemy forces there, caught between two forces and unable to retreat through the crush of bodies behind them, surrendered en masse. Pembroke's men herded thousands of prisoners toward the valley's eastern slope where the captives could be watched.

But the Crown left and center still fought. Maybe two thousand men, backed against the valley's western wall, formed a rough defensive line. They had nowhere to run. Behind them, more soldiers clogged the defile trying to escape. The narrow passage had become a death trap. Men at the rear pushed forward while men at the front, seeing Alwin's cavalry sealing the exit, pushed back. The crush killed more than any sword.

William signaled for his reserves. Three hundred men who'd held position at the ridge crest throughout the battle now descended in tight formation. They advanced on the Crown defenders with locked shields and at a steady pace.

"One more push," William said to Baldwin. "Break them and this is finished."

The fresh troops hit the Crown line. The defenders, already exhausted from hours of fighting, couldn't hold. They broke. Some threw down their weapons and begged for mercy. Others fought until they were killed. A brave few tried to cut their way to the defile, hoping to force passage through the packed escape route.

Alwin's cavalry stopped them. The narrow defile, jammed with fleeing soldiers, became a killing ground as mounted men rode along its edges and cut down anyone trying to push through. The Crown soldiers trapped inside couldn't fight back and couldn't retreat. They could only die or surrender.

William walked through the carnage. Bodies covered the valley floor. The living stumbled through the dead, too exhausted to do more than lean on their weapons and breathe. His veterans rounded up prisoners and separated the wounded from the dead. The sounds of battle faded to groans, curses, and the cries of men calling for water or mercy.

"Your Highness!" Pembroke rode up, his armor dented and blood-spattered. "They're finished. The ones who didn't surrender are running into the hills as individuals. No formation, no leadership."

William nodded. "Send cavalry after them. Small groups. Hunt down any groups larger than a dozen. I want this whole army routed."

The battle had been closer than any of the recent ones, more because of the size of the force than any spectacular generalship.

Which was why he had to keep moving fast. His father had proven that he could keep pouring men into the fight, outnumbering them at every turn.

There were still armies out there, but this was Edmund's biggest army, and it had fallen.

William needed to keep moving to get to Starhaven fast before another army could be formed.

Chapter 21

Grimshaw River, Ice Lands, Sidor

The Ice Landers had fallen in clusters, cut down as they tried to form their shield walls or scattered where his cavalry had run them through. He counted the banners as he passed them, noting which houses had committed forces. There would be a time when this war would be over, and he would remember those who took up arms against him.

The information would prove useful when the time came to redraw the map of the North.

His own wounded sat or lay in rows near the tree line, organized by severity. The disciples moved among them with water and bandages, doing what they could. Garris moved to the next man, then the next, speaking briefly to each. He may not have the reputation that the prince had, but he knew the value of such gestures, how they bound men to a cause beyond coin or duty.

Sir Odran approached as Garris finished with the third row. "My lord, the prisoners."

"How many nobles?"

"Seventeen that we've identified. Two barons, the rest knights and minor lords. They're asking about ransom terms."

"Send out the wyverns and see who agrees."

He left Odran to manage the details and continued across the field. The battle had been closer than he'd let his men believe.

A part of him knew that, had William been here, he would have figured out some strategy to reduce his casualties while still winning the day. For all of the boy's short-sightedness and soft heart, he did have a flair for tactics like no one Garris had seen since Gavric.

The smaller medical tent stood apart from the main encampment, guarded by four men of his personal guard. Garris had ordered it set up specifically for high-value prisoners, those whose wounds required treatment but whose presence demanded isolation from the common soldiers. The guards straightened as he approached.

Garris pushed through the tent flap into the dim interior. Three cots lined the canvas walls, two empty. Duke Isaac Cadogan occupied the third, his massive frame making the cot seem small despite its sturdy construction.

Bandages wrapped his torso where a spear had pierced him, and his right leg was splinted below the knee.

"Baron Sinclair," Cadogan's voice said, sounding tired. "Come to gloat?"

"Gloating is for children." Garris pulled a stool close to the cot and sat, studying the wounded Duke. "I came to discuss terms."

"I'm in no position to negotiate."

"Then you'll listen. Your army is destroyed. Almost a thousand dead on the field, another nine hundred too wounded to fight, the rest scattered into the hills or captured. Your brother Torben escaped with perhaps two hundred horse, not enough to defend even a minor keep. Your son sits in Shieldshome with a garrison that can't possibly hold against what I'll bring if you force me to siege."

Cadogan said nothing, looking off at the wall of the tent, mute.

"Your position is this," Garris continued. "You can watch your duchy burn while you heal in this tent, see your towns put to the torch and your people starved, or you can end this now with a message. One wyvern to Shieldshome, ordering your son to open the gates and surrender the city. The bloodshed stops, your lands remain intact, and we can discuss what comes next."

"And if I refuse?"

"Then I march west tomorrow with my army, and I burn every village between here and Shieldshome, I put every fighting man to the sword, and when I finally break your walls, I hang your son from them. You know I'll do it. It's less than your people did when you invaded Iron Keep and no less than you deserve."

Cadogan closed his eyes briefly. "You're asking me to surrender my duchy."

"I'm giving you the chance you didn't give me. I'm asking you to be practical. The war is over. You lost. The only question now is how much you lose in the losing."

"The King still holds Starhaven."

"I received word from the prince's army this morning, shortly before our battle. The grand army he had sitting in Penvale is shattered, ten thousand dead, wounded, or scattered by the warrior cub. Only a small force remains between him and the capital. Edmund Whitton will not remain on the throne for long."

The color drained further from Cadogan's face. "Ten thousand ..."

"And he beat an army of six thousand just a week before. And an army before that. And an army before that. The Crown is out of fighting men. You have lost even if I do nothing. Now is the time for you to salvage what you can."

Cadogan stared at the tent ceiling, his jaw working. Finally, he spoke. "The message. What exactly would it say?"

"Just as I said. You order the immediate surrender of Shield-shome and all Ice Land garrisons. You order your son to cooperate fully with my forces and ensure no further resistance. In exchange, I guarantee that your wounded receive proper care, that your prisoners are treated honorably, and that your lands aren't put to waste."

"My son ..."

"Lives. Rules Shieldshome in your name while you heal. When you're recovered, you return to your seat, and we discuss the duchy's future in the new order."

Cadogan's laugh came out as more of a wheeze. "Who will you give my lands to?"

"That hasn't been decided."

"If you could guarantee my position. My family's position ..."

"Why, by the ancients, would I do that? You have shown how ready you are to invade your neighbors. Kill your countrymen."

"I did what I had to. Edmund was the king, and Serwyn before that. What was I supposed to do? When he summoned me to war, I came because that's what dukes do. We answer our king's call, we send our men, we follow the law and custom of the realm. I don't want my loyalty to the proper order of things used against me. Don't want my sons to lose everything because I honored my oaths."

"That kind of loyalty comes with no rewards," Garris said. "Not when the king you serve was a usurper and a kinslayer."

"It doesn't. You're right about that. But that is not the consideration I am asking for. I know you, Sinclair. You have your honor and morals, but you're a practical man above all else. It's that part of you I want to make a deal with."

"Then stop beating about the bush and say what you have to say."

"I have information that I want to exchange for guarantees of my family's position. I will step down if you demand it, but I want my son to retain my seat."

"For something like that, what you have to offer will have to be like news to the kings of old, before the fall of magic."

"It is. You mention the kings of old. Edmund has made himself one of those, in effect. He has an artifact from the time of magic."

"The house of Whitton has several. The sword, the staff of binding."

"Those are trinkets in comparison. This one influences people, bends their will to the one who possesses it, makes them feel things that aren't real. From what I was told, it allows the user to shape emotions, to make crowds love what they should hate and support what they should oppose. That's how he raised such vast funds from common folk who can barely feed themselves and recruited fresh soldiers faster than you could kill them. That's how he kept barons loyal even when they saw their neighbors imprisoned or executed."

While on the face of it, that seemed impossible, the kind of thing a man facing his own demise might make up to escape his fate.

And yet, it explained everything.

The rebels had almost won at the start of winter. The Crown armies were routed and the way to Starhaven was mostly open.

They'd freed Iron Keep and the River Mark, and it seemed to all of them that the war was almost over.

And then the Crown suddenly began recruiting huge hosts. True, most of that army had been peasants, but conscription has its limits. An army still had to have enough professional soldiers in it to keep it together. The only exception was when these forces were defending their homes, but a lot of these peasants were from other areas of Kingsheart not impacted by the war.

Sinclair, and everyone else, had wondered how the king had not only enlisted that many people but kept them loyal when under arms.

If he really had such an artifact, this would explain everything.

"He could do that?"

"He could. It's how he's done all this."

"What is this artifact? Where is it?"

"Promises first," Cadogan demanded. "Guarantees about my family's future."

"Will you be able to tell me where it is?"

"Yes. And how to get more information about it. But first, I want your word."

"Fine. If this proves true, your family can hold the Ice Lands after the war. You have my word on it."

"He keeps it on his person at all times. That much I know. Beyond that, there is a man in the dungeons, kept separate from the other prisoners. An acolyte, of all things. He knows about this artifact, which I assume is why Edmund keeps him locked in a cell. He is still there, unless something has changed in the last few weeks. If what you say is true, and your people will have Starhaven soon, then you will have the disciple also, and he will be able to tell you everything."

"But this thing, this artifact, it can do what you say? Bend men's wills to his control?"

"Yes. Not, I don't think, single people. Not individuals. But it can do it for groups. For crowds. Again, I don't understand how it works exactly, but if he could use it on one man, he would have used it on me. I have been delaying his orders, seeing the writing on the wall, to the point where he imprisoned my son to force my obedience. He wouldn't have had to do that if he had something that would have forced my acquiescence."

"Still, that is a powerful thing."

"For a man who knows how to use it," Cadogan said, and the two exchanged a look.

This was valuable information. Kingdoms were built on rallying the peasantry. Just look at what that man Fletcher had done, bringing the Crown to its knees without a single noble in the fight. A man who possessed an artifact such as this and titles of nobility could control a kingdom.

"You were right, that is valuable information indeed. If it's true."

"It's true. We have an agreement."

"We do." Garris moved toward the tent entrance, his mind already working through how to use this new knowledge. "I'll have that parchment and ink brought immediately. Write your message to Shieldshome, and I'll see it sent at first light."

Garris left the tent and stood in the fading afternoon light, watching his men organize the captured equipment and tend their wounded.

This changed everything.

Port Ilston, Barony of Stonehill, Kingsheart, Sidor

The bodies had been cleared from the quay, though blood still darkened the wooden planks between the warehouses. William stood at the edge of the wharf and looked out across the Tharnfell where it widened into the sea. The river mouth churned brown with silt, and beyond it, the Sea of Kings stretched gray and endless under the late spring sky.

Behind him, his men moved through the port. They'd taken it in less than an hour. The garrison commander had surrendered after the first assault broke through the river gate. Smart man. His fifty guards would have died for nothing.

"Your Highness."

William turned, seeing Pembroke approach along the wharf dock.

"We've secured the warehouses. Found grain stores, salted fish, some iron ingots ready for shipping. The harbormaster's tallying it now."

"Good." William gestured to the ships moored along the docks. "How many are seaworthy?"

"Eight merchant vessels," Pembroke said, still sounding confused by the task. "Two small warships, though they're barely worth the name. Fishing boats beyond count."

"It should be enough."

Pembroke walked twenty paces closer, lowering his voice so it was covered by the sound of the water, and said, "We need to talk."

"Say what's on your mind."

"This was a mistake."

William didn't reply. He only waited.

"We came out of the Stonehills," Pembroke continued after a moment. "Left a strong defensive position to march west through Drunwald Forest, where we then took a port that's not even on our route to Starhaven. It's not a strategic target, which is exactly why it was so poorly defended. We've won nothing here but a week's delay."

"You feel like I am wasting time? Perhaps putting us in danger?"

"I'm saying I don't understand the plan. You've fought brilliantly so far. Every battle, you've chosen ground that favored us and forced Edmund's commanders to fight where they couldn't use their numbers. This breaks that pattern. I don't see what we gain from this."

"Have we heard from the scouts about the positioning of my father's remaining forces?" William asked in a sudden non-sequitur.

Pembroke's frown deepened. "William, I ... yes, we have. They've pulled everything from across the duchy back here, abandoning the ground they picked up when we moved away from our supply lines, concentrating between Starhaven Bay and the Stonehills. Seven thousand men, near as we can tell, maybe more, holding position next to King's Bay in the Stone Gap. And I get your point. We all thought it was a mistake when you marched into the Blackheath and left Iron Keep and the River Mark unguarded. And yes, this has worked. Instead of breaking into our home territories, they have pulled all their men away from there. But this is different."

"And how many men do we have?"

"Just over three thousand, although a lot of those are lightly wounded and won't be back to fighting shape in a month or two. And yes, you have done a good job fighting with such a small force, but that won't continue if we make the wrong moves."

A fishing boat glided past, its single sail catching the wind. William watched it disappear around the bend where the Tharnfell curved north, not answering right away.

Pembroke almost fidgeted, waiting for William to say something.

"You want to go back to the hills," he finally said, turning back to Pembroke.

"I want to use what's worked. We've beaten them twice using the terrain. We should do that again. We need to pull them into the Stonehills, force them to come at us through narrow valleys where their numbers don't matter. Just like before. Yes, it's what they'll expect, but that doesn't make it wrong. Sometimes the obvious choice is obvious because it's the right one."

William shook his head. "And that's how they'll counter it. We win because we don't do exactly what they expect us to do. You taught me that."

"I also taught you that the military realities are what they are, and you stick with what works. Your tactics have worked."

"Because my father's commanders are incompetent. Like many nobles placed in command, they have no artistry. They charge headlong into battle and smash into the enemy until they win or lose. It's how Sinclair fights. But we haven't killed every commander, and they have learned. Seven thousand men concentrated between here and Starhaven, and they haven't marched in to get us. They're holding in open plains. Why? Because they're not panicking; they're waiting. If we go into the hills, they will wait us out while my father recruits more men and surrounds us again, except this time pressed up against the sea."

"Then what's the alternative?"

"We march toward Starhaven."

Pembroke stared at him. "You just said they're going to sit on the plains and wait for us, forcing us to choose their ground to fight on. Now that's exactly what you want to do with three thousand men against seven thousand in prepared positions? That's not clever. That's suicide."

"Not the way I'm planning to do it."

"Then explain it to me. I've followed you this far on faith, but I need to understand what we're doing here. Why did we take this port?"

William moved to the edge of the wharf. He crouched down and used his finger to trace lines in the dried blood on the planks.

"This is the Tharnfell. It flows down from the Stonehills and empties here into the Sea of Kings." He drew another line. "Here's the coast running south. Twenty miles down, the mouth of King's Bay opens up here. It's small, and not as used, with Starhaven Bay just another thirty miles south, with both the capital and Hven's port, which feeds directly onto the Tradesway. I spent some summers here when I was younger, mostly because my father wanted me out of sight. It's a good bay, widening up nicely with deep moorings."

"Okay, but that still puts us north of the capital. We have to march across this outcropping here, and then cross the bay itself to get to Starhaven. All with a larger army right behind us."

"I didn't say we were going to march straight on Starhaven, only toward it. We're going to split our forces. You take a thousand men on ships from this port. Sail south down the coast and into King's Bay. While I march south with the other two thousand men. I will wait for your signal that you're in the bay, just inside the Stonehills, where they will think I am dithering, trying to figure out how to counter them. When you are there, I attack, straight at them. Once I have them engaged, you hit them hard in the left flank and roll them."

"And if they don't wait? If they see your forces just inside the hills and decide to come for you?"

"Then I do the same thing to them that I did to the last army, and you get to land peacefully and help me mop up."

Pembroke stared at the dock turned mental map, and thought for a moment before nodding.

"Okay, it is a good plan. Your uncle would have been proud. Aldric, I mean. He always said wars were won by thinking three moves ahead."

"Thank you, my friend," William said. "Now we just have to make it work."

Chapter 22

Eastern Sea, Near Inos

The Inosian coast rose dark against the eastern horizon, a jagged line of cliffs that marked lands Alistair had never visited and never planned to. He stood at the rail, watching the distant shore slip past. Behind them, that damned merchant vessel held its course, no longer gaining but not falling back either. Six days now. Six days that ship had hounded them.

He turned from the rail and crossed the deck to where the duchess sat beneath an awning his men had rigged near the mainmast. Her hands were no longer bound, though. She wasn't going anywhere. Not out here.

"We'll reach Starhaven for sure now," he said. "Even if that ship back there plans to follow us around the world, it's not going to catch us."

Alyssa looked up at him. Her face showed nothing. No fear, no anger, just that same cold regard she'd worn since they'd taken her from Kenna.

"I don't care where you take me. I won't give in to any demands you or your master make."

"We'll see."

"You should throw yourself over the rail, beg the ancients for forgiveness. You are an oath breaker, doomed to be barred from the halls of our ancestors, never to join them. You murdered my husband, your friend. You are the vilest of deviants. No better than a Purifier."

Alistair raised his hand to strike her but paused. The king had made it clear he didn't want her injured in any way. Since he'd first met her, she'd always had a smart mouth and had needed someone to put a hand to her, to teach her her place.

And that's what she wanted. She was trying to provoke him. He wouldn't give her that satisfaction.

"You talk about oaths. I believe you also swore an oath when you became duchess. Swore your fealty to the Crown. And now you, your dead husband, and your nephew are all in rebellion. You have no room to talk."

"Keep trying to convince yourself, oath breaker."

He turned away before he could say something he'd regret. Arguing with her served no purpose. Edmund wanted her alive and relatively unharmed. That was all that mattered. The rightness or wrongness of it, that was for others to decide.

"Ship ho!"

The cry came from the lookout in the crow's nest. Alistair's head snapped up.

"Where away?" the captain yelled from the stern castle.

"Three points off the starboard bow! Three ships, making sail!"

Alistair took the short ladder to join the captain. "What is it?"

"Inosian warships," the captain's aide said, lowering the glass. "Three of them and coming out fast."

"Pirates?"

"No. There are few pirates in this area. The Inosians patrol it too heavily, and these are coming from that port. Those are kingdom ships."

Alistair took the spyglass and looked for himself. Three vessels, larger than the one they sailed on. It took a moment, but he finally saw the Inosian flag on their top mast.

"You think they mean to stop us?"

"I don't know, but it might explain those wyverns that ship behind us sent flying toward Inos two days back."

Alistair nodded. They'd wondered about that. At the time, he convinced himself that the merchant wasn't after them, that it was just a coincidence. Merchants in River Mark and Shadowhold did a lot of business with Inos, so there could be business reasons for it, but of course, he'd been fooling himself.

That ship was after them.

He looked back at the merchant ship still trailing them, then forward at the three Inosian vessels cutting across their path. His mind worked through the possibilities. Someone on that merchant ship had contacts in Inos, someone with enough influence or coin to convince a foreign kingdom to intervene.

"If we're going to avoid them, we need to turn around now. In the next few minutes," the captain said.

"Right toward the ship following us."

"Better one merchant ship than three Inosian warships. The choice is, of course, yours, Sir Alistair. But the decision must be made fast."

Alistair stared at the approaching warships. They were still perhaps two miles off, but closing rapidly. If they wanted to intercept them, they'd manage it easily. And Inosian warships meant soldiers, lots of them. Fighting through three shiploads of Inosian marines with his ten men was suicide.

"Turn," he said.

The captain shouted orders and sailors scrambled up the rigging, hauling on lines as the boom swung across. The ship heeled, turning in a wide arc that pointed them back the way they'd come, back toward that pursuing merchant vessel.

Alistair watched the Inosian ships slow their approach. They weren't chasing, just blocking, which meant they had been called by a person on that merchant ship.

But who?

The merchant ship grew larger as the distance closed. Alistair could now make out figures on the deck, more than he would have expected for a simple merchant vessel. The captain noticed too.

"That's not a normal crew complement," the captain said.

"How many?"

"Hard to say from here. But more than they need for sailing, and some of them look to be wearing mail."

The two ships drew closer. Alistair could see the merchant's crew working their own rigging, adjusting their course. Not trying to avoid them. Coming right at them.

"Will they ram us?" Alistair asked.

"No. They're preparing to board."

As they closed, Alistair could see men gathering at the merchant ship's rail, armed with swords and what looked like grappling hooks.

Alistair strode back down to the main deck, calling his men to arms. They came quickly, drawing swords and taking positions along the starboard rail. Most wore leather jerkins or light gambesons. He wished he'd had his mail, but only a fool wore plate on a ship. If you went overboard, the weight would drag you to the bottom before you could shed it.

The merchant ship closed to fifty yards. Forty. Thirty. Alistair could see their faces now. A mixed group. A knight he recognized, serving one of the smaller houses in River Mark, a handful of men who carried themselves like trained fighters, some household guards in livery, and several who looked more like dock brawlers than proper soldiers.

"Brace!" the captain shouted.

The merchant ship crashed alongside them. Wood groaned and splintered. Grappling hooks flew across the gap, biting into rails and rigging. Men hauled on the lines, pulling the vessels together. The hulls ground against each other, locked in an embrace neither could easily break.

"Repel boarders!" Alistair drew his sword.

The first attackers came across while the ships were still closing. The knight led the charge, sword already drawn, two household guards flanking him. Behind them came the rest, scrambling over the rails and across the hooks' connecting lines.

Alistair's men met them at the rail. Steel rang on steel. A guard went down with a sword through his belly. One of Alistair's men took a blade across the face and fell screaming.

The enemy knight pushed forward, cutting down one of Alistair's men with a strong overhand strike. This man might be a lesser knight, but he knew his business, and he could take most of the men Alistair had brought with him. Which meant it was up to him to stop him. Alistair moved to intercept the man.

Their blades met with a sharp crack. The knight pressed the attack, forcing Alistair back two steps with a series of quick cuts.

Alistair caught the rhythm of it. The knight fought well but conventionally. Nothing surprising. Nothing unpredictable. When

243

the next cut came, Alistair didn't parry. He stepped inside it, letting the blade pass over his shoulder, and drove his pommel into the knight's face.

The man staggered. Blood streamed from his broken nose. Alistair followed with a low cut that opened the knight's thigh through the leather, crippling him. The knight's leg buckled. He tried to recover, raising his sword in a desperate guard, but Alistair beat the blade aside and thrust for the throat.

And then his blade was stopped.

A new figure interposed itself between them. A man in his forties, thick around the middle but moving with surprising speed. His sword met Alistair's, deflecting the thrust away from the wounded knight.

Alistair stepped back, reassessing for a moment. The newcomer didn't look like much, with a soft face and merchant's clothes under a leather vest, hands that had clearly held ledgers more often than swords in recent years. But the way he held his weapon told a different story. He'd had a harder life before he'd become a merchant, that was for certain. The stance was right. The balance was right.

"Get back," the man said to the wounded knight, not taking his eyes off Alistair.

The knight pushed himself away, helped by one of the household guards pulling him toward the rail. Alistair circled, watching this new opponent. Behind them, the fight raged on. His men were holding, but barely. The attackers had numbers.

The merchant attacked first. A testing thrust that Alistair parried easily, followed by a cut that had more conviction behind it. Alistair gave ground, reading the man's style. Quick hands. Good footwork despite the weight. Someone had trained him properly once, even if the years had softened him.

But Alistair had spent thirty years keeping his edge sharp. He caught the next attack on his blade, twisted his wrist, and nearly took the man's sword from his grip. The merchant recovered, but Alistair was already moving. A low feint drew the man's blade down, then Alistair reversed into a high cut that opened the merchant's shoulder.

The man grunted, blood soaking into his shirt. But he didn't drop his sword. Stubborn.

Alistair pressed harder. Another cut. And another. The merchant parried, blocked, gave ground. His breathing came harder now. Sweat ran down his face. He knew he was losing.

Around them, the battle tilted, Alistair's men going down. The attackers were taking casualties too, but they had more bodies to spend, and they were generally better trained, it seemed. If this went on much longer, they'd be overwhelmed.

But if Alistair could finish these fighters quickly enough, he could break them before they broke his crew ...

He drove the merchant back against the mast, raining down cuts that left the man barely able to defend himself. One more good opening and this would be over. One more and he could turn his attention to the rest of these bastards.

The merchant's blade came up slowly, too slow to catch Alistair's next strike. Alistair went for the throat. The merchant twisted desperately, taking the cut across the collarbone instead. He fell against the mast, sword slipping from his grip.

Alistair raised his blade for the killing blow.

Pain exploded through his back, cold and hot at once. He looked down and saw steel jutting from his chest, red with his blood. The blade had punched straight through him, between his ribs, missing his spine by inches but finding his lung and probably his heart.

He tried to turn. The sword wrenched in the wound, tearing more flesh. His own blade fell from nerveless fingers and clattered on the deck. He had gotten halfway around when he saw her.

The princess. The boy's damn Lynesian bride stood behind him, hands red with his blood. Her face was set, hard and cold, all the soft nobility burned away by something darker.

"This is for William," she said as he dropped to the deck.

Barony of Canford, Kingsheart

William positioned his force at the base of the rolling hills where stone outcroppings broke the grassland into uneven terrain. Two thousand veterans formed loose battle lines across a quarter-mile front, their ranks deeper than the Crown army's, but far shorter.

It wouldn't be hard for the enemy to wrap around him on either side, to flank him.

The main body deployed in three divisions: eight hundred heavy infantry in the center, six hundred on each flank, with crossbowmen positioned in the gaps between formations. Behind them, the ground rose in gentle slopes dotted with boulders and scrub that would break cavalry charges and funnel attacks into narrow approaches.

The enemy host spread across the plain like a dark stain, their numbers dwarfing William's army. Banners fluttered above packed formations that stretched beyond the edges of his vision. Seven thousand men, perhaps eight. Conscripts filled most of their ranks, as they had with all of the Crown armies his father had sent after him, although there were a few more disciplined blocks scattered throughout their ranks.

The Crown deployment troubled him. Their commander had positioned his best troops at regular intervals along the front, using them as anchors to maintain cohesion among the less reliable conscripts.

It was smarter than the other commanders he'd faced, sound tactics that suggested experience rather than mere noble birth. William counted at least twelve separate blocks of royal infantry, each perhaps two hundred strong. That meant twenty-four hundred professional soldiers backed by nearly five thousand militia and conscripts.

The small fraction of professionals in this army was greater than his entire force.

"Crossbows forward."

Four hundred crossbowmen moved through gaps in the infantry lines, their weapons already spanned and loaded. They formed two ranks fifty paces ahead of the main force, close enough to retreat quickly but positioned to deliver maximum casualties during the enemy's approach.

"They're moving scouts along our position, my lord, probing for weak points," Commander Haverhill said, riding up to the command group.

William nodded, having noticed the same movement. Small groups of enemy cavalry ranged along his front, staying just beyond crossbow range while they studied his formations.

"Let them look. They'll see what I want them to see."

The Crown army began its advance. Their line wavered as conscripts struggled to maintain formation, but the core of royal troops held steady. Officers on horseback rode behind the formations, shouting orders and using the flats of their swords to keep stragglers in line.

William raised his arm and held it high. The crossbowmen lifted their weapons to their shoulders. Eight hundred yards. Seven hundred. The enemy formations grew larger, individual faces becoming visible beneath steel caps and leather helms. He could see the fear on some of those faces now, the wide eyes of men who had never faced professional soldiers in battle. But he could also see the grim determination of the veterans mixed among them.

Six hundred yards. The front rank of crossbowmen took aim, their weapons trained on the densest sections of the approaching host. William watched the advance carefully, judging distance and timing. The enemy officers were maintaining good control, keeping their units dressed and preventing the line from becoming too strung out.

His arm dropped.

The first volley released, four hundred bolts arcing through the air before punching into the advancing ranks. Men stumbled and fell, gaps appearing in the front line as bodies collapsed. Screams rose from the wounded, but the advance continued.

The second rank of crossbowmen stepped forward while the first began reloading. Another volley, another rain of death into the packed formations.

The enemy advance faltered as officers shouted orders and tried to close the growing gaps. Conscripts stepped over fallen comrades, some beginning to waver, their formations wavered as men instinctively tried to avoid the areas where bolts had struck. But the royal infantry maintained better discipline, and that held the conscripts together.

Damn whoever was on the other side for finally getting smart.

Five hundred yards. Four hundred. The crossbowmen continued their deadly work, reloading and firing in steady rotation. Each volley sent dozens of men to the ground, and the carpet of bodies behind the Crown formations grew thicker. William could see officers trying to maintain order by riding behind their troops and preventing anyone from fleeing. One captain struck down a conscript who tried to turn back, his sword taking the man's head clean off.

Three hundred yards. Two hundred. The enemy formations were ragged now, their neat lines disrupted by casualties and by the natural tendency of men under fire to bunch together for mutual protection. But they kept coming, driven forward by their officers and the momentum of their own advance.

"Crossbows withdraw!" William shouted.

The missile troops began falling back through prepared gaps in the infantry lines, their job done for now. They had bloodied the enemy and slowed their advance, buying precious minutes and reducing the numbers his infantry would face. But the real work lay ahead.

The Crown army struck his line like a breaking wave. The impact sent shock waves through both formations as thousands of men collided in a deafening crash of metal and flesh.

William's veterans held their ground, their superior training evident. The front rank locked shields while the second rank thrust spears over their shoulders, creating a wall of steel that the enemy assault broke against. When gaps appeared, reserve fighters stepped forward to fill them before the enemy could exploit the openings.

But the enemy had weight of numbers, and that weight pressed forward relentlessly. Conscripts threw themselves against the veteran lines in human waves, accepting horrific casualties in exchange for gradual progress. Behind them, the royal infantry applied steady pressure.

William watched from his command position as the battle developed along his entire front. His left flank bent backward under pressure from a concentrated attack by three blocks of royal infantry. As he had worried, the enemy was using their larger frontage to try to wrap around him, turning his flanks.

William's section commanders were doing the only thing they could do: bend the line back, which would work right up until his line bent in on itself.

Then he'd be surrounded and crushed.

"They're stacking their veterans on the left. Have the right try and push forward," William ordered, sending signalmen scurrying.

That wouldn't last. The enemy would readjust and put more weight on the right, causing him to roll back.

But it was about buying time, not just winning.

As he'd hoped, they started to have some success, pushing the enemy line on that side back, but William could see that advantage was temporary. Royal infantry were moving to reinforce that sector and would soon restore the balance.

The casualties mounted on both sides. For every veteran that fell, two or three enemies died, but those numbers favored the Crown. The enemy could afford to trade bodies.

A runner reached his position, blood streaming from a cut on his forehead. The young man had obviously fought his way through enemy infiltrators to reach the command post.

"My lord, Haverhill requests immediate reinforcement on the left. The Royal infantry has broken through our first line in two places."

William studied the battle line. His left was buckling visibly now, the defensive formation bowing inward as the enemy assault intensified. If he pulled troops from other sections to reinforce it, those areas might collapse in turn. And Pembroke should be in position by now. Where was his flanking force?

"Tell Haverhill to fall back to the second position. Fighting withdrawal, maintain formation."

The runner nodded and sprinted back toward the fighting, dodging between knots of combat as he made his way across the chaotic battlefield.

The pressure intensified as more enemy troops entered the battle. William could see reserve formations moving up behind the Crown front line, fresh men ready to replace those who had fallen or grown too exhausted to fight effectively. The enemy commander was managing his forces well, rotating units to maintain constant pressure while preventing any single formation from becoming too weakened.

His own reserves consisted of barely two hundred men, not enough to make a decisive difference in a battle this size. Every deployment had to count; every decision carefully weighed against the possibility that it might be his last.

A horn sounded from the enemy lines, and William saw fresh troops advancing toward his weakened left. Another thousand men at least. If they struck his battered flank now, the entire position would collapse.

"Sound the withdrawal."

His troops began falling back toward the hills, maintaining formation but yielding ground.

The veterans executed the maneuver with professional skill. The front rank fell back through gaps in the second rank, which then became the new front line. The process repeated as they withdrew, always maintaining a solid barrier between themselves and the pursuing enemy. The crossbowmen provided what cover they could.

Unfortunately, the Crown commander proved cautious. Instead of pursuing into the broken terrain where his numerical advantage would count for less, the enemy army halted at the base of the hills. Their officers shouted orders as they reformed their ranks, unwilling to follow William's force into what they clearly suspected was a trap.

The enemy deployment remained strong. They had taken casualties, but they were still intact, and their morale seemed unshaken. William could see reserve units moving up to fill gaps created by their losses.

William cursed under his breath. He had counted on their pursuit to buy time and reduce the enemy's advantage. Their stopping was the last thing he wanted. He needed them focused and engaged for when Pembroke arrived.

"Reform the line!" he shouted. "Prepare for an assault!"

His veterans pulled back into a tighter formation, anchoring their flanks against rocky outcroppings that would prevent envelopment. The position was defensible but cramped, forcing his men into a compressed front that reduced their tactical flexibility. It was the kind of position armies occupied when they had no other choice.

The infantry in the center pushed forward again, back onto flat ground.

The crossbowmen took positions on higher ground where they could fire over the heads of their own infantry, which at least gave them the ability to hit the middle rows of the enemy lines.

The renewed fighting began with fury, and this time there was nowhere to retreat, at least not without selling out Pembroke and any chance he might have of pushing through to Starhaven.

The fighting became desperate, his line thinning out more than it should.

William drew his sword as a group of Crown soldiers broke through the line near his position. A sergeant led them, his blade already bloody from earlier fighting. William cut through a spear from one of the conscripts and opened the man's throat with a return cut, then spun to slice an axe in half. His guards moved to support him, but William made short work of the attackers, his sword ignoring armor, shield, and sword.

His line managed to reform, but he was losing too many men. God help him, if he made it through this battle, he might not have enough men to continue the fight.

Then salvation arrived.

A horn sounded from the west. William looked up from where he fought in his lines to see banners cresting a low ridge perhaps half a mile away. Pembroke's force, a thousand strong, appeared on the enemy's left flank like an answered prayer.

The Crown army was completely exposed. Their entire force faced north toward William's position, with no troops positioned to guard against a flank attack. Every man was committed to the assault, officers and reserves alike thrown into the grinding battle in front of them.

The combined weight of five hundred mounted men, concentrated into a narrow front and moving at tremendous speed, slammed into the Crown army's left flank at full gallop, their lances and swords cutting through packed formations like scythes through wheat. Men died by the hundreds in the first seconds of contact as the heavy cavalry carved deep into the enemy ranks.

Panic spread through the Crown formations faster than wildfire. Units at the point of impact simply disintegrated, their survivors streaming away from the slaughter in mindless terror. The contagion spread to adjacent formations as fleeing men carried tales of disaster and death. Officers tried desperately to maintain order, but their commands were lost in the chaos.

They were ready to break.

"Forward!" he roared. "Advance!"

His veterans, sensing the shift in momentum, surged from their defensive positions with renewed vigor. They struck the wavering enemy line just as Pembroke's cavalry completed their initial charge and wheeled to attack again.

The Crown army collapsed. They had held on through a staggering number of casualties because they saw victory at hand. With that suddenly taken away from them, the conscripts broke. Men threw down their weapons and ran, trampling their own comrades in their desperate flight. The Royal infantry tried to maintain some semblance of order, but they were islands of discipline in an ocean of panic.

And even they didn't last long. They saw the writing on the wall and made good their escape as well.

Pembroke's cavalry ranged freely across the battlefield now, cutting down fleeing enemies and preventing any attempt to rally. The knights had reformed into smaller groups after their initial charge, allowing them to pursue multiple targets simultaneously. Their horses were still fresh, easily running down foot soldiers who tried to escape across the open plain.

The slaughter continued for an hour before William finally called a halt. The field lay carpeted with bodies, and his men were exhausted from the pursuit. Prisoners huddled in frightened groups under guard while his troops began the grim work of sorting through the dead and wounded.

One thing William knew, his casualties this time would not be light.

Chapter 23

Port Otleigh, Barony of Canford, Kingsheart, Sidor

William stood near the windows of Port Otleigh's harbormaster's office, watching ships unload supplies at the docks below. The port had fallen three days past, barely a fight at all once the Crown's last organized army shattered on the plains outside Starhaven Bay. The garrison commander had surrendered the moment William's scouts appeared on the coastal road.

Now the only thing that remained was Starhaven itself.

His father had gambled everything on that last battle and lost. But taking the capital itself would be another matter entirely.

Baron Pembroke entered the cramped office, ducking beneath a low beam as he approached the table where William had spread charts of Starhaven Bay and the surrounding lands.

"We'll be able to get the ships you asked for," Pembroke reported, settling into a chair that creaked under his weight. "We also came into a bit of luck. Looks like Edmund was stockpiling supplies here for a coastal defense that never materialized."

"Good, although with our losses, we actually have more material than men to use it. Still, it shouldn't matter, except for the garrison left on the island, there isn't anything else standing in our way. Of course, actually taking it is another matter entirely."

"The island's still holding close to one thousand men, maybe more. They've had time to prepare, and they know we're coming. We can also guarantee none of these will be conscripts. It's just like Edmund to hold back the best men to protect him personally."

"True, but they know they're trapped. My father may not be one to lead men into battle, but he's read his histories. He knows what happens to kings who allow themselves to become isolated on the island and encircled. He'll remember the fate of King Talford, his men resorting to eating each other when the rebels left them on the island to rot. It's why he made Serwyn surrender during the peasants' revolt and why he had his main army holding in Penvale until we got too close. I assure you, he's panicking."

Before Pembroke could respond, the door burst open without ceremony. Both men turned in surprise, although not worry, since the building was well guarded and they would have heard a fight before someone got this far. Still, William was surprised to see that Garris Sinclair was the one who came through the door.

"Well, well. It appears the whelp has learned to bite."

William made a face but didn't take the bait. "Garris. I didn't expect to see you here."

"I imagine not, considering you left me to handle the Ice Landers on my own," Garris said, stepping into the room and closing the door behind him. "But it all worked out and I come bringing gifts, young prince. Three hundred of my best men sailed with me to assist you, and the rest of my army follows. They'll be here within the week, if the war isn't done by then."

Pembroke leaned back in his chair. "That's welcome news. How fares the north?"

"Isaac Cadogan surrendered Shieldshome rather than watch me burn his lands. The Ice Lands are finished as a fighting force. A few holdouts in the eastern baronies, but nothing that can't be handled by a garrison. Which leaves us just the capital."

"That is what we were just discussing. My father has pulled the remainder of his veterans to him and is more or less alone on the island, since he knows any force he sends to try and stop us from blockading it is now too small to matter. The scattered remnants of his last armies might pull together and reform for a new battle, but we're close to the end now, and I'm not sure how many barons will risk their necks."

"None of them will. No, the real fight will be taking the island itself. This won't be like your clever ambushes in the hills," Sinclair said.

"No tricks this time," William agreed. "If we want Starhaven, we'll have to take it head-on, if we have to take it at all. The morale of the men there must be low. They've watched every army Edmund sent get broken. They know they're alone."

"Alone and well-supplied," Pembroke said.

"There's only so much food they can have cached there, and with one thousand extra mouths, that have to stay in fighting shape, they will go through that food very fast. I think our first move is to cut off their supply." William's finger moved across the chart, tracing the shipping lanes that converged on Starhaven's docks. "We blockade the bay, making sure no food or fresh water reaches them. We're coming out of the rainy season and the island has no fresh wells. They rely on collected rainwater and water shipped in from the mainland. Give it a few weeks, and the people will become restless. The soldiers might revolt, or at least they'll be hungry and weak when we finally land."

"That's really the only plan," Garris said. "Until my men get here, there's not much I can do to help you, but I can take my three hundred and hold the gates, block the mouth of the bay."

"That works. When your main force gets here, they can bolster our numbers or act as a ready reserve if any of those scattered remnants try to reform."

"Sounds good to me," Sinclair said.

William was a little worried about how quickly the usually prickly baron agreed, but asked, "Then we're agreed?"

"We are." Garris moved toward the door. "I'll send word to my army to make haste."

The baron left as abruptly as he had arrived, leaving William and Pembroke as stunned as when he'd arrived. Pembroke rose from his chair and moved to close the door Garris had left open.

"You trust him?" William asked.

"I trust him to act in his own interest. Right now, that means taking Starhaven."

"That was my thought, but I wanted to be sure."

Pembroke returned to the table but remained standing, his hands braced on the wooden surface. "William, I need to speak plainly with you."

Something in the older man's tone made William look up from the charts. "What is it?"

"You've run an amazing campaign. The men are calling it the best generalship they've seen since your grandfather's day. But you've kept us all in the dark too much about your plans."

"My plans worked."

"They did, but even I felt at times that you kept plans secret until the last possible moment. There was no reason I couldn't know about the plan to attack the coast until right before we enacted it."

"Plans change quickly in war. What looks possible one day becomes impossible the next."

"That's true, and we all understand that, but involve us in the changing plans. Include us in the planning. We might even offer alternatives or thoughts you hadn't considered."

"The barons question every decision. They argue about everything. Sometimes there isn't time for discussion."

"These men all want to see the kingdom in a better place, and they're putting their lives and the lives of their people on the line to do it. For you to make them feel as if they're no better than common soldiers ... it's wasteful. In spite of the victories, some of the nobles feel like they've been kept out of the glory, that you're piling accolades on yourself while treating them like mushrooms."

"Mushrooms?"

"Kept in the dark and fed shit."

Despite himself, William's mouth twitched toward a smile. "I see."

"I continue to support you wholeheartedly, but I've heard the grumbling. Not just from the more serious malcontents that sided with Sinclair. From men who have staunchly supported you."

"Perhaps you're right. It wasn't intentional, but ... I've found the barons harder to deal with of late."

"They're proud men who've given up everything to follow you. They deserve to feel like partners in this war, not just swords to be pointed at the enemy."

"I hadn't thought of it that way."

"Then reach out to them. Try to smooth the ruffled feathers. You'll need their loyalty after this war ends, and kingdoms aren't held by force alone."

William was quiet for a minute, thinking.

Finally, he said, "When Garris's army arrives, I'll convene a full council. Let them all contribute to the plans for taking Starhaven. Even if we end up with the same strategy, they'll feel ownership of it."

"That would be a good start."

Kenna, River Mark, Sidor

The docks of Kenna came into view as the *Wayfarer* rounded the final bend of the Von River, and Isolde felt her heart lift at the sight. A crowd had already gathered along the waterfront, word of their return having spread faster than their ship could sail. She could see people pointing and calling out as the vessel slid into its spot by the main pier.

"There's quite the welcoming party," Roth observed, securing a rope as his crew prepared to dock.

Isolde spotted Alyssa's personal attendant, Maris, whom she'd met a few times during the previous weeks but never had an extended conversation with. She did know the woman had served the duchess faithfully for over twenty years, and Isolde could see relief written across the woman's face when she caught sight of her mistress standing at the bow.

The gangplank dropped with a solid thud against the dock, and immediately the pier erupted into motion. A half dozen people didn't wait for Alyssa and the rest to descend from the ship; instead, they rushed up the gangplank onto the ship to check on their duchess.

"Your Grace, thank the ancients you're safe," Maris said, her voice trembling with emotion. "We thought we would never see you again."

"I'm well, Maris," Alyssa assured her, patting the woman's hands. "Thanks to Princess Isolde and Master Roth, I'm home."

Isolde turned her attention to the wounded men who were being carefully helped from the ship. Several of Roth's guards, two of Lady Harkow's men, and Sir Colstorm, who served Baron Egerton, bore serious injuries from their fight with Alistair's men. Two others, one of Roth's men and one of Lady Harkow's, had died in the fight on Alistair's ship, their bodies now wrapped in sailcloth and awaiting proper burial.

"These men need immediate attention," Isolde called out to the attendants and guards waiting for Alyssa on the dock. "They fought bravely to rescue the duchess, and they deserve the finest care we can provide. I want them taken to the keep immediately and housed in the best quarters available. Send for the finest healers in Kenna and spare no expense for their treatment."

Alyssa joined her at the railing and said to Maris, "See that it's done exactly as the princess commands. These men risked their lives for me, and I'll not have them want for anything during their recovery."

"Of course, Your Grace," Maris replied, bowing and rushing off to carry out her task.

As the attendant hurried off to make arrangements, Isolde turned back to Roth, who was overseeing the unloading of their gear.

"I must thank you again, Master Roth. Your assistance went far beyond anything I could have expected when I first came to your offices."

"Your Highness is most gracious, but I was merely protecting my investment."

"You were protecting far more than that," Isolde insisted. "Your willingness to risk so much has not gone unnoticed. And I'm still amazed that you were able to convince your contact in Inos to send those warships. Without them turning Alistair's ship, we might never have caught him."

"Trade relationships are built on trust and mutual benefit, Your Highness. My contact understood that helping us served Inos's interests as well as ours. A stable Sidor under Prince William's rule means better trade opportunities for everyone involved."

"Still," Isolde said, "I won't forget what you've done."

Roth inclined his head respectfully. "I was happy to do it, Your Highness. And I'm particularly glad that Her Grace is back safely. River Mark has need of steady leadership in these uncertain times."

"Your concern is appreciated, Master Roth," Alyssa added. "I hope my absence hasn't caused too much disruption."

"Nothing that cannot be easily remedied now that you've returned," Roth assured her. "Though I suspect there will be much work ahead for all of us."

Before anyone could respond, more people were coming up the gangplank, including Baron Egerton and Lady Harkow, pushing past the men unloading supplies from the hurried trip. Both nobles looked as though they had rushed to the docks the moment word of the ship's arrival reached them.

"Your Grace!" Egerton said as he reached them. "Welcome home. We feared ... well, we feared the worst when we learned what had happened."

Alyssa embraced them both, getting a surprised squeak out of Lady Harkow from the ferocity of the hug she gave the smaller woman.

"I must thank both of you for putting your men at risk on my behalf," Alyssa said. "I know the danger you accepted when you agreed to help Princess Isolde pursue my captors."

Egerton waved off her concerns. "Your Grace, any risk was worth taking to see you safely returned. Though I'm sorry we lost good men in the effort."

"Their sacrifice will not be forgotten," Alyssa promised. "The families of the fallen will be provided for, and the wounded will receive the best care possible. I've already given instructions to that effect."

"You honor their service, Your Grace," Lady Harkow said.

"You come at a good time, compounding fortuitous news," Egerton said. "I've received word from my men who are with

Prince William's army. They have made it to the shores of Starhaven Bay. The prince has routed Edmund's forces completely. My men write that the Crown army has been shattered, and it's only a matter of time before Starhaven itself falls."

Isolde felt a warmth rising in her chest. After all the weeks of uncertainty, of not knowing whether William's campaign would succeed or fail, to hear that he was so close to victory filled her with relief.

"That is excellent news," she said. "If William has Edmund's forces routed to that degree, then the war is nearly over."

"Indeed," Egerton agreed. "My men expect that within days, perhaps weeks at most, sanity will be restored to the kingdom."

Isolde turned to look out over the river, thinking through the situation, considering.

"I'm sorry, Alyssa, but I must leave," she declared, turning back to face the group. "If William has the area around Starhaven Bay secured, it should be simple enough to take a ship across Kingsheart Bay and join him there."

Alyssa's eyebrows rose in concern. "Isolde, William will be focused on the siege and wanted you here. There may not be time for ..."

"That's perfectly fine," Isolde interrupted. "I don't need his attention to be constantly on me. I simply want to be with him as this war comes to an end. Whatever happens in these final days, we should face it together."

Alyssa opened her mouth to argue and stopped. Isolde could see something in the eyes of the duchess, an understanding of a woman married to a man at war and the desire to be with him.

Isolde turned back to Baron Egerton and Lady Harkow. "I want both of you to know that I will forever be indebted to your service."

"Your Highness, we did only what honor demanded," Egerton said.

"You did far more than that," Isolde insisted. "And I want you to know that no matter how the final resolution of this conflict unfolds, no matter what the future holds for Sidor, you will always have my support. If there is ever anything I can do for either of you, you need only ask."

Lady Harkow, who had initially been one of Isolde's harshest critics, seemed genuinely moved by the declaration.

"Your Highness is most gracious. We are honored to have served alongside you."

"The honor was mine," Isolde replied, then turned her attention back to Roth, who had been quietly watching the conversation while his men finished securing the ship.

"Master Roth, thank you again for everything. I'll make certain that my people in Rendalia are ready to receive your factors as soon as trade can resume. The appropriate facilities will be made available, and I will personally ensure that all the agreements we've made are honored to the letter."

"I look forward to it, Your Highness," Roth replied with genuine warmth. "I anticipate a long and profitable working relationship between us."

"As do I," Isolde said, meaning every word.

The merchant had proven himself to be far more than just a businessman, but rather a capable ally.

"I know there is still much you have to do to fix everything that happened, but I'm going to make my preparations and leave as soon as possible," Isolde said to Alyssa. "If I'm to reach William while the siege is still underway, I cannot afford to delay."

"I understand," she said quietly. "If I were in your position, I would make the same decision."

"Thank you," Isolde said, genuinely grateful for the understanding.

Alyssa reached out and took both of Isolde's hands in her own. "You have shown more courage and determination in these past months than most people display in a lifetime. Aldric would have been proud to call you family, and I am honored to do so."

The words brought unexpected tears to Isolde's eyes.

"You'll always have a home here in River Mark with us," Alyssa continued. "No matter what the future brings, no matter how the winds of politics may shift, you will always be welcome here."

"Thank you. I pray it won't be long before we can all be together again in better times."

"As do I," Alyssa replied, releasing her hands with obvious reluctance.

Isolde took a step back, looking around at the small group that had gathered on the pier. She had been against coming to the River Mark, but these people had become true allies, and she found she liked all the people she'd met here. Or most, at least.

She would miss them.

Chapter 24

Starhaven, Sidor

"Your Majesty, I bring reports from the harbor defenses," Baron Elsow said, bowing as he entered.

"Speak."

"The blockade holds firm. Three rebel ships patrol the northern approach. Four more are anchored at the bay's mouth. We attempted a sortie at dawn with what vessels remained, but between their ships and the men on the shore, we lost two ships before we could retreat. Your Majesty, the captains say there is no passage, not without losses we cannot afford."

"Then they are cowards."

"The rebels control the waters, and every supply ship we send is turned back or captured. The fishing boats dare not leave port. The city's reserves ..."

He faltered.

"Continue."

"Three weeks. Perhaps four if we ration severely. Food we still have, but fresh water begins to grow scarce."

Edmund rose from the throne and descended the steps, causing Elstow to take an involuntary step backward. Edmund studied the man's face, noting the fear there, the resignation.

"You come before your king to tell me defeat is inevitable."

"I merely report the situation, Your Majesty. The decision remains yours."

"How generous of you. What of reinforcements from the mainland baronies?"

Elstow's silence answered before his words did. "The barons no longer respond to summons, Your Majesty. Most say they have no more men to give."

"Excuses. They abandon their rightful king in his hour of need."

"Perhaps if Your Majesty were to consider negotiations ..."

Edmund turned. The look he gave Elstow made the baron blanch.

"Leave."

"Your Majesty, I only meant ..."

"I said leave. Send Orlan to me."

Elstow bowed and retreated, his footsteps quick across the marble. Edmund returned to the window, his mind racing through possibilities. His hand went to the Key under his tunic. With it, he had raised armies from nothing, filled his coffers with donations given willingly by men who wept with joy to serve him.

But here, trapped on this island, what use was the Key?

The doors opened again. Orlan entered, bowing low.

"Your Majesty summoned me?"

"Any word on Alistair?" he asked, not that it mattered now.

Not with everything falling apart.

"We received a wyvern this morning from one of our friends in Kenna. He is dead, Your Majesty."

"Damn," Edmund said.

He didn't care so much for Everwood himself. The man was a turncoat, had sold out his liege lord, and murdered his commander to gain status. Still, he had hoped at least something would go right.

With Alyssa here ... not that it mattered.

"And the messenger who arrived under flag of truce?"

"He's still here, waiting, Your Majesty."

"From my son?"

"No, Your Majesty. From Baron Sinclair."

"Bring him."

Orlan departed and returned moments later with a young man wearing Sinclair's colors. The messenger bowed deeply, then extended a sealed letter. Edmund took it, broke the seal, and read.

Safe passage from Starhaven for Edmund and any who wished to accompany him. Ships will be supplied to carry them to any port of their choosing on one condition: that he surrender the Key.

How did Sinclair even know of its existence?

Edmund read it twice, then looked at the messenger. "This is Baron Sinclair's offer?"

"It is, Your Majesty. The baron asked me to convey that the terms are not negotiable, but that he will honor his word if you accept. Safe passage, unmolested, to wherever you wish to go."

"How generous. And if I refuse?"

The messenger's throat worked. "Then the blockade continues until Starhaven falls. The baron said ... he said you know what happens when cities fall after a long siege."

Edmund folded the letter slowly. "You may tell Baron Sinclair that I will consider his offer. Return tomorrow for my answer."

The messenger bowed and departed. Edmund handed the letter to Orlan, who scanned it quickly.

"Your Majesty, this could be ..."

"A trap. Obviously." Edmund walked back toward the throne but did not sit. "Sinclair wants the Key. They all do. They must have learned of its existence somehow. They'll kill me the moment I step onto their ship. I don't trust his word. The word of a traitor. What value does such a pledge hold?"

Orlan said nothing. He understood the rhetorical nature of the question.

"Still," Edmund continued, "there is something in the offer. They want the Key more than they want my death. For now." If they kill me immediately, they gain nothing. Better to let me go, take the Key, and hunt me down later at their leisure. Or perhaps they fear what the Key might do in battle, think it some great weapon that could turn the tide."

"Could it, Your Majesty?"

"No." Edmund shook his head. "Still, I wonder why it's Sinclair and not my son making the offer. Last I'd heard, he was in the Ice Lands fighting Cadogan, and now he's here and demanding the Key. Is it possible William doesn't know about it? That this is Sinclair's play alone?"

"It's possible, my lord."

"Leave me."

"Your Majesty, there are decisions that must be ..."

"I said leave!"

Orlan bowed and withdrew. Edmund waited until the doors closed, then slammed his fist against the nearest wall. Pain shot through his knuckles, but he welcomed it, a physical sensation to anchor him against the tide of fury threatening to overwhelm his reason.

Everything was falling apart.

He forced himself to breathe slowly, to master the rage and fear. Emotions were weakness. He had taught himself that long ago, had learned to present whatever face the situation required while his mind worked coldly through problems. He was intelligent enough to see the pattern, to understand where this path led.

Without the Key, he had no means of raising new armies. The artifact's power had been his greatest advantage, letting him turn the common folk into devoted followers who gave everything to his cause, but keeping the Key meant staying in Starhaven, meant waiting for the inevitable fall of the city and whatever fate William had planned for him. A trial, perhaps. A public execution to satisfy the rebels' thirst for justice.

All his plans, all his ambition, reduced to a simple choice: keep the artifact and die, or surrender it and flee.

The thought of fleeing galled him. He was Edmund Whitton, Duke of Kingsheart, rightful King of Sidor. He had plotted for decades to reach this throne, had removed every obstacle in his path, had even killed his own nephew to claim what should have been his from the beginning. His brother Gavric had been given everything: the crown, the loyalty, the love of the people, simply because he was born first. Edmund had been pushed aside, dismissed as the spare, the one who would never matter.

But Edmund was smarter than Gavric, more capable, more willing to do what was necessary. He had proven that by outlasting his brothers, by taking the throne that should have been his by merit if not by birth.

And now William.

Was it fate, that he would remove those in his way and the boy he adopted would then do the same to him? Were the ancients playing a game on him? Showing him his hubris?

Not that it mattered. Now he only had one decision.

The Key was power, but it was not the only power. Edmund had his intelligence, his ruthlessness, his willingness to do whatever was necessary. He did not have the Key when he got the throne initially, so he could do it again.

He turned from the wall and walked back across the audience chamber.

Edmund climbed the steps back to the throne and sat, the carved wood hard against his back. He'd made his decision. This room had witnessed Gavric's long rule, and Serwyn's much briefer one, had seen Edmund take his place as rightful king. Now it would witness his departure.

It wasn't an easy decision, giving up everything he'd ever wanted, but it also wasn't a hard one once he'd considered the alternative.

Without fresh water from the mainland, the island's wells would run dry within weeks. The granaries held perhaps a month's supply, and after that, starvation. The garrison numbered barely fifteen hundred men, and while veterans all, they were not enough to defeat William's army.

Once the water ran out, the nobles would turn on him immediately.

He could not win. The truth of it was plain.

"Orlan, get back in here," he bellowed, knowing the man was hovering just outside the door.

Orlan entered almost immediately, proving him right, anxious as ever.

"Your Majesty, I ..."

"Be silent and listen. Send for Conservator Chatwell and request his presence here immediately. Tell him I require an oath-binding ceremony for a prisoner exchange with Baron Sinclair."

Orlan's eyes widened. "Do you mean you plan to ...?"

"This is not a conversation, Orlan. Go now."

Orlan opened his mouth as though to protest further, then closed it and bowed. "As you command, Your Majesty."

He withdrew, and Edmund was once again alone in the vast room. The decision was made. Now came the hardest part, the waiting.

He had never been good at waiting.

Edmund rose and descended from the dais, pacing the length of the audience chamber. Around him, the tapestries on the walls depicted scenes from Sidor's history: Charles Whitton establishing the dynasty, Edgar Whitton the Second leading the First Alliance, and Alther the Bold conquering Kingsheart and establishing Sidor as a kingdom. But nothing lasted. Power shifted, dynasties rose and fell, and the only constant was change.

He stopped before one tapestry showing his grandfather, King Aldwyn, receiving tribute from defeated enemies. The old man had been ruthless in his way, had crushed rebellions and executed traitors without hesitation. But Aldwyn had ruled in simpler times, when threats came from outside the kingdom rather than from within the family itself. Edmund's challenges had been more complex, requiring more subtle solutions than simple military force.

And now those solutions had failed him. William had proven too capable, too quick to adapt, too willing to take risks that should not have succeeded. The boy was a better warrior than he would have ever imagined, leading Edmund, for the hundredth time in just the last week, to curse himself for not strangling him as a child.

He turned from the tapestry and walked back to the throne, climbing the dais once more. The seat felt colder now, less welcoming. It knew he was leaving, perhaps. Or perhaps he was simply projecting his own emotions onto carved wood and ancient stone.

Time passed with agonizing slowness. Edmund counted his breaths, measured the light shifting through the windows, and listened to the distant sounds of the keep around him.

Finally, footsteps approached. Edmund straightened in his seat as Orlan returned, but the scribe was not alone.

"Your Majesty, the Conservator Chatwell," Orlan said, standing aside for the Acolyte Elder.

"Your Majesty." Chatwell's bow was perfunctory, the bare minimum that courtesy required.

"Conservator." Edmund descended from the dais, crossing the chamber to meet Chatwell on level ground. "Thank you for coming so quickly."

"Your scribe indicated urgency regarding an oath-binding ceremony."

"I require such a ceremony for a prisoner exchange with Baron Sinclair," Edmund said, not wanting to explain directly that he was exchanging an artifact for his life.

"The Covenant takes no position on matters of war and succession."

"This is asking no different. This is simply two parties seeking binding terms for an exchange, which I believe is the purpose of the ceremony. I am not asking you to take sides; I am asking you to fulfill the traditional role your order has always maintained."

"I see. What guarantees are you asking from the Covenant?"

"Safe conduct to the agreed meeting for both sides and a binding of the agreement that is struck there, with both parties swearing to honor the exchange and not attempt any deception or betrayal during the ceremony itself."

"That is permissible. I will conduct the ceremony, provided both parties agree to the terms and appear before me with genuine intent to honor their oaths. The Covenant cannot prevent men from breaking their word, but we can ensure the consequences of such betrayal are understood and enforced. Any man who breaks a bound oath will find himself exiled from civilized lands, unable to trade, unable to seek refuge, unable to call upon any kingdom for aid."

"That is acceptable."

"When would you wish this ceremony to occur?"

"I am making arrangements for a meeting under truce now, and would hope the peace of that meeting could also be assured by your offices. It will probably be in the next day or two."

"I will make the necessary preparations. You must send word to Baron Sinclair outlining the terms and requesting his agreement, informing him of the Covenant's participation. The ceremony requires both parties to appear voluntarily and swear their oaths in person."

"Of course." Edmund inclined his head in a gesture of respect he did not entirely feel. "Thank you, Conservator. Your assistance in this matter will not be forgotten."

"I assist the traditions of the Covenant, Your Majesty, not any particular king or rebel," Chatwell said, and then departed.

Edmund watched him go, then turned and walked back to the throne. He climbed the dais and sat, the chamber once again empty save for himself.

The message to Garris Sinclair would determine everything that followed. It must be worded carefully, must convey strength even in surrender, must make clear that Edmund was choosing this path rather than being forced into it. Desperation would invite exploitation. Calculated pragmatism would earn respect, even from an enemy.

Edmund called out to the guards. "Bring me writing materials. Parchment, ink, quill, wax, and seal."

One of the guards departed and returned several minutes later with the requested items. Edmund accepted them and dismissed the man, then arranged the materials on the arm of the throne. Not ideal for writing, but he would not leave this seat until the message was complete.

He dipped the quill in ink and began to write, the words formed slowly and deliberately.

Baron Sinclair,

I have received your terms regarding the exchange of prisoners for the artifact known as the Eclipse Key. After careful consideration of the military situation and the welfare of those under my authority, I am prepared to accept these terms with the following conditions.

The exchange will be conducted through an oath-binding ceremony overseen by Conservator Chatwell of the Covenant of the Ancients. This ceremony will ensure both parties honor their agreements and provide protection during the exchange itself. By your request, I assume you do not want this meeting to happen in the light of your other rebels and offer a meeting under a flag of truce tomorrow at midnight. After the ceremony, I will surrender the Eclipse Key intact.

In return, you will swear before the Conservator to provide safe conduct for myself and any men who choose to accompany me, guaranteeing no pursuit, attack, or imprisonment of any party departing under these terms. You will further swear not to interfere with our passage from Starhaven or attempt any deception during the ceremony.

If these terms are acceptable, send confirmation by return wyvern.

Edmund Whitton

He read the message twice, checking each phrase for weakness or ambiguity. The words struck the right tone: firm but not aggressive, clear but not desperate. Edmund set the quill aside and waited for the ink to dry, then folded the parchment carefully. He melted wax over a candle brought by the guards, pressed his seal into it, and held the sealed message.

"Summon the Master of Wyverns," Edmund called to the guards.

One guard saluted and departed. Edmund remained on the throne, the sealed message in his hand.

Sinclair would accept. Edmund knew men, knew how to read their ambitions and motivations. The baron wanted the Key, and Edmund had a good idea why. If he was right, this would be his final shot at William. If he could not have the throne, the least he could do was ensure the boy did not keep it either.

The Master of Wyverns arrived, an elderly man whose hands trembled slightly as he approached the throne. Edmund descended the dais and handed him the sealed message.

"This goes to Baron Garris Sinclair at his camp at the gates. Use your fastest wyvern. I need confirmation of receipt by tonight."

"It will be done, Your Majesty."

The man withdrew, and Edmund climbed back to the throne. He sat once more and looked out over the empty space, alone in the vast chamber where thirty-seven Whitton kings had sat before him.

The throne would be his again. Garris and William would not get along once this was over, of that Edmund was certain. And their disagreement would open the door for his return.

Chapter 25

Garris stood in the narrow space on one side of the castle wall, a small green area there to maintain a firm holding for the city walls that also served smugglers as an out-of-the-way place for people to meet out of the view of others.

Tonight, however, it was a place of kings and barons.

Shadow covered the entire area; what little moonlight there was blocked by the wall. The docks themselves were silent, and no boats were on the water, as the siege bore on into its sixth day.

People stayed home, rationing what little fresh water they still had, afraid of being filled with arrows by one side or the other.

Edmund picked this location because it was hard to see from the land, and no one from the city could see what was happening there. If the people here knew what he was planning, there would be riots, mostly among his own soldiers, and if William learned what Sinclair was doing, he would try to take the city now, blood-shed be damned.

Sinclair's guard, an Iron Keep veteran named Cullum, waited three paces behind him with a hand resting on his sword hilt. The man had fought at Four Corners and the Darien Hills and was not one taken with honor and oaths. He was a good fighter, but more importantly, Garris trusted him to keep his mouth shut about whatever transpired here.

Footsteps approached from the small path leading around to the harbor. Three figures materialized from the darkness: one tall and straight-backed despite everything, one slouched with a pockmarked face, and the last shorter and hunched in the robes of the Covenant. The soon-to-be-deposed king showed the same arrogance he always had, even now.

And of course, he'd chosen Colm to guard his back. Ever the loyal lapdog. Unusually, though, Colm carried a small table, its legs folded up into it so that he could carry it in one hand, leaving his sword arm free.

"Let's get this done," Edmund said impatiently.

Chatwell held out his hand, and Colm gave him the small, well-crafted folding table that he set between them before producing a small leather case from within his robes and held it out on the palm of his hand.

"The binding of oaths is among the most sacred rites preserved from the time before the Fall. The Ancients themselves witnessed such promises, and their judgment falls upon those who would break faith."

Garris watched the conservator arrange his implements with care. He had witnessed oath-bindings before, though never under circumstances quite like these. The ritual itself dated back more than one thousand years, to the very early days of the Covenant.

"The terms have been agreed upon?" Chatwell looked first at Edmund, then at Garris.

"They have," Edmund said.

"Then we shall begin," Chatwell said, unstopping the vial and pouring a small amount of oil into the clay bowl. The scent reached Garris even from several feet away, something so pungent as to almost be rancid. "Baron Sinclair, step forward and place your right hand over the bowl."

Garris moved closer to the table. The oil in the bowl reflected no light, appearing as nothing more than a dark pool against the pale clay. He extended his hand, holding it steady above the surface.

"Your Majesty, please do the same."

Edmund joined him, his hand hovering opposite Garris's own. The two men stood close enough that Garris could make out the lines of exhaustion around Edmund's eyes. He could see the defeat in them.

Chatwell took a white cord and began to wrap it around both their wrists in a pattern that formed loops and knots. His fingers tying bindings that Garris supposed had been passed down through generations of the Acolytes.

"You come before the Ancients and the Covenant to swear oaths that will bind your actions and your honor. To break such oaths is to place yourself beyond the protection of sacred law, to mark yourself as one who has abandoned the old ways and the wisdom of those who came before."

The cord tightened as Chatwell continued his work. Garris felt the pressure against his wrist, not painful but insistent.

"Should either of you violate the terms sworn here, the consequences will be immediate and absolute. The Covenant will declare you excommunicated, cast out from the community of the faithful. No oath sworn to you thereafter shall carry weight or obligation. Any man who made promises to you before your violation shall be absolved of those commitments, free to act as though they had never been bound. The lords of the Shattered Lands, all who hold title and territory, will be enjoined to pursue your capture and deliver you to justice. The full power of the Covenant, which has endured since the Fall itself, will be brought to bear upon you until you are brought low."

"Do you both understand these consequences?" Chatwell asked.

"I understand," Garris said.

"I understand," Edmund said.

Chatwell reached for something else in his case, withdrawing a small knife with a blade no longer than a man's thumb. The handle appeared to be carved from bone, yellowed with age.

"Then speak your oaths."

"I, Edmund Whitton, rightful King of Sidor and Duke of King-sheart, do swear before the Ancients and the Covenant that I will surrender into Baron Garris Sinclair's possession the exact artifact we have agreed to exchange. In return, Baron Sinclair will permit one ship carrying myself and my chosen men to pass through his section of the blockade without challenge or interference. This ship will be allowed to proceed to whatever destination I choose, and Baron Sinclair will take no action to prevent our departure or reveal our movements to others."

Garris couldn't help but notice Edmund had phrased his oath, claiming still to be the rightful king even as he prepared to flee like a common criminal. The man's pride knew no bounds.

Chatwell turned his attention to Garris. "Baron Sinclair, speak your oath."

"I, Garris Sinclair, Baron of Stormhaven, do swear before the Ancients and the Covenant that upon receiving the artifact we have agreed upon, I will permit one ship carrying Duke Edmund to pass through my portion of the blockade without challenge or interference. This ship will be allowed to depart, and I will take no action to prevent its departure or reveal its movements to others."

Edmund scowled at Garris's chosen title for him but said nothing. Neither man wanted to say what the artifact was, not here in front of the elder.

Chatwell lifted the bone-handled knife. "Extend your left hands."

Both men obeyed, offering their free hands palm-up. The conservator pressed the blade against Edmund's palm first, drawing it across the flesh in a swift motion that left a thin line of blood welling up. He repeated the action with Garris's hand. The cut stung but remained shallow, more symbolic than truly harmful.

"Join your palms together over the bowl."

Garris pressed his left hand against Edmund's, feeling the warm slickness of blood between their skin. Their clasped hands hung suspended above the clay bowl as drops of mingled blood fell into the oil below.

"By blood and oath, by the witness of the Ancients and the authority of the Covenant, let these promises be binding until death or fulfillment releases you." Chatwell began unwinding the cord from their right wrists, his movements as deliberate as when he had tied it. "To break faith now is to condemn yourself to the judgment I have described. Let no man say he did not understand the weight of what he has sworn."

The cord came free, and Garris pulled his hands back, wiping the blood from his left palm on the cloth Chatwell offered him. Edmund did the same, neither man looking at the other during this mundane act of cleaning away the physical evidence of their oath.

"The binding is complete." Chatwell gathered his implements and returned them to their case with the same careful attention he had shown in removing them. "What is bled cannot be un-bled;

what is sworn cannot be unsworn. May the Ancients judge you both according to your adherence to what you have sworn."

Edmund reached inside his cloak, his hand re-emerging holding a leather pouch, small enough to fit in a palm. For a heartbeat, he held onto it, squeezing it tight in his palm.

Garris waited. He let the silence build. Let Edmund feel every second of this surrender.

Finally, he held it out, offering it to Garris, who took it from him quickly. It was so light, feeling like there was almost nothing in the small package. He opened the back and looked into it. It was as Cadogan had described.

Moreover, he could feel the power from it as his hand touched it, as if the artifact was reaching inside of him, sealing itself to him. There was no doubt in his mind that this was the artifact they agreed on.

"And my ship?" Edmund asked. "I don't want your men getting jumpy and trying to make a break for it."

"It must go at night, and soon, before more men get here and the Gates are reinforced with too many eyes for me to keep quiet. You have until dawn the day after tomorrow, and then I cannot guarantee your son will not see your escape and try to stop you."

"You swore ..."

"I swore I would not stop you; I made no promises about William. But, to uphold the truth of our binding, I am telling you now, two days, and the odds of that go up significantly. If you want to get out of here, do so soon."

Edmund scowled at him but said nothing. Garris had upheld his part of the agreement.

"He will suspect. William is a lot of things, but he is not an idiot. He will know you let me through."

"By then, I will have consolidated my position."

Edmund gave a small shrug and turned to leave. Garris had no illusions about William's reaction if he discovered this bargain. The young man would see it as betrayal, as Garris choosing personal advantage over the alliance that had brought them this far. William would be right, by a certain measure, but righteousness never really mattered. Only power did.

The conservator, Edmund, and Colm departed, disappearing back into the night. Garris watched him go, still feeling the power from the small pouch clasped in his hand.

"My lord," Cullum prodded.

"We return to the ship," Garris said, turning toward the ship. "And you will speak of tonight's events to no one, not even under direct questioning from William or any other baron. What transpired here remains between those who witnessed it."

"Understood, my lord."

Garris nodded once and thought to the future. He'd done it, and soon he would have his reward for being the one to start all this. The one with the courage to stand up to the Crown.

Shores of Starhaven Bay, Havensport, Barony of Penleigh, Kingsheart, Sidor

Soldiers hauled open the inner gate and the keep's yard came into view. Isolde stepped down from the saddle and passed her reins to Galer without looking at him. The stone stairs to the great hall rose on her left and she took them two at a time, crossing quickly to where one of the guards said her husband was.

She knew he was planning. William never stopped planning.

Sure enough, she found him in a large council room, maps covered a long table where he bent over them with Pembroke and two captains she knew by sight. He had taken off his mail but still wore the padded jerkin. A squire stood near the hearth with a pitcher in both hands and eyes fixed on his prince like a dog fixed on a thrown bone.

William looked up as she came in, and for a moment, she froze, seeing his warm eyes and face, now with more lines.

"Isolde?"

"Hello, husband."

He came around the table without a word and closed his arms about her. She pressed her cheek to his chest, felt the heat through linen, and the fast rise and fall against her skin.

"I got the wyvern about Aunt Alyssa. Thank the ancients you brought her back safely."

"She's well, back resting in Kenna with Maris fussing over her."

"Pembroke, see to what we discussed, and see if we can't find more boats. We're going to need them," William said to the baron, stepping away to retain proper decorum, who in turn nodded, taking the other men and the squire with him, leaving the couple alone. "I'm glad you got her back, but ... you put yourself in personal danger by doing so. You should never have boarded a ship full of armed men. That was so dangerous."

"I stabbed that danger in the back while he was occupied with Roth. He's dead now."

"That's not what I mean."

Isolde moved to the table and poured herself wine from a pitcher. "Then what do you mean?"

"You could have been killed."

"But I wasn't." She drank, letting the wine steady her. "You put yourself in danger all the time, for the good of the realm. That's all I was doing."

"That's different."

"How so?"

"Because I'm a soldier. I was trained for battle."

"And I took no undue risk." Isolde set the cup down. "I pulled together every fighting man I could in the time available and had more than enough to win. We lost two men in the fighting, and Sir Alistair and his crew are dead. By any measure, that's a decisive victory with minimal cost."

"You still ..."

"I took only the actions absolutely necessary, nothing more. What would you have had me do? The River Mark barons refused to help; they were more concerned about their own lands than saving your aunt. There was no one else."

He studied her face for a long moment, then his shoulders dropped. "You're right."

"I am?" she said, surprised he gave up the point.

"You did what needed doing and brought her home." He rubbed his face. "I just don't like knowing you're in danger."

Isolde moved to stand beside him. "I feel the same way about you. Every time you ride into battle, every report of fighting ... but I can't ask you not to fight. I know what this all means to you."

"I know."

She moved past him to the window, looking out over the water toward Starhaven.

"How are things going here?" Isolde asked.

William's expression darkened. "Not well."

"Not well?" She turned to face him fully. "You have the king trapped on an island with no food and no water. I would think all you need now is time."

"The war itself is going well but the political situation ... that's the disaster."

"Tell me."

"I've had issues with the barons the entire campaign, constant arguments about strategy, going off on their own, complaints about what they want that is greater than winning, constant petty squabbles. Every decision becomes a debate, every plan gets challenged."

"That's the nature of leading nobles."

"It's more than that. They don't trust me, or they don't respect me as more than a commander, and I'm not sure which is worse. And now Garris has suddenly reappeared."

"Your update said he split off to fight the Ice Landers."

"He did, and he won. Came back with three hundred men and promises that his full army will soon follow. Showed up at like nothing happened, like we're all united."

Isolde watched him pace. "You don't believe that."

"I know Garris Sinclair wants the throne; he doesn't try to hide it. He's older, more experienced, has a reputation as a landholder, and he left me when I needed him most. Took two thousand men north in spite of the situation and now that I am on the verge of taking the capital, he's back in time to participate in its fall."

"You think he's positioning himself."

"I'm certain of it, and he's been talking to people, gathering support among the other barons, building a case that he should rule instead of me. Worse, if things are at all how they were in the Blackheath, he might succeed. My father is the man we are deposing, after all."

"You're right," Isolde said. "Nobles are difficult to command. But William ... these are men of pride. Great lords who expect to be consulted, to have their counsel heard. If they're pushed aside too many times, they take it personally. They hold grudges long."

"What should I have done differently?"

"I keep telling you; include them, ask their opinions even if you already know what you'll decide. Make them feel invested. You get too focused on your own goal, too sure of yourself in battle, but they aren't just soldiers. They're lords with lands and families and futures at stake. They need to believe their voices matter."

"Even when they're wrong?"

"Especially then. You can guide them to the right conclusions. Make them think it was partly their idea." Isolde touched his arm. "Let them share the glory."

"I'm glad you're here to help me manage these things. I can win battles. But this other part ..."

"Is just as important. More important, maybe. You need to remember that when it comes time to assume the throne. The battle for Starhaven might be ending, but the real war starts after. Convincing the barons to follow you, building a government, healing the kingdom. That's going to take both of us."

"What do I do about Garris?"

"I'll ask around, find out what he's planning and who supports him."

"What if it's already too late? What if he's already built enough support?"

"Then we deal with it, but first, end this siege. Get Edmund to surrender. Finish the war so we can focus on what comes next."

William rose as well. "The blockade should force it soon. We've cut off all supplies. He can't hold out more than a few days."

"Good. Then we have work to do."

Chapter 26

Starhaven, Sidor

The crates required two men each to lift, and Edmund watched a pair of his remaining soldiers struggle with one that held gold sovereigns sealed in canvas bags. Behind them, Orlan supervised two more men carrying a smaller chest filled with platinum wyverns and various imperial seals Edmund had collected over the years.

Orlan hurried up the gangplank once the men had the chest secured below. His thin face held that perpetual expression of nervous eagerness, like a hound desperate to please.

"The manifest shows twenty-three crates loaded, Your Majesty. Another six wait on the dock. We also have thirty crates of trade goods, five more of art and artifacts, and three containing as much of your father's collection as we could fit."

"How long?"

"An hour."

Edmund turned toward the island city behind them. Starhaven's high tower caught the morning sun.

He'd hoped to be off before the sun came up and people came out of their homes only to see their king fleeing. Not that many would be out. The city had all but shut down since the start of the siege.

"Your Majesty?" Orlan's voice intruded on his thoughts.

"What?"

"The men ask if we should bring the tapestries from the throne room. They're quite valuable, and ..."

"Leave them." Edmund moved to the ship's rail, his hands curling around the wood. "Bring only what holds practical value that we can use when we get to Werna. Gold, seals, documents. The rest means nothing."

Orlan bowed and scurried back down the gangplank. Edmund heard him relay the orders in that reedy voice that had grated on Edmund's nerves for years, yet the man's absolute loyalty and willingness to perform distasteful tasks had made him indispensable. Orlan would follow Edmund to Werna and beyond if necessary. Some men craved purpose more than principle.

Colm emerged from below decks. Another who had agreed to come with him, leaving their past behind. Colm possessed neither Orlan's intellect nor his talent for administration, but he excelled at violence and intimidation.

"The hold's near full," Colm said. "Captain says any more weight and we'll sit low in the water."

"How much can we take?"

"Three more crates. Maybe four."

Six crates remained, two of which held personal effects he could sacrifice. The other four contained either gold or treasures; those were what mattered.

"Bring the four crates marked with red wax seals. Leave the others."

Colm nodded and returned below decks without comment. Edmund appreciated that quality. The knight never questioned orders, never offered unsolicited opinions, simply executed commands.

The sun climbed higher as the final crates were loaded aboard. Edmund retreated to the small cabin the ship's captain had vacated for him, a cramped space with a narrow bunk and a desk barely large enough to hold an open map. He'd need to purchase a larger vessel once they reached Werna, something suitable for a king in exile. The Wernans respected power and wealth. Edmund possessed one and carried enough of the other to establish himself in their mercantile society.

A knock on the cabin door interrupted his planning.

"Enter."

Orlan slipped inside, closing the door behind him. "The loading is complete, Your Majesty. The captain says we can depart whenever you're ready."

"Then tell him to push off."

"Of course, Your Majesty," Orlan said, turning to a ship hand and passing the message, but not leaving the doorway. "May I speak freely?"

Edmund gestured permission while studying the map spread across the desk. Werna's coastline showed multiple port cities, each marked with notes about their primary exports and political affiliations. Rikshof served as the capital, seat of the Chancellor and the Directorate. Edmund would need to establish connections there first.

"I worry about our reception in Werna," Orlan said.

"They'll welcome anyone with sufficient gold. They don't care about anything else. But only if we leave this place before my son notices and tries to stop us."

Orlan ducked his head in agreement and scuttled away, taking the hint.

The crew moved to their positions, casting off mooring lines and raising sails. Edmund returned to the deck to watch Starhaven recede as the ship caught the wind and moved toward the bay's narrow mouth. The Gates rose on either side, two massive fortifications that controlled access to the bay and protected the capital from seaborne threats. Edmund had dined in those forts dozens of times, had appointed their commanders personally, had stood on their walls surveying his domain.

The ship passed between them without incident. Edmund watched soldiers in Sinclair's colors standing on both fortifications. None of them called out or made threatening gestures. They simply watched as the vessel sailed past, carrying their defeated king into exile.

Colm joined Edmund at the rail, his scarred face expressionless. "We'll be back."

It wasn't a question. Edmund appreciated Colm's certainty even as he recognized it as empty loyalty rather than strategic analysis. But loyalty, even the empty kind, had value when one's position required rebuilding from nothing.

"Yes," Edmund said.

The open sea beckoned beyond the Gates. Edmund had sailed these waters before, knew how hazardous it could be, at the mouth of the Leviathan Straits. Even in summers, some of the giant creatures remained, able to escape the pull of the maw, making it an all but impossible stretch of water for ships to pass through unharmed. Captain Strom seemed competent enough, barking orders to his small crew as they adjusted sail angles and prepared for deeper waters.

Orlan emerged from below decks carrying a leather folder stuffed with documents.

"I've organized the most important papers, Your Majesty. The agreements with the Alchmaran shipwrights are here, along with correspondence from several Wernan merchant houses we've dealt with previously."

Edmund took the folder but didn't open it immediately. The ship's motion increased as they left the bay's protected waters, the deck rolling beneath his feet in a rhythm he'd never particularly enjoyed. He preferred solid ground and had never enjoyed sailing much.

"Your Majesty, should you rest?" Orlan hovered nearby, always hovering. "The voyage to Werna will take days ..."

"I'll rest when I choose to rest."

Orlan retreated, chastened. Edmund heard him descend into the crew's quarters, likely to fuss over the stored crates and ensure nothing had shifted during departure. The man's nervous energy sometimes proved tiresome in close quarters.

The ship sailed north along Sidor's western coast. Edmund remained on deck, watching the shoreline pass. He'd walked that coast as a young man, before Gavric became king, before Edmund had learned to transform ambition into power. The memories felt distant now, belonging to a different person. That Edmund had died slowly over the years, sacrificed piece by piece to necessity and pragmatism.

Pragmatism, like giving up the throne to save his own neck, and start trying to find a way to take it again. It wouldn't be easy, but he would find a way to make it happen. He'd done it once, he could do it again.

With one last look, he turned and headed back to his borrowed cabin, leaving Sidor behind.

William and his men swarmed off the ship, ready to fight their way into the city. A thousand men were under strength compared to the forces he was mustering, now that Sinclair's men had joined them, but it was still going to be a fight.

Or it should have been.

Instead, they found men with banners pulled down, weapons stacked, and hands in the air, surrendering. Row after row of Crown soldiers, just giving up without a fight.

For all the buildup to this fight, it was anticlimactic enough to leave his men just standing there, staring at each other, the Crown soldiers staring back, no one sure what to do about each other. Just shocked.

"Take prisoners and hold them until we can figure out what's going on," William commanded, his men hopping to it now that they had straightforward orders.

"Your Highness!" Eskild said, pushing through the men. "The garrison commander wants to meet you. He's a knight named Balmar."

"Show me to him," William said.

Eskild led William and a guard detachment back through the surrendering men to one of the warehouses that had been turned into a command post at some point. In front was a man in fine armor, but no helmet.

"Sir Balmar?" William said.

"Yes, my prince. I was left in charge of the soldiers in the city when the ki... former king and his closest allies left the city."

It did not surprise him that his father was gone. The only way his father would have allowed his throne to be taken from him without a fight was if he'd already given it up and run for his life.

Although it left a lot of other questions in its wake.

"Were you given orders on what to do after he left?"

"No, my prince. I had the impression from our former commander, who left with him, that we were to fight to the death but ... it seems pointless now."

"I am glad you came to that conclusion. Enough Sidorians have died in the last two years. How did he leave? Where did he go?"

"I don't know, Your Highness. Our commander had us hold a cordon around the docks early in the morning two days ago just as the sun was coming up, keeping everyone away from it, telling us smuggled food and water were being brought in, and they were concerned that there would be a rush on the docks. So our orders were to protect the docks and face the city, keeping people out. For a time, our officers would check on us, give updated orders. At one point, they even had us push further back toward the city. People had heard there was a shipment and were starting to gather. But then, the orders stopped. An hour passed, then two, and we heard no word, but my orders were clear. Stay out by the cordon and don't let any of my men leave there. I'd guessed they were concerned that the men were hungry too and might break to get to it themselves and then there would be a rush. After three hours, though, I got concerned. I sent a man to check, just to get updated orders. But they were gone. The king, the men with him. All gone. There was no food. There was no water. There was nothing. Since then, we've been trying to figure out what happened."

"But it was at the docks, correct?" William asked. "That must mean a ship."

"That's what I assumed, but you controlled the entire bay. Where would a ship go? How would it get out? Maybe a rowboat, but the king had thirty men with him. Honestly, I have no answers for you, Your Highness."

"I appreciate your telling me everything. We're going to hold your men in custody for a time, just to make sure there's no violence while we settle the situation. I've already discussed it with my commanders, and we want this war to end as much as anyone. I expect to give all those not taking part in atrocities pardons and send them back to their baronies and their lives."

"Thank you, my prince."

William left the disposition of the soldiers to his men and went to find the command group. Sinclair was nowhere to be seen, still holding the Gates, but he found Pembroke and a few of his knights, still trying to think through what could have possibly happened. If there had been a ship large enough to carry thirty men, his men would have reported it.

"Have you heard?" he asked Pembroke when he got to them.

"That your father fled with his men? Yes."

"How is that possible, though?"

"I don't know," Pembroke said. "But it's concerning. We are pretty sure all of his personal guard left, the cutthroat Colm, and his scribe, based on what we've been able to get from the soldiers, descriptions and whatnot, but we will keep interviewing them to see if we can find out anything else."

"Not that it matters now. He's gone. I want him found, but right now we have to figure out what to do about the city. We need to start bringing in water and foodstuffs. The soldiers look fed, so I'm sure he starved the city's populace. He wouldn't give up a meal, but I know my father would have no qualms about starving others."

"I've already ordered supplies brought up."

"Thank you, Baron. Let's go see the city, I guess."

They walked through the gates into Starhaven's lower city, where Pembroke's men were already distributing bread and salted meat to crowds of grateful citizens. Families who'd been hiding in their homes, fearing a battle, slowly came out of their homes and hiding places, mothers clutching infants.

Word was spreading that relief supplies were coming with William's forces.

They continued up the winding streets toward the middle city, where the merchants and minor nobles lived. Here too, William saw signs of recent hardship. Shop windows stood empty, and the usual bustle of commerce had been replaced by an oppressive quiet.

They climbed the steep streets leading to the upper city, where the great lords kept their mansions and the royal palace dominated the skyline. Here, at least, the buildings showed no signs of want or neglect. These men had wanted for nothing, even with the blockade.

288

But as they approached the palace gates, the usual crowd of petitioners, merchants, and minor functionaries was nowhere to be seen. The courtyard stood empty except for a few servants sweeping debris.

"I'm heading up to his office to see what was left behind," William said. "Secure the palace and find the stores I know he was hoarding for himself so we can release it to the people."

"I'll take care of it," Pembroke said.

William climbed the steps of the tower, this place that had been his home for so long seeming both familiar and completely foreign. He'd been in these hallways so many times, but it had been two years since the last time. Now he was here as its conqueror.

He found the king's study looking much like it had when his uncle Gavric held it, except that many of the artifacts that had been there were missing. Ashes filled the chimney, probably where Edmund had burned letters and documents he couldn't take with him, but beyond that, much was missing.

His father had cleaned the office out, clearly not expecting to come back.

William walked around the desk and sat in the chair his uncle, his cousin, and his father had sat in, and worried. How had he gotten out? There was one obvious answer, but it made no sense. Sinclair had held the Gates, but the idea of Sinclair letting his father go was preposterous. This whole thing started because of an animosity between his father and the baron. The two men hated each other completely.

The thought of Sinclair helping his father escape was impossible to wrap his mind around. And yet, if he hadn't taken a ship through the Gates, then how could he possibly have gotten out? For all appearances, he loaded up a ship and then that ship vanished into thin air.

He was still there when Pembroke, almost breathless, rushed in.

"We have a problem."

"What's happened?"

Pembroke closed the door behind him and said, "The treasury has been emptied."

"What?"

"It's empty. There's nothing left. No gold, no silver, even the crown is gone. The entire treasury has been cleaned out."

For a moment, William had nothing to say. He should have seen this coming, should have predicted it. It was exactly the sort of thing his father would do. But the ramifications of his robbing the kingdom blind were going to be large, and he was sure they couldn't foresee all of them.

William stood slowly and said, "Show me."

They descended through the palace corridors, past the familiar tapestries and portraits that had watched over William's childhood. The irony wasn't lost on him that he was returning to claim his birthright only to discover it had been stolen from under his nose.

The treasury lay deep beneath the palace, reached by a narrow staircase carved into the living rock. Pembroke produced a heavy iron key.

"The assistant steward gave me this. Said your father's lapdog ordered him to stay away from the treasury for the past month."

William stepped into the vast chamber and stopped. Where once golden crowns in rows upon rows of boxes on shelves to keep the coinage and grates where solid bars of the precious metal were, now only dust remained.

"How much was taken?"

Pembroke consulted a piece of parchment. "According to the steward's records, nearly three hundred thousand gold sovereigns in coin alone. Plus an assortment of artifacts and other valuables."

William walked slowly through the chamber. Here and there, scattered coins caught the torchlight, but they were dregs dropped in a rush, the remnants of what had once been an empire's worth of treasure.

"There's more."

William looked up. "More?"

"I sent men to the dock warehouses to inventory what is still in the city so we can figure out what our options are."

"Don't tell me."

"Empty. It seems as if not just the grain and preserved meat, but oil and any other portable trade goods that could be shoved into a hold like cloth was stolen on the way out."

William sank onto one of the empty chests. The magnitude of what Edmund had done was beginning to dawn on him. This wasn't just theft. This was deliberate, systematic destruction of the kingdom's ability to survive.

"How much grain was stored there?"

"Enough to feed the entire guard through winter, according to the harbormaster. Maybe six months' worth for five thousand people."

William closed his eyes and tried to calculate. His army had brought some supplies, but nothing close to what would be needed.

"The people have been squeezed dry already," he said. "Edmund's tax collectors took everything they could give and then more, if what we heard during the campaign is right. There's nothing left to extract from them, even if I was willing to do it."

"Which you're not."

"Of course not. I didn't fight this war to become another tyrant bleeding the people white."

Pembroke studied the empty shelves around them. "The irony is that Edmund probably has enough wealth now to buy food for the entire kingdom."

"And is now probably already halfway to Werna or Alchmara, planning how to use our gold to buy himself a new throne."

They climbed up from the treasury and back to the palace courtyard. Servants and minor functionaries had begun to emerge, cautiously approaching William's men to offer their services.

People who didn't want to lose their place in the palace with the switching of regimes.

William looked out over the city. They had a few months until the harvest, and it was going to be difficult to find the money to buy the vast amounts the Crown bought every year. Without that revenue, the farmers would have trouble finding buyers for all of it.

Grain would rot in storehouses, which meant starvation would make it to the cities. There were options to fix it, but none of them good and none of them would be popular.

Chapter 27

William climbed the palace's central stairwell, making his way toward the council chambers, still furious that Sinclair would have the audacity to demand a council meeting, as if he held any authority to call for one. The city had been in their hands for only three days, and the focus had been on getting the populace fed and the Crown army disbanded.

No king had been crowned yet, let alone Sinclair.

William turned down the corridor to the council chambers and found Pembroke waiting for him, lurking.

"Your Royal Highness."

The fact that he was here, waiting, was not a good sign.

"Can you believe him?" William said, needing to vent his frustration.

"We need to talk before you go in there."

William studied his face. The baron was rattled and in all the time he'd known him, he'd never seen Pembroke rattled, not even in battle.

"Tell me."

Pembroke glanced down the corridor, then moved closer. "Sinclair has been meeting with the barons since the moment we took the city. Large groups of them, and with their knights and captains, too."

"Meeting about what?"

"That's what worries me. No one will say. The men have suddenly become tight-lipped about everything that happened when Sinclair called them together."

William felt something cold settle in his stomach. "How many barons?"

"He's met with most of them. Farrow, Donnington, Ansell. Even Rokeby and Bellamy. Whatever Sinclair is planning, he's been building support for it while we've been trying to feed the city and restore order."

"We both know what he's planning," William said. "He's never done a good job of hiding what he wants."

"I know, but this is different than his earlier grumbling."

William looked toward the council chambers at the end of the corridor. The doors stood closed, but he could hear voices beyond them. Many voices.

"Then let's find out."

He started forward again. Pembroke fell into step beside him.

"William, be careful in there. Something has changed. I can feel it."

William reached the doors and pushed them open.

The council chamber was full. More barons than William had expected, standing in clusters around the long table that dominated the room's center. Garris Sinclair stood at the table's head, where the king would normally sit during such meetings. He looked up as William entered, and something that might have been satisfaction crossed his face.

"Prince William. Thank you for joining us."

William walked to the table. "You summoned me to a council meeting, in the king's palace, despite the fact that no king currently sits in Starhaven, and you certainly hold no authority to convene such gatherings."

"Someone needs to lead, even in uncertain times." Garris gestured to the assembled barons. "We have matters to discuss that cannot wait for crowns and ceremonies."

William counted them. Almost thirty barons, perhaps more, and not all from the rebels.

"What matters?"

Garris smiled. "Why, the future of Sidor, of course. We've just finished a war that nearly tore this kingdom apart. Edmund's rule, and Serwyn's before that, was a disaster. The Whittons have brought nothing but chaos and bloodshed to Sidor for years now."

"Garis was a good king. Edmund murdered the rightful king and seized power through treachery," William said. "That's not the fault of my family. That's one man's crime."

"What matters is what we are recovering from. The barons are tired, the people are tired. This kingdom needs leadership that doesn't come wrapped in Whitton ambition and Whitton wars."

"What are you saying?"

"I'm saying the barons have made a decision." Garris straightened. "We're grateful for your service in this rebellion. You fought well, won important victories, but Sidor cannot have another Whitton on the throne."

"How dare you," William said.

"How dare I? I dare because this kingdom needs strong leadership, it needs a different direction. We just fought a war to change the fate of our kingdom, and we aren't going to start the cycle over again with the deposed king's son on the throne. We are done with his bloodline."

"Edmund may have adopted me, but he did not raise me, and I am not of his blood. My real father died when I was a boy. I am not responsible for his crimes."

"No, but you carry his name. You were raised in his house, taught by his tutors, given his resources. The people see you as Edmund's son, regardless of blood."

"This is treason."

"So was the rebellion we just finished, but we did it because it was the right thing to do." Garris straightened. "We are not angry at you, William, and we all know what you've done for this kingdom. It's why we have all agreed that you should have the new Duchy of Rendalia. It's small, I know, but wealthy, and you already know it well. It's yours by marriage anyway, and it's a suitable realm for a prince with a Lynesian wife. And it allows those of us worried about your history some breathing room, giving you space to show you are your own man."

William looked around the chamber. Baron after baron met his eyes with expressions that ranged from apologetic to defiant. None of them looked like they were about to back down.

Garris had been politicking these men since the rebellion started, even as William focused on the war. Isolde and Pembroke
warned him, but he'd needed to ensure they won first.

"And if I refuse?"

"Then we'll have another war. I have the barons. I have the
backing of Kingsheart, Iron Keep, and the Ice Lands. If you try
to take the Crown by force, you'll find yourself facing the same
united front that just defeated Edmund."

William wanted to point out that he was why they'd defeated
Edmund, but he'd also spent a large part of the men he'd come
with from Rendalia on the fight to remove his father.

His forces had taken the brunt of the damage near the end.

"You can't do this."

"I already have." Garris moved around the table, stopping a few
paces from William. "This isn't a negotiation, this is reality. You
can accept it gracefully and take what's being offered, or you can
refuse and watch Sidor descend into another pointless conflict.
How many more need to die for Whitton pride?"

"You have no right."

"Don't take it personally. You're a good commander, William,
you've proven that, but commanding an army and ruling a kingdom are different things. Let someone else bear that burden. Take
your wife, go to Rendalia, and build a life there."

"And you'll take Sidor's throne."

"Someone has to. I started this rebellion, was the first to stand
up to Serwyn and then your father. The barons have put their trust
in me. I held the east together when Edmund's forces should have
overwhelmed us. I've earned this."

William looked at Pembroke. His friend's face was carefully
neutral, but his eyes held a warning.

"Think it over," Garris said. "You have until tomorrow to give
me your answer. But understand this decision is already made. The
only question is whether you accept it peacefully or force us into
another war."

He gestured to the other barons, and they began filing out.
Some looked relieved. Others couldn't meet William's eyes as they
passed. Within moments, only William and Pembroke remained
in the chamber.

The silence stretched.

"I can't accept this."

Pembroke moved to the window, looking out over the city. "Garris has the upper hand."

"He's a traitor."

"He's a baron who spent the entire campaign listening to the other barons' complaints. I've been hearing them too, William, but now that the war is won, those complaints have become something more. Something louder." Pembroke turned back. "The men Garris has been speaking to, they're more insistent than I've ever seen them. If you tried to counter this, you'd find yourself with very few allies here."

"What about you?"

The question hung between them. Pembroke's face didn't change, but something in his eyes grew pained.

"I'll always be your friend, but we can't fight another war. The kingdom can't survive it, and neither can the people." He moved closer. "Garris has a point about the barons. You did ignore them. You made decisions without consulting anyone, kept your own counsel, treated them like pieces on a board instead of lords with their own interests and concerns. This is the consequence."

"I did what had to be done, but this is more than that. It feels like there's more going on here. Like Sinclair didn't just convince them. Like something changed in them."

"Perhaps. But that doesn't change the situation. We would be on our own, and the River Mark is in shambles." Pembroke joined him at the table. "What will you do?"

William stared at the wood grain, at the scratches and marks left by years of councils and arguments. His family had sat at this table for centuries. They'd built Sidor from fragmented territories into a unified kingdom.

And now he was being told to walk away.

"It doesn't look like I have much of a choice."

"You always have a choice."

"Not good ones." William straightened. "If I fight this, how many will die? How much more of the kingdom will burn?"

Pembroke didn't answer. They both knew what another civil war would cost.

"I'll return to Rendalia."

The words tasted like ash. Pembroke's expression didn't change, but his shoulders dropped slightly.

"I'm sorry."

"Don't be. You were right about the barons. I should have listened to you. I should have listened to Isolde. But this isn't over. Garris thinks he's won, thinks he can take Sidor's throne and rule peacefully. He's wrong."

"What do you mean?"

"The same barons who just betrayed me will betray him eventually. They'll remember that he was a baron too, not a king. They'll question his decisions, argue with his policies, scheme for more power. That's what barons do." He shook his head. "Garris won a battle today. But he doesn't understand what ruling actually means. He'll learn. Let Sinclair have his throne. Let him deal with the barons and the empty treasury and the kingdom Edmund gutted. I'll take what's mine by marriage and build something better in Rendalia."

They walked in silence until they reached the palace's main hall. Servants moved through the space, trying to restore order after days of occupation. Everything looked tired, worn down by years of conflict.

"What will you tell the men?" Pembroke asked.

"The truth. That I'm going home." William stopped at the palace's main entrance, looking out over Starhaven. The city sprawled before him. "This was never really my home anyway."

"And Rendalia is?"

"It can be." He turned to Pembroke. "What about you? Back to your barony?"

Pembroke's expression shifted to almost guilt.

"Sinclair offered me the River Mark. Well, he said he would back my being Duke of River Mark. At the time, I thought he just meant his support, but now I see he was trying to buy me off. I tell you honestly that if you chose to stand against him, even though I think that would be foolish, I would stand with you."

William was struck by the words, but after a moment, he found the idea did not gall him. Pembroke was the right choice to follow in his uncle's footsteps.

"I know, and I think it the right choice. You'll do well."

"Stay in touch and listen to your wife. Sinclair isn't wrong. Ruling is different than commanding. Send me a wyvern if you need an ear, and I will offer what counsel I can."

"Thank you, Rowan," William said, taking his offered hand.

William descended the palace steps. The sun had climbed higher while they'd been inside, and Starhaven's morning bustle filled the streets. People went about their lives, unconcerned with what happened in the palace at the center of the city, as if thrones and crowns and kingdoms didn't matter compared to food and shelter and survival.

Maybe they were right.

He'd spent a year fighting for Sidor's throne without ever asking himself why he wanted it. Was it because he thought he'd be a good king? Because he believed the kingdom needed him specifically? Or was it just because everyone kept telling him it was his birthright, his duty, his destiny?

William had won those battles through tactics and timing, through reading terrain and understanding his enemies. But he'd never won the barons. He'd never made them trust him, never gave them reason to follow him beyond military necessity.

Garris had done that. Even men who'd supported William against Sinclair when it came to military necessity stood against him now, backing Sinclair.

How they could change allegiance like that, he would never know. He'd been warned, and he'd ignored those warnings. He'd needed to win the next battle, and the next, and the next. He'd needed to win the war.

Now, the war was over, and everything Isolde and Pembroke had warned him had come to pass.

He'd won the battles and lost the war.

To Be Continued...

About the author

Travis writes science fiction, fantasy, and thriller novels (and the occasional coming-of-age story), with the hope of transporting and enthralling readers. Publishing novels since 2015, Travis's passion is creating worlds and characters that live and breathe, and experiencing the joy of those stories with his readers. When not writing, Travis enjoys connecting with readers and other writers, managing the popular Complete Marvel Reading Order website, where he works on his other passion for comics and graphic novels, and spending time with his family. If you have enjoyed this book, please consider taking a moment to rate or review it wherever you found your copy, as it helps new readers find my works and ensures I can continue writing book into the future.

Find out more at:
amazon.com/TravisStarnes/e/B072YBDC3S/

Or visit
https://tstarnes.com

Maps available at
https://tstarnes.com/book-series/imperium/

Signup to get free previews and notifications of upcoming books at
http://tstarnes.com/preview-notification-newsletter/

Also by

John Taylor Stories

Rebirth
False Signs
The Wrong Girl
Burying the Past
Family Ties
Election Day
Danger Close
Extraction
Designated Target
Border Crossed
Desperate Rendition
Broken Ground

Country Roads Series

Playing by Ear
Fanfare
Dissonance
Elegy
From the Top
Center Stage

Imperium Series

Volume 1
The Sword of Jupiter
The Trumpets of Mars
The Sands of Saturn
The Depths of Neptune
The Fires of Vulcan
The Triumph of Venus
Volume 2
The Wings of Mercury
The Plains of Pluto
The Clouds of Caelus
The Masks of Janus

Shattered Lands Series

In the Shadow of Lions
An Ending of Oaths
The Barons' War
Heavy Lies the Crown

False Start Series

Second Down
Scramble
Loss of Down

The Veilguard Saga

Threads of Destiny
The Blackstar Legacy

Stand Alone

Going Home